THE DEATH OF JUSTICE

DI BLISS BOOK 5

TONY FORDER

Print ISBN 978-1-912986-77-4

B liss followed the three young men from the Crab and Winkle pub, pushing on through the estate of pleasant-looking detached and semi-detached dwellings – no long rows of terraced homes in this residential neighbourhood. A piercing white LED glow from overhanging streetlights added to the softer light which emerged from various properties close by, illuminating the entrance to the park. The deeper they moved into the wide-open playing field beyond, the more the glow receded behind them.

It was a warm night for late September, though low cloud hung like a pall over the city, it blocked out the stars and prevented the day's heat from escaping. Bliss wore a thin blouson jacket over a plain polo shirt. He'd never felt comfortable in jeans, but at least the dark grey cargo trousers he wore did not hiss as he moved. As he continued to follow the trio, it was neither the temperature nor the physical exertion that brought a film of cold sweat to his brow. It was anger.

With every step he took, Bliss's wrath increased. It ripped through his blood and thrummed in both temples, causing his head to ache. He was glad of the walk, fearing what he might have been capable of if pressed into action the moment he stepped out of his car.

The three youths came to rest by a knot of skinny young trees and a line of dense hedgerow fringed by undergrowth and a fresh carpet of fallen leaves. They now stood less than ten yards off the open field, virtually hidden from view in the deepening dusk and formless shadows. Bliss followed their voices as he inched his way towards them, taking care not to disturb the scattering of crisp golden leaves beneath his feet. He recognised the hunger feeding their simmering excitement, understanding they would be skittish and alert. Their regular dealer would soon appear out of the same gloom in which they currently skulked.

And Bliss would be ready for him.

A light, warm breeze brought with it the tang of smouldering autumn, and the merest hint of an approaching rainstorm still way off in the distance. Bliss hung back in the darkness, breathing in the air and observing the scene with mounting fervour.

The skinny, scruffy-looking trio of wastrels traded banter and insults as if their callow words were laden with wit. Their mutual laughter became increasingly raucous as their adrenaline flow increased. They had already spent good money becoming nicely mellow on alcohol. Now they wanted to get themselves high and were impatient to begin the process.

Bliss shared their frustration, but tonight he was piqued neither by the sensation of time dragging with exaggerated slowness, nor by irritation at its slow passing. Having built towards this moment for a month or more, a wait of a few extra minutes was not about to discourage him. Concealed and comfortable in what remained of the unseasonably warm day, he had his rage for company. The youths became his unknowing and unwilling bait, luring in the true object of his ire.

Whispering leaves and snapping twigs gave away the approach of the dealer. Moments later, Bliss heard the eager chatter of greeting, slapped high fives, and the heightened sense of fearful anticipation. Every exchange came with its potential dangers, from either the police or any of the youths involved in the trade of money for drugs. The deed was something usually carried out swiftly and with an economy of fuss.

Bliss shuffled further to his left, approaching the dealer at pace from behind. In his hand he held a small steel tube, which he jammed into the dealer's back as his other arm snaked around the young man's throat.

'Move and you die,' Bliss whispered in his ear, though loud enough for the three buyers to overhear. 'I pull this trigger and that's you done. You understand me, Jake?'

The dealer stiffened at the sound of his real name being uttered. On the streets, people referred to him only as Demon, and he revelled in his anonymity. Bliss needed the boy to realise the man behind him was serious, with good intelligence backing him up. It would slow his reactions should he offer any resistance.

Bliss squinted over the young man's shoulder. He put real weight into his voice. 'You three, piss off. And I wouldn't come back if I were you.'

Each of them stared at the dealer.

'Don't look at him,' Bliss spat. 'Don't wait for him to give you the nod. Fuck off now while you can still walk.'

Two of them said nothing. The shortest of the three decided he would put on a show. 'There's four of us, or can't you count?'

'I can. Let me prove it to you. The gun pressed into this scum-bag's spine holds sixteen rounds. By my calculations that's four bullets for each of you. Am I right? Do I win a prize?'

Bliss was holding onto his temper despite the pain spearing through his head and the acid squirting in his gut. A decade ago he might have beaten the shit out of all of them, but his focus now was to accomplish only what he had come for.

The three youths he had followed from the pub looked at each other in despair before bolting, leaving the dealer stranded and confined by Bliss's harsh embrace. As soon as they were far enough away and unseen once more in the darkness, they called out their threats and vowed to return mob-handed to make him sorry he was born. Bliss ignored them, because by then it was just him and Jake Watts, who had so far said nothing at all.

Bliss leaned in, his lips less than an inch from the kid's left ear. 'Carrie Dixon,' he said.

He felt the jolt. Watts struggled a little in his grasp, but a tightening of the grip around the man's neck and a grinding of the cylinder into his spine quelled any thoughts the lad might have had about trying to escape.

'Carrie Dixon!' Bliss said again, more urgently.

'What about her, man?'

'You killed her.'

'It was an accident.'

'You were drugged up and pissed out of your tiny brain, yet still you jumped into your farty little pimped-up hatchback. Then you drove it so fast and so recklessly you left the road and ploughed into the garden wall behind which Carrie Dixon was playing. That's six-year-old Carrie Dixon I'm talking about.'

'It was still an accident,' Watts protested with a dismissive snarl.

'No. You took drugs. You drank alcohol. Then you chose to drive. That's three strikes, you fucking little maggot.'

'What the fuck you want with me, man? Nothing I can do about it now.' The Peterborough born and bred youngster spoke with a fake gangsta-style patois more associated with London suburbs.

Bliss closed his eyes for a moment. Told himself to maintain the mental strength and composure not to snap the runt's neck.

'I saw you in court, Jake. Tell me what you did while Carrie's parents sat there sobbing as the long list of their daughter's fatal injuries was read out. Go on. Explain it to me!'

'I don't know, man. I don't fucking know!'

'Yes, you do. But you're too much of a coward to admit it. So I'll tell you instead. You smiled as you stared straight at them. Then you yawned. Meant nothing to you, right? It bored you having to listen to such a sorry tale of misery. After that it was the exaggerated roll of the eyes. A six-year-old's death was totally unimportant as far as you were concerned even though you caused it, yes? And then, as Carrie's mother howled with grief, you laughed. You laughed at them, Jake. You laughed at their loss, at their grief, at their impotence. Is it all coming back to you now, Jake?'

Without realising it, Bliss punctuated each sentence with a jerk on the youth's neck, and a deeper stab in the back with the steel tubing. The rage burned inside him like molten lava, spilling from every open pore.

Carrie Dixon's death earlier in the year had been reported both locally and nationally, and although the investigation had not landed across Bliss's desk, his interest in it began immediately. He felt outraged by what Jake Watts had done, more so by his obvious lack of remorse afterwards. Because Jake had somehow managed to crawl out of the wreckage of his devastated Peugeot and subsequently go into hiding for three days, the prosecution had ultimately rested on a charge of dangerous driving while under the influence of controlled substances; this despite witness testimony to the fact that Jake had been drinking heavily and smoking meth from a glass pipe all day. Without an admission of guilt or any bloodwork to prove the allegations, the judge postponed court proceedings to allow the prosecution time to enhance their case.

Bliss saw the trial heading in only one direction. The dangerous driving charge would probably stick, but the "while under the influence" aspect would fail. It could even get dropped altogether to allow the jury to focus on the solitary element they believed might earn Watts some jail time. Even then, the defence team cited temporary loss of control: Jake claimed he was being chased by another vehicle driven by his competition.

Bliss thought about how easy it would be to end it. Choke the life out of the kid, maybe even snap his neck. Easy for some, perhaps, but not for him. He knew how much pressure to apply to get the job done. He had the rage required to pull it off. But he was no killer. He wanted this kid to suffer, for as long as Carrie Dixon's parents would endure their own agony. He even yearned to inflict a little pain along the way, to see terror aligned with suffering in Jake's eyes. But that was not his purpose here. Not this time around.

'Did you sense me coming, Jake?' Bliss asked. 'Did you have any clue that I was creeping up on you intending you harm?'

The kid made no reply, but his body quaked. Bliss had put a scare into him. But was he scared enough? 'I know you didn't, Jake. It was easy. And it will be just as easy the next time I pay you a visit. You understand that, don't you?'

Bliss clamped his arm tighter, inducing a response this time.

'Yeah! Yeah, man. What you want from me?'

'What I want is for you to call your brief tomorrow morning and tell him you've decided to admit to each charge against you. You can claim whatever you like. That you found God over the weekend, or somehow grew a conscience in two days. I don't give a shit. Provided you cough to everything.'

'And if I don't, you come looking for me again, yeah? Who the fuck are you, man?' Jake's voice faltered all the way through the bluster. It betrayed him, revealed his fear.

Bliss ignored the second question. 'That's right. Only there's one major difference, Jake. Just like this time, you won't know when I'm coming, you won't see me and you won't hear me. In fact, the only time you'll be aware of me is when I jam this gun against the side of your head and pull the trigger. You got that, Jake? Do you under-stand what I'm telling you here? Believe me when I say there will be no further chances. You killed Carrie Dixon just as surely as if you'd stuck a gun in her mouth and shot her dead. I can't allow you to go unpunished for that.'

He paused, summoning any and every power in the universe to prevent the dealer from calling his bluff, and waiting for his heart to stop smashing itself against his ribcage. He swallowed back some foul-tasting bile. Despite loathing everything Jake Watts stood for, behaving this way was not something Bliss enjoyed. It was the only move he could think of to ensure Carrie Dixon's parents received a small measure of justice.

And maybe a little peace.

'So what's it going to be?' he asked. 'A prison sentence that sees you back on the streets in less than fourteen years, perhaps as few as six or eight? Or checking out with a bullet through the brain? Your choice, Jake. Just understand it has to be one or the other. No alternatives. No second chances.'

'You don't scare me, man.'

Bliss recognised a terrified voice when he heard one, and he was listening to one now. 'Oh, I think I do. Check your shorts when you get home, Jake. You've got a fair bit of leakage going on there by the smell of it.'

The kid tried to wrestle himself away one more time, but then became still, at which point Bliss felt Jake's shoulders lose all of their tension.

'So I do what you say and you leave me the fuck alone, yeah?'

'That's right. It really is that simple.'

'Why are you doing this, man? What was she to you, that kid?'

Bliss squeezed and jabbed for all he was worth. 'That *kid* has a name. Carrie Dixon. Remember it and use it in future, you disgrace of a human being. She was only six years old. Never forget that. Never!'

'All right, all right. Take it easy, yeah? I'll do what you ask, man. I'll do what you tell me to do.'

'You'd better not be fucking with me, Jake. You fuck with me and I might take my time with you instead of killing you quickly. The way I feel about you, I reckon I could stretch out your pain and misery for days.'

'I said I'll fucking do it, man!'

'That's good. So, when I release you, carry on facing the same way you are now. You turn round and you'll suffer for it. Count to a hundred and then you can bugger off. If I don't see or hear about

7

you confessing to all charges tomorrow, consider yourself on notice.'

He moved out of the park as swiftly and silently as he had entered it. Alert to the possibility that the other three youths might be lingering, he hurried back to his car. He encountered nobody, saw nobody. As Bliss's chest rose and fell and his hands clenched and unclenched, the tension slipped away from his neck, his breathing becoming less laboured. Gut-wrenching rage was replaced by an inner calm, a sense of peace and purpose.

The shrill tone of his mobile phone caused him to jerk upright. He blew out some pent-up air and thumbed the green button to accept the call.

'How soon can you get here, Bliss?'

The voice of Detective Chief Inspector Edwards was unmistakable.

'That depends on where you are,' he replied.

'In my office.'

'I can be there in ten or fifteen minutes.'

'Make it ten.'

Bliss was puzzled by his boss's tone and attitude. He and Edwards had ridden through some personal difficulties, but they now enjoyed working together on relatively decent terms. Her manner suggested he had either fouled up somehow or that something serious was going on.

'You do realise I'm neither on duty nor on call, boss?'

'We need you in, Bliss. As soon as.'

'We?' he said.

'Meet me in Superintendent Fletcher's office, Bliss. Believe me, you'll want in on this.'

Bliss killed the call, turned the engine over and set off with tyres smoking and screeching, Jake Watts dismissed from his thoughts.

2

Bliss had left his service-allocated Airwave communication device at home. The beaten-up handset ran on ageing and unreliable technology, but having use of it now would at least provide access to crime-related chatter taking place in the city. Bliss did not enjoy the thought of going in blind without it. Decrepit system or not, he wished he carried the Airwave with him now.

Having briefly considered calling his regular partner, Penny Chandler, Bliss left his phone where it was. The DS tended to keep herself well-informed, but as she was back on shift rotation the following morning after a week of annual leave, he decided not to disturb her until he had further information.

Roadworks held him up on Lincoln Road. He found himself tapping his thumb against the steering wheel in an increasingly agitated fashion. It had a rhythm to it, but the drummer clearly fancied himself to be a cross between Animal from *The Muppet Show* and The Who's Keith Moon at his most extravagant. As he finally weaved his way up onto the parkway, Bliss tore through the traffic as if the other vehicles were standing still.

Finding room in the ground-level car park made for a nice

change. Chandler often berated him for complaining about having to search out tight spaces beneath the Thorpe Wood police station. Given the sense of dread lying in his stomach like a dead weight, Bliss doubted whether his steering wheel would have survived hunting out a vacant slot this evening.

Sliding out of the seat and using the fob to lock the doors, he glanced up at the superintendent's brightly lit office windows on the third floor. The clench inside his gut became more of a pinch this time. He wondered whether it was a bollocking or a job waiting for him up there. With his track record it could easily be either. Or both.

Bliss ignored the sluggish lift in favour of the staircase. Having recovered from injuries received in two vehicle-related incidents early in the summer, he had returned to full fitness four weeks ago and found the exercise useful in building up both his strength and stamina. He often enjoyed standing on a landing peering out of the window at either the nature reserve below or traffic whipping by up on the dual carriageway. Tonight it was stuffy and uninviting, and Bliss wondered if the foreboding he felt was to blame for that. He did not linger, gaining time by jogging up the stairs.

He could tell by the stern countenance of the two women in Detective Superintendent Fletcher's office that something major had occurred. Bliss nodded a greeting as he took a seat alongside his DCI at the super's desk.

'Twelve minutes is as quick as I could legally make it,' he said apologetically. 'So, am I in trouble or are we?'

Marion Fletcher met his gaze and raised both eyebrows. Judging by her casual attire and lack of make-up, she had also dragged herself into work when off duty. Her T-shirt and slacks were grey, the usually immaculate short hair now mussed if not entirely unkempt. On her feet she sported a pair of grubby tennis shoes. The super also wore spectacles rather than her contacts. When she spoke, Fletcher's voice was grave.

'Inspector, there has been a fatal shooting in Farcet. That alone is awful enough, but sadly I have to inform you that the victim was a member of our police family. Kelly Gibson worked in the communications suite. I'm sure you probably knew her quite well.'

Bliss felt a hand grip his heart and give it a squeeze. 'Kelly?' he half-whispered. Gibson had been a calm and knowledgeable operative. Not a police officer, but regarded as one of their own by those who worked with her. Bliss had spoken with the pleasant and cheerful woman on a regular basis. As far as he could recall, she had a husband and young child. 'What on earth happened?'

'Details are sketchy at this point,' DCI Edwards said in a voice choked with emotion. 'The report from our first responders came in only minutes before I contacted you.'

'Which was why, exactly?' Bliss asked. 'Not that I mind now that I know what occurred. I'm just wondering why I've been called in.'

'It's been one of those nights,' Edwards explained, turning to face him. 'We have a team attending a drug-related stabbing, another at the scene of a ram raid on a cash machine in Bretton. The wounding incident is why I happened to be here when the call came in about the shooting. First uniforms on scene there recognised Kelly. I phoned you because you were next up in terms of rank.'

'Okay.' Bliss moistened his lips. 'Then if it has to be anyone, I'm glad it's me.'

'I thought you might say that,' Superintendent Fletcher said to him with a nod of approval. 'Look, I'd make you silver commander on this but I know you would much prefer to be operational rather than tactical.'

Unable to fully disguise a stifled groan, Bliss said, 'With respect, ma'am, I'd rather be left to do my job, which makes me both tactical and operational. Call it salmon pink for all I care, but I need to be both silver and bronze on this.'

He winced and shook his head at the thought. GSB terminology – gold, silver and bronze – had existed for many years. Its structure indicated the pyramid of command levels, gold having strategic oversight of a major incident from a remote location. Silver represented the most senior officer on scene, providing the tactical hub for the emergency response. Bronze commanders directly controlled resources on the front line, and were usually the most experienced in terms of hands-on know-how.

Bliss was not a fan of the strategy. He considered it to be yet another superfluous hierarchical structure. If used merely as a shorthand in place of names and ranks then it had its uses, but in his opinion the system only added complexity and ended up wasting time. During his years with the Met its use had been mandatory, but now that he was back in Peterborough, Bliss ignored the arrangement and made plain his disdain for its deficiencies. Orders from Alec Stroud, the chief constable himself, were currently being enforced, however.

'Your reluctance to embrace the system has previously been noted, Bliss,' Fletcher remarked with a shake of the head.

'And I'm not wrong, am I?'

'I happen to agree with you,' DCI Edwards chipped in, much to Bliss's surprise. 'And to be perfectly honest, the thought of referring to you as salmon pink commander has a nice ring to it. However, practically speaking, it's simply not possible.'

Edwards raised a hand to forestall any further complaint from him. 'The super and I discussed this very issue while we were waiting for you to arrive. The solution appears to lie in the flexibility of ranks.'

'How so?' Bliss sat forward eagerly.

'The GSB system allows for it, so why not make use of it appropriately on this occasion? We could, for instance, have DS Short back here in gold command. As silver out at the scene you might opt for either DS Bishop or Chandler. Which leaves you as bronze. And although there are probably two other bronzes out there already, you are being given some latitude on this one, Bliss.'

'Latitude?'

'Yes. The theoretical structure is in place, but of course we expect you to indulge in some form of alchemy and become a combination of all three. Provided it is not reflected on the official records, we can live with it. The super and I are agreed that the chain of command in this instance may slow us down, and nobody here wants that.'

Bliss swallowed, unused to getting his own way without a battle. He felt as if he had muscled into a knife fight only to be handed a flamethrower.

'Just to be clear,' he said uncertainly. 'I take control of the scene, make whatever decisions I deem to be appropriate, and report back to you as soon as I have anything worthwhile. Is that correct?'

'Within reason,' Fletcher said. 'The usual demands for a media briefing are bound to flood in, and we have to allow time for developments to filter through the system so that we can formulate a response. So, although you have autonomy, Bliss, you need to provide feedback on a more regular basis than you usually do. Is that understood?'

'It is, ma'am.'

'I hope so. Keep DCI Edwards fully briefed. Our reaction to the public clamour for information needs to be both transparent and accurate. We cannot do that if you neglect to maintain contact.'

'I agree. The moment I have anything of use to the boss I'll call.'

'Very well. You need to get yourself over to the scene. Would you like one of us to pull your team in?'

Bliss had already undertaken the same internal debate with himself. He shook his head decisively. 'No, thank you, ma'am. I'll take DS Chandler along with me for now. No point in pulling everyone in until I know what's what and how best to use them.'

Fletcher indicated the door with her right hand. 'Then you be on your way. And Bliss, I of course recognise the fact that Kelly Gibson was one of us, and as such we all feel a sense of duty to make sure her killer is apprehended swiftly. However, and I'm sorry if this comes across as overly harsh, your reputation precedes you and it would be remiss of me not to instruct you to act professionally at all times and not – and I mean this, Bliss – not to even consider taking matters into your own hands.'

Already getting to his feet, Bliss paused for a second before continuing to stand fully upright. He stared down at the super. 'Of course, ma'am. It would never cross my mind.'

Fletcher fixed him with a thin smile. Said, 'We both know it will. What I'm telling you is that, for once, you allow it to pass across your mind and let it go. Expect enormous scrutiny on this case, both internally and externally. Do what's right for Kelly Gibson, but make sure you do your job at the same time.'

Bliss thought back to what he had been doing moments before receiving the call from DCI Edwards. Jake Watts would have a thing or two to say about his methods.

Working on the very edges of legality in order to achieve results was a given. Bliss had operated that way since first making detective, and nobody in the room believed he was about to change now. Not at the age of fifty-six, with decades in the job behind him. Edwards always insisted she gave him only sufficient rope with which to hang himself, but no one had yet slipped the noose around his neck. It had come close at times, but Bliss was intelligent enough to realise that he needed to select the right time and place in which to step over those blurred lines.

The shadows there were deep and dark and nothing ever remained wholly black or white, right or wrong, good or bad. There was only success or failure, and the varying degrees of each. A killer was arrested and convicted or a killer evaded capture. On occasion they met a worse fate, but Bliss had never knowingly instigated such an event. He lost no sleep over hardened, despicable criminals who died as they had lived, but equally he enjoyed making a difference in ensuring they did hard time behind bars.

What he had done and said to Jake Watts would see him summarily dismissed if it ever became known. But he expected the thug to do as instructed the following day. A little pressure applied in the right place, and a length of steel tubing with the shape and heft of a gun barrel, seemed like a small price to pay in Bliss's eyes.

Now, with the gunning down of Kelly Gibson having become his case, once again Bliss acknowledged to himself that some things were worth the risk.

3

Detective Sergeant Chandler lived on the exotically named Viersen Platz, in a five-storey apartment block whose shadow often draped itself across the river Nene. Rather than negotiate a secondary one-way system, Bliss parked illegally on the London Road side of the building, bumping up onto the pavement to allow other vehicles to flow freely around him. The streets were well lit as he drew up at 8.45pm. Chandler was waiting for him a few yards beyond the traffic lights. She hurried across to yank the door open, long dirty-blonde hair streaming behind her.

'Sorry for disturbing you on your last day off,' Bliss said as Chandler slipped into the Insignia's passenger seat and clicked her belt into place. 'But you look as if you scrubbed up well enough in the ten minutes I gave you.'

'Yeah, we both know I look as rough as a badger's arse, so drive on.' Chandler motioned with her fingers for him to go.

Bliss checked his mirrors then dipped the accelerator and got them moving. He slid a sidelong glance at his DS and smiled. 'Now that you mention it, I think that's unkind to the badger.'

Chandler gave him one of her looks. The kind that told him she would happily strangle him if she could only be bothered to get her hands dirty. 'We're not like you men,' she explained. 'A quick squirt of deodorant – if that for some of you – and you're done. You don't give a stuff about your appearance. We women like to look presentable when we're out in public.'

Smiling, Bliss chuckled. Chandler was such an easy wind-up.

'Anyhow, where are you taking me?' she asked, growing serious. They had forced the initial humour in light of the grim duty awaiting them.

'Farcet.'

'And it's definitely our Kelly Gibson? No change on that status since you called? No chance the victim was misidentified?'

'Unfortunately not. It's Kelly, I'm afraid. Shot dead as she walked towards home from her car it seems.'

'How awful. I didn't know her well, but she seemed nice and good at her job.'

'She was both. And now she's gone. Just goes to show – you can never predict how you exit this world.'

Chandler's professional mask slipped into place. 'Been a while since I attended the scene of a shooting.'

'Me, too.' Bliss gave a reflective grunt. 'Had a few when I was working organised crime.'

'You ever have a gun pulled on you?'

'Yeah. Tests out the old rusty sheriff's badge, that's for sure.'

Chandler turned her head, frowning. 'The what?'

'Your ring-piece. Your anal sphincter.'

His colleague allowed that to permeate before puckering up her face. 'Oh, that's gross.'

He shrugged. 'It's just language, Pen. That's all.'

'Well, it's disgusting language.'

Bliss caught the smile turning up the corners of her mouth. He knew Chandler would file the phrase away in her repertoire for later. Jocular verbal exchanges at such times offended the sensibilities of some, but Bliss always found it to be a necessary release. Theirs was a dark enough job, and any light shone upon the gloom was welcome.

He circled around by the court building and back onto Rivergate before heading towards the Old Fletton area, beneath the vast concrete structure of the Frank Perkins Parkway, on past Stanground and into the small village of Farcet. The drive gave them a few minutes to chat.

'So how are things out in Turkey?' Bliss asked, understanding how important this most recent trip out there had been for his colleague.

Seventeen years ago, Chandler's two-year-old daughter, Hannah, had been abducted by her Turkish father. He then disappeared into that vast country taking the girl along with him. Chandler had travelled there every single year since, searching for some news about her child, attempting to negotiate with embassy staff, Home Office and the Foreign and Commonwealth Office. Bliss's intervention on her behalf earlier in the year had paved the way for a possible reunion, after his MI6 contact confirmed that Hannah was still alive and well and living in her father's homeland. Chandler's visit on this occasion had been arranged to smooth the waters between her legal representative in Turkey and those working for her ex.

'Good. Very good, in fact.' Chandler's expression revealed genuine enthusiasm. 'It's a slow process, but Hannah knows about me now, so it's worth every step no matter how minor.'

'You think she will allow you to use her original name? Or do you have to call her Anna?'

'Anna is her name now. It's all she's known since the age of two. I guess I'll have to get used to it.'

'Must be tough.'

'Not as tough as it was when I didn't even know if she was still alive. It's only a name. And not so different.'

'I suppose. The main thing is there's now every chance of her being in your life again.'

'Thanks to you.'

Bliss crinkled his nose. 'I did nothing really. Other people put in the real time and effort.'

'Don't do that,' Chandler told him, turning her face towards him. 'Anna will come to understand the role you played in bringing us back together again. If it happens. Please don't belittle it. If she visits me, I will want her to meet you.'

'I'm sure she'll have much better things to do with her time than spend it with a grizzled old git like me. But I'll be happy to if that's what you both decide. From the little I know about her, she seems like a very level-headed young woman. A lot like you. Sometimes genetics finds a way.'

When the pair arrived at the scene of crime, the emergency vehicles remained scattered along the short, narrow street. Their lights lapped against the walls of neighbouring properties with a flickering blue glow, and shadows danced across the night sky. A firearms unit stood by, having cleared the area ahead of the ambulance crew and further uniformed police officers. Twelve in all, they appeared alert yet relaxed at the same time. The immediate threat no longer existed, but they stayed behind in case it returned.

'How come you got the call on your day off?' Chandler asked Bliss as they climbed out of the car.

'They're a bit short-handed back at HQ. I was volunteered.'

'Which in turn volunteers me.'

'You could have said no. That you were too busy applying face masks.'

'You'll need a bloody mask of some sort if you carry on,' Chandler muttered.

The pair pushed their way through the gaggle of onlookers and ducked below the cordon tape gently fluttering in a light autumnal breeze. A white tent with its blue fringe was lit from inside and

19

stood out like a beacon, though it concealed the potential horrors beneath.

Bliss admired the speed at which every component of the emergency response had sprung into action. Lack of staff and reduced budget notwithstanding, when it came to major crimes the services still had the chops to get things done right.

As he and Chandler approached the tent, Bliss recognised two men of inspector rank. One was in uniform, the other wore full 'RoboCop' attire. The pair chatted animatedly as they stood outside the tent's entrance flap. As the two detectives reached the staging area, a male uniform jotting something down on a form attached to a clipboard stopped them at an inner cordon of ribbon. They both held out their warrant cards for his perusal.

'DI Bliss and DS Chandler,' the officer said with a stiff nod. 'We've been expecting you. Will you want to examine the victim *in situ?*'

'We will,' Bliss told him, signing in. He passed the clipboard to Chandler, who did the same. They each picked up a full forensic body suit from a pile sitting on a fold-out table. Wedging the plastic-wrapped garment beneath one arm, Bliss strode across to the two senior officers who remained engaged in their conversation.

'Evening, troops,' he said, interrupting them. 'Are you two bronze command on this so far?'

The pair nodded in unison. For incidents during which weapons were used, it was usual for both a firearms and uniformed senior rank to act as the third rung on the ladder of command. The former was responsible for the armed response, the latter working on public order.

'Anything we need to know before seeing the body?' Bliss asked.

The firearms officer was the first to respond. 'Nothing out of the ordinary. How's tricks, Jimmy?'

'Not so bad, Eric. You and yours?'

Eric Price hailed from the same area of London as Bliss, though he was at least twenty years younger, so their paths had never crossed in the capital. They had worked together on one previous occasion during which firearms officers were summoned. A single projectile was fired during the incident, the weapon holder somehow managing to shoot himself with what proved to be an air pistol during an angry dispute with a neighbour. Bliss both respected and liked Price immensely, his cool demeanour a calming influence on those around him.

'All good, pal. All good,' Price replied. His expression remained solemn. 'So, what we have here is a woman identified as Kelly Gibson, aged thirty. Gunned down as she made her way from her car towards her own front door. Parking is bad on these streets, so she'd left her motor about fifty yards down the road from her own property. Witness saw a vehicle roll along the street and heard three or four shots fired from inside it. Our victim has three rounds in her body. We're waiting on forensics to locate the fourth – if there was one.'

Bliss raised his eyebrows, perplexed by the account. 'A drive-by?'

'Looks that way.'

'You know Kelly Gibson was one of us?'

'I do, yes.'

'So was she, or her husband perhaps, known to us at all? In terms of criminal activity.'

'First thing I checked on. No record for either of them. Nor have they come up in any previous investigation I could find. Obviously there's the fact that she works at Thorpe Wood, but it's not as if she's ever put anyone away or got herself known to organised crime. Strictly backroom staff offering no threat. I don't see this as being down to her job.'

Bliss didn't, either. He swore beneath his breath. The majority of gun crime was drug-related, or in some way involved with gangs. The gunning down of a female victim with no apparent affiliation to organised crime or drugs did not fit the usual pattern. As irregular as shootings were in the United Kingdom, they almost always fell into one of very few categories.

As if reading his mind, Inspector Price said, 'This may be the result of something more personal. Either way, it's going to leave a very bad taste in the mouth.'

4

B liss knew what Price meant. Any murder, no matter who the victim was, deserved the investigation team's best efforts. And they usually got them. Even so, some were more palatable than others. Bliss had a 'live by the sword, die by the sword' attitude towards some homicides. It was the killing of complete innocents that stung the most.

Inspector Stringer, the uniformed officer that Eric Price had been talking to, leaned in and said, 'She doesn't appear to have ever been on our radar at all. Plus, she's a civilian doing good work. I think Eric is right when he suggests it could be a personal matter. A love affair gone wrong, perhaps, that sort of thing.'

Bliss agreed. It was the next logical conclusion. 'Did our witness happen to get a plate?'

Stringer shook his head. 'No. White SUV of some description. Maybe a Range Rover, but that was a guess on his part. The witness is at the city hospital being checked out for signs of shock. Afterwards, we'll get him over to Thorpe Wood for an interview and gunshot residue swabs. Hopefully, more will come to him after he's calmed down.'

'Saw and heard the entire thing,' Price confirmed, with a slow shake of the head. 'He was just a few yards away, on his way to the boozer. Saw the victim, saw the vehicle, heard the shots, saw her go down. The SUV laid tyre marks on the road as it took off afterwards. The poor bloke thought they might circle around and come back for him, but he couldn't be certain they'd even spotted him. His first movement was to duck when he heard the shots, so my guess is he wasn't noticed as they drove down the street looking for their target, and they sped off without being aware they'd left a witness behind.'

'Lucky for him,' Bliss said. His mind ran through the processes as the night pressed in on them. 'Okay. Well, obviously we'll want to have a chat with him later. Time for Kelly Gibson, I suppose.'

Bliss pulled on the lilac one-piece suit and a pair of nitrile gloves and followed Chandler, who was already inside the tent, having clambered into the protective coverall while he was chatting. He found his partner squatting beside the body, her hair tied back to prevent strands from hanging down as she closely studied their victim. A single lamp illuminated the scene. Bliss shuffled around to the other side and took his first look at their murdered colleague.

Thankfully, their victim's face was untouched. Gunshots could often be so much more destructive than TV shows and films portrayed, and head wounds often left a person unidentifiable. Gibson's upper body was naked. Bliss assumed the paramedics had removed clothing in order to locate her wounds. Her jeans had also been stripped or cut off, but her underwear remained in place. The three separate wounds were immediately obvious; one in the left breast, a second just beneath the right breast, another in the lower abdomen.

It was perfectly natural for a hand holding a gun to travel on a slight downward arc when firing, so his guess was that the first bullet to enter Gibson's body did so through the chest. The entry wounds themselves appeared innocuous, but Bliss was aware of the devastation almost certainly wrought internally. A significant volume of blood had pooled around the stricken woman, suggesting Kelly Gibson had not died instantly. The lack of gunshot residue blackening around the three entry wounds confirmed the witness statement: the rounds travelled a distance before felling the victim.

A fresh appendectomy scar reminded Bliss of Gibson's recent absence from work, and he also noticed another weal around her armpit. He wondered if there had been a cancer scare at some point in her life, resulting in an investigation of her lymph nodes. Bliss let his gaze drift back to the woman's face. Her hooded eyes were not fully closed. They contained no revelations, no answers for him. They saw nothing, they revealed nothing. Dead eyes seldom did.

Bliss wondered if, in the last moments of her life, Kelly Gibson had been aware of the vehicle's approach, the hand holding a gun, a weapon pointing in her direction. The scene of crime and forensics reports would provide a clearer picture of what had occurred, but drawing upon the location and angles in his mind, Bliss put the white SUV's driver on the side of the road on which Gibson was walking. Despite the witness claiming to have seen the vehicle rolling by, the grouping of the bullet wounds suggested it was more likely to have paused long enough for the triggerman to fire the shots.

Three of them. In as many seconds. Maybe even a little less.

'Could have been the driver,' Bliss said quietly.

Chandler looked up at him. Her eyes roamed as she attempted to hook into his thought process. Something she was becoming increasingly expert at. Eventually she nodded and replied, 'It's possible. My initial assumption was this had to be the work of a passenger, but you're right. Could just as easily have been the driver.'

'Early thoughts?' Bliss asked, nodding towards the body.

'I have no idea. She seemed to be an ordinary woman living an ordinary life. I can't begin to imagine why anyone would do this to her.'

'Wrong time, wrong place, maybe. Could have been some form of gang initiation.

'That's a possibility. And if not, what's her story do you suppose?'

Bliss explained everything relayed to him by Price and Stringer. He shook his head and said, 'If this wasn't a chance shooting, then our best theory is this is a relationship gone badly wrong.'

'She's no age. Such a tragedy. Which reminds me, where are her husband and son?'

'I'm assuming they are both tucked away inside their house with a uniform or two. Most likely the first responders. I'll check in a moment, make sure an FLO is either here or has been arranged.'

Having a family liaison officer available to the bereaved was one of the few relatively modern policing measures Bliss approved of. The primary purpose of the FLO was to act as a conduit between the investigating team and the victim's loved ones, while at the same time obtaining information relevant to the case from the family members. In some circumstances, the role was invaluable.

Bliss continued discussing the wounds with Chandler as they exited the tent and removed the protective garments. Their conversation reminded Bliss of something he had forgotten to ask as he stripped off the gloves and discarded them in a plastic bag set aside for such items. The uniformed officer was nowhere to be seen, but Price was standing alone cradling his Heckler & Koch carbine. He looked pensive as his eyes scoured the locals gathering outside the cordon.

'I meant to ask about the casings,' Bliss said to him. 'Did you find any on the road?'

Price shook his head. 'Could have used a revolver, but I doubt it. The wounds looked like nine mil to me, and we don't see too many nine mil revolvers. Those who prefer revolvers tend to go for the large calibre. Big fuck-off 44s, like Dirty-bloody-Harry.'

Bliss thought about it, his mind immediately pulling up the stark image of Kelly Gibson's broken body. Nine millimetre bullet wounds in the UK tended to come from pistols, so he agreed with Price. But the lack of expelled casings concerned him.

'From what our witness said it doesn't sound as if the driver stopped to pick up his brass. Which suggests his hand was inside the vehicle when he pulled the trigger.'

Price shrugged. 'Or very close to it. Most casings are ejected to the right and rear of the weapon, so it's possible for the hand to have been a little outside the window, but unlikely as I doubt all three casings could have made it back through the opening into the SUV. Given the probable angles we're working with here, the gun was quite possibly pointing out of the smallest area towards the front angle of the window. Making it more likely that the hand was inside when firing. Even so, the shooter got lucky.'

'Or used a revolver after all. What might we be looking for if that's the case?'

The firearms officer pursed his lips. 'Smith & Wesson, of course. Various Chiappa models. Ruger. The Taurus is popular with those who like smaller calibre revolvers.'

'How about the KBP Kobalt?' Bliss asked.

He received a nod of appreciation from the expert. 'That might be a good shout. Plenty of those around if you ask the right people. You seem to know your weapons, Jimmy.'

'I did some firearms training when I was with the NCA.'

'I've not heard of the Kobalt before,' said Chandler.

'It's an old Russian piece,' Price said. 'Looks a bit like a Smith & Wesson J-frame revolver. There are a lot of them knocking around in Eastern Europe, with a fair few ending up over here. Organised crime emerging from Russia, Lithuania, and the Baltic nations tend to favour them because they're cheap.'

Bliss inclined his head. 'Are the bullets themselves still inside the victim?' he asked.

'They are. It's by no means certain because of the distance but I'm betting they'll be hollow-points.' He turned his insight to Chandler before continuing. 'Hollow-point slugs are designed to fragment once they've hit their target. They're extremely destructive, and they don't often go right through the body.'

'Sounds almost professional,' the DS observed, raising her eyebrows.

'Might be,' Price admitted. 'But I doubt it. A pro is likely to get closer than twenty feet or so. Wouldn't rule it out, though. Hold on...' The inspector raised a hand then put it to his ear. Someone was communicating with him through the speaker bud. His eyes widened, taking in the two detectives, before narrowing again as he cast them downwards.

'Damn!' he said sharply. 'What are the bloody odds? There's been another shooting. Just outside Crowland this time. The other side if you're coming from this direction.'

'Another one,' Bliss snapped back, a large V appearing above and between his eyes. 'Can that possibly be a coincidence?'

'Unlikely. I've been asked to scramble another team. Bloody jurisdictional horror show out there, though.'

Although it fell within a Peterborough postal address, like many towns and villages in the northern reaches of the outskirts, Crowland physically lay in the adjoining county of Lincolnshire. Bliss understood precisely what Price meant about the nightmare of crossing boundaries and entering another service's territory, but while the firearms leader was duty bound to remain at this scene, Bliss was not.

'Come on,' he said, turning to Chandler. 'Let's get out there.'

'Are you sure?' she asked him. 'Are we done here so quickly?'

'No.' Bliss shrugged. 'But we're going anyway.'

'How come?'

'A second shooting on the same night? That's raising a big red flag inside my head, Pen.'

Price winked at him. 'Good luck, Jimmy. You'll need it out there. Bring me back a stick of rock.'

As the detectives hurried towards his car, Chandler harangued Bliss about the bird in the hand principle. He said nothing. His mind was focussed on the shooting in Crowland and what, if anything, it had to do with the murder of Kelly Gibson.

5

Bliss pushed the car hard along the Frank Perkins parkway, turned towards the city recycling depot, then hit the A16. It was a twenty-minute drive in normal conditions, but he knew he could shave at least five off on a Sunday night in good weather. On a straight stretch of road with wide, flat grass verges, he called DS Short by thumbing a speed-dial number on his phone which was in its holder affixed to the dashboard.

'Mia,' he said as she answered. 'Sorry to haul you away from the family on your day off, but we have a situation.'

Bliss quickly explained the scene he and Chandler had been summoned to, and then the second shooting out near Crowland.

'Are we certain Kelly is the Farcet victim?' Short asked, a tremor in her voice.

'Sadly, yes.'

'You think the two shootings are connected?'

'Wouldn't you?' Bliss knew Short would already be on her feet and moving around the house to prepare herself to go to work.

'Pretty huge coincidence if not, boss. So, what do you want from me?'

Smiling to himself, Bliss was confident in Mia Short's abilities.

She was going places within the job and getting there quickly. He gave it some thought before identifying her role.

'Sorry, but first up is to call in the rest of the team. I'd do it myself but I'm about to be extremely busy. Our witness is coming in from the city hospital as soon as they've checked him over. I want you to get his statement. Focus on agreed distances between him and Kelly, and concentrate on the vehicle – a white SUV. Have Bish work with CCTV. I doubt there will be any along the street itself, and scarce throughout the village, so have him look at the entry and exit points immediately prior to and after the shooting. Tracing this SUV is clearly a priority task. Have Ansari take door-to-door at the scene. See that she spreads it out into neighbouring streets just in case anyone saw a vehicle come or go. I want Hunt to spend time on our victim profile, and make sure he goes deep on this one. Gratton can hold the fort and get the operation ball rolling.'

Short was one of life's note-takers, habitually carrying a leather-bound notebook with her everywhere she went. But she was also sharp, easily capable of retaining the information he had thrown her way in quick-fire fashion. She had no need to repeat it back to him for clarification. Her mind was like flypaper to his words.

'What about Kelly's husband, boss?'

'Leave him to me. Contact the FLO, tell them Penny and I will be back there just as soon as we're done with whatever we find in Crowland. Shouldn't be too long.'

'Who are gold and silver commands on this?'

'Superintendent Fletcher and DCI Edwards have agreed to a large amount of flexibility. In theory, you're gold command. Penny will be silver, and Bish our bronze. I'm a kind of salmon pink for the duration, which means we'll run this like any other major crimes operation and do without all the bullshit.'

'Okay, boss. I'm on it.'

Secure in the knowledge that the early phases of the team's

primary investigation were in safe hands, Bliss set his mind back on what lay ahead.

The further they moved away from the city the less its amber glow impinged on the dark night sky. This allowed them to see the flashing lights of the emergency services in the distance, painting that same sky in vivid hues of blue. While Bliss pushed the car as fast as safety concerns allowed him to drive, Chandler listened on an open channel to the chatter arising from the crime scene ahead.

'A car was earlier discovered in a roadside ditch,' she told Bliss. 'No word yet as to whether the shot came before or after the vehicle went into the ditch.'

'Any witnesses?' The road running east out of Peterborough was the main link to Boston, and was often well-travelled.

'Not so far. Certainly not at the scene.'

His hopes were dashed but not crushed. People often came forward some hours after witnessing something inexplicable or frightening, delaying either because they believed somebody else would report it, or because they were wary of becoming involved. It might take notices at the side of the road, perhaps even a media request, but the chances remained high that this incident had not occurred in isolation and eventually a witness would emerge.

Although the road further ahead was blocked by the road traffic collision crew, and traffic was being turned away as diversion signs were distributed, some vehicles blundered on until they were stopped and the drivers instructed to turn around to find an alternative route through. Bliss waited for a couple of minutes for the queue to disperse, before he himself became impatient. He put on his siren and front grille lights, making his way along the wrong side of the road to get to the incident more swiftly. The first vehicle he encountered tried to play chicken with him, but he was not turning for anything, and the smaller car brushed up against a hedge to avoid a collision.

Chandler carded them through a flimsy barrier of tape. Beyond, a dozen vehicles sat scattered across the road or up on grass verges.

Bliss manoeuvred his car as close as he could before they had to park up and walk the final fifty yards.

In addition to liveried police patrol vehicles, roads policing unit SUVs, and an ambulance, a pump ladder fire appliance stood at the scene with its engine running noisily. Crews from all units discussed priorities and protocols, while others went about their clear-up duties. Work on the vehicle itself appeared to have finished, and Bliss wondered what that meant for the victim. He knew by now there would be an investigator from the roads policing unit in amongst the group, plus two more third-layer command officers. This all took place beneath the harsh glare of halogen lamps encircling the immediate area.

It was a road policing unit officer they encountered first. A ruddy-cheeked Lincolnshire-based sergeant who introduced himself as Barry Smyth. In addition to his RPU status, the officer also carried a semi-automatic carbine as part of a mobile unit that provided an armed response throughout the county. He puffed away on a cigarette, though it was against regulations to do so while on duty.

'Surprised to see Peterborough's finest here,' he said by way of a greeting. Smyth stood some distance from the other responders, taking in the entire scene as it unfolded around him. His was the air of a man finished with his initial role in the incident and now waiting for everyone to move on so that he could get down to the nitty-gritty business of hunting down a killer. The end of his cigarette glowed in the dark as he took a long drag on it.

'We happened to be closer than anyone else, I guess,' Bliss offered with a tentative smile. 'I dare say the Lincoln team will be with us soon enough. It's a bit of a trek if they're coming all the way from your HQ in Nettleham.'

'So you decided you'd pop over to have a sniff around first,' Smyth said. His fluorescent jacket was grubby and ill-fitting. Bliss thought he detected dried blood smears, also.

'Actually, we just came from the scene of our own shooting in the city, and two in a single evening bothered me.'

'Hmm. I can understand why.' The armed officer took a deep breath, blew out some smoke. 'But I warn you both, there is nothing ordinary about this one. I doubt you'll have the same problem with yours.'

'How's that?'

'For starters, our victim is missing his head.'

Chandler let out a horrified gasp and put a hand to her mouth. Bliss gazed over towards the side of the road. He noticed the rear end of the crashed vehicle still protruding from the ditch. The car was well-illuminated. There was no obvious sign of crumpled bodywork, nor trees or signposts looking as if they had been struck as it came off the road. The roof had not been detached in order to free the victim.

'Doesn't look bad enough from here,' Bliss said to Smyth. 'Not to decapitate somebody. So where did you end up finding the poor sod's head? Back seat?'

Smyth jiggled his eyebrows. 'Ah, that's just it. We've searched the entire area and still haven't found it.'

6

B liss closed his eyes for a moment and blew out a long breath. Now this no longer sounded as if it could possibly be connected with his own new case; a coincidence after all. And given what he had just been told, he was glad of it.

Smyth explained the working hypothesis of the chief road policing investigator, backed by the existing physical evidence and measurements taken. They believed the victim's car was initially struck from the back, accounting for two short bursts of braking and the resulting tyre marks on the road. The two vehicles then pulled over onto the verge, after which the driver of the lead vehicle was shot three times through the open side window. The car was later pushed off the road and into the ditch, where the head was swiftly and savagely removed, probably by an electrical saw of some description.

'Sound anything like your own case, Inspector Bliss?' Smyth asked unnecessarily, a slight grin thinning his lips.

'Only the bit about three shots fired, sergeant.'

The two incidents were nothing alike if you excluded the shooting. Still, Bliss thought even the vague possibility of a connection was worth pursuing. The number of bullets fired at each incident stuck with him. 'When your team checks out CCTV or witnesses eventually come through, will you do me a favour and keep an eye and ear out for any mention of a white SUV, most probably a Range Rover?'

'Consider it done. Your suspect vehicle, I take it?'

'Yeah. We have a decent witness by all accounts. I should know more later tonight or early tomorrow. If I think there's any connection at all I'll pass any relevant information your way.'

'The head thing is worrying, though,' Smyth said, turning to gaze back at the ditch. He finished his cigarette and pinched the end, snuffing out the burn. 'Why go to all that trouble after you've already shot someone dead?'

'I take it the victim still has both his hands,' Bliss said. 'You'd have said otherwise.'

'Yes. You're thinking identification removal.'

'Not anymore I'm not. Not unless the victim's prints are not on file and the killer happens to know that.'

'We have the owner of the vehicle down as Anthony Mainwaring, at an address in Durham. But shortly before you arrived we received confirmation that he sold the vehicle five months ago. Says he sent the slip into the DVLA, but it's still registered to him. Expired MOT, no insurance on it. Sold to an Eastern European whose name was, apparently, unintelligible. The victim does have a tattoo on his left forearm. It's faded, but it may tell us something.'

'I don't suppose you have a photo, do you?' Bliss asked.

The officer pulled his mobile from his back pocket, loaded up an app and showed the screen to Bliss. He could make out an eagle clasping a cross in its beak, head turned to the right, bolts of lightning emerging from its talons. In the centre was a white anchor on a blue background. On a scroll beneath the figure there were five words. The first was 'Statul', the fifth 'Navale', the central three were indistinct, although one looked as if it might have been 'Major'. Bliss had seen the coat of arms before.

'Romanian armed forces,' he said solemnly. 'Naval forces, to be precise. The land one is similar, but instead of the anchor it has two crossed swords. The air service emblem has wings and some weird type of propeller.'

Smyth was staring at him hard.

'NCA,' Bliss explained with a lopsided grin. 'A good proportion of the Romanian organised criminals are ex-forces, and a fair few of them are operating over here.'

'You were National Crime Agency?' Smyth said, his tone quietly respectful.

'For a number of years. Serious Organised Crime Agency beforehand, from its inception.'

'Why did you give it all up for this place?'

Bliss sneaked a glance at Chandler. 'Running major crimes in Peterborough has its charms,' he replied. 'Besides, working organised crime has a habit of catching up with you. If you outstay your welcome it can be bad for your health.'

'I hear that. You must have seen some action.'

'Just ask him about his rusty sheriff's badge,' Chandler chimed in with a perfectly straight face. 'Apparently, it's not quite as tight as he'd hoped.'

'Don't take any notice of her,' Bliss told the armed officer. 'She's not all there, poor thing. Care in the community, and all that. So, any chance we could get a look at the body.'

Smyth raised his eyebrows. 'You up for that?'

'I've seen worse.'

'Okay. Give me a few minutes to clear it with the crew, then you can wander over.' He swivelled on his heels and started making his way back towards the ditched vehicle.

Bliss turned to Chandler. 'It's entirely up to you if you want to peek in under the canopy, Pen. I won't blame you if you decide not to.'

'That bad is it, boss?'

'It's not so much the gore that gets to you, although it's decidedly grotesque. More a question of what it does to your mind and how long it lingers. Thing is, our brains are predisposed to seeing fellow human beings with heads. When you see a body without one, it's as if the brain can't compute any of the information coming from the eyes. Initially the glitch lasts only a few seconds, but it then replays it for you every so often. It's a bloody weird sensation on top of the ugliness of it.'

Chandler's chest rose and fell. She swallowed once. 'I'll come with you. All part of the job.'

'If you're sure.' Bliss set his jaw. 'Just don't say I never warned you.'

7

During the drive back from Crowland, both detectives were largely quiet. After seeing what remained of the body, Chandler acknowledged her difficulty in reconciling the nightmarish figure inside the vehicle with a human being. Despite Bliss's warning about how the sight of a headless corpse played tricks on the mind, in her opinion he had underplayed the gruesomeness factor by a wide margin.

The raw and still-glistening disarray of severed muscles, veins, arteries, and subcutaneous tissues, was grotesque enough. The ragged edges of meat left behind by a saw resembled anything but a human being. But it was the stark clash between the dark and bloody pulp of tissue, and the hard white nubs of exposed cervical vertebrae and spinal cord, that jarred most of all. Some things were never meant to be displayed anywhere other than on an operating or autopsy table. Finally, there was the gaping trachea to conjure with, looking for all the world as if it might find a way to start aspirating blood-tainted air at any moment.

To her credit, Chandler had merely swallowed thickly a couple of times, managing to keep down her dinner. Bliss knew his partner had seen something which would live with her for some time to come, and he let it percolate as they drove back to Farcet on the south side of the city.

The familiar multiple spires of the cathedral came into view, by which point in the journey, Bliss had dismissed from his thoughts the horrific image of the Crowland victim's neck. Instead he focussed on the gunshots. Crime scene investigators confirmed three small calibre entry wounds to the chest, with only a solitary corresponding exit injury. This nagged at him. On hearing about the second shooting victim being subsequently decapitated, Bliss wondered if the murders were linked after all. Two shootings in a single night was the kind of statistical rarity and coincidence that occurred every now and then.

The bullet wounds themselves bothered him, though.

The truncated ex-Romanian serviceman was shot from a much closer distance than Kelly Gibson had been. Gunshot residue stippled the victim's T-shirt at the point where the three bullets entered him. Bliss was aware of the ballistic documentation suggesting shots fired from more than twelve inches away allowed for far greater forensic misinterpretation. Both Smyth and Bliss agreed, however, that the trigger had most likely been pulled outside the driver's door while it was open, as the projectiles had clearly not passed through either glass or bodywork before striking the victim.

Three shots with a small calibre weapon. No casings found. One exit wound.

Bliss asked himself what the chances were of two similar shootings occurring on the same evening around the city and the incidents not being connected.

Not impossible, he decided. *But highly unlikely.*

The question now was, in what way could the two murders be linked?

The street in Farcet remained sealed off to anyone other than residents and emergency service personnel. In addition to standard elevated halogen lamp rigs used to illuminate crime scenes, forensic specialists also held Labino white light torches, whose piercing beams flashed around on the road and pavement like an under-rehearsed display. Bliss assumed the techs were continuing to look for expelled firearm casings, despite realising their search was almost certainly futile. The CSI unit were nothing if not thorough.

Detective Constable Gul Ansari led the door-to-door canvassing, and stationed herself close to the crime scene. Bliss and Chandler found their colleague standing outside the door of Kelly Gibson's narrow terraced home. Hands buried deep inside her pockets, head down, Ansari cut a forlorn figure. The young DC jerked to attention as she heard footsteps approaching. Sad, moist eyes greeted them.

'How are things here?' Bliss asked, keeping his tone casual. The personal element of such investigations was something less experienced detectives struggled with. Bliss was having difficulty with it, so he could only imagine how Ansari was coping.

'Nothing much coming in from the canvas, boss.' Ansari shrugged before hunching back into herself. 'Crime scene techs not turning up anything, either.'

'How about Kelly's husband? How's he doing?'

'He's not here. He's away on a business trip to Dubai. He was informed by local police and is flying home, but for now we have Kelly's sister indoors with the son. The boy was being looked after by a babysitter when the shooting occurred. She gave us a brief statement, and then we had her taken home as soon as the sister arrived.'

'Who interviewed the sitter?'

'One of the uniforms. The sitter is only just nineteen and she was pretty hysterical so I hear.'

'Do you happen to know if the officer asked her where Kelly was this evening?'

'They did. According to the girl, Kelly met up with a couple of old friends for an early dinner and drinks in Holbeach.'

Bliss grimaced and said, 'Shit! Quickest route home from there is the A16, which puts her driving past the scene we've just come from.'

He drew in a deep breath. Something clicked inside Bliss's head which gave him pause for thought. He glanced at Chandler, then back to Ansari.

'Either of you ever watch the film *Fargo*?' he asked. 'Not the TV show, the film.'

Chandler nodded. 'Yeah. Frances McDormand, Steve Buscemi.'

'That's the one. Well, in the film a cop is shot to death on the side of the road, and as the killer attempts to dispose of the body, a car coming in the opposite direction slows down as it goes by and a young couple spot what's going on. They speed off, but the killer jumps back into his car and gives chase. The couple are going so fast on the icy surface they run right off it and he shoots them both dead.'

Bliss paused, sighed. 'I'm wondering if we have a similar occurrence here. That maybe Kelly drove by the scene just outside Crowland, saw something she should not have seen, and was then chased down by the killer.'

'That's a little speculative, boss,' Chandler said. She nudged him with her elbow. 'Even by your standards.'

'Perhaps. But is it any more fanciful than having two separate and unconnected fatal shootings so close together on the same night? Especially when it seems certain one of those victims was in the same vicinity as the other?'

His partner tilted her head to one side. 'Well, when you put it like that…'

'It gives us our motive. It also explains both the similarities and the differences between the two murders. Someone planned the first, but not the second. Because the call about the Crowland shooting came in after this one, we assumed it had occurred afterwards. Now I think it's the other way around. And if we can place a white SUV along the A16 somewhere earlier tonight, then who knows?'

'I see where you're going with that, boss,' Ansari said, nodding as she spoke. 'But if Kelly saw something bad out there, why did she not call it in, or even drive directly to Thorpe Wood if she felt she might be in danger?'

'Well, first of all we can't know exactly what happened. It could be that she saw something, but nothing which overly concerned her. It may be she was entirely unaware of the pursuit going on behind her.'

'So then why did somebody follow her and kill her if what she stumbled across caused her no concern?' Chandler asked.

'Maybe they were unsure as to what exactly the driver saw as they passed by. Didn't want to take any chances. Look, it's pure speculation for now. It fits, I think. But if we expand the CCTV search, it will hopefully tell us a great deal more.'

'That would make for a welcome change.'

'Pen, give Bish a call and have him request the appropriate footage. We want the A16 from Holbeach to Crowland, and Crowland to Farcet. There is the back road route via Thorney and Whittlesey to consider, but the quickest way is A16 to A15, and then the Frank Perkins parkway from the Eye roundabout at Parnwell. Have him consult with the investigators out in Crowland as to timescale, with special attention on the three vehicles involved.'

Bliss turned and dipped his head in the direction of the front door. 'How's the sister holding up?'

'As well as can be expected. For the child's sake more than her own. Keeping him calm is helping her control her own emotions. FLO is with them.'

'Excellent. And how about you, Gul? How are you doing?'

Ansari seemed surprised to be asked. 'I'm fine, boss. It's hard to take when the victim is familiar to you, but the job remains the same.'

'Good answer. But you let me know if it starts weighing on your mind. Pen and I have to get back to HQ to interview our main witness. Meanwhile, have a quick word with the sister and then the sitter. I want to know more about Kelly's evening out, and especially any names and contact details if at all possible. We need to interview whoever she was with, and I want particular focus on how she was behaving and what time she left them.'

'You really think these two shooting incidents are connected, boss?'

'I do. More so now that I know where Kelly was earlier this evening.'

'Even though the other victim was beheaded?'

'If I'm right about why Kelly was shot, then yes. I'm pretty sure it's incidental to the original murder.'

'You reckon there's anything more sinister to the beheading, boss?'

Bliss met the young DC's wavering gaze and held it. 'Let's not wander down such a path just yet,' he said. 'The city was rocked hard enough a few months ago with the fear that terrorists might have struck so close by. I don't want to stir it all up again if I don't have to. Besides, a Romanian ex-serviceman is not exactly your typical terrorist victim in this country.'

Ansari appeared satisfied with his response. Bliss started walking back to the car and motioned for Chandler to join him. As she drew level with him, he said, 'I'm beginning to think Kelly was simply all out of luck here tonight. She sets off for home ten minutes earlier and I reckon she's sitting indoors now with her son tucked up in bed.'

'So you think your *Fargo* scenario is what took place, then?'

'I do, Pen. Who knows what she actually saw as she drove down that road earlier. It was just her misfortune to cross paths with a killer hell-bent on covering his tracks.'

Chandler shuddered as she opened the passenger door and started to climb in. 'Somehow that makes it all the worse.'

Bliss agreed. Now it was his job to prove his gut right.

8

L ate on Sunday night was usually a quiet and relatively peaceful time to be inside the Thorpe Wood police station. Not this particular Sunday night, however. Tonight the city had, for reasons known only to its seamy underbelly, immersed itself in an explosion of major crimes after the sun fell away over the horizon. Light leaked from every window, and the moment Bliss and Chandler stepped through the doors up from the underground car park they were met with scenes of furious activity.

'The taxpayers are getting their money's worth tonight,' Chandler observed caustically as they took the stairs up to the major crimes unit.

'They do every night as far as I'm concerned,' Bliss responded, his mind drifting elsewhere. The checklist of jobs and actions related to a fatal shooting was pretty much the same as any investigation that came across the team's desks. However, the high probability of a link to the murder in Crowland added further layers of complexity and difficulty.

The small border town lay in the South Holland district of Lincolnshire, but only a mile or so outside the Peterborough city boundary. Its four-roomed police station was staffed by both

Cambridgeshire and Lincolnshire officers, and the crossing of jurisdictions had proven problematic on several previous occasions. The winter before, a significant drug bust in the town had fallen foul of the breakdown in communications that occurs occasionally between separate police organisations, resulting in the dealers escaping into the Fens. Two of the four were still at large as far as Bliss knew.

In his absence, DS Short had worked her magic since his earlier phone call. The team who had initially commandeered the largest incident room for their ATM raid were relocated at Short's insistence, backed up by some considerable clout from DCI Edwards. Bliss was glad of the extra space, and he thanked his sergeant for acting decisively.

'We're up and running, boss,' she told him. 'DS Bishop is working closely with tech-ops to collate all of the relevant CCTV footage you requested. DC Ansari just called to let me know she'd spoken to you and had started work on interviewing the sister to gather the info you wanted. I hope you don't mind, but I took DC Hunt off the victim profile and sent him to interview the sitter before it got too late. It's close to midnight as it is, but I figured the poor kid won't be getting much sleep tonight anyway.'

Colour in her cheeks, Short paused for breath before continuing. 'Phil Gratton is managing the office and doing a great job keeping the log and timeline going. As you can imagine, there are a lot of moving parts, but he's coping well. I've already liaised with command at the Crowland scene, and they will be sharing all relevant information with us, plus they have their county CCTV people on the case for the A16 footage.'

Smiling his appreciation, Bliss said, 'Thank you, Mia. Great work. You've made my life so much easier.'

'It's why I get paid the small bucks, boss.'

'You're worth your weight in printer ink to me at the moment.'

'Um… thank you. I think.'

'It's a good thing, Mia. Believe me. Printer ink is more expensive than gold and a hugely valuable commodity.'

'Just doing my job, boss. Speaking of which, I'm told you believe the two shootings might be connected, yes?'

'I consider it a viable working theory. It also makes more sense than anything else I can think of right now.'

'So where do we stand in terms of the Crowland murder? In respect of access and command, I mean.'

'That all depends. Lincolnshire police will view the murder of Kelly as the secondary scene, and from their perspective they'd be right to do so. We would if the roles were reversed. As for what it does to command I have no idea, because someone has to figure out if we are working with them or they are working with us. One of us has to take lead, only I'm not sure which it will be. I'll be nipping up to see DCI Edwards shortly, so I hope to know more by the time I leave her office.'

'How do you want me to proceed from here?'

'For now, put all of our resources into Kelly. Oh, and I want to speak with the witness as soon as I'm done with the DCI. Not sure we'll get any more out of him, but I want a crack at the bloke before his mind starts shutting it all down.'

Out in the major crimes area, Bliss caught up with Gratton. 'DS Short tells me you're doing a fine job,' he said to the young constable. 'Look, Phil, DC Carmichael has put in for a transfer to counter-terrorism, so this post is yours on a permanent basis if you want it. Take a day to think about it if necessary.'

Gratton beamed. 'No need, boss. I'm chuffed to bits by the offer. I really like it here.'

'Well, we like having you. You're a good fit for the team. Put in the paperwork, I'll sign off on it.'

Gratton stood in place, seemingly uneasy now. Bliss met the man's anxious gaze. 'Is there something you want to get off your chest, constable?'

'Sir?'

'Something you'd like to tell me about your sudden appearance in my team a few months ago, perhaps linked to DC Carmichael's rapid shift to the CTU?'

'You know, don't you?' Gratton looked horrified.

'What? That you were posted here in June to spy on me, on us, by those idiots from the IOPC ahead of their investigation into me? Yes, I figured it out.'

'So then why… why are you asking me to stay on?'

'Because you didn't do as they asked. You took the posting because you had no choice. But you fed them nothing. Instead you got stuck in here and worked with us rather than against us. I don't care why you came here, only about what you do now you're one of us. Understood?'

Gratton fought against a trembling bottom lip. 'Yes, boss. Thank you. Thank you so much. And the rest of the team?'

'Need know none of it.'

'But, boss. How… how did you know?'

Bliss smiled. 'There was something about the way you introduced yourself. Couldn't put my finger on it at first. A look in your eyes, maybe. So I asked around about you.'

'And you never said a word to me about it.'

'I was waiting to see how you acted. I got a sense you were uncomfortable with the whole thing, so I let it play out.'

'Well, I'm very glad you did, boss.'

'Yes. Me, too,' Bliss replied, turning away.

He was back out on the staircase about to head up when Bishop called him. He caught sight of his reflection in the window on the landing, lit up against the darkness outside. As with all cities, the night was never fully black, but the streetlights and the glow from local housing estates softened the impact of forty-year-old architecture. As for himself, Bliss turned his eyes away.

'I have a white Range Rover entering and exiting Farcet inside our timeline,' Bishop said. 'We're back-tracing it now, and so far we have it coming in along the route you suggested.'

'And the bad news is?'

'How do you know there is any?'

'Because you don't sound anywhere near as excited as you should be by the news you just gave me,' Bliss told him. His pulse was racing, but he thought he knew what his DS was about to tell him.

'The plate is false,' Bishop confirmed. 'Belongs to a Range Rover right enough, but one which was destroyed a year or so ago following a bad RTC in which the driver and two passengers were killed.'

Bliss sighed and thumbed the scar on his forehead. It was a mannerism he returned to whenever an investigation turned up unwanted news. He took a breath and tried not to sound too disappointed.

'Good work anyway, Bish. It's still progress. As soon as you and the people in Lincs confirm the same vehicle was on the A16 around the time of the Crowland murder, let me know. Also, trace the motor as far as you can after it left Farcet. I doubt we'll get too far with it because whoever did this tonight is no mug and they'll have a route out where eventually our cameras can't follow.'

'Will do, boss. It's looking as if you were right, though. Same man responsible for both shootings.'

'Yeah. Though I wish I was wrong on this one occasion. He's no fool this bloke we're dealing with. Certainly not a man dead from the neck up.'

'Boss?'

Bliss huffed a humourless laugh. 'Nothing. Bad taste. It was a saying my old man often used to describe people he considered stupid. Just popped into my mind and I thought it was appropriate. But it wasn't. Forget I ever said it.'

'Hard to now, boss. It's stuck there in my brain right alongside all your other homilies and witticisms. Actually, I rather like it. Might use it myself. In different circumstances, of course.'

'Of course. And you're welcome. Have that one on me. By the

way, you said you have the Rover moving in and out of Farcet. In which direction did it leave?'

'Left onto Broadway and through into Yaxley.'

Closing his eyes, Bliss pictured the vehicle's movements. His guess was that rather than continue on and head for the A1, or travel through towards Peterborough, the SUV had detoured earlier, into the centre of the village and out the other side, disappearing off camera into the Fens. Implying their shooter was familiar with the area if so.

He cut the connection after Bishop confirmed he would call back the moment any further news came in. Bliss then turned his thoughts to Edwards, knowing that eventually he might have to convince her to fight for the major crimes team taking the lead on both murders. It was a hard sell, but maybe this time his DCI would accept that she owed him one.

Bliss did not relish the prospect of investigating a case in which some nutjob had removed the victim's head from both its body and the crime scene itself, but if the same person was also responsible for gunning down Kelly Gibson then he wanted to own it. He would have his say, and intended to stand his ground. It was time to find out if his boss was willing to stand with him.

9

Born and raised in a landlocked country, Paul did not see the ocean until he was nineteen years old. He had loved the sea ever since, acquiring a particular fondness for English coastal towns. He visited many along the eastern coastline, from Margate in Kent all the way up to Yorkshire's Whitby. Mablethorpe was new to him, and from the moment he had discovered his destination that day, Paul's intention was to enjoy mixing business with pleasure.

He arrived at high tide shortly after 6am. Finding a parking space close to the front was easy enough at that time of morning, and he ended up a short walk from the fairground and amusement parade. With the temperature not quite hitting double digits, and a salty breeze coming in off the sea, Paul took a quiet stroll along the promenade. Wrapped up tight in his favourite leather jacket, gloved hands stuffed into its pockets, he embraced the buffeting gusts with deep breaths and long exhalations of building excitement.

Nothing was yet open as he walked past the fairground and the lifeboat station further down, encountering only a few hardy dog-walkers and joggers along the way. He kept his head down as they passed by, though they paid him little or no attention. Although

Paul appreciated the hustle and bustle of tourists clamouring for sandy beaches and entertainment for their children, he much preferred the relative solitude afforded by early mornings. It was quite something to experience the reawakening of a seaside town; the change in sounds, smells, moods, and the ever-colourful visual stimulus as the day wore on. Overnight, the detritus left behind by thoughtless holidaymakers had been flushed away, and the resort was reborn anew around him. Paul felt as if he were part of its reanimation, and there was comfort in that.

Though the outer shell of the town was tranquil during those early hours, behind the scenes he knew the townsfolk were busy, preparations being made for another long day ahead. There was still some money to squeeze from the season, and a hive of activity started taking place behind closed doors well away from the public gaze. Today this knowledge was especially useful to Paul.

There was nothing particularly unique or interesting about the architecture to keep him exploring, so he found a café whose garish advertising boards mentioned hot tea and toasties. The toasted sandwich was something else he liked about England, and over the years he had tried many filling combinations. On this morning he settled for cheese and ham, and a large mug of tea which was as hot as advertised. He chewed his food slowly in order to appreciate the different flavours. The tea was good and strong. When he was done, he felt better prepared for what lay ahead. He thanked the woman behind the counter and left the café, content with his day so far as he made the short journey to his ultimate destination that morning.

The frontage of Pete's Plaice was clean and inviting, its location little more than a hundred yards from the sea front itself. Paul was less interested in the customer entrance as he was the one at the rear, given the intelligence provided to him in a text shortly before midnight which suggested staff tended to use the scuffed and faded blue door at the back of the premises.

It was a little before 8.30 when he made his way around the

corner into a quiet side street, and on through an alley servicing several properties, expecting only one person to be working inside the shop at this time of day.

The single-storey red brick extension held only two windows, both small with frosted glass panes and steel bars fitted on the inside. Paul paused to listen by the blue door, smiling at the sound of a woman singing to herself somewhere behind it. He recognised the tune: 'Perfect', by Ed Sheeran. Paul was not a fan and did not care for the song much, but he listened along for a few beats before rapping his hard, bulbous knuckles on the door.

When Mariana Iliescu pulled it open, her narrow inquisitive eyes swiftly became wide with horror. Paul had no idea who or what she might have been expecting when she answered his knock, but he knew it could not possibly have been either him or the gun he now pointed at her face.

'Don't scream,' he warned. His voice was low and untroubled. 'Just move back inside and remain calm.'

Mariana had no clue who he was, but he thought she might have a terrible idea of exactly *what* he was.

The Clujian woman did as she was told. She said nothing as she stepped backwards into the painted brick passageway, her eyes never leaving the steel barrel of the weapon he held on her. The confined space reeked of fish and cooking oil. Paul smiled as the cloying odours washed over him; his favourite meal these days was fish and chips, and the smells inside the shop immediately made him feel warm and comfortable. Despite the digesting toastie, his stomach burbled.

Originally from Cluj-Napoca, the unofficial capital of the Transylvanian region of north-western Romania, Mariana's features were delicately chiselled, as if a great artist had been employed to sculpt them from the finest porcelain. Even with her thick hair tied up and hidden beneath a white protective cap, and without any trace of make-up on her face, Paul could see she was a fine-looking woman. Tall and slender, with a full bust filling out her sweater, the sight of Mariana up close caused him to question whether there might be more fun to be enjoyed here than first anticipated. When eventually he glanced up into the woman's eyes, he could tell she knew what he had been thinking. He saw hope spark there for a moment, and knew then that she would submit to anything he asked of her in exchange for her life.

Dismissing for now the possibilities her firm body might offer, Paul took a look around what appeared to be a preparation room for the food about to be cooked and served. It was small, not particularly hygienic and cracked plaster bulged obscenely from the walls. Dark smudges of mould lay exposed to the air beneath thin slivers of paint peeling from a patch of ceiling in one corner. Happy not to be eating here, Paul passed by two other rooms along the narrow corridor to check out the service area, where he noticed the hatches on both fryers were open, the sound of boiling oil bubbling away inside. He nodded absently to himself.

Turning back into the dark passage, Paul squeezed past the young woman. As he did, he lowered himself slightly so that his chest brushed against hers and their groins meshed. He lingered briefly until his hardness twitched, and revulsion replaced fear in her gaze. He then added flint to his gaze, put a hand inside his jacket and came out with a photograph, which he turned and showed to Mariana.

'You know who this is?' he asked.

The woman looked at the photo for little more than a second before averting her gaze. This told Paul that she knew the man in the snapshot, though her head shook in mute denial.

He flashed a crooked smile. 'I know that you do,' he said. 'Listen to me carefully now. I will allow you one lie. But only the one. So, tell me Mariana, do you know where he is?'

This time there was a lengthy pause. Paul understood. The woman was torn between loyalty and her fear of what this stranger pointing a gun at her head might do to her if she lied. In the end she did what most people do when they are unfamiliar with the kind of person they are dealing with. The shake of her head was less certain now, but still the gesture was clear.

Paul took a deep breath. His eyes narrowed. He glanced at the preparation room, and then back towards the service area entrance. When his gaze returned to Mariana, it was not kind.

'Potato chipper or fryer?' he asked casually, as if he were enquiring as to her preference between tea or coffee.

This time her own eyes seemed not to know whether to narrow or widen further still. The question had confused her, and she made no reply.

'Mariana,' he said softly. 'I know you understand English, but I could just as easily speak to you in your native tongue if you preferred it. So, let's not waste time with pretence. I need to know where I can find the man in the photograph. I believe you know the answer. I also believe you have no clue what I am capable of doing to you in the event you keep lying to me. So, what I am asking you is very clear: if you do not tell me what I want to hear, I will put your left hand in either the potato chipper or the deep fat fryer. In an act of kindness, I am offering you the choice as to which. But, and let me make this clearer still, if that is not enough to prise the truth from you, then I shall continue with your other hand, only I will not then be so kind. Understood?'

Mariana nodded as her eyes blazed and her body started trembling. 'Yes! Yes, I understand you.'

'There. That was not so difficult, was it?'

'N… no.'

'So, then. Tell me, Mariana, do you know where I can find this man?'

'I do.'

The terrified woman told him exactly where he could find the man in the photograph, and what he did for a living. When she was done, Paul tucked his gun away inside his jacket pocket and put his large hands on both of Mariana's trembling arms to steady her.

'Thank you,' he said. He sighed, long and deep. 'Such a shame you needed that final persuasion.'

'Wh… what do you mean?' she asked, barely able to choke out the words.

'I was fair with you, was I not? I told you right from the beginning. I allow only one lie. The second I cannot forgive.'

'What do you mean? What does that mean?!' she cried.

Paul's grip tightened as he shoved her back against the wall with enough force to drive the air from her lungs. Then he leaned closer to whisper in her ear. 'Only that while I do thank you for eventually telling me what I wanted to know, there has to be suitable punishment for your second lie.'

'No…' The woman's legs buckled beneath her, and she began wailing and sobbing.

'It's okay,' he said softly, using the thick fingers of one hand to delicately push back strands of hair which had escaped the elastic of her hat. 'It won't be as bad as you might imagine.' He switched his gaze between the serving area and prep room once more. 'I like you, Mariana. We will have a little fun first. After which, you still get to choose.'

10

B liss was awake early, dawn's tentative light encroaching across the garden toward the rear of the house. For the first time in as long as he could remember, the night temperature dipped to such a degree that when he awoke shortly after 5am his exposed arm was cold enough for him to immediately withdraw it beneath the duvet and rub some warmth back into his flesh with his other hand.

When he glanced at the clock on the bedside cabinet, Bliss groaned. It had been a late night, and with barely four hours' sleep behind him he had an early briefing to deliver. Snoozing only ever seemed to make him feel worse later in the day, so he dragged himself out of bed, hit the shower and luxuriated beneath its powerful jets for a good twenty minutes. If nothing else, his skin felt hydrated.

Taking his time over coffee, Bliss stood by the living room sliding glass doors looking out at the garden. The sight of it always made him feel more relaxed, and often he caught himself smiling as his eyes took in the various plants, koi pond, bamboo bridge and rough standing stones. It was the one place in which he was ever able to find true peace. He soaked it all up, wishing it could seep through his flesh and into his bones.

For once, the Zen garden failed to work its charms on him. Overwhelmed by the feeling that the current investigation was only going to get worse, he was unable to relax and tension started building in his neck and shoulders.

His meeting with DCI Edwards in the remaining minutes of the previous night had not lasted long. After apprising his boss of progress made, Bliss dropped the first hint that he would be keen for his team to have a foot in each of the two murder investigations.

'How convinced are you that these incidents will eventually be connected?' Edwards asked.

'Virtually a hundred per cent.' Bliss gave a confident nod. 'DS Bishop has so far been able to track the Range Rover back along the route I suggested it may have taken had it come from the direction of Crowland. I need the confirmation from Lincs, but I'm as certain as I can be.'

The DCI's response was to ease back into her chair, the subsequent head-nodding less assured. 'We have two things working for us, one against,' she said objectively. 'The latter being the wider implications of the Crowland murder. This man who was beheaded is clearly the primary target, and the sheer brutality of what was done to him after he was already murdered suggests a potential fallout to follow. In our favour is the fact that Kelly Gibson is part of our family, and also that we are the closest major crimes unit to the scene.'

'You think you'll be able to swing it if the time comes, boss?'

Bliss no longer assumed Edwards to be the kind of leader who chose to fight against him and every request he made. Their relationship had improved immeasurably in the ten months during which he had worked under her command. Whilst he would never presume them to be friends, the occasional friendly exchanges were now more commonplace.

'I may yet need the super to run with this on our behalf, Bliss. If you verify the connection, then I will certainly make the initial request on behalf of the team. However, it could well depend on who this other victim is. Perhaps even on our suspect if we arrive at one in the next day or so.'

'How d'you mean?'

'Well, you are the ex-NCA officer, Bliss.'

'You're thinking organised crime?' Edwards was right to ruminate along those lines. It was the same direction his own thoughts were taking him.

'I am. However, if Lincs already have open cases on either the victim or the shooter, then it will most likely be their investigation to handle.'

'We'll keep hold of our own, though, yes? We get to chase down Kelly's killer.'

Edwards's nod carried conviction with it this time. 'You can count on it. We will offer any and all assistance in the Crowland killing, but we deal with Kelly ourselves.'

Bliss liked this version of his boss. The fact that she referred to Kelly Gibson as 'family' and also used her first name was the kind of touch he had hoped for from the DCI, and for once she seemed more in tune with the case itself than the political quagmire surrounding it. Bliss ended the meeting by offering assurances that he would steer clear of the Lincs team until the connection between the two killings had been firmly established. That appeared to satisfy Edwards.

Raymond Gantry, the forty-five-year-old man who witnessed the gunning down of the police administration worker, had ultimately offered Bliss and Chandler nothing more than they already knew from his statement taken earlier by DS Short. Following Short's briefing about the interview, Bliss decided to take Gantry through it one more time to see if there were any inconsistencies.

Having overcome his initial shock at what had happened on the street where he lived, Gantry was understandably reluctant to revisit the incident in his mind. But with Bliss gently steering him through it, from the moment the vehicle's presence first caught his attention to the point at which it roared away with its tyres screeching, the witness made it all the way through the harrowing story for a second time.

The one change to his original verbal statement was that the white Range Rover had probably stopped in those few brief seconds when the gunman opened fire, which tied in with Bliss's own line of thinking. Gantry revealed how he first noticed the SUV because it felt closer than usual as it glided past the parked cars lining the street. He insisted it was virtually silent on a still and soundless street, and at first had appeared huge. It had taken a moment or two before he realised its size was exaggerated because the vehicle was driving on the wrong side of the road.

By the time the shots started ringing out in rapid succession, Gantry's attention had switched towards the figure making its way hurriedly towards him. He did not know the eventual victim, he attested, but recognised her as a near neighbour and was about to nod and bid her a good evening. The sound of gunshots broke the stillness and reverberated along the street, confusing Gantry as to how many shots had been fired. He first ducked and squatted, and then threw himself to the floor. He only heard the Rover driving away, his view obscured by the parked vehicles belonging to neighbours. But by then his focus was on the woman lying spread-eagled on the pavement ahead of him.

Her face turned his way, the woman's mouth hung open in an endless scream that would never be heard. Her eyes appeared to bulge in their sockets, the whites almost seeming to glow in the dark. She was still, not even groaning. Gantry admitted that was the moment he realised the intended victim was not him, and that the neighbour was dead. When he spoke about this to Bliss and Chandler he paused, before revealing that for a brief few seconds before the first shot, the street behind the Range Rover had been stained in blood red.

'Brake lights?' Bliss suggested.

Gantry closed his eyes, gave a stiff nod, and then fell silent as his shoulders heaved and fresh tears spilled down both cheeks. Bliss lowered his head and ended the interview. When a witness reached such an emotional stage, it was pointless carrying on. There was also their own welfare to consider. Every mention of Kelly Gibson's murder felt like a dagger being driven into his own heart.

As he and Chandler left the room with the still-sobbing man being comforted by a uniformed officer, Bliss expressed his hope that the babysitter and the sister might yet provide further information whilst giving their formal statements, but he was convinced that neither were going to offer any clues as to the identity of Kelly's killer. He was as certain as he could be that her murder was unplanned, and that she was simply an innocent motorist who happened to be passing by an incident at which a monster had taken notice of her.

The cold morning brought with it no comfort or respite from the thoughts burrowing inside Bliss's mind. After churning over the previous night's events, he decided there was time for a second cup of coffee. He also knocked up some scrambled eggs on toast. Bliss sensed it might be a long and hectic day, which invariably resulted in him forgetting to eat.

11

U pon arrival at HQ, Bliss headed straight for the incident room assigned to the case. Detective Sergeant Short was the only person there, and she appeared drawn and pale. She had every right to be, having worked through the night to ensure that, by the time the first briefing came around, the boards were ready, case logs as current as possible, statements and information collated, and relevant staffing arranged. Bliss thought she looked spent, and he felt a pang of sympathy.

'Why don't you get yourself off home,' he suggested, pulling across a chair and sitting by her side. 'We can take the next step forward while you get some sleep. Join us later this afternoon if you feel up to it.'

Short refused, as Bliss had guessed she would.

'I'm fine, boss. I'll grab a shower and a change of clothes and I'll be as right as rain. I'd really rather not lose track, if that's all the same to you.'

'Of course. You've done a great job by the look of things, Mia. You're welcome to stay, but if you change your mind just let me know. So, how about you bring me up to date?'

Short indicated the whiteboards. 'Starting with the crime scene itself, CSI tell us they found no casings. So, chances are good that a revolver was the weapon used. You've spoken to both the witness and Bish, so you already know about the Range Rover and how the shooting went down. It was obviously a deliberate hit on Kelly, and although we can't yet confirm the motive, everything points towards your theory that she may have seen something she shouldn't have when driving home from an evening out with her friends. Door-to-door has come up with no more witnesses.'

'Nothing in Kelly's background to suggest any other reason why somebody might want her dead?' Bliss asked.

'No, boss. Not that we expected to find anything.'

'Any word yet from Lincs? I'm waiting for CCTV confirmation that the Rover was seen on the A16 around the time of the Crowland murder, and an update from Sergeant Smyth, their lead RPU and firearms officer on the scene.'

'We're expecting the CCTV information any moment. They will contact Bish directly, and if there is anything worth viewing they'll send it on. Your RPU man left a message to say he'll be putting the word out about a missing ex-forces Romanian, as well as his interest in a white Range Rover.'

'Is the scene clear over there now?'

'Not quite. They have it sheeted and cordoned off still, but have opened up the northbound lane to traffic, managed by temporary lights. Is there anything you feel we might gain by revisiting in daylight?'

Bliss shook his head. 'No. I suspect the Lincs detectives will be there, and I don't want to bowl up and ruffle any feathers unnecessarily. Smyth was a little leery of us at first, but he opened up as soon as he realised we weren't looking to steal the case away from them. We can't afford to lose any flow of information right now, so let's just keep a watchful eye on it. If it reveals what I expect it to reveal, then the moment we have the CCTV in we can put forward a request to officially link the two investigations. The DCI seems up for it.'

At that moment, Chandler barged her way into the room, carrying a wilting cup holder with three large coffees planted in it. 'Good morning, fellow crime-fighters,' she said. 'I have arrived armed with liquid sustenance.'

'You're in a good mood,' Bliss said, reaching over and twisting the black coffee out of its slot. Someone had taken time to mark the side of the cup, so he knew which was his.

'Somebody obviously got some sleep last night,' Short joined in. Then she gave a wide grin and narrowed her gaze. 'Or did you get lucky?' She accepted the offered latte and raised it in salute.

Puffing out her lips, Chandler said, 'Chance would be a fine thing, Mia. I might as well be wearing a chastity belt for the all action I'm seeing.'

'Woah,' Bliss cried, wincing and turning his head away. 'Too much information, thank you.'

'Sorry, boss. Did we invade your safe space? Have you become a tender little snowflake overnight?'

'I don't know about a snowflake, but I can see an avalanche of shit jobs coming your way if you're not careful.'

Chandler laughed and pinched his cheek. Bliss glared back, which only increased the laughter.

'So how was Turkey?' Short asked her.

'Different. It's the first time I've been over there with any sense that I might actually achieve something. The Turkish national security bloke I met with seems to be a reasonable sort. The MI6 agent is closer to fifty than forty, and really knows her way around the system out there. I travelled over in hope, and returned in confidence.'

They chatted for a while longer. Short remembered something and yanked open her drawer. She took out two plastic tubs. 'Cake in one, cookies in the other,' she said, grinning from ear to ear as she pushed them across the desk. 'I've started baking again.'

'You bake?' Bliss said. It was news to him.

'Oh, yes. Back when I was on maternity leave I got into it. I spent a lot of time awake, and I went baking crazy. I hadn't done any for a while, so did some yesterday morning. I forgot all about this batch.'

Bliss was full of breakfast, but he took a slice of cake and a chocolate chip. The fluffy and moist lemon drizzle went down a treat, and the cookie was so moreish he wantonly eyed the open container.

Short caught him looking and laughed. 'Good?' she asked.

Bliss closed his eyes and purred. 'Mmm. Delightful.'

'Go on then. One more. As you're the boss.'

'What about me?' Chandler looked up, still savouring her slice of cake.

'Sorry,' Short told her, pulling the tub close to her chest. 'But I don't need to suck up to you.'

DC Ansari was next through the door, beating Bishop and Gratton to it by seconds. Others filtered through over the next few minutes, including several uniforms, and eventually they were joined by Hunt who was last to arrive. Bliss noted the DC's tardiness before allowing Short to run the briefing in his stead.

He observed her performance closely throughout. An idea came to him, and as he ruminated he watched his DS at work, taking note of the way Short engaged with the team, admiring how she used words sparingly yet still somehow managed to deliver all the facts in a concise and even-handed manner.

The only new update from the team arose from Hunt, who had formally interviewed the babysitter. The young girl had not heard the shots, most likely because she was at the back of the house at the time. She told Hunt that, although she had been a little concerned by the delay in Kelly reaching home, the first she had become aware of anything amiss was when she went back into the living room and saw all the flashing lights from emergency vehicles outside.

Hunt handed back to Short when he was done. Bliss stepped up only after the DS had walked the team through every salient point of the investigation so far.

'The assigned operation name is Observer,' he told them, providing the only item of news Short had not touched upon. 'Thanks to Mia you now all understand what we may be up against here. For the time being we focus on Kelly Gibson and only Kelly. If, or when, the moment comes to broaden our investigation, I'll let you know. But if any of you happen to bump up against the Crowland op along the way, you speak to me before going any further. Evening briefing at five. Thank you all.'

As he walked by Short, who had remained standing to one side during his address, he inclined his head. 'Join me in my office please,' he said. 'I want to run something by you.'

When they reached the tiny room and Bliss asked her to take a seat, Short frowned at him. 'Have I done anything wrong, boss?' she asked.

'No. Why do you assume that?'

'I've just never known you to ask anyone to sit in here before.'

Bliss grinned. 'Only because the room is so bloody small. Anyway, I'm hoping you will find what I have to say to be a positive step.'

Short seemed to remain cautious as she took a seat opposite him. She had to close the door before there was room to pull the chair out from beneath the desk.

Bliss decided to put his DS out of her misery quickly. 'Mia, I am considering approaching DCI Edwards with a recommendation that you are made up to acting DI. I know it's a track you're keen on, and I think we can both agree you're ready. The usual process is for you to apply, take your exams and then if you pass those and the subsequent interview stage, you get to go for any relevant posts coming through the channels. With DCI Harrison having handed in his papers, we're a senior officer down. Ultimately I'm sure the super and the DCI will replace like for like, but for the time being I thought I might suggest this move as a temporary compromise. What do you reckon?'

Short's response was everything Bliss had hoped for. She shrugged off her anxiety at being summoned to his office and her face broke out into a huge smile. 'Boss, I don't know what to say. I'm extremely grateful to you for bringing this to me, and for the suggestion itself, of course. But… with all due respect, am I your first or second choice for the role?'

'You mean have I already offered this to Penny and had her turn it down? The answer is no. Mia, you were promoted to sergeant before Penny, and your work since I've been back in the city has been exemplary. There is no reason why you would not have been first on our list.'

'I thought perhaps Penny's secondment down in London with Operation Sapphire might have given her the edge over me. A year down there in a different and challenging environment is great experience to add to the CV.'

'It is. And there's no doubt she will eventually be a terrific candidate. But let's be truthful here: first, I know you two are close friends, so I must assume you know Penny currently does not want the step up. Second, with the way things have gone over in Turkey in relation to Hannah, Penny's mind is nowhere near focussed enough to accept the challenge even if she wanted it. But third, and most significantly as far as I am concerned, you are the best person for the job.'

'And this is not just because you got a second cookie?'

Bliss smiled. 'Well, not *just* because of that.'

Short glanced down at her hands neatly clasped together in her lap. When she looked up again, however, her grin faltered. 'I'm blown away by your faith in me, boss. But there may be a slight fly in the ointment.'

'Oh. How so?'

'Well, you see, by the time all of this promotion stuff is over, I won't be around anymore.'

'Whatever do you mean? You're not ill, are you?' Bliss grew immediately concerned.

A look of pure joy was now back on Short's face. Bliss read it and knew what was coming.

'No, boss. Actually, I'm pregnant.'

Bliss laughed, a whoosh of relieved air escaping his chest. 'Well, that's terrific news. Congratulations to you both. Are you eating for three again?'

'Not this time, no. It's not twins again.'

'So how far gone are you?'

'Eight weeks. Starting to show, too.'

'That's such wonderful news, Mia. But when you say you won't be around, you are intending to come back after maternity leave, aren't you?'

Short nodded. 'Oh, of course. In fact, the old boy and I are sharing the leave, so I'll be gone for a month before the due date and three months afterwards.'

'Then we can go ahead as I've suggested.'

'Thank you so much, boss. It means an awful lot to hear that coming from you.'

'You're welcome, Mia. You deserve it. You earned it. Look, I wanted to run my idea by you before I spoke to the DCI about it. I can't imagine she will have a problem with it at all. Without wishing to denigrate the woman, she'll like the fact that the budget won't take such a big hit, and she is extremely keen to see more women promoted. I also happen to believe she will consider it a decent move. Bish is a good DS and he's certainly running you close, but I have every confidence in you.'

'I won't let you down, boss.'

'I've no doubts whatsoever where that's concerned. I consider myself extremely fortunate in having the three of you sergeants at such a stage in your careers. My only disappointment will be the eventual loss of one, two or even all of you at some point. But I think if you spend some time now acting up as DI, it can only work to your advantage in the long run.'

Short got to her feet. She held out her hand. Bliss rose and grasped it firmly. 'Congratulations once more on the new family member,' he said.

'Thanks. And for now, can we keep this between us? I don't want to tempt fate and jinx things before the first twelve weeks is up. I felt I had to tell you, but I don't want anyone else to know just yet.'

'Of course. As for the promotion, I know you'll make the most of this opportunity. And when you do, I will be very proud.'

He could have sworn Short grew an inch in that moment. She thanked him again and left him standing there feeling better than he had in several days.

Then Bliss thought about Kelly Gibson and his mood darkened once again.

It took Paul over two hours to make the journey between Mablethorpe and Peterborough, but he was in no rush. He made a couple of phone calls during the drive, and long before he arrived in the city his plans were fully developed. He had been right about Mariana. She had opened up to him like a spring flower in the vain hope that he might spare her any pain afterwards. But Paul kept his promise, having drained himself inside the woman before making good on his threat.

The industrial complex he drove to was in the Orton Southgate district. Mariana had told him that in one particular estate populated by a garage, several distribution centres and a number of warehouses, the extensive parking area was used by van drivers who wished to leave their vehicles away from the bays outside their own front doors in residential streets. Paul recognised it as a tactic often employed by those who claimed incapacity benefits despite making deliveries during the week on a cash-in-hand basis. On this occasion, he made the system work for him instead.

Paul parked up in a prime location, from which he could see every vehicle entering and exiting the estate. As he sat in contemplative silence, his thoughts turned back to Mariana Iliescu.

Getting better acquainted with her had been an enjoyable experience, but he had felt no guilt whatsoever in the final outcome. People needed to know that when he promised something he also delivered. There was no such thing as an idle threat in his world. He lived by that maxim, or he might very well die otherwise.

Although it had been a fine start to the day, he was eager to return to his accommodation. There his little beauty awaited him, and Paul was desperate to see her. With her by his side, his favourite booze to quaff, and music to delight in, he had everything his heart desired. He had no need of luxuries, and certainly he craved no other company. In the weeks or months to come his current state of contentment might very well alter, but for the time being he was a happy man going about his business and looking forward to heading home with his work completed.

Paul sat perfectly still for a little under half an hour, stirring only when he recognised the sharp, angular features of the driver of a white Renault van coming towards him as it reached the T-junction ahead. Moving swiftly, Paul exited his own vehicle and dashed across the centre of the parking area over to the distant block in which the majority of vehicles standing idle were also vans. There he tucked himself behind one of the larger Transits and turned his ear towards the sound of an approaching diesel engine.

The white van passed by and pulled into a bay two rows further down. Paul stepped out into the open, took a good look around for any sign of movement, and decided there was no better moment to act. By the time the man in his photograph had stepped down out of the ageing Renault Trafic, Paul was standing directly behind him. He leaned in and jabbed the revolver hard into the man's back.

'I know you were once military,' he said. 'But so was I. And believe me, I am better. So listen to me and do exactly as I say. I want you to open the sliding side door of your own van and step into the rear compartment. Now.'

The man made no reply. Instead he did as instructed. He did not look back over his shoulder. Paul understood why. In a situation like this, if you did not see the face of your assailant then he might just allow you to live.

The rear of the van was empty save for a few flattened cardboard boxes, a length of rope, and a coil of jumper cables. Once he had joined the man inside, Paul slid the side door closed. This was the point in movies where the gunman distracted himself with banal chatter, allowing his potential victim time to think and react and maybe even force an escape attempt.

Paul was not about to make such a mistake.

Without uttering a single further word, he fired three shots.

The man whose face was in the photograph he carried fell forwards. His padded jacket puffed out blood and nylon filling in unequal measures from the multiple holes that had appeared in it. He lay still and silent on the boarded floor of the van, head turned sideways, eyes wide and blank.

Paul kicked him once. Hard in the side of the upper torso with a steel-capped boot. No need to check for a pulse – it didn't matter how good an actor you were, nobody remained silent and perfectly rigid while their ribs were being snapped.

He then slid the side door back open, stepped down out of the target's van, and walked in his usual composed manner across to his own vehicle. From its rear compartment he retrieved a large cooler box, inside which was a change of clothing wrapped in an opaque plastic bag, and a cordless Bosch power saw with a new six-inch blade. He then made his way back to the Renault van, whistling the chorus to Ed Sheeran's 'Perfect' and thinking about the fish and chip dinner he was going to tuck into later.

13

B liss was feeling both impatient and frustrated in equal parts by the Lincs CCTV people taking their time in responding to Bishop's request. That sense of impotence usually resulted in him grabbing Chandler and heading off somewhere in pursuit of leads, but today he was stumped.

Everything that could be done was already being done, except for interviewing the friends Kelly Gibson had driven to Holbeach to see the previous evening. An internal debate raged inside his head. He felt like getting out of the office, taking a drive to blow away the cobwebs. Often the simple act of conversing with Chandler whilst driving at speed opened up previously obscured pathways in his mind.

Only now there was his therapy to consider. More to the point, the words of advice given to him by his therapist.

Weekly sessions with the Cambridgeshire Constabulary occupational health psychologist was the solitary non-negotiable part of Bliss's return to work agreement with Superintendent Fletcher. This arrangement came at the conclusion of an investigation into his own past which had lured Bliss back to London, resulting in a final stand-off with the man who murdered his wife almost seventeen years earlier. In Fletcher's opinion, the level of stress and strain placed upon him during that period, in which he also led the team in solving a stalker-related murder, could not be left unaddressed.

Bliss accepted she was acting in the best interests of the team as a whole. In the space of ten days back in June, he had been rendered both mentally and physically devastated. Fletcher's concern was that he might have burned himself out to the point of exhaustion and collapse. Privately, Bliss wondered the same thing. Therefore, he had not fought the instruction, although his respect for either therapy or the individuals whose career relied upon delivering it, was negligible.

To his mind, the setting for the sessions was totally wrong. He could not understand the point of talking about anything in a quiet room entirely dislocated from the very stressors which might well trigger the responses he was there to discuss. He wondered why it was considered best practice to place a person requiring therapy in a serene environment before drilling into their head. In the therapist's position, Bliss would demand to observe patterns of behaviour by seeing the patient in action, while under duress, in the thick of things where it could get dark and messy and a soul could become splintered.

Jennifer Howey was younger than Bliss had anticipated, but he had also expected a woman more officious and staid. He was therefore pleasantly surprised to find Howey to be neither of those. Her manner was both relaxed and charming throughout their sessions together.

The therapist's words came to Bliss now as he pondered how to proceed. Her overall emphasis with him so far had been to try teaching him to focus more on his own responsibilities and accountability. Howey insisted that the pressure Bliss heaped upon himself was ultimately self-defeating. That in seeking to be both responsible and accountable for everyone else's outcomes, he was setting himself up for an inevitable fall.

'There is more than enough going on with your own job, your own heavy workload,' she told him halfway through their first session. 'You can't possibly hope to be accountable for your entire team as well.'

'But I am,' came his immediate response. It was a fact, at least in his eyes. 'They are my team, I am responsible for their welfare and outcomes, and I am liable when it fails to produce results.'

Howey pointed out the presence of higher ranks to whom he was ultimately answerable. The chain of responsibility currently tethering him did not end with him at all, she insisted. The therapist also believed he would never resolve either of those issues if he constantly took on the burden of doing everything himself.

'Take advantage of your team,' Howey advised him. 'Deploy them more appropriately, delegate more thoughtfully. Encourage them to express themselves. You never know, they may actually flourish.'

'But I do let them play their part,' Bliss argued. 'They each have a role, each have their strengths and weaknesses which I utilise. I don't try to stifle that.'

'And what I am suggesting is that you allow it to happen even more. For example, the next time you are inclined to dash off to a scene, or to interview somebody of some importance, take a step back and ask yourself a question: *does this have to be me?* If not, and provided others are available, let them do it in your stead.'

'But I'm not the kind of detective who enjoys sitting behind a desk. That's not my way of running a successful team.'

'Understood.' Howey maintained her insightful scrutiny of him. 'But neither can you carry on as you are. If I have read you correctly, you would very much like to continue doing the job for a number of years yet. Well, I'm here to tell you that at your current pace and levels of stress, the force of pressure you pull down upon yourself will eventually break you.'

'Eventually?' Bliss took heart from the single word.

Howey pursed her lips for a moment, before saying, 'You've

probably heard the old joke, Inspector Bliss. A doctor tells his patient he has good news and bad news. The good news is he has ten years to live, the bad news being that he should have been told nine years ago. My own version is, if you continue to operate in the way you have been, you will eventually burn yourself out both mentally and physically. And the bad news is, I wish I had been treating you a year ago, because the "eventually" I referred to is just around the next corner.'

Though not entirely convinced by the assessment of his well-being, Howey's words now gave Bliss pause for thought. He considered the task in hand. It did not necessarily require him to personally carry out the interviews with Kelly Gibson's friends. Any one of his detectives was more than capable of asking the right questions, using their experience to read body language and instantly analyse responses. Whoever he sent to do the job was not going to fall off the edge of the planet, and the case would not start to unravel without his own presence.

Moments later, Bliss stepped out into the major crimes work area and summoned DCs Hunt and Ansari. He told them what he needed.

'John, you take lead on this. Hit them with the usual questions. Remember, whichever one of you is doing the asking, the other monitors the person giving the answers.'

'Yes, boss,' Hunt said. He gave a firm nod. 'Of course.'

They knew how to do their job. Bliss knew they knew. He felt a little foolish in even second-guessing himself. This was their chosen career. It was what they were trained to do. And if he had led by example at all over the past ten months, they would do it well.

He busied himself catching up on admin, occasionally sneaking glances at the open case log as it updated following every insertion of new data. After a while he threw down his pen and made a call, connecting with the National Crime Agency in London.

In his time there he had garnered a good reputation, and Bliss knew his name would prompt co-operation. There was little to go on, but he asked whether they were running any organised crime investigations involving Romanian nationals in or around his patch.

The response he received was to the point: the agency was often interested in Romanian men and women, especially those living in eastern counties where indentured slavery was a common practice. Critically, they were also able to confirm that nobody even close to the city had been under NCA surveillance at the time.

Satisfied that his ex-employers were a dead end, Bliss headed back out of the office. He swung by Bishop's desk first. 'Still nothing from Lincs about the CCTV?' he asked.

The burly sergeant cracked a smile. 'Just this second got off the phone with them, boss. They think they have our Range Rover. They took a bit longer to get back to us than anticipated because they were good enough to edit the footage first, splicing together every camera that picked up the vehicle. Our tech-ops people would have done it otherwise, so no time was lost.'

'Terrific. How soon do we get it?'

'Within the next few minutes. They say we'll be happy with what's on the video file.'

'That's good enough for me. I'm off to have a word with the DCI. Find Chandler will you, and meet me in the canteen in thirty. I'm buying.'

He found Edwards busy but welcoming, which was another shock to his system. Bliss did not enjoy being at loggerheads with his superiors, it was just the way things often ended up. He seldom worked under anybody he respected, which had been difficult for him to handle in the past. These days, provided they were civil to him, valued his opinions, and did not try to screw him over, he could make it work. Bliss even found himself less guarded when speaking to the DCI.

'First up, looks like the confirmation we were waiting for is on its way through. The way Lincs tell it, there is a trail on the right road at the right time for the right vehicle. The two murders were carried out by whoever was inside the Range Rover. One more thing. I've been turning over a plan of sorts. It's to do with appropriate staffing and DS Short. Do you have ten more minutes for me?'

Bliss was feeling extremely pleased with himself by the time he walked into the canteen. He spotted his colleagues at a table in the far corner, and fetched himself a tea and a large sausage roll, before joining Bishop and Chandler who were already tucking into their own lunch.

'I put them on your tab, boss,' Bishop said, almost without breathing as he devoured a bacon butty. Grease left a slick trail on his lips.

Nodding, Bliss took his seat beside Chandler. It occurred to him that no matter where they sat or who else was at the table, the space alongside her was always vacant. As if without any conscious thought, everybody regarded the two of them as a couple who could not be separated. Bliss could not decide whether this bothered him or not, given he still felt a little uncomfortable with the memory of a drunken shared kiss back in June. Jokes about Chandler being his work wife notwithstanding, he did not want their working relationship to become a subject for mockery.

'We have movement at last,' he told them, shrugging the negativity aside. 'Edwards is already stepping up. She's calling her opposite number in Lincs to get the conversation started. She made the point earlier that identifying either the victim or the killer might be the deciding factor as to who takes the lead on this. Other than that, she thinks she can make a good case for it being us.'

Mugs raised in celebration, but the response was muted due to the amount of chewing going on. His sausage roll consumed, Bliss then told Bishop and Chandler about his second discussion with the DCI.

'I think it's a terrific idea,' Bishop said without any trace of envy or malice. 'Mia is absolutely ready right now. Stick her into any situation and she'll thrive.'

Chandler agreed. 'You know you have my backing where Mia is concerned, boss.'

Bliss was unsurprised by their enthusiasm. 'Edwards seems to agree. It's only an acting-up post, but Mia will have to endorse it officially and then spend some time with HR. I mentioned it to her before and she is game. I regard it as the next logical step before she makes the move on a permanent basis. Like I told her, I am resolved to losing all of you eventually.'

It was not his place to mention Short's pregnancy. Such good news was for her to share in her own time, and Bliss respected the confidentiality.

'You're not losing me.' Chandler shook her head firmly. 'I'm happy right where I am.'

Bliss shrugged. 'But young enough to change your mind as circumstances in your life vary. How about you, Bish?' He turned to face Bishop.

'I wouldn't want to leave major crimes, boss. But yes, I am looking to make the step up to DI.'

'Naturally. It's a good career move for you, and you have a family to think about. I don't know if it'll come to anything, but when I was in with Edwards, another idea popped into my head. I mentioned it, and she said she'd discuss it with the super.'

Both of his colleagues now squinted at him. 'Go on, then,' Chandler prompted. 'Don't be a tease.'

'I asked her if whether, instead of replacing DCI Harrison with another DCI, we opened up another DI position.'

'You mean two DIs for major crimes?'

Bliss nodded. 'It struck me that there was a significant lag when the super promoted Harrison to DCI. I know you had a few temporary DIs in, but no permanent replacement. Then suddenly Harrison wasn't available because of what happened to his poor wife getting sick, I take over his assignments and somehow cover the lack of a more senior post. By rights, the DI would look to move up into Harrison's post, then we promote internally, DS up to DI. But I'm that existing DI and I have no intention of moving up a rank, even if they'd consider it – which they wouldn't. So the DCI post needs filling, and I'm suggesting we fill it with another DI instead.'

'And Edwards went for it?' Chandler said, unable to hide her astonishment.

'She's considering it, yes. Enough to run it by Fletcher.'

'Won't that leave us a little unbalanced as a squad?' Bishop asked.

'As far as I can tell it's been this way ever since Harrison himself was promoted. It would be on a trial basis anyway. But I thought if my idea was accepted, even if only for a short while, then at least one of you will get to stay on here as part of the team if that's what you wanted.'

There was enthusiasm for the idea, and Bliss decided he would fight for it to work if word came down from the super that his suggestion had been passed over. He did not want to lose both Short and Bishop in quick succession. The impact on the team would be immense, and he thought he might win the day with his argument if he got to make it.

Bliss had started to relax and enjoy the notion when Mia Short blasted through the doors, scouring the canteen room for him. She strode briskly across the floor, and he stood to meet her. The look on her face told him it was going to be more bad news.

'We have another victim, boss,' she said, eyes hooded.

'A shooting?' Bliss asked.

Short grimaced. 'And a beheading.'

14

Nobody was left in any doubt as to whose crime scene this one was. The industrial complex in Orton Southgate lay firmly within Peterborough city territory, and Bliss's only thought now was to wonder who would be handed overall control of the investigation into the two decapitation murders. He wanted it; no question. This fresh killing would only provide further backing for his claims.

The murder had been discovered by pure accident, triggered by a homeless man causing trouble in the nearby Orton Centre. Building and renovations work had blocked his regular pathway into the central quad. The workmen he encountered laughed off the abuse they received from a man carrying his total worth in a large black bin liner. As he followed diversion signs around the side of the shopping centre, still loudly cursing, the man came across a group of school children accompanied by a member of the teaching staff. The adult deemed the man's language unacceptable, and immediately summoned the police.

Twenty minutes later, two police community support officers tracked the homeless man down outside Greggs bakery, where he moved from person to person begging for either money or food or both. As the officers discussed the matter with him, the man told them through a long stream of epithets that they should leave him be and instead concentrate on what he had seen happen over on the industrial estate. The incident he described, and the way he described it, set off flares in the minds of the two PCSOs. They invited him to show them where the odd behaviour had occurred, offering him a hot meal and drink in exchange for his assistance.

Standing yards away from the Renault van back at the car park, the homeless man went over it all again. He had been nestling down beside a vehicle which acted as both firm support and a wind break. At some point – the man had no idea how long ago – he saw the van he was now pointing at pull up and park. As the driver climbed out, another man appeared from out of nowhere and forced the driver into the back of the vehicle through the sliding side door. The homeless man described how, barely moments later, he heard three sharp sounds, before the second man reappeared through the side door on his own.

At first the homeless man thought there was something 'queer' going on, but then the second man came back with a light blue cooler box and climbed inside once more, after which there came a loud whining and high-pitched buzzing noise from the back of the van. At that point he decided it was best for him to get out of there. He said he didn't know what was going on in the back of the Renault, but it scared him and he didn't want to know more.

One of the officers made sure the man did not run off again, while the other approached the Renault with caution. He first peered in through the side windows, finding nothing of interest, but when he reached the rear doors the glass in them was opaque. The PCSO walked around to the side door and pressed an ear against it. Finally, he glanced over at his colleague, they exchanged nods, and he pulled on the door's handle.

Both the PCSOs and the agitated homeless man had since been removed from the scene. Bliss, Chandler, Bishop and Short now gathered in the hub of activity, the crime scene management undergoing its usual rituals and protocols. With the entire car park cordoned off, several arguments broke out between uniformed police officers and people demanding access to their vehicles. The senior uniform on site, Inspector Kaplan, wasted no time in summoning reinforcements to deal with any malcontents. Two dozen or more vehicles were caught inside the perimeter of the crime scene, resulting in a lot of angry confrontations with the public.

Bliss and Kaplan were long-time friends, having worked together many years earlier in both London and Essex. The two plotted how things might pan out ahead of the inevitable media rush. Though the air around them was warmer than it had been during the morning, a low grey cloud was rolling in from the east and the sky was beginning to darken.

'Doesn't seem five minutes since I was handing that mutilated body over to you at Ferry Meadows,' Kaplan said to Bliss. His voice was uneasy as his eyes worked the crowd.

'Yeah, that was a bad one.' Bliss remembered it well. An ugly crime scene, followed by an uglier investigation. 'Poor woman. I pop by their house from time to time to see her husband. The bloke was distraught enough to be right on the edge, and I guess I'm still worried he might step over it.'

'You can get too close to a case, Jimmy.'

'Some cases demand that you do.'

'I suppose. Let's hope this one doesn't turn out to be quite so complicated.'

Thumb to the tiny scar on his forehead, Bliss replied, 'Lennie, I have a terrible feeling this is going to be even worse.'

'You thinking another serial?'

'I'm not sure what I'm thinking right now. And that's what bothers me.'

Bliss explained how certain he was that the killer had broken away from his first murder to follow and shoot down Kelly Gibson.

'I can't tell you how uneasy it makes me feel,' he continued. 'It suggests to me that whoever did this is cold, calculating, and has no fear whatsoever. The only thing I am convinced of right now is that he has a purpose. Did you clock the tattoo on our victim's left arm? I snapped a quick photo and sent it to the Lincs RPU officer I met last night. I recognised the ink, just as I did on yesterday's victim. Romanian Land Forces. The first was navy. There's a pattern emerging.'

'You think they were part of the Romanian travellers' community?'

'You mean GRT? That's how we're supposed to refer to them now, apparently. Gypsy, Roma and Travellers. I get so confused with these sort of things. I thought we weren't allowed to call them Gypsies anymore. Apparently, Travellers usually refers to the Irish, whereas either Gypsy or Roma covers the Eastern Europeans.'

Kaplan shrugged. 'The only thing I know for sure we can't call them is pikeys.'

'Another word that's been bastardised.'

'Shame. What do we call West Ham fans now, then?'

'Wankers?' Bliss suggested with a grin.

Kaplan laughed, but quickly grew serious once more. 'These beheadings, they could be part of some Gypsy feud.'

'Perhaps. Possibly OC.'

'I suppose. If it's organised crime it should be right up your alley.'

'It might give me a way in. I've already had a word with someone at the NCA, but I can always call them again and see if they have any intelligence on specific GRT communities in the area.'

'You really think this could be OC?'

'Decapitation tells me a message is being sent. So it certainly fits.' Bliss was confident that if something was going on within the local Romanian OC world, such as a power struggle at the top or a feud between rival factions, his old colleagues at the NCA would be aware of it.

Kaplan took a deep breath. He glanced around at the crowd gathering beyond the taped perimeter. 'The natives are certainly restless,' he said.

'It's national have-a-pop-at-a-copper-week, Lennie. We're all fair game.'

'I thought that was last week.'

Bliss chuckled. 'It's every bloody week, mate.'

'True enough. How's your mum, by the way?'

'Doing well, as it happens. Loving life in rural Ireland. She has a bunch of friends, many of whom are on their own. I keep asking her if she's found a replacement for dad yet, but she just laughs it off.'

'Would it bother you if she did?'

'What, a bit of companionship in her old age? Not at all. I'd probably worry about her less.'

'You? Worry less? That'll be the day.'

Bliss knew his friend was right, though not entirely. 'I'm mellowing, Lennie. I keep telling you that. Right, I'll catch you later. I better see how many of my team are still green around the gills having clocked our headless corpse inside the back of the Renault. Luckily the poor sod was dead before his head was lopped off, or it would have been even more of a bloodbath in there.'

The two men shook hands. Bliss strode back across to where his partner and their two other colleagues stood in deep discussion. Bishop looked up as he approached.

'We were just saying, boss, how none of us have ever seen anything like this before. Now we have two in as many days. What's your angle on it?'

Bliss walked them through his theory, revealing his knowledge concerning the tattoos, and the organised criminals he had encountered in the past. 'My money is on OC,' he told them. 'But I'm not ruling anything out right now. I'd be more certain if it wasn't for what happened with Kelly. I've run across several Eastern European gangsters, some stone-cold killers among them, but I can't think of any who would have jumped in their motor to follow a passer-by the way this bloke did. Scarper away, yes. In the opposite direction, most likely. But pursue and then gun them down… that's a new one on me.'

He broke off from the discussion as his mobile rang. He checked the name on the screen. It was Sandra Bannister, a journalist from the local newspaper. For a second he considered ignoring the call, but his inquisitive nature got the better of him. He wanted to know what she knew.

'Good afternoon, Ms Bannister. Something I can do for you?' Bliss kept his tone light and easy as he moved several paces away from his colleagues.

'Are you ever going to call me "Sandra"?'

'That depends, Ms Bannister.'

'On what?'

'I haven't yet decided. So, what's up? I arranged our appointment, so it can't be that.' Bliss had agreed on the first of three officially sanctioned interviews to take place the following week. Each represented partial payment of a debt he owed the reporter, who was writing a book about the implosion of the local police service and his part in it back in 2005.

'You know full well what I'm calling about. Something major is going off over in the Ortons.'

'Look, I appreciate your help previously. But I have repeatedly told you that when I am in the early stages of a case I am not slipping you any confidential information.'

'Not unless it helps you, correct?'

'Absolutely. We both have our jobs to do. Mine is to catch criminals. Killers, even. I'm sure we both want the same thing where that's concerned, yes?'

'Of course.'

'There you go, then. Look, I have no problem feeding you something ahead of your competition at the appropriate time. But we're not there yet, and we never will be on any investigation which is less than an hour old.'

After a moment of silence, Bannister said, 'That's fair, I suppose. So how about Kelly Gibson? Are we far enough down the line for you to be offering me anything there?'

Bliss realised he had been caught out by his own words. He considered the matter for a few seconds, eventually deciding there was something he could give the woman that would do the investigation no harm.

'Ms Bannister, let me just say this: it will not hurt you to start suggesting there may be a link between the shooting of Kelly Gibson and two other fatal shootings in or around the city since last night.'

The silence went on a little longer this time before Bannister responded. 'That's very interesting. I'm hearing all kinds of rumours about the murder in Crowland. Are you able to confirm–'

'Let me stop you there,' Bliss cut her off. 'I am unable to confirm anything until my boss gives me the nod. All I am willing to say at this stage is that if you explored the possibility of a link between the three shootings, you will be heading down the right path.'

'So, the incident in Orton is another shooting, then?'

'It is.' He saw no reason to keep it from her.

Bliss killed the call before the journalist was able to respond. He had never met Bannister on a one-to-one basis. Until now she had merely been a face in a sea of journalists trying desperately to ask questions, and a disembodied voice on the phone. He had not been allowed to attend any formal briefings since the previous winter, which he had stormed away from after the questioning became personal. That suited Bliss, but the media invaded virtually every major crime investigation in one form or another, so he had caught glimpses of her since.

He liked Bannister. So far she had played the game with him, providing useful information of her own when requested. He wasn't looking forward to the forthcoming interviews with the woman, but she seemed pleasant enough and he was no longer dreading being in a room alone with her.

'Who was that?' Chandler asked as Bliss returned to the group.

'Peterborough's answer to Lois Lane.'

'Looking for a scoop was she?'

'Aren't they all?

'We were just saying that even though the ex-servicemen lead is interesting, we can't think how to make it work for us.'

Bliss shook his head. 'Me neither at the moment.'

He was about to add more when his phone rang again. He blew out a long breath as he took the device from his pocket once more. This time it was DCI Edwards.

'We need you back at the ranch,' Edwards said without pleasantries.

'We?'

'We're in the conference room, Bliss. Myself, the super, plus a couple of guests who have some information for us which I think you will find extremely interesting.'

'On my way.'

Bliss grimaced as he turned back to the other detectives. 'A summons. Fletcher, Edwards, and guests.'

'This case?' Bishop asked.

'I think so, yes. I'm hoping it's the team from Lincolnshire. Edwards didn't sound exactly happy, so I have to wonder whether it's being taken away from us.'

'I'm sure you won't give it up without a fight, boss,' Short said.

'If there's one thing you can count on,' Bliss replied, 'it's that.'

15

DCI Edwards was the first to glance up when Bliss entered the conference room on the third floor of the Thorpe Wood building. Her expression was every bit as sombre as her voice had been on the phone. Alongside her and Fletcher sat two figures, one of whom Bliss recognised.

Superintendent Fletcher flashed a thin smile as he walked across to join them at the large bespoke walnut table. She spread her left hand and gestured towards the male officer seated next to her.

'Thanks for coming so quickly, Inspector Bliss,' she said. 'I believe you and Sergeant Smyth from the Lincolnshire roads policing unit have met.'

Bliss responded with a nod. 'Yes, ma'am. Last night over in Crowland.'

'Then let me introduce you to DCI Warburton. Diane is running the Lincs side of things. They've been working flat out on this together since first thing this morning, and have already taken things forward. Diane will explain further.'

The DCI from Lincolnshire was perhaps fifty-ish, Bliss thought. Natural auburn curls framed a pleasant narrow face. The gleam in her eyes suggested both intelligence and warmth, and though her smile was muted as she turned to him, it lit her up as if from the inside. She offered her hand to him, and her grip was firm and strong as she spoke.

'Inspector Bliss, Barry and I have made significant advances today, mainly thanks to your swift identification of the tattoo. So thank you for that. We contacted the Romanian Armed Forces headquarters in Bucharest, and asked them for the names of naval servicemen covering five years either side of our victim's estimated age. Men who were still alive according to their records. The Romanian officials proved to be extremely helpful, and their pensions department were able to offer us the data we required.'

'Sounds like a significant list,' Bliss observed.

'It was. Fortunately, it was the naval services and not the land, whose records we were assured would be considerably longer.'

'And presumably you then cross-checked the list with all known Romanian nationals currently in the UK.'

'Within reason. As you might imagine, we covered documented illegals as well as economic migrants. Once again, however, we were able to filter the list down further still.'

Bliss narrowed his gaze a little. It was good work, but he could not see how it helped them identify this specific victim. It occurred to him that there was something else in play here. He chose his next words carefully. 'Even so, absent other individual identifying marks, you'd still be struggling. Impossible to narrow down without DNA, and I know you can't have that at this early stage. Unless you already happened to have an idea of who it might be.'

Warburton's smile was broader this time. 'Spot on,' she said. 'We ran a cross-check of our own, and a name from their list popped up on ours. That alone meant nothing, of course. But it was food for thought.' She looked across at Smyth, allowing him to pick up the story.

'We were at the station in Crowland when your message came in containing the photograph of today's victim. We set the ball in motion to obtain the same result from Romania, and decided to immediately head over here to await the results. Our guts told us this might be starting to go our way.'

'And I take it your guts were right,' Bliss said.

'Yes. Between the call asking you to come in and your arrival, we got the news we'd been waiting for. All I can say is thank heavens for electronic data and a helpful computer operator. It allowed us to confirm a name on their list as also being on our own.'

Bliss was unable to hide his surprise. 'Really? That's great work. But all we have to go on are two victims with forces-related tats, so I'm still not following how you narrowed things down to the point where we might identify them. Not unless... tell me, how many names are on your own list?'

Smyth's eyes almost squeezed shut as he answered. 'Only seven.'

'Ah. I see. So not a coincidence, then?'

'We don't believe so, no.'

'Okay. This all sounds good so far. You have two matching names, and presumably you're still waiting to identify which of the corpses is which. But I'm sensing a negative undertone here. What exactly is the source of your list?'

'Let me answer that,' DCI Warburton interjected. 'Tell me, have you ever heard of the Baker's Dozen case?'

Shaking his head, Bliss said, 'Not that I recall. Are we talking about a local investigation?'

'Lincolnshire, yes. It dates from just about nineteen months ago.'

'I wasn't posted back here until last autumn. That one certainly bypassed my radar.'

'I'm not surprised, even though it received nationwide publicity. International interest, actually.'

'Are you able to bring me up to speed now?' The reference to an old case intrigued Bliss. Progress had been rapid, especially given the point from which they had started. He wondered why they were now peering back in time.

'Of course. We have video footage to show you. Neither Super-intendent Fletcher nor Alicia have seen it, because we wanted to wait for you.'

Smyth pulled a laptop from a backpack nestling by his feet on the floor. Less than a minute later he had an app displaying the first still frame of film on the large digital monitor affixed to the far wall. He jogged across to the lights to kill them, then quickly back to his seat.

'What you are all about to view is footage from a road traffic camera opposite a T-junction at which there are sets of traffic lights. It's not great quality, but decent enough for our purposes. When I play the film, you'll see four vehicles pull up in a line at the lights which have just turned red. A fair bit of action takes place in a very short space of time. The best vehicle to focus on is the second to stop; a dark Audi Q7 SUV. Let me run it through in full, then we can play it back piece by piece afterwards.'

Bliss sat forward, his curiosity blazing. This was an unexpected turn of events, and he could feel the excitement building in the flow of his blood.

Nothing much happened until all four vehicles were in place. Then the first car's passenger door opened, somebody climbed out and walked around to the offside door of the Audi. As it arrived, Bliss saw the figure yank the door open and launch what at first looked like a punch aimed at the driver. After just the one blow, the indistinct form turned and headed back to the car in front. At which point, the remaining doors opened and three more people exited. The same occurred from the two cars idling behind the Audi. During the following thirty-three seconds, each of the figures repeated the actions of the first. Only now Bliss could see flashes of light glinting off metallic items held by each of them. When they were done, they returned to their cars and drove away.

There was complete silence in the room as Smyth stopped the video.

'It continues,' he said. 'Other vehicles arrive, flashing lights at

THE DEATH OF JUSTICE

the Audi as it fails to move on green, the discovery of the body inside, emergency services arriving, etcetera. None of which is of interest to us here and now. So, initial thoughts?'

'I counted thirteen,' Bliss said. He had no need to recalculate. 'Hence the Baker's Dozen reference, I assume.'

Warburton let go a long sigh. 'You assume correctly. What's more, the victim's name was Charlie Baker.'

'Can that possibly be a coincidence?' Fletcher asked. Bliss was wondering the same thing.

'You mean he was stabbed precisely thirteen times by thirteen separate people because he was called Baker and those responsible considered it a decent pun?' The Lincs DCI shrugged. 'I have to say we asked ourselves the same question over and over again at the time. We also questioned our thirteen suspects over and over again. We are none the wiser to date.'

For ten seconds nobody spoke. Until DCI Edwards asked, 'Exactly where did this take place? I remember the case, I just can't recall the town.'

'Sutton End,' Warburton replied. 'South-west of Boston.'

Edwards snapped her fingers. 'Baker was the town tyrant as I recall. He was suspected of being responsible for a number of crimes, both major and minor, he bullied people in the town, fought with them, abused them, forced some out of business, stole from others, and acted as a bookie and a loan shark. There were also drugs involved, of course, and allegations of much worse. An all-round piece of human garbage. But he somehow ended up always being squeaky clean when it came to the law being enforced.'

'That's the man,' Warburton said. 'We'll come back around to the police involvement shortly, but for now let's look at the incident you all just saw on the film. It was eventually agreed that locals united together to commit this bizarre murder because they were sick and tired of Baker getting away with his crimes and outrageous behaviour. Baker had recently been cleared on a rape charge, and feelings were running hot in and around Sutton End. So, yes, our investigation led us to conclude this was a case of people taking matters into their own hands.'

'That is astonishing,' Fletcher said, echoing Bliss's own thoughts. 'Thirteen local people coming together to commit murder in such a manner. You must have been wading through tips and rumours galore.'

'We were.' The Lincs DCI nodded and shook her head by turns. 'At first it was like that scene from the movie when everybody steps forward claiming to be Spartacus. The entire town seemed to want to confess in the beginning, and of course we knew what their intention was. The obfuscation delayed us, but we stuck to the task. Eventually, we narrowed things down and arrived at our list of thirteen suspects.'

'Seven of them being Romanian nationals,' Bliss said, making an educated guess based on an earlier admission.

'Correct. Which is where our own list came from, of course. Of the remaining six local people, one was a woman whose husband was allegedly beaten so badly by Baker that the poor man was confined to a wheelchair afterwards.'

Sergeant Smyth leaned forward to rest his elbows on the table, steepling his fingers and tapping them against his chin. He looked tired, a little dishevelled, but there was a grim determination in his demeanour that Bliss liked. 'Ben Franklin said the only way for three people to keep a secret is if two of them are dead. I'd argue the only sure way is if all three of them are. But if you accept his version, you might well ask how it is that not one of the thirteen suspects has to this day said a word to us. No, tell a lie. Each of them have said two words, repeatedly. "No" and "Comment".'

'So their silence and the lack of hard evidence left them in the clear.'

'Precisely.'

'Only now you think somebody is coming after them?' Edwards said.

'It certainly looks that way. The DCI and I suspected as much when the first name popped. The second merely confirmed it for us.'

'Why now?' Bliss asked. 'I know the old cliché about vengeance being a dish best served cold, but even so, nineteen months is a long time to wait.'

Warburton cleared her throat. 'We think the breakdown of our case against the thirteen suspects might have been the trigger,' she said. She moved her mouth as if chewing on the inside of her lower lip. 'Our problems from the very beginning have been many and varied. There was not, I have to admit, a huge appetite from within the team to find justice for Charlie Baker. I doubt everybody brought their best game to the table. Other than a few notable exceptions who we believed to be in Baker's pocket, the people of Sutton End were uninterested. The accused remained unified in their silence. The three vehicles used came back as salvage items, purchased for cash at an auction held on farmland out near Ely. We had no leads and nobody was talking, other than misleading us with tales of supernatural events and even military involvement.'

'I've never heard anything quite like it,' Bliss said, glancing around the table. 'But okay, I'm following what happened from the night of Baker's killing to the present date. What I am hazy on is how the man came to be so untouchable in the first place.'

Again it was DCI Warburton who spoke up, and Bliss could see that what she was about to reveal hung heavy on her. 'Unfortunately, a cabal of sorts, we believe including several police officers, a Euro MP, and a number of business owners, set themselves up as some kind of local dictatorship. It's by no means unusual for such a group to organise itself, often under the guise of community leaders or a chamber of commerce, but this one appears to have been heavily influenced by Charlie Baker. Or, more probably, Baker's money.'

'And how exactly did he make a living?' Fletcher wanted to know.

'Legally, through farming, building, haulage, and salvage. Illegally, we suspect he was as close to organised crime as you can be without raising alarms, and we also believe he was involved in people trafficking.'

Bliss felt all eyes flick across to focus on him. He flashed a sardonic crooked smile. 'I thought that might raise its ugly head again. We nailed one of our own local traffickers back in the spring, and if this Baker arsehole is even half as bad then I can see why the investigation team dragged their heels trying to find his killers.'

'I'm not sure I was quite as blunt when it comes to the efforts of my team,' Warburton demurred. 'But I do take your point. He was a repellent character by all accounts and the world is a better place without him in it. Despite that, I'm satisfied we did all we could.'

'And even if you'd got them all to confess, how would you have known which of them, or which combination of them, were responsible for murder?'

'Our thoughts exactly. The legal ramifications of trying to prove which of those thirteen stab wounds were landed by which of the thirteen suspects, was mind-boggling. The Crown Prosecution Service were desperate for us not to drop it in their laps.'

DCI Edwards said, 'All of which appears to leave us in the position of finding out who is taking revenge on Baker's suspected killers. I assume family and friends are the most logical places to start.'

Warburton appeared to agree. 'I imagine so. Baker has two sons and a daughter, aged between twenty-seven and thirty-two. Not nice people, believe me. And an extended base of friends, many of whom are known to us and I should think also feature in your own records.'

Bliss followed the flow of logic. There was a structure and form to every investigation, some of it easier than the rest. This was the stage where notions were plentiful, methods equally so, and he could feel the familiar pull towards it. There were a couple of things on his mind, however.

'Where do the Romanians fit in?' he asked, looking over at Warburton. 'I'm going to take a punt and guess they were part of the Roma community living out there in the Lincolnshire Fens. It doesn't strike me that they and the townsfolk of Sutton End would usually mix together.'

'Good question and point well made,' the DCI responded. 'The simple answer has its roots, we believe, in the rape mentioned earlier. The female victim was from the GRT community. She was known to be… sociable, especially when she had a few drinks inside her. She often strayed outside her own people. It was said that Baker got her drunk deliberately and took advantage of her after a long session in one of Sutton End's pubs. A tough case to prosecute under the best of circumstances, but impossible it seems where Charlie Baker was concerned.'

'Then I can well understand the Roma men taking matters into their own hands,' Bliss said. 'In fact, I'd expect it of them. What I'm still having trouble piecing together is the liaison between them and six other people from the town. That aspect doesn't fit.'

'We think it began during a gathering held in the church hall. The locals were outraged and up in arms about Baker and the dropping of the rape case. We have confirmation of a Roma couple attending that first meeting. It's possible they were the girl's parents, but we have no way of knowing for certain at this point. Either way, our opinion is that the conspiracy to murder Charlie Baker grew from there.'

'Sounds plausible enough. What about the victims' families? I assume we'll want to talk to them sooner rather than later.'

'Neither man was married as far as we can tell. None of them were. The only traceable family are still in Romania.'

'Okay. I have another question.'

'Fire away.' Warburton's eyes blazed, seeming to be almost enjoying the grilling.

'Why didn't the Audi's security lock work?' Bliss asked.

The DCI opened her mouth and closed it again immediately.

She turned to the RPU officer to her left. Smyth eyed Bliss cagily as if to imply he was not about to get caught out so easily. 'We believe it may have been deactivated by the first figure to approach the vehicle. A compromised security code according to our engineers. A fairly simple device to build, requiring a precise script to unlock the car at the press of a button.'

'So some tech skill required, and someone had to have obtained a code for the Audi.'

'We thought of that. Our people tell us there are ways and means, neither of which require specialists. Just the right people in the right line of work. We followed it up, but got nowhere.'

Bliss mulled it over for a moment, then said, 'Perhaps there was no device. Maybe they relied on Baker's aggressive nature, certain of him opening the door himself if challenged.'

Smyth exchanged glances with Warburton and then shrugged. 'Now that's something we had not considered. But I suppose it's possible.'

'So where do we fit in now?' Bliss asked, finally delivering the question he had been waiting to ask since first walking into the room.

Warburton took over once more. She met his direct gaze and said, 'If what happened in Sutton End under Baker's rule proved anything, it is that the police service in the area is compromised. The poison may even have spread further afield, to Boston, Spalding maybe. The truth of the matter is, we don't know for sure who or where. Only that a certain level of corruption exists.'

'And you want us to… to do what exactly?'

'We want you to work with myself and Barry here to tear it down, to weed out the bent and the dirty. And, of course, to find out who is going around shooting and beheading our suspects.'

'Because there are eleven more on the list,' Bliss said.

'Precisely.' DCI Warburton leaned back in her chair. 'Because there are eleven more people on that list.'

16

Slipping his hand through the open flap of a small wire cage, Paul removed one of the wriggling, squirming creatures, before closing and locking the door once again. He sat down heavily on the only item of soft furnishings inside the caravan – a tired, sagging sofa whose springs were broken and floral upholstery torn, faded and stained so it was not possible to recognise its original colour. Yellowed foam bulged through many of the apertures, and in places the wooden framework itself was exposed.

Paul did not dwell on the condition of his surroundings. Instead, pinching its tail between his forefinger and thumb, he dangled the mouse he had removed from its cage over the arm of the sofa. It hung down almost to the floor, front feet wildly pawing the air. The rodent wriggled itself and continued to squirm, clearly both uncomfortable in such an exposed position and also wary of danger. He knew it sensed the close proximity of a predator, just as the predator reacted to the presence of the animated little creature.

Come on my beauty.

Do your thing.

The adder was not hungry. The evolution of such animals meant they could reduce their metabolic rates to such an extent that they were capable of surviving without food for several months at a time. His beautiful pet consumed treats regularly. Even so, despite not craving a meal, he was certain she would not pass up on the opportunity to devour something set before her.

Paul had no idea of her whereabouts, only that his beauty was out there somewhere and probably winding her way towards him now. One of her favourite resting places was behind the TV cabinet, but he refused to so much as glance down. He did not wish to see her approach. Which she would do with utmost caution, anticipating a trap yet sensing another tiny creature's wild contortions as it fought to escape. Such was the hunting instinct of his darling pet, whose anticipation never ceased to amaze him. Paul gripped the mouse's tail tighter still as he lowered his hand an inch or two further.

This was the moment of greatest danger. The wise course was to drop the mouse onto the carpet and let it scurry off to seek a hiding place. That was a game Paul had enjoyed on a couple of previous occasions, but it quickly became tiresome because there was only ever one winner. He had since discovered that the best way to add interest to the feeding ritual was to put himself in peril at the same time.

To the snake, the difference between a squirming furry creature and Paul's wriggling fingers was miniscule; both were moving sources of heat and agitation. The strike had only to be off by a centimetre or two and it would be Paul's hand bearing the full impact of dual fangs puncturing flesh, followed by the swift injection of venom.

But Paul had faith in his little beauty. She had never so much as reared back in his presence, let alone struck for him. If she did happen to attack him rather than the mouse, it would be nothing more than a simple mistake. Paul believed in his beautifully simplistic pet – she would not deliberately bite him. They did not have that sort of relationship.

He closed his eyes, anticipating her silky movements as she slid closer before becoming motionless once the target was identified. He could almost sense her coiling in preparation, and the seconds dribbled away like minutes, minutes like hours as the three of them waited for the inevitable. When she was ready – always in her own sweet time – she struck so swiftly that it was over before Paul could even blink. Certainly he had no opportunity to react. The mouse may have, though it would have been futile. In a single whiplash motion, the adder snapped forward, bit, injected its venom and retreated again into its coiled position. Paul felt all of this activity vibrate through his fingers, at which point he breathed a gentle sigh and opened his eyes again.

The mouse tumbled to the floor, and this prompted Paul to look down for the first time since sitting on the sofa. After initially attempting to stand, its hind legs quivered and eventually buckled, leaving the front claws to scrabble aimlessly at threadbare tufts of carpet. Moments later it was still for good. The beautiful creature he had made a pet of almost a year ago glided forward, and in a motion that took Paul's breath away, unhinged its jaw and slid its open mouth around the entire circumference of the mouse, swallowing it whole in two further movements. It was a thing of such exotic splendour to watch, and Paul could not avert his eyes from such a perfect display of nature at work.

The adder slithered off with her prize and seconds later Paul began to reflect on his own current predicament. The police would eventually realise what was happening. Of that he had no doubt. It was a logical process and only to be expected. This knowledge did not faze him at all. He was neither discouraged nor daunted. He carried out his work in strict order of priority until something occurred to derail the plan, and he was not about to be deterred.

Taking out the most dangerous targets first was the main objective. Before long, the police would discover he had been busier in that respect than they were aware. He also accepted that from the moment they realised he existed and subsequently began hunting him, his job would become much more demanding.

Paul was indifferent to this.

The merely difficult was not as hard to overcome as the wholly impossible.

He poured himself a second glass of rakija. The fruit brandy made from plums was almost fifty per cent alcohol by volume, but he had acquired a taste for it at an early age, which dulled its effects now that he was in his forties. He allowed it to sit on his tongue and inside his mouth before swallowing, savouring every drop. Such a fine drink deserved his patience. Besides, only four bottles had travelled with him to England, and he did not want to run dry before his mission was complete.

His temporary accommodation came equipped with a variety of electrical items, including a TV, multi-media player, and a decent radio. He listened only to Classic FM, favouring the likes of Grieg, Bach and Schubert. It played in the background the whole time he was in the standard cream-coloured ERIBA mobile home, even as he slept. The constant thrum of sound at night did not bother him. In fact, it both disguised the noise of the generator out back and often lulled him into dropping off.

Now, basking in the afterglow and heady rush of the feeding, Paul allowed the music to wash over him as he gave weight to his options. When a particularly raucous Beethoven track came on, Paul set down his glass and slipped a sheet of paper out of the breast pocket of his chequered shirt. He unfolded the list and ran his eyes over it one more time.

Paul felt it was only right to congratulate himself on a job well done so far. But doing well was not the same as being wholly successful. From this point on he would have to be even more vigilant and resourceful. He had been fully aware of the difficulties involved when accepting the task. The volume and complexity of risks entirely reflected in the remuneration he was receiving. Those theoretical complications had finally become a reality, and it was time to analyse the plan all over again.

Paul was in no doubt that the authorities had by now established a connection between all three murders. The woman in Farcet might throw them for a while, but that shooting offered neither him nor them any advantage.

He was not a monster, so he felt a pang of remorse over the death of the woman who had driven past him on the road just outside Crowland. Unforeseen casualties were to be expected – unlike the woman he had shot, Mariana Iliescu would recover in time, though use of her left hand might not be possible again. He had muffled her screams of pain by forcing a cloth towel into her mouth, while the hot oil in the deep fryer first devoured the epidermis of her hand, then the thick living tissue beneath, followed by the subcutaneous fats, before finally eating its ravenous way deep into the muscle. The flesh bubbled and separated as it reddened, peeling off in long, thin strips before the outer layer seemed to slide off her hand like a translucent glove.

For Mariana, Paul felt no sympathy whatsoever. She had lied to him and she had not taken his words seriously. People needed to know that you said what you meant and you meant what you said. There were consequences for disobeying. It was only right and proper. As for the woman in the car, she had done nothing wrong and her punishment was perhaps harsh. But standing in that ditch at the side of the road he could not be certain what she had seen as she drove by, and he could not take chances.

With the police now investigating, Paul imagined there would be other victims in the near future whose only crime was to have become involved in his world as part of their job or maybe even as an innocent bystander. He had no desire to make superfluous kills, or to leave unnecessary wounded lying in pools of blood. However, if they got in his way, then the alternatives were limited.

In fact, there were none.

17

At the rear of the open-plan major crimes area there was a small meeting room. Nowhere near as grand as the conference room on the third floor, it was nonetheless functional and could comfortably seat six people around a table formed by shoving two desks together. A seldom used space, Bliss decided it was the ideal location from which this particular group should operate.

He first introduced his senior colleagues to both DCI Warburton and Sergeant Smyth. The structure of the modest task force was limited, mainly due to the potential for information leakage. But also because Bliss had decided to initially keep the splintered operation entirely separate from the team looking into the murder of Kelly Gibson. It was Warburton who requested the condition limiting the number of officers in the group, explaining that at all costs the officers most under suspicion of being associated with the Sutton End cabal, could not discover they were under investigation. Despite having complete faith in the loyalty and discretion of his entire extended team, Bliss nonetheless agreed to keep things simple.

Some compromises made sense.

Although Bliss was not the senior officer in the room, the case was officially under Peterborough command, which meant it was his to run. He briefly laid out the plans discussed upstairs at the earlier meeting, providing concise details relating to Charles Baker, his toxic relationship with influential figures in the Sutton End community, his murder, and its subsequent investigation.

'Together with our two colleagues from Lincolnshire,' Bliss said as the group settled into their creaking and overly flexible chairs, 'myself and Mia will work the cross-county investigation. Bish, Penny, I want you to run with Operation Observer.'

'What about the inevitable overlap?' Chandler asked. Her face betrayed no emotion at DS Short being selected to accompany Bliss rather than her.

'That's when this task force can easily expand to the six of us. I see it as something fluid. I'll brief the wider team, inform them that you and Bish are taking the lead on the murder of Kelly Gibson. For now, all they will know about the cross-county task force is that we are looking into the other murders.'

Bishop coughed into a balled fist. 'So this group here will actually be investigating not only the current murders, but also the Baker's Dozen case, plus Baker's connections prior to his death.'

'That about sums it up,' Bliss confirmed. 'Because they are all probably connected in some way. Now, of prime importance are the eleven remaining people suspected of being involved in the murder of Charles Baker. I'm opening this meeting up to thoughts and ideas about how we proceed from here.'

'We can't offer them protection,' Short said immediately. 'There's no budget for it.'

'Nor has there been an explicit threat made against any of them,' DCI Warburton pointed out. 'So even if money was no object, it wouldn't be sanctioned based on what we have at the moment.'

'But we can warn them, yes?'

'If we can trace them, sure. It is our understanding that, of the seven Romanian men involved, only three remained in the local area. As itinerants, the missing four could be anywhere, so I'm wondering whether our best bet is to focus on their home country to see if they returned there.'

'Good plan,' Bliss said. 'Which leaves seven remaining people on the original list who may still be living in or around Sutton End. Finding them ought not to be too difficult.'

Warburton continued, 'Inspector, I imagine of the four of us you have the most experience dealing with the GRT community. In which case, it's probably best if you speak with the final Romanian national once we've managed to identify him. Interviewing in pairs also seems logical to me, each pair including one from Lincs, one from Peterborough, with a male-female split. I think that covers all bases.'

Bliss liked Warburton's suggestions. They felt like something he might have thought of, had his mind been focussed on how the task force would handle those meetings.

'Which puts you with me, and Barry with Mia,' he said. 'We all okay with that?'

'I realise it doesn't fit in with those plans, but if you want to cut down on time, me and Pen can chip in,' Bishop suggested. 'Three pairs take two people each, leaving the Roma as the extra for you and DCI Warburton.'

'Please,' she said, putting a hand to her chest. 'Call me Diane. No need for formality here, I don't think.'

'Agreed,' Bliss said, nodding. 'And, actually, Bish's idea makes a lot of sense. I know I just said he and Penny should focus on Kelly Gibson, but there's little to go on that won't eventually cross over into our task force aims. So, this way we get through the list much more quickly, and given this gunman's current pace that would be no bad thing. Everyone on board with that?'

They were.

'Excuse me for a moment,' Warburton said as her phone started to ring. She walked outside into the open-plan area and Bliss noticed her find a quiet corner. When she returned a minute or so later, she wore a broad smile.

'That was one of my team members,' she said. 'We have an ID confirmed for both of our Roma victims. The man with the navy-related tattoo was called Florin Budescu, and Constantin Benzar was the other.'

That put a few smiles on faces. The task force was buoyed by the news. 'Great stuff,' Bliss said. 'You already got a photo array from Bucharest I assume?'

'We did. And we're in close contact with them regarding the other names on our list. A further three have been identified as having served, so this is terrific progress.'

Bliss divided up the names, deciding the final Romanian national known to be still living in the area could wait until last. Attempting to speak to someone inside the Roma community was likely to be a difficult and lengthy process, so it was better to get the others out of the way before taking on that particular unenviable task.

'One final question,' Bishop said, looking at Warburton. 'You say these Roma men are Romanians. Are you certain of that? All of them? Only, my understanding of Roma is that they originated from northern India, becoming a fairly nomadic group of people swallowing up all nationalities.'

'I'm sure your own inspector can clarify the issue of the Roma people,' Warburton replied. 'But I can assure you these men on our list are Romanian nationals.'

'And you're right about their background,' Bliss said, nodding at his sergeant. 'They are Indo-Aryan by ethnicity, but as you quite rightly say, over many hundreds of years the Roma have pulled in all manner of nationalities.'

'I just wanted to be certain who and what we were dealing with,' Bishop said. 'I know the tattoos helped identify our two decapitation victims as Romanian, but I didn't want there to be any misunderstandings about anyone else.'

'It was a fair point,' Warburton said. The others nodded their agreement.

Looking around the table, Bliss saw only good people. Their presence ought to have instilled confidence. Yet, despite his faith in them as individuals and their greater strength as a group, he was unable to rid himself of the sense of unease that had crept into his stomach, where initially it flapped about like a startled crane fly before settling stone-like deep in his gut.

18

The Green Fingers nursery lay just over a mile outside the picturesque Lincolnshire town of Sutton End. After making enquiries inside the main building, Bliss and DCI Warburton eventually tracked down Alan Brewer who was using a small forklift truck to transport sealed bags of compost from a delivery vehicle to the storage shed twenty yards away. Seeing that he had only four pallets left to shift, Bliss decided to wait until Brewer was done and the lorry driver on his way before speaking to the man.

While they waited, the two detectives chatted amiably. 'You ran the original Baker's Dozen inquiry?' Bliss asked.

Warburton shook her head. 'Not at first. I came in quite near the end, following a colleague's retirement. I saw what it did to him, though, and I have to say it's my toughest case so far.'

'In what way?'

'Well, from the very beginning there was either a wall of silence or a torrent of misinformation flooding in. Then there was the likely involvement of some fellow officers, though we lacked evidence against any of them at that stage. The Baker family are awful people to deal with, their business friends not much better, and the community of Sutton End largely treated the police with both suspicion and animosity. It was one of those lose–lose cases you get from time to time.'

'I've known a few myself. Given everything that's happened, I'm surprised you've been so accepting of us running this investigation.'

Warburton smiled. Again, Bliss was drawn to its warmth and the way the DCI's entire body seemed to generate heat and light from it. 'The last thing I want is to trade blows with a neighbouring county,' she admitted. 'If there is co-operation to be had, then I'm all in favour of it. If the result prevents our leads from leaking out to those on the Baker family payroll at the same time, then taking a back seat is a price I am more than willing to pay. Besides, from what I hear you have a cracking team we can both rely on.'

'We do. I'm lucky to have them, though I doubt they'll all be with me for too much longer.'

'Oh, why's that?'

'It's time for them to spread their wings. Onwards and upwards.'

'I see. So a good thing for them, not so good for you or your unit as a whole.'

'That's about the size of it. Tell me, though, do you know who these bad apples of yours are?'

'We have strong suspicions, yes. Hard evidence? None whatsoever. It's virtually impossible to run financial checks on them legally without first informing them they are under investigation. Which is the last thing we'd want to do.'

Bliss understood. He was certain he would feel the same way in Warburton's shoes. He looked up as the lorry driver climbed back into his cab and started up the heavy diesel engine. As the large vehicle engaged first gear and Brewer jumped out of the forklift, Bliss stepped forward holding out his warrant card.

The man was surprised when they introduced themselves, and instantly on edge. Bliss reacted swiftly to quell any fears he might have. 'Mr Brewer, we're not here to accuse you of anything,' he said. 'Far from it, actually.'

'I'm due a break. I can give you five minutes.'

Brewer stood over six feet tall, with a huge barrel chest. Mid-fifties was Bliss's estimate. The man's hair was unkempt, and he had not shaved in several days. The stubble around both cheeks and chin was the same grey-white colour as the tousled thatch on his head, which was thick and swept back from his brow. The weight on Brewer's eyelids and puffiness beneath suggested he was not sleeping well.

In a box-like grubby office tucked inside to the left of the main doors into the storage area, Brewer uncapped a thermos flask and poured himself a hot drink. The bitter smell of coffee beans wafted around the enclosed space. He took a sip and jerked his head at Bliss to get on with it.

'Mr Brewer,' Bliss said. 'The names Florin Budescu and Constantin Benzar are familiar to you, yes?'

The man's eyes narrowed suspiciously. 'What is this? Why are you bringing them up again?'

'I'll take that as a yes. Sir, in the past twenty-four hours, both Mr Budescu and Mr Benzar have been murdered. Each shot three times.' Bliss did not mention the beheading at this stage. The task force had decided to keep one or two pieces of information away from the potential victims for the time being.

Brewer was visibly rattled by the news, but he recovered quickly. 'So what, you want to fit me up with those murders, too?' he asked, setting down his plastic cup.

'Not at all, sir. However, with you being one of the remaining eleven suspects in the Baker's Dozen murder inquiry, you may also be being targeted.'

'Targeted? By who?'

'That we don't know. We're in the process of piecing information together, sir.'

'So you reckon that just because those two Gypsies were shot and killed, the rest of us are in danger, too?' Brewer shook his head dismissively. 'Shows how little you knew them.'

'I didn't think you did, either,' Warburton said sharply. She had spent time recently with the suspect statements, Bliss knew, and it was obvious from her outburst that Brewer had previously claimed no knowledge of the two Romanian men.

'I know their type,' the man snarled. 'The kind you'd be surprised to learn didn't end up in an early grave.'

'They had enemies, did they?' Bliss asked.

'Including their own kind.' Brewer picked up his cup and began drinking once more.

'And what kind might that be?'

The man's lips twisted as he snorted his derision. 'Gypsies, of course.'

'So you don't think there's anything more to these shootings?' Warburton asked, her tight gaze not leaving Brewer's face. 'You don't think family or friends of Charlie Baker could be looking for justice?'

Brewer's head jerked up. His eyes darkened. 'Justice? That piece of filth made the lives of so many people around here a living bloody nightmare. He treated us worse than the dogs he fussed over. We were the shit on his boots and one by one he scraped us off. Justice? What happened to him *was* justice. For our town.'

'And what was it he did to you, Mr Brewer?' Bliss asked.

'Baker made my wife ill. She daren't even step outside the house towards the end. He swore he'd burn our place down one time after he and I got into an argument. Said he'd make sure us and the kids were all tucked up in bed when he did it. He had me beaten up. I was on sick leave for four weeks, and by the time I was fit again my boss decided there was no longer any work for me. I learned later he'd been threatened. Now I do this sort of shit to earn a crust.'

'You have farmland, don't you?' Warburton said.

'Yes. But no equipment or capital to farm anything there.'

'You must have been angry with Baker. Did it end there?'

'No. The bastard wasn't satisfied with having me done over and then ruining me. The harassment started soon afterwards, my wife and kids included. That was when Helen stopped going out. Three nights on the trot our windows were bricked. The fourth one came with a message written on it, saying how next time it would be a petrol bomb and not a brick. Then one day Helen opened the back door to put something out in the bin and saw a man standing there holding a knife. He just stood there, looking at her, she told me. The next day, when we heard something out in the garden, Helen got into such a panic she couldn't breathe.'

Alan Brewer shook his head and his chin slumped almost to his huge chest. He made a choking sound in the back of his throat. Without looking back up he said, 'She died in my arms before the ambulance reached us. Stress-induced heart attack as far as they could tell.'

Pain came off the man in waves. Bliss sympathised. 'I'm sorry to hear that, Mr Brewer. Baker was responsible? No doubt in your mind?'

'None whatsoever.'

'Then you must have felt great anger towards him. I know I would. You must have at least considered getting back at him, somehow. Again, I'd've felt much the same.'

This time Baker did look up. 'Don't even go there,' he said in a flat monotone. 'Your boss here didn't get anything out of me, and you won't, either.'

Bliss did not bother correcting him about who was leading the discussion. 'That's neither my case nor my concern,' he said. 'I'm investigating three murders, and hoping to prevent there being any more.'

'Three?' Brewer's frown was deep. 'You mentioned two before. Can't you even get your own story straight?'

'Yes. One innocent victim got caught up in whatever this is, unfortunately.'

'Really?' Brewer scoffed. 'Only one? What makes you so bloody certain the other two weren't innocent as well?'

He was right. Bliss regretted his choice of words. Neither of the Romanian victims had been so much as charged with the murder of

Charles Baker, yet ever since hearing about the case from DCI Warburton he had made assumptions about the two murdered men.

'I apologise. I have no excuse. Thank you for reminding me.'

Brewer eyed him strangely, as if unable to work out his angle. 'Like you care. None of you people care about us. If you did, Baker would never have been able to get away with it all those years.'

'Well, somebody put a stop to that,' Warburton said.

'Thirteen somebodies.'

'Indeed. And was one of them you, Mr Brewer?'

'I thought you weren't here about ancient history. I thought you were here to warn me about some mad killer going around hunting down the thirteen.'

'Which we have done. But for some reason you seem to think we are trying to trick you. Our investigation into the murder of Charles Baker remains open and ongoing, and you remain a suspect. I won't lie to you about that, Mr Brewer. Two fellow suspects have been shot dead, and we are in the process of person-ally informing the rest of you. So if you have anything you wish to say, anything at all to offer us in the way of intelligence concerning these events, now is the time to do so.'

'Intelligence?' Brewer regarded Warburton as if she were insane. 'Love, please don't talk to me about something you know nothing about.'

Bliss cleared his throat and said, 'We came here to warn you, to advise you, and to help you. If you wish to remain hostile, that's your choice. Our work here is done.'

'Good. Now let me get on with mine.'

Bliss told him to take care, advising him one last time not to dismiss the warning. He turned round before the man could reply, ushering DCI Warburton away ahead of him. He did not offer to shake Brewer's hand, adding the suspect to a very long list of things and people he did not care about.

19

J ane Monkton was an unemployed thirty-four-year-old living at home with her parents in Sutton End. Their bungalow was one of a dozen on an estate of new builds, backing onto hundreds of acres of prime farmland. As Bliss turned off the main road into the tract of private land, he caught sight of a billboard outside a showhouse on the corner to their right.

'Did you see that?' he asked Warburton as they passed by.

The DCI nodded. 'I did: "A Charles Baker development".'

'Interesting.'

'Very.'

Bliss glanced sidelong at his companion for the day. Warburton was a woman of few words, yet he could tell there was a lot going on behind eyes that were constantly alert as she sucked in information like a sponge soaks up liquids. He thought it would be a pleasurable experience working as her subordinate, imagining the DCI to be both hard but fair. Their conversations limited to the investigation so far, he knew nothing of Warburton's private life, and had revealed nothing of his own. Which was more than fine by Bliss, who considered sharing to be overrated.

The Monkton residence was a wide, square property with a

drive large enough for three vehicles, though Bliss's Vauxhall Insignia was alone on it when they pulled up. The pair remained inside the vehicle for a few minutes while Warburton made a call. Nodding her head as she ended it, the Lincs DCI turned to Bliss and said, 'The Monktons have owned this place for four years. Apparently, not happily.'

One of the reasons for the Monkton family's unhappiness became obvious from the moment the two detectives stepped out of the car. The stench of raw sewage was overwhelming, causing both officers to wince and clamp a hand over their nose and mouth. They were greeted by a sky speckled with roiling clouds of flies, and the buzzing sound of beating wings filled the warm, still air. As he and the DCI approached the front door, Bliss noticed large cracks in the block paving driveway, several of which continued up the walls of the bungalow's exterior.

The woman they had come to see was the only person at home. She wore a shapeless tracksuit, with sweat and food stains forming darker patterns on the thin, pink material. Her long hair was greasy and tangled, shiny wan face flecked with pimples. Bliss wrinkled his nose in distaste as her body odour replaced the stink of sewage in his nostrils. He thought Monkton looked at least ten years older than her documented age; someone who appeared to have lost all hope of a better life, and given up even trying.

DCI Warburton opened up as they had agreed on the drive over. 'Your husband not at home, Jane?'

'We don't live together anymore. Our lives changed the day he got put in his wheelchair.'

'I'm sorry to hear that.'

'Yeah, I bet you are.'

Warburton asked the woman about the property, and it became immediately apparent as to why Jane Monkton held further grudges against Baker. Putting her husband in a wheelchair for the rest of his life was a despicable act, but her hatred of the vicious bully did not end there. Her parents had sunk every penny they had saved and from the sale of their house into the bungalow, due to her mother's failing health and inability to use stairs on a regular basis. The many faults only came to light shortly after the couple moved in. Far from being sympathetic and co-operative, Baker's building company had taken an aggressive approach towards the owners.

Jane's father subsequently threatened legal proceedings. He only did so once. The following day he was the victim of a hit-and-run, left lying in the road with two broken legs, a dislocated hip and internal bleeding. He survived, but had never fully recovered from the trauma. Jane railed publicly against the unfairness of the situation, but less than a week later she was bundled into the back of a van and intimidated by four masked men with both rape and torture if she did not stop her protests.

'Sounds horrendous,' Bliss said, genuinely sympathising. 'You must have been delighted when you heard about Baker being murdered.'

'Oh, I was.' Monkton could not hold back a smile of satisfaction. 'Not quite so much when you filth came after me for it, though.'

'That's not why we are here, Mrs Monkton. Not to rake over old ground. Even so, the reason for our visit is connected.'

Bliss went on to inform her about the two fatal shootings. She shook her head as if to ask what any of it had to do with her. He obliged by explaining. 'Our working theory is that somebody is looking to avenge Mr Baker's murder, and they appear to be going after the thirteen suspects interviewed under caution by the police. As you pointed out, you are one of them. We think you might be on his list.'

Unlike Alan Brewer, Monkton was not sceptical. Her eyes grew wide, and Bliss saw she was immediately terrified at the prospect. 'Are… are you two here to protect me?' she asked, vulnerable for the first time since they had arrived.

Warburton shook her head, responding in a gentle voice. 'I'm sorry, Jane, but that's simply not possible. We don't have the resources, I'm afraid. We cannot provide round-the-clock protection indefinitely to all eleven of you. I doubt our boss would grant permission even if we received an overt threat. But the truth is, this is just our theory at the moment. There is little for us to take affirmative action on. We are here to warn you. To tell you to be on your guard. Do you have anywhere else you can go?'

Monkton was virtually speechless. Clearly it did not compute that she could be in danger from a gunman and the police were not going to do anything about it other than offer words of advice.

'But you… you have to protect me,' she cried, getting to her feet and marching across to the bay window, where she drew back the curtains. Monkton turned, stared them both down. 'You can't just leave me here on my own when there's someone running around with a gun killing us off one by one.'

'We don't have any option,' Bliss explained. 'I'm sorry.'

The woman jabbed a finger at the DCI, her face a twisted scowl of rage. 'This is you, isn't it, you bitch! This is your way of getting us to confess – to something we never even did! Is that how you're going to provide protection, by banging us all up?'

Bliss heard a slight pause before the final sentence. He glanced across at Warburton, whose subtle nod suggested she had also picked up on it. He took a step forward. 'Mrs Monkton, I can assure you that's not why we are here. Frankly, I'm not sure it would make any real difference at this point. It's unlikely that you'd be held on remand even if you confessed, because your defence solicitor would justifiably claim you posed no further threat to society due to the subject of your anger being dead.'

'So you wouldn't just lock me up?'

'The legal system doesn't work that way. Besides, are you likely to confess? If not, then this discussion is moot.'

'I'm not guilty, so why should I confess?'

'You've just alluded to a possible reason. That by confessing you could be held under lock and key and therefore out of this gunman's reach.'

Bliss let the implication hang there for a moment. As much as he wanted the woman to believe he and Warburton were not there looking for her to cough to anything, the truth was that her doing so might prove to be a significant breakthrough not just in the Baker's Dozen case, but also in their current task force investigation. The domino effect was something all police officers eventually became familiar with, and if the two cases were linked, then Monkton confessing might cause the rest to fall.

Jane Monkton was wrestling with a decision. It was written all over her face. Bliss knew then that she was guilty of stabbing Charlie Baker. The issue now was whether she feared this gunman more than arrest and prosecution. As her features changed from anger to resentment and then to resolution, Bliss realised she was not about to deal.

The woman sank down into her seat, leaning forward, hands clasped together as she rocked back and forth. 'So what now?' she asked.

Bliss rubbed a hand over his mouth before replying. 'As I have made plain, two of the people among the thirteen suspected of killing Charles Baker have been murdered. We strongly believe that all remaining suspects are in danger. Our job is to advise you of this and then return to continue hunting for the killer.'

'I know this has something to do with you,' Monkton said, pointing accusingly at Warburton. 'Just because you could never get us to talk.'

The DCI shook her head. 'I can assure you that my only thoughts right now are to find whoever is doing this and catch him.'

'But you think we're all killers ourselves.'

'That's true. I do. But just as I went after you for murder, so I'm going after this man.'

Bliss glanced at his partner for the day, admiring her steadfastness. 'Jane,' he said, returning his gaze to the slovenly woman. 'There is nothing to be gained by you making wild accusations. You must do what you can to protect yourself until this is over. If you have somewhere else to go, then I suggest you make arrangements to do so. Other than that, be alert and if you do see anybody around who looks suspicious, you call triple nine. Mention our names and someone will get here as soon as they can.'

'Yeah, I bet.' Monkton sneered at the pair. 'You'll break your necks getting here to stop *me* being killed, I'm sure.'

'Believe what you want, Jane. We can do no more.'

As they walked outside, Warburton took a call. Her voice first lowered and then became clipped as she spoke urgently. By the time she was done they were back inside the car with the engine running. She looked across at Bliss and shook her head. 'That was Barry Smyth. He just took a call of his own from Bucharest. Our four missing Romanian males are no longer missing.'

'Well, some good news at last.'

'Not really. They had each returned home to Romania, where all four of them were shot dead last week. And yes, they were each also decapitated.'

The Boathouse, gabled and weather-boarded, looked every bit the late-eighties architecture it was. It overlooked a narrow tributary of the Nene river in Thorpe Meadows and Bliss returned to the pub often. Its beer garden and decking alongside the water's edge provided seating appropriate to fine weather, and when inclement the high ceilings inside gave the bar the impression of a vast and airy space. With its relaxed atmosphere, Bliss never felt uncomfortable there. Plus, it offered the serious advantage of selling both cask ales and craft beers, so he was never short of choice. On more than one occasion he'd had to take a taxi home and leave his car parked outside overnight.

The Lincolnshire duo of DCI Warburton and RPU officer Smyth had headed off as soon as they were able to, but Chandler, Short and Bishop accepted Bliss's invitation of a drink to unwind. It had been a gruelling night and day, and Bliss wanted to gather up his team's immediate thoughts before any of the darkness crept in unannounced and uninvited. He understood the importance of times like these, when you could both relax and discuss the investigation without any pressure to deliver a firm lead.

It was a pleasant evening, so they chose a table outside on the decking. Bliss waited until they were all seated with drinks before revealing DCI Warburton's latest news. His three colleagues were aghast, each understanding that with these four additional murders the initial investigative notion had now moved from probability to certainty – somebody was working their way through the thirteen people suspected of killing Charles Baker, and was almost halfway towards achieving their goal.

'If it's the same killer, then he's ruthless and astonishingly proficient,' Short said, concern deepening a vertical line in the centre of her forehead.

Bliss agreed. 'This is no local yokel with a grudge and a Stanley knife. We're looking at a contract killer here.'

Nobody at the table disputed his assertion. 'The Baker family have the wealth,' Bishop said. 'And it makes perfect sense for them to bring someone in from the outside rather than get their own hands bloodstained.'

'It does. Make that your first-up job tomorrow, Bish. A contract killer needs paying. See if you can trace the money back to the Bakers. Check all their funds, look for large recent cash withdrawals or deposits into other accounts.'

'It's not going to be so easy,' Chandler warned. 'They've bided their time. Clearly they've given it a lot of thought. I'm guessing they prepared well for this.'

'True. But I doubt any of them are as savvy as Charlie Baker was. By all accounts he was as bright as he was monstrous. Perhaps whoever arranged it left a door open for us somewhere.'

'Why the heads?' Short asked after knocking back half her blackcurrant and soda in one go – nobody had questioned her choice of a non-alcoholic drink on this occasion, but Bliss wondered if the others had noticed. 'And why three shots each?'

'The old double-tap has become a triple,' Bliss explained. 'The age of personal bullet-proof vests has led shooters to use two rounds to put their victims down, with a third to the nut sealing the deal. Neither of our victims here were shot in the head, probably by design. The face needs to be recognisable to count.'

'So why not just photograph the body afterwards? That's proof enough, surely?'

'Perhaps not. If it's the buyer's choice, then maybe they are wary of their hired assassin staging shootings in order to get paid, especially if each kill triggers a fresh payment. I hear you can work miracles with Photoshop. If the killer has decided to use this method, maybe it's a sign of his professionalism. The head being offered as absolute proof.'

Chandler puffed out her lips. 'All the same, it's a pretty sick way of going about it. Why take the chance?'

'If he's using an electric saw, it wouldn't take long to carve a head off,' Bishop said. His expression was grim, mouth curving downward. 'No more than a few seconds each.'

Bliss felt his skin crawl. Just as seeing a human body minus its head played tricks with the mind, so the very thought of it sent chills racing through the bloodstream. There was something disturbing and remorseless about the act.

The team moved on to discuss their visits to various suspects. The interviews carried out by Chandler and Bishop had pretty much replicated Bliss's own experience, with one of the intervie-wees dismissing the threat out of hand, the other demanding police protection.

'What sense did you get from them in terms of the Baker murder?' Short asked.

'Both as guilty as fuck,' Bishop responded. He sounded indig-nant. 'And both with good reason to want the man dead. Listening to their stories, I can't say I blame either one of them for wishing it on him. He comes across as having been the most odious and callous of men.'

'Which is pretty much what we picked up as well,' Short said. 'Barry Smyth and I briefly chatted about both visits after we'd finished with them, and we came to the same conclusion. Baker had it coming, and the suspects we spoke to were involved. Neither of us were left in any doubt about that. On the other hand, neither of us are entirely unsympathetic.'

'How did they react to being on someone else's shit list?' Bliss asked.

'Surprisingly cool. I think both see themselves as hard men, or at least had before the Baker family arrived in Sutton End. Whether they were competitors, I can't be sure. But they are both dodgy characters, and I wouldn't be at all surprised to find an element of business rivalry in what occurred the night Baker was put down.'

'We have two people who have requested protection,' Chandler confirmed. 'Is there any way we can do so, given we don't have so many to keep an eye on? I mean, eleven may have been out of reach, plus we had no evidence of a genuine threat. Both of those circumstances have now changed considerably.'

Bliss hitched his shoulders. 'I'll have a word with Edwards and Fletcher. Now that we know for certain these people are in danger, I can make a better case. If the others aren't interested then there's not a lot we can do about it, but we should consider putting the two suspects under full-time observation. It's also looking as if it may be our only way into our killer, because he's giving us nothing else. Maybe him going for the next person on his list is our best chance of snatching him up.'

Short drained her glass and got to her feet. 'I'm not stopping for food,' she said. 'Hubby's cooking tonight. So, if me and Bish dig into the Baker financials first thing in the morning, you'll speak to the DCI about protection, yes?'

Bliss was swallowing back the last few dregs of his beer. He wiped his lips before replying. 'That's the plan. We'll catch up as soon as I have an answer. Diane and Barry are due into HQ by eight. I'll attend the Observer briefing, check on any progress made there. I think we can now safely follow the line that poor Kelly was killed by the same gunman, but I don't want her to become some sort of by-product of what we're doing. This Baker's Dozen thing is messy, so if it's also possible to nail this bastard on Kelly's murder then I'll be a lot happier.'

'What about the last Romanian, boss? You didn't mention him.'

'He wasn't around. Diane knew who to speak to, having been there on several occasions during the Baker's Dozen case. She made a couple of calls while we were on the road. It turns out that she had not only interviewed the bloke we're looking to talk to, but also one of the victims discovered murdered in Romania. Providing that piece of news to the community welcome wagon bought us some co-operation from them, and we both felt it was genuine when they said our man wasn't there. We'll try again tomorrow.'

A few minutes later, DS Bishop also announced he had dinner plans at home with his family. Bliss and Chandler checked out the menu and both went with the chef's chicken, which came in strips with melted cheese and a tomato and herb sauce. Bliss realised he had missed being with his usual partner during the day, despite having struck up a comfortable relationship with DCI Warburton.

'How did you get on this afternoon without me there to hold your hand?' he asked.

'It was good, actually. Olly is a great bloke to work with. And he doesn't give me shit like you do.'

Bliss laughed. 'That's because he's terrified of you.'

'Good. That suits me just fine.'

'Bish is a bloody good copper. As I said to you before, it won't be long before he makes the step up. He'll be hard to replace if he has to move on.'

'He has all the right instincts. Not to give you an even bigger head, but he mentioned today that he's learned a lot from you.'

'Good. I'm glad something is rubbing off.'

Her eyes widened. 'Yeah, not only the good, either.'

'What d'you mean?'

'He said he's also learning from you how not to do things.'

'Which is just as invaluable. We each have to find our own unique way to make progress, Pen. Bish has a good head on his shoulders – no pun intended – and it's only right that he chooses the best of my influence to follow and leaves the worst behind.'

'It's certainly a very different ride. You and me are pretty similar in that we have little going on in our lives other than the job. Hence the reason why it's just the two of us left here now. Olly mentioned his wife and kids quite a bit, and it did make me think even more about Hannah.'

'It's bound to. But it's not quite as bleak as you make it sound. Don't forget your wider family, including your parents. And I still have my mum around. We're not exactly alone in the world.'

'But they're not present in our daily lives. Not a physical presence in our homes, family we wake up to every day and who are there when we come home again at night. It's hard to deal with sometimes.'

Bliss understood. Having come this far over the past few months, the wait for final arrangements to be made must feel like purgatory to his partner.

'Knowing you, Pen, you'll be focussing on the positives and ignoring the negatives.'

'I try to. It's in my nature. But I swear it's getting harder with each passing week. I know everybody is doing their best, and that the situation out there is volatile, but it feels like torture at the moment.'

'Is there anything I can do?'

Chandler shook her head. 'God, no, Jimmy. I couldn't ask more of you even if there was something I thought you might be able to influence at this late stage. You've already stuck your neck out enough on my behalf.'

He shrugged. 'There probably isn't a great deal left for me to do. But if you need a call made or just want to vent, you know where I am.'

'Yeah. And how sad is that? I mean, the fact that I always know where I can find you. Are you ever going to put yourself out there again, Jimmy?'

Bliss knew exactly what Chandler meant. Since the murder of his wife some seventeen years ago, his relationships with women had been scarce. He had got as far as living with someone whilst posted to Bedford, but the situation fell apart due to his lack of further commitment. Previously, a potential relationship with a specialist his team had come to refer to as the Bone Woman, ended when he was sent packing back to London after his first stint in Peterborough ended badly for him. Other than those two brief flings, a short dalliance with a DI working in the sex crimes division was all he could point to in terms of failed attempts at moving on.

Back in June, however, time had caught up with Bliss. With the darkest shadows of his past threatening to overwhelm him, he unexpectedly managed to turn the tables in his favour and subsequently found the strength to take a few uneasy steps forwards. But opening up your heart and being willing to embrace the possibility of a new relationship was not the same thing as finding one in the first place, and Bliss's dry spell was in danger of taking on drought proportions.

'Perhaps you've ruined me where other women are concerned,' he said, stifling a grin. He felt his twitching lips giving him away. 'Maybe I'll never get over that one snog.'

Chandler rolled her eyes and groaned theatrically. 'Oh, my God. Are you ever going to let that go, Jimmy Bliss? A solitary drunken kiss when I was worried about you and thinking I might lose you does not a snog make.'

'You used your tongue on me, Pen. A man doesn't forget things like that.'

Her expression changed to one of utter disgust. 'Ugh. That's a damned lie and you bloody well know it.'

Chuckling now, Bliss's broad shoulders heaved. 'Are you sure? Pen, it was like being French kissed by a giraffe. It felt like a demonstration of true love to me.'

'Yeah, you wish. Don't delude yourself, old man. I'm more woman than you could possibly handle.'

'You're right about that.'

The drunken incident with Chandler was etched upon his mind. The memory of their kiss had taken a day or so to fully filter its way through the alcoholic haze, but it remained with him for quite a while afterwards. At the time, he worried that a single crazy moment might ruin their friendship. For a couple of weeks they were a little awkward around each other, but eventually their relationship eased back into familiar patterns. Within a month they were making wisecracks about it.

Bliss relented, holding up a hand to call for a truce. 'Seriously, though, I have made progress,' he said. His gaze wandered absently to the water being gently stirred by the warm evening breeze. A crimson sunset made this part of the Nene look like a river of blood. 'I've turned my sterile house into a home just as you suggested, family photos are now on display instead of sitting inside cardboard boxes, including those of me and Hazel. That's a serious move in the right direction, and precisely what you told me I needed to do. A good start, I think you'll agree.'

'I do,' Chandler acknowledged with a nod.

'And to be fair, I've not exactly been in the best of circumstances to meet anyone since.'

'I understand. I know how tough that can be.'

'But the barricades are down, right?'

'Right.'

'So give it time.'

'You're coming along, I suppose. And while we're on the subject, Diane seems very nice.'

'She does. I also clocked the gold and diamonds on her finger, so there's nothing going to happen there.'

'She could be in the throes of a divorce for all you know, Jimmy. And she is definitely your type.'

'Which is?'

'She has that sultry, brooding thing going on.'

Bliss laughed and shook his head. 'You don't give up, do you? Anyway, you're a fine one to talk. Has there been anyone in your life since your ex-boss on the Sapphire team?'

Chandler sighed as if it didn't matter, though he knew it did. 'Not really. Same problem as you I suppose – lack of opportunity.'

'It'll end up being someone in the job.'

'Oh, please.' Chandler gave a mock shudder.

'How about Gratton? He seems a nice enough bloke, and he follows you around like a puppy.'

'Phil? Sorry, but he's DC Gratton to me remember, and there's no way I'm getting involved with a junior rank.'

Bliss spread his hands palms upwards. 'I understand. Before long, you and I may have to make the pledge.'

'What pledge?'

'The one where friends decide to settle for each other when they haven't found anyone else to share their life with.'

Chandler's eyes widened and she stabbed a finger at her own chest. 'You cheeky bugger. First of all, this lady isn't about to *settle* for anyone. It'll be love or it won't happen at all. Secondly, you'll reach that stage long before I do, you fossil.'

Chandler had a point. Bliss refused to give it up straight away, though. 'All I'm saying is, there's more sand in the bottom half of the hourglass than the top these days.'

'Jimmy, I'm not even forty. Not quite. Don't measure me for my coffin just yet.'

He sniggered. 'Well, at the rate you're going it won't need to be a Y-shaped one, that's for sure.'

'You cheeky bastard. I'll pay you back for that one, Jimmy Bliss.'

'Oh-oh. I'm in trouble now. You only use my full name when you're angry with me, and that's the second time tonight.'

Chandler laughed and waved his observation aside. His own laughter continued. This was everything Bliss had missed during the afternoon. Diane Warburton was a charming, easy-going woman with a seemingly lovely nature. Intelligent and outgoing, she had proven to be a wonderful companion. But the sparking chemistry between him and Chandler helped get him through the days, especially those that were filled with the very worst humanity is capable of.

'You'll miss me when I retire,' Bliss said. He took a sip from his glass, nodding at her as if emphasising the import of his words.

Chandler grunted. 'Not that old bollocks again. You threatened to retire back in June. Three months on and you're still with us. Still tormenting the life out of me.'

'But not sucking the life out of you. Which is the important bit.'

'True. I dare say I'll miss you when you're no longer around.'

'You bloody well better had. Not that I'm ready to jack it in just yet.'

'Now, is *that* a threat or a promise?'

Bliss gave a snort of derision but made no reply. Their food arrived, and the banter stopped. They were both hungry, and as they ate, his mind had already wandered back to the investigations and the tasks that lay ahead.

21

The ancient sewage system of Kirton Drain cut straight through the Roma camp. It was now more of a stream than a river in Bliss's view, but as DCI Warburton reminded him, if the locals referred to it as a river then he should respect their opinion. He was, after all, in their own backyard. By the time they arrived at their destination, Bliss had yielded to her point. Perhaps the drain held more water in the spring.

Warburton filled him in on who they were about to meet. The Roma people had initially taken up residence on the plot of land by the river back in 2013. Following a long-running and bitter feud with the owners, the community eventually purchased two entire acres, an area twice as long as it was wide. The families who lived there had no intentions of moving on anytime soon, and so excavated half the property, laid hardcore to provide foundations, skimmed this with tarmac, built brick supports set into concrete to support the expansive mobile homes which arrived in two separate pieces each on the back of huge flatbed lorries. A few months later they added the final touches, with utilities being fed in from local spurs. It was a settlement that was there to stay and built to last.

According to Warburton, Tudor Chipcui was the elected elder

of the community. His was the first home you came across when entering the site, and if you knew your business you stopped there to ask permission before venturing any further into the camp. Non-compliance often met with aggressive resistance, though seldom physical violence. The community was a largely peaceful one within its own boundaries. Its leaders leaned towards a Vegas-like philosophy in regard to what happened away from the immediate area.

Bliss waited in the car while Warburton spoke with Chipcui at the man's own front door. Having elected to dress down a little today, the DCI's casual-smart crew-neck sweater and boot-cut slacks looked nonetheless stylish, and pretty expensive. The change in style softened her all the more, and Bliss felt himself drawn closer to the woman during the forty-five-minute drive north-east from HQ. He thought about Chandler's observation regarding the rings on a woman's finger not necessarily meaning anything, but closed his mind to it as he saw Warburton striding hurriedly back to the vehicle.

'They have a community hall,' she told him, easing into the passenger seat. 'Nicolai Stoian will meet with us there in a couple of minutes, but three community leaders will accompany him, including Tudor. They want to know more about what happened to the other victims, as well as how it all relates to Stoian and the local Roma people in general.'

'I expected as much,' Bliss said with a nod. 'Anything which may eventually impact on the community as a whole is a problem best shared as far as they are concerned.'

Warburton pointed ahead. 'You take the first left and then a right. The community hall is the only structure painted yellow, apparently.'

'We're already the subject of great scrutiny.' He stared out through the windscreen at the children – toddlers mainly – now standing on grass verges around their homes. No horse-drawn gypsy caravans of old stood looking forlorn and aged, and even the non-mobile homes came in the form of large and expensive modern caravans. As Bliss looked on, several adults also wandered outside to see what was going on, their expressions inquisitive.

'They've seen me talk with their elder, so they'll leave us be.'

'This place is a lot cleaner and tidier than many I've visited,' Bliss observed.

'It's run well. I don't think the community as a whole will ever allow the site to become a dump.'

As Bliss nursed the car around the site, his thoughts drifted back to the morning briefing. The team focussing on the Observer op were in full agreement that both they and the task force were all hunting down the same man. Bishop revealed that all the relevant security and automatic number plate recognition footage was spliced together to reveal the timeline of events leading up to Kelly Gibson's murder.

It was DC Hunt who took them through it verbally, describing how the white Range Rover pursued Florin Budescu's vehicle along the A16, and pointing out that neither appeared when they ought to have done on a camera at the Crowland junction. The next vehicle through was the Skoda driven by Kelly Gibson, followed shortly afterwards by the Range Rover.

At that point, Bliss asked to see the footage. Ansari set it going on the pull-down white screen and a uniform extinguished the lights. There was complete silence in the room as the evening unfolded in front of the squad. Bliss watched closely as both the Skoda and Range Rover were picked up at various points all the way through to Farcet. By the end of the video, Bliss found himself troubled by what he had noticed.

He jerked himself out of his reverie, spotting a parking space outside the low building that comprised the Roma community hall. Less than five minutes later they sat in the centre of a large area made up of two double-width mobile home shells. An arrangement of six chairs formed a circle, no table in the middle. Bliss recognised the philosophy; no table ensured there could be no head of table, and therefore no leader amongst those meeting.

Stoian was a thin, almost gaunt-looking individual with dark hair shaved close to the scalp. Shabby clothes hung on him like rags, and his neck was inked with a variety of symbols and what Bliss assumed to be words in either Romanian or, if Stoian came from Transylvania, possibly Hungarian. The young man's right foot tapped nervously, and his hands seemed to claw at each other as he sat with them clasped in his lap. To Bliss he had the fraught appearance of a junky desperate for his next fix. Not a man who fit in with the clean-cut image this community were at pains to promote.

'Officers,' Chipcui said in heavily-accented English. Unlike Stoian, the elder was a small and wide bull, whose dark eyes were almost lost in shadow. 'We have concerns to raise based on the information you gave me yesterday. A number of us discussed this matter overnight, and we have questions for you, yes?'

'Of course,' Warburton said, taking the lead. 'Fire away.'

'Good. First, our friends who recently returned home. I have no word other than yours that these men are now dead. You say this is true, though, yes?'

'There's no reason why we should lie to you, sir. Just as we were looking to trace Mr Stoian here, so we were searching for the others as well. We had no information indicating their return to Romania, but as we were in touch with officials out there in Bucharest we asked anyway. This is what we were told, and indeed their deaths mirror the two that have taken place here since Sunday evening.'

The three community leaders exchanged glances and nods. Bliss noticed they avoided looking at Stoian. He wondered why that might be.

'You say this is because of Baker, yes?' Chipcui sought to clarify.

Nodding, the DCI replied, 'That's right. At least, that is the theory we are basing our investigation on.'

'But these men… all innocent, no?'

Warburton paused, and Bliss knew she was weighing her words carefully. 'That's not technically correct, sir. None of the thirteen suspects have yet been found either innocent or guilty. At this stage of the operation we have not yet charged anybody. Do you understand the difference?'

The man nodded. An elder he might be to these Roma people, but he looked to be no more than forty. 'My English is good. I understand. Not innocent... not guilty. So why you say they are killed because of Baker?'

'As I explained yesterday, sir, even the two murders here convinced us because both victims were also suspects in that investigation. The murder of four other men from the same suspect pool only increases our confidence. We are as certain as we can be at this stage, having spoken to all of the remaining accused, with the exception of Mr Stoian. We'd like to do so now.'

The elder leaned back in his chair and whispered something into the ear of the man to his left. In response he received a single nod and a brief huff of breath.

'Nicolai does not have good English. He speaks with me earlier, before you come. He no wants protection from police.' Chipcui made a circling movement with his hand. 'We keep safe. Here in Roma community.'

Bliss was watching Stoian closely, and he noted the man's reaction as the elder explained the situation. He might not be able to speak good English, but he certainly understood every word being said. Bliss accepted discretion was required here, yet still he felt the need to poke the bear.

'Is that really what you want, Mr Stoian?' he said, immediately drawing the Romanian's gaze. 'You believe these men will protect you better than the police can?'

'He not understand,' Chipcui said, adding a little edge to his tone. 'I tell you this.'

'Yes, you did. But I think he understands more than you say he does. In fact, I think he understood every word.'

Stoian looked over at the three community leaders, his eyes glistening and fearful. He found only hard stares in return. When he turned back to Bliss he shrugged his narrow shoulders and seemed to shrink further into his own slender frame. He gave one final shake of the head before looking away again.

Bliss was about to say more when he felt a sharp tug at his sleeve. Turning his head, he saw a warning flash in DCI Warburton's eyes. She was aware of the other men in the room looking at them, and so did not tell him to stop pushing. Her meaning was clear all the same.

Drawing in a deep breath, Bliss took the hint. As he exhaled he said, 'Six of your fellow countrymen have been slaughtered so far, Mr Chipcui. I sincerely hope the confidence that you have in yourself and your community to keep this man safe and secure is justified. I genuinely have no desire to call on you again with a mortuary vehicle behind me next time.'

'We protect,' the elder repeated, folding both arms across his chest. 'We protect.'

'Then how about Florin Budescu and Constantin Benzar?' Bliss pressed, leaning forward in his chair. 'It would be useful to us if we knew more about them. Especially useful to learn what they were both doing in the hours before they were killed. Will you help us with those two men?'

'I will ask. If I have answers, I pass on. If not... not.'

As Bliss drove out of the site and began threading his way back along the serpentine route towards Kirton, Chipcui's words echoing inside his head, he swore in exasperation.

'Fuck! What the hell was all that about?' The question was as much for himself as it was his companion.

'That was them looking inwardly and taking care of themselves,' Warburton answered. 'You must have seen it before when you worked for the NCA.'

'Of course. But I didn't mean them. The three so-called pillars of the community I understand all too well. It's him I'm having trouble with. Stoian. He sat there, not even speaking up for himself, although everyone in the room knew he could, and everyone in the room knew that everyone else in the room knew it.'

Warburton looked sidelong at him and laughed. 'Inspector, that's just about the most sensible thing you've said all morning.'

Bliss shook his head. 'Hey, if you're Diane, then I'm Jimmy. Okay?'

'Fair enough. So what are your thoughts, then?'

'I don't know. I don't understand him remaining silent throughout. He's an adult, not a child.'

'He was terrified. Simple as that.'

'Even so. Why not speak up for yourself? It's his life at stake, not theirs.'

'He's one of them, though. A true Roma, you can tell. To receive protection from the community, you have to obey the will of the leaders and, especially, the elder. They will have told him it was in his best interests to keep quiet, and the easiest way not to get drawn into a conversation is to pretend not to understand the language being used.'

Bliss smacked a hand on the steering wheel. 'It's not bloody right, Diane. That man might well be safe in there with that lot around him, but what happens when he steps outside? Will they accompany him wherever he goes?'

The DCI glanced across to her right. 'Would we? *Could* we? Besides, they may not let him go anywhere. And meanwhile, you can bet they will have their people out asking questions of their own. They may believe they're capable of finding our killer before we can.'

'And they could well be right about that. They can intimidate in a way we can only dream of doing.'

'Oh, I suspect you're capable of intimidating others when you put your mind to it.'

'That may be true, only I'd never get away with it. You know, I came close to telling them about the beheadings, just to see their reaction. Or even if they reacted at all. Fact is, I wondered if they already knew.'

Alongside him, Warburton began to nod. 'I have to say, the exact same thought crossed my mind. Charlie Baker was able to keep police officers on his payroll, and I have to ask myself whether the Roma elder does, too.'

'Which leaves us where?' Bliss asked.

Warburton gave a slight shrug. 'I don't really know, to be honest with you. But we do have two other suspects to focus our attentions on.'

'We do. That and what we saw on the video footage earlier of the Range Rover tracking the Skoda.'

Bliss thought back to his initial concerns following the viewing of that video file. When the light went back up, Bliss had risen out of his chair, holding up a hand. 'Does anyone else have a problem with what we have just seen?' he asked.

There were some puzzled looks tossed his way, but the eager DC Gratton sprung to his feet. 'Boss, there was something that occurred to me.'

'Well, then let's hear it.'

'All right. It might just be me, it may even be that the splicing of the footage isn't synchronised properly, but something was worrying me and by the time it ended it grated on me all the more.'

Bliss offered encouragement. 'Go on, then. Spit it out.'

'Boss, it just felt to me as if the SUV wasn't following closely enough to actually be following. What I mean is, at times I wondered how it was able to follow because it didn't seem to keep the Skoda in view throughout. It was when it reached Farcet that I was most concerned, though. I was pretty sure that when Kelly Gibson turned off the main road, the Rover did not have it in view. Even more curious, when it eventually slipped down the road where Kelly lived, it entered from the opposite end to the one Kelly drove into. You may want to play it back, but right there and then I told myself there was no way they could have followed her there.'

Bliss wagged a finger at the young DC. 'No need to replay it, Gratton. That was an excellent spot. I noticed the very same thing, and it worried me, too. Now, we all know how good they are in tech-ops, but while DCI Warburton and I are out interviewing Mr Stoian, I want you to pop over there and ask them to check the synchronisation. Because if what we're seeing follows a precise timeline, then like you I don't think there is any possibility that Range Rover followed the Skoda all the way to the street in which Kelly was murdered.'

'Then how did they know where to go?' Ansari asked, beating several others to the punch by the look of it.

'That,' Bliss said, 'is a very good question. The answer to which I fear is going to make us all very angry indeed.'

22

The incident room was still buzzing by the time Bliss and DCI Warburton returned to Thorpe Wood. Gratton was at his desk, but jumped up the moment Bliss came through the door.

'I've been working with tech-ops, boss. They are one hundred per cent certain that the video sync is spot on, and therefore what we saw was an accurate representation of the entire journey from the A16 onwards.'

Having already drawn the most logical conclusion, he and his partner for the day had been discussing the matter during the drive back from Lincolnshire. It was the news Bliss had been expecting to hear, yet feared most of all.

'Our killer got Kelly's address from us,' he said, anger filtering through into his voice. He took a moment to compose himself. 'He made a call, gave somebody on the job the Skoda's plate, and they in turn told him where she lived.'

DS Short was already standing close to one of the two white-boards currently in use. In the now hushed room she said, 'We've all just been discussing the same thing, boss. We think you're right. It's the only way it makes any sense.'

Bliss shook his head and pinched the bridge of his nose. 'Bastards! I'll flay the skin off their backs for this when I find them.'

'It doesn't end there, though,' Bishop said. His jaw was jutting, barely able to draw the words out. 'We now have to ask ourselves what else our man is being fed.'

'And from whom?' Ansari added.

'Of course,' Bliss agreed. 'Which makes it all the more urgent for us to find whichever scumbag amongst our ranks is providing this sick fuck with information. We don't plug that leak, we don't stop any of what's about to happen.'

It was a bleak picture he was portraying, but it was also a realistic one. Everyone in the team now needed to digest the evidence from the perspective of the worst case possible. Bliss looked around the room and noted a particular absentee.

'Where's DS Chandler?' he asked.

'She stepped out to take a call,' Short told him. 'I think she was going for a hot drink afterwards.'

'Thanks.' He had left Warburton in the major crimes meeting room with the RPU man, Smyth, and was in a hurry to get back to them. 'Anything else I need to know right now?'

'Gul and I spoke to Kelly's friends,' Hunt said. 'The early dinner and drink was arranged via Facebook Messenger on the spur of the moment on Saturday morning. According to each of them she was in a great mood and had no obvious worries. They all left the pub at the same time and Kelly was the first to drive away. Her mates are genuinely stunned by what happened.'

'Nobody noticed anyone lurking or following? Specifically a white Range Rover.'

'No, boss.'

Bliss wrinkled his nose. 'Thanks. I really didn't expect anything from that source. We know how it went down, I think.' His mind latched onto something else. 'Bish, how are Baker's financials looking?'

'Still ongoing. Nothing so far to suggest recent payments have gone out to anybody, but we're continuing to dig.'

'All right. Is that it everybody?'

'It is,' Short answered. 'I think our next move is to find out if we can provide security for the two suspects to have requested it.'

Bliss tutted through clenched teeth, angry with himself. 'Damn! I forgot all about that. I could have called DCI Edwards earlier about it.' He fastened his gaze on Short. 'Tell you what, come upstairs with me now. If she's able to spare five minutes, you and I can have it out with her.'

'Me?' Short touched a hand to her chest.

Smiling, Bliss said, 'Yes, you. You're an acting DI now. So act like one.'

They walked along the corridor and up one flight of stairs. Bliss heard his DS taking deep breaths and expelling them slowly. It was Short's way of psyching herself up. Her next move would be to pluck a rubber band from somewhere about her person, pull her shiny blonde hair back and fashion a tail. By the time they reached the DCI's office, Short had done exactly as he'd predicted.

'What?' she asked, noting his smile as they approached the door.

Bliss shook his head. 'Nothing.'

'It must be something. You don't go around smiling for no good reason unless you're a simpleton.'

'Well, then either there *is* a good reason for keeping it to myself, or I am simple.'

Short grinned. 'I'm not taking bets on which.'

'You spend far too much time with Penny Chandler.'

'You've said that before, boss.'

'Yeah, and I meant it before, too.'

Edwards was at her desk. She beckoned the pair inside. Bliss remained standing, and Short did likewise.

'What's this?' Edwards asked, frowning. 'Some sort of deputation?'

'Not quite, boss, but we do have something we'd like to put to you,' Bliss said. 'I thought acting DI Short could do with experiencing this side of the job as well.'

'You mean the one where you grovel and beg me to allow you to take some foolhardy action?'

Bliss shot her a broad grin. He had previously considered the DCI incapable of making such a crack in his presence. It was yet another positive step in the right direction.

'Something like that, boss. Only this time, I'm not the only one who believes it's the best move.'

'Go on then. I'm listening.'

'Boss, we have a couple of the Baker's Dozen suspects who are not only willing to be placed under protective surveillance, but are actually beseeching us to do so. I know resources are stretched, and unfortunately, we'll require three teams of two to cover each twenty-four-hour period, but I'll happily take on one of those shifts at no cost to your budget. I'm expecting DCI Warburton to make a matching offer, but I haven't asked her yet. I wanted to run it by you first.'

'Well, thank you for that, Bliss. Usually your methods rely on the old cliché of asking forgiveness rather than permission. I assume you're hoping our killer will approach one of these suspects, at which point we can apprehend him.'

'That's precisely my thinking, boss. We know it's only a matter of time. The Roma community insist on providing protection for their own, leaving us with six civilians out there making themselves easy targets. Those are decent odds in our favour I'd say.'

After a moment of deliberation, Edwards nodded. 'I'll approve seventy-two hours at the outset. Come to me again if there's no show in three days.'

'Thank you, boss. I doubt we'll need it. This man is in a hurry to get the job done.'

'Agreed.' Edwards looked up at Short and said, 'Please don't be fooled into thinking it's always this easy. The reason your boss goes around me so often is that I don't usually give it up without a fight.

On this occasion, however, the budget is secondary. Just… well, be careful. Keep your wits about you at all times.'

'Of course,' Short said gratefully. 'Thank you… ma'am.'

Edwards acknowledged Short's hesitation with a smile. 'Temporarily I am only the one rank up from you at the moment, so let's make it "boss" for the time being.'

'You okay?' Bliss asked Short as they stepped back out into the third-floor corridor.

'I am actually. I thought that went well.'

'It did indeed. DCI Edwards and I have recently mended some fences which once lay in disrepair and, I'm sorry to say, disarray. Six months ago I'd have been arm-wrestling her for that same result. I'm hoping you will get to see her better side more often than not, Mia.'

'Me, too. I need all the help I can get.'

'We all do. It's why we're part of a team. But she's right when she warns you to take care on this one, Mia. We all now know what this man did to Kelly Gibson, so it stands to reason he'd not hesitate when it comes to pulling the trigger.'

'I understand.' Short tried to smile, but it was crooked and weak. To Bliss she seemed just about the right amount of nervous.

'I'm going to head down to the task force room,' he said. 'Would you mind stirring Penny out of the canteen? And if you'd bring me back a cup of coffee, I'd be ever so grateful.'

'Will do. Was that a DI to DI request, or DI to DS?'

Bliss thought about it for a moment. Said, 'How about friend to friend?'

This time, Short's smile was full and wide.

On his way down the stairs, Bliss took out his mobile and placed a call. There was something he had forgotten to take care of the day before.

'Is this Colin Tracey?' he asked.

'Speaking. How can I help?'

'This is DI Bliss. I was wondering whether there was any movement on the Carrie Dixon case today.' Tracey was the prosecution solicitor handling the briefs.

'Ah, Inspector Bliss. As a matter of fact, the case has spun on its heels. Jake Watts walked into his local police station yesterday morning and confessed to being both drunk and having taken drugs shortly before the offence took place. Police immediately took his new statement, which was also taped. Needless to say, the Dixon family are delighted.'

As was Bliss. The threats had worked, and he did not feel the least bit guilty for having used them in order to help achieve a small measure of justice for Carrie and her family.

In the meeting room temporarily assigned to the task force he caught up with Warburton and Smyth, filling them in on his discussion with DCI Edwards and the updates from his team. 'I mentioned your services only as leverage, Diane,' he told the Lincs DCI. 'I genuinely don't expect you to join us. I'm sure Penny, Mia and Bish will pitch in with an extra shift each.'

But Warburton held up a hand. 'No, no, no. I wouldn't want anyone to suggest we Lincolnshire officers are not willing to put in the time and graft.'

'I'll throw my hat in the ring as well,' Smyth offered.

Bliss thanked them both, adding, 'Barry, it would actually be good to have one or two ARVs floating around the general area over the next few days. I'll also have a word with Eric Price's team down in Huntingdon, see if they can spare a unit.'

Smyth seemed pleased with that suggestion. 'Having an armed response close by is the only way to go where our man is concerned. He's far too dangerous to approach in terms of arrest without armed backup.'

'I agree.'

'You said you underwent firearms training while you were with the NCA. Did you ever acquire full authorisation to carry?'

'I did. I passed my last physical, and both tactical and shooting tests to retain my permit just before I left the agency. It must expire in a few weeks, but it's still current.'

'Have you considered signing out a weapon for yourself until we nail this prick?'

Bliss gave a deep sigh of frustration. 'Sadly, I am currently receiving mandated psychological therapy. It was stipulated in the terms of my returning to work a few months ago following an IOPC investigation. My AFO certificate is current, but it won't be valid with a psyche monkey on my back.'

'Sounds like quite a story behind that statement.' Smyth eyed him with a glint of wry humour.

'There is. But these days such tales are strictly between me and my therapist.'

When the task force had reached its full complement with the arrival of his sergeants, and Bliss was enjoying the fresh stimulus provided by black coffee, he set about other issues relevant to their assignment.

'Other than the killer and the list of thirteen, we also need a strong focus on the Baker family and their friends,' he suggested. 'After all, if we are correct in assuming that one of them hired this gunman, then finding out which of them is responsible could give us the lead on the man we're looking for.'

Bliss was pleased to see nods of approval around the compact room.

'We have obviously been working that aspect of this case for quite a while now in Lincolnshire,' Warburton said. 'We have a lot of good intel on the people who orbited Baker's circle. To my knowledge, Charlie was the only one who was overtly dangerous and aggressive. He simply did not give one fuck what anyone thought of him. He and his wife involved the kids in everything, but they kept their heads down. Nasty, snidey characters each and every one of them, but nowhere near as despicable as the patriarch. For my money, I'd say we look hard at those on the fringes. The kind of hired muscle the Baker family regard as disposable.'

'Which will be one of three,' Smyth said emphatically. 'Wayne Harvey, Jon McLaren, or Eddie Vincent. Small-time wannabes, work for peanuts, proud to boast of their allegiance to Charlie Baker, and entirely expendable.'

'Good.' Bliss was delighted at having moved the operation forward. 'Then as soon as we have sorted out the protective details on the two Baker's Dozen suspects who requested it, I say we pay a visit to each of these three men. Same partnerships as yesterday, taking one interview each.'

It took no longer than ten minutes to organise the shift rotation, after which, Bliss instructed Chandler to action it all. Before he left to head back into Lincolnshire, Chandler asked him for a word in private. He met her in the car park at the rear of the building. Her features were soft and relaxed, but Bliss recognised the look of scrutiny that told him he was in for a grilling.

'I heard a whisper about the Carrie Dixon case,' she said.

'Really?'

'Yes. It's odd, because I remember you being all steamed up about that scrote Jake Watts being such a callous bastard. Then I happened to hear from the prosecution that you'd taken an interest in the court case. Now, all the talk is about Watts coughing to the lot sometime yesterday.'

'Yes. I seem to recall hearing something about that, too. A great result in the end.'

'Isn't it just?' Chandler's gaze narrowed and her voice took on the edge of scepticism. 'I don't suppose you know anything about Jake Watts's change of heart, do you?'

'Me? Is there any reason why I should?'

'No reason. It's just that things rarely turn out so well for us, and given it's exactly what you told me you'd like to happen in this case, I was thinking what a miracle it was.'

'I assume the little tosser's conscience got the better of him.'

Chandler folded her arms beneath her chest. 'You do? Somehow I doubt he has a conscience.'

'Perhaps he found God.'

'Yeah, or maybe he was… persuaded into confessing all.'

'Then if that was the case, let's be thankful for it, shall we?'

Bliss felt the strength of his partner's gaze. He knew Chandler well enough to realise that even if he told her about his involvement, she would not judge him. Her problem was probably the fact that he had not invited her along to help.

'You didn't actually deny being involved,' she said then.

Bliss winked as he saw Warburton striding across towards his car. He said, 'You know, Pen, I think you're right about that. Sorry, but we need to get going. We've had one thing go in our favour. Now we all have to work hard at getting another.'

23

Less than five minutes into their interview with Eddie Vincent, Chandler was certain she and Bishop had drawn the short straw. Vincent looked and behaved like a 1950s spiv, or perhaps the type you'd find hanging off the pole on the tail end of your bumper car at a fairground. His duck's arse haircut was slicked back and shiny, and he sported a pencil moustache. On a swan-necked coat and hat stand just inside the entrance to Vincent's dilapidated thatched cottage, whose orange-tinted stone exterior was built from local limestone, hung a range of coats and jackets and two Trilby hats which fitted the overall image the small-time villain was attempting to recapture. When he spoke, his accent was pure Lincolnshire, which softened the impact of the role he sought to portray.

'Charlie was as good a man as ever drew breath,' Vincent assured them when speaking of Baker. 'He was a diamond. A rough one, mind, but a diamond for all that.'

'Not everybody felt the same about him,' Bishop insisted. 'He rubbed a lot of people up the wrong way.'

Vincent waved a hand as if shoving some invisible object aside.

'Ah, that's just haters being hateful. You couldn't genuinely dislike Charlie if you tried. Not if you knew him well enough.'

'Thirteen separate people stabbing him to death suggests otherwise, Mr Vincent.'

The man ran a thumb and forefinger over his heavily waxed moustache. 'If you were inside his circle of friends you could do no wrong,' he snapped. 'Outsiders saw things differently.'

'So you regarded yourself as being inside the circle, then?' Chandler asked.

'I was.' Vincent jerked his chin up. 'And proud to be so.'

'But isn't it true to say that you mostly remained on the fringes of his circle? You weren't close to Baker or his family. The way we hear it, they treated you like a dogsbody, gave you all the menial tasks.'

Leaning forward, Vincent tapped the side of his nose. 'And that's just how I want you people thinking of me, too.' He finished with a conspiratorial wink.

'Are you telling us you held a more important role working for the Baker family, sir?'

'I worked for Charlie Baker, not his family.'

Chandler noted the change in the man's demeanour. He stiffened, clearly irritated by something.

'So after Charlie was killed did you lose your job?' Bishop asked, perhaps also having spotted the shift.

Vincent shook his head. 'It was never like that. Never our arrangement, if you know what I mean. There was no P45, no contract. When Charlie had a job for me to do I did it. Simple as.'

'Okay, but then his death obviously left you without that particular source of income. Must have made you almost as angry as losing your friend.'

'Bloody right it did.'

'So you want to punish whoever murdered Charlie Baker. Or see them punished, at the very least.'

'Wouldn't anyone?' Vincent shrugged, rolling his eyes at the suggestion.

'So is that what you did, Mr Vincent? Did you decide to go after the people suspected of killing the man who fed you work from time to time?'

Vincent hesitated before pleading ignorance. 'I've no idea what you're talking about. What people? Why would I get involved?'

Chandler edged closer to him, though repelled by the oily slickness of the man. 'Are you telling us you don't know about the murder of two men suspected of killing Baker? I find your story hard to believe in a small town like this.'

News of the four additional men murdered in Romania had yet to be released, and the task force agreement was to share only widely known information during their interviews.

'I… I heard something about it, yes.' The man shrugged. 'A couple of foreigners. What's it to me? Opens up some fruit picking jobs for locals, I reckon.'

Chandler decided to push a little harder. 'So, Mr Vincent, you are trying to tell us that thirteen individuals decide to kill your friend and boss, costing you a living in the process, but neither you nor any of your own friends bear the suspects any ill will? Seems highly unlikely to me.'

This time the nouveau-spiv thrust himself back in his chair and cackled. It quickly became a coughing fit, after which he reached for a packet of cigarettes on a sideboard whose wooden exterior bore the kind of sheen you could see your reflection in.

'Do you mind waiting until we're done, sir?' Chandler asked him. 'We won't be more than a few minutes.'

At first she thought Vincent was going to object, his eyes hardening and his stained teeth showing through a thin smile. But then he allowed the packet to fall from his grip and he sniffed as if it made no difference to him.

'Say what you came here to say then,' Vincent insisted. 'Ask what you came here to ask.'

'Mr Vincent,' Bishop said, shifting in his chair. 'Where were you on Sunday evening and at around lunchtime yesterday?'

The man's grin grew wider. He slicked his moustache one more time. 'Well now, why didn't you start with that question and save us all a lot of time? The answer to both is exactly the same. I was in the pub. The Lion and Key, not a five-minute walk from here. Plenty of witnesses. You go ask.'

Chandler glanced across at Bishop. She thought Vincent seemed genuine in terms of where he was when both murders were committed. They would follow up with the staff and landlord of the pub, but to her mind this was not their man. Intelligence from Lincolnshire police appeared to be accurate – Eddie Vincent was a man desperately trying to live up to his flash name, but thus far had clearly failed miserably. He was a nothing anywhere other than inside his own head.

W ayne Harvey ran his second-hand car empire out of a scruffy old corrugated tin shed held together by fibres of rust. It stood on what had once been the forecourt of a petrol station, the shell so fragile a structure it was weighed down by breeze blocks in all four corners. The fuel pumps had long since been removed, but Bliss noticed the steel blanking plates sealing off the storage wells below ground. The building itself had also succumbed to the bulldozer, leaving room for a dozen vehicles spread around the site.

From what Bliss could see at first glance, the cars Harvey was looking to sell were in a similar condition to the hut he used as an office. The kind of motors you were likely to pay more for in repairs to get them through the MOT than the asking price on the stickers adhered to the windscreens. Bliss doubted there was a single thing legal about this enterprise, which he thought might provide some leverage over the man he and DCI Warburton had come to talk to.

Bliss regarded Harvey as a heart attack waiting to happen. When the businessman rose from behind his desk to shake hands, he towered over the two detectives. But his six-foot plus frame was carrying close to three-hundred pounds, and the colour of Harvey's face suggested his arteries, heart, and lungs struggled on a daily basis to cope with shifting the load around.

Flashing his warrant card, Bliss introduced himself and Warburton.

'I booked you as coppers the moment I laid eyes on you,' Harvey said, causing the entire unit to judder as he retook his seat. The cushion on his chair let out a whump of air through a gash in its stitched seam. 'So, what can I do for you today?'

The big man was a Londoner from what Bliss could tell by the voice; Essex at the very least. The walls of the compact office were littered with flyers offering a variety of services, and for décor Wayne Harvey had opted for hubcaps resting on screws half buried into the metal crossbeams. On top of a narrow filing cabinet stood a coffee pot with a thick rind of sludge in the bottom. Bliss glanced around and saw only the twin back seat of a car for them to sit down on, its once grey velour cushions now covered in oil and grease stains. One glance at them and both he and his colleague chose to remain standing instead.

'Business good?' Bliss asked, raising his eyebrows.

'So-so. I doubt you're looking to buy, though. Not unless you want to have a look at a little run-around for the Mrs here.' He indicated Warburton with a nod of the head, grinning at his own pathetic joke.

'If I was,' Bliss said in a flat, cold tone, 'I wouldn't be going anywhere near any of those death-traps you have outside.'

'Cheap and cheerful is what we offer here. My vehicles suit the pockets of the people who drive them.'

'Yeah. Mostly foreigners is my guess. The kind you can take advantage of more readily. Young men and women who don't have a clue about the rules regarding, say, MOTs and insurance, car tax even.'

'Is that why you two are here? I doubt it, somehow. A couple of detectives being sent out here to bend my ear about a small second-hand car business don't ring true.'

'It's not why we came here to speak with you,' Warburton confirmed with a bright smile. 'But since we are, we might find ourselves becoming extremely interested in what we've seen. I'm sure there's plenty here for our uniformed colleagues to get their teeth into if we give them a bell. Taxman, too, I should imagine. Ultimately, whether we bring them in or not probably depends on the answers you provide to our questions, Mr Harvey.'

'Well, why didn't you say so in the beginning? I'm always happy to help. Fire away?'

'I take it you are aware of the murders of two Romanian nationals over the previous couple of days. Two suspects in the Charles Baker murder.'

The huge head bobbed up and down, several chins wobbling beneath. 'What about it?'

'Baker was a colleague of yours, right?'

'Sure. Me and Charlie went back a long way.'

'You did some work for Baker, so his death must have put you out of pocket.'

'Yeah. I felt the pinch. So what of it?'

'Were you ever tempted to act against the people suspected of killing him?'

Harvey laughed. The flesh on his face turned an even darker shade of red as his whole frame shook and rattled. 'Are you serious?' he asked. His eyes became almost invisible behind narrow slits. 'Me take on thirteen of them? Including a bunch of Roma pikeys. Look, sweetheart, I don't know what you're on, but I could do with puffing some myself.'

'No need for you to be rude, Wayne,' Bliss said, taking a step forward and glowering down at the man. 'My partner has been nothing but pleasant to you so far. I suggest you respond in kind, or DCI Warburton here will rip you apart piece by piece if she feels the urge.'

Bliss managed to yank himself back from a thoughtless reaction. His natural instinct was to step up on behalf of the DCI. Not because she was a woman, but because she was a colleague. Following the initial outburst, he had allowed wriggle room for Warburton to have her own say if she thought it was warranted.

'You'd better listen to him, Mr Harvey,' Warburton said so softly her voice was almost a whisper. 'Because if I don't fuck you over, DI Bliss here most certainly will. Now, do yourself a huge favour, stamp down on your ego like you were putting out a cigarette, and answer my damned question.'

Bliss felt the chill of her words. They impressed him.

Harvey was clearly a good listener. He held up his hands in deference. 'All right. Fair play. I don't understand why you're paying me a visit, is all. I was always low-level, given the donkey work, just the hired help to Baker. Truth is, I may have said otherwise but I couldn't actually stand the man. He was a bully, which was one strike against him, but he was also a psychopath. A bloke who enjoyed hurting people, who really took pleasure in it. He was a sadist, but also protection for those of us making a living in the margins.'

The man's words smacked of genuine antipathy towards Charlie Baker. Bliss did not see Harvey exacting revenge for the murder of such a man, whose influence was wide-ranging but who did not appear to have lined with gold the pockets of the men who acted as his muscle.

'Any ideas as to who might have felt differently?' he asked. 'Somebody has started to pick off the thirteen suspects. Either they really loved Baker or someone is paying them a decent amount of wedge. We'd appreciate your thoughts on the matter.'

The big man took a deep breath before replying. 'I very much doubt it's anyone employed by Charlie. He hardly treated us any better than he did other people in the town. Difference was, we sucked it up because we earned out of him. If it was me, I wouldn't look further than Charlie's kids. Seemed to me all three have the same psycho gene in them. You know the sort, nothing going on behind the eyes.'

Bliss did know. Just as he also understood that a meeting with the Baker family could not be put off any longer. But he did have another line of inquiry to develop.

'Mr Harvey, even on the fringes of Baker's reach you must have known he was being protected. We've heard rumours of a group of interested people. Some of them are businessmen, there may be at least one councilman and also an MEP. But of greater interest is the intelligence suggesting Baker had one of us or even several of us on his payroll. What can you tell me about that?'

'Other than the fact it's true, not much,' Harvey admitted. 'We knew he had bent coppers in his pocket. We just had no idea who they were. Leastways, I never did. And I never spoke to anyone else who did, either. I think you needed to be pretty close to Charlie to be trusted with the full strength of his dealings.'

Bliss nodded. 'If you do suddenly discover more, you'll give us a bell, right?'

'Of course.'

Bliss knew they would never hear from the man again about the subject. But then Wayne Harvey said something interesting.

'What I can tell you, is that Charlie Baker was a member of the local Masonic lodge. Along with a few businessmen, a councilman, and an MEP. The very people you just mentioned to me. As for coppers, that I don't know. But it'd be a good bet now, wouldn't it?'

The look of pure cunning and spite on his face almost enticed Bliss to wipe it off.

Almost.

25

Paul enjoyed what he liked to think of as eclectic tastes. Good food and fine drink, a love of travel, and taking great delight from his music. Then there was his little beauty who kept him company, of course, and he could devour hour after hour of TV box sets or movies. That he also had both an interest in and a talent for the more macabre, darker side of the human condition, was simply part of the wide range of choices he made and desires he followed.

For a nine-month period during his eleven years in the armed forces, Paul worked in the mortuary attached to the hospital which catered for current and ex-service men and women. So it was that he came to know by heart the processes and different stages involved in embalming and preparing a corpse.

The majority of people are unaware that one of the mortician's jobs is to check the individual for vital signs, after first laying out the naked body in preparation for the procedure; it wouldn't do to embalm someone who retained even the most tenuous grip on life.

The body is then bathed in a disinfectant and germicidal solution while stretching and massaging the limbs to ease any lingering indications of rigor mortis. At this point, facial hair is shaved off unless the deceased naturally wore it in life. Before making the first incision, the embalmer sets the features of the deceased to make the expression appear as relaxed and natural as possible. The mortician does this by using an eye-cap which keeps the eyes closed, wiring the jaw shut and adding shape to its contours, followed by suturing the lips and gums.

Afterwards, the body's blood vessels are drained while simultaneously injecting embalming chemicals into the arteries by means of a centrifugal pump. The fluids comprise a mixture of formaldehyde, glutaraldehyde, ethanol, humectants and other wetting agents. Cavity and hypodermic protocols follow, first to remove any traces of natural gases or fluids, and then to seal up cavities and treat any areas where the arterial fluids are unable to reach.

After surface embalming to restore post-decomposition damage, thorough moisturising of the entire body takes place, before applying make-up to the face, neck and hands.

Paul remained absolutely fascinated by the transformation from bluish-grey, marbled and obviously lifeless cadaver, to what appeared to be a sleeping person capable of awakening and rising up off the table at any moment. He remembered being struck by the pungent odour of fluids during the procedure, which could often be every bit as foul as the decomposing flesh and internal gases themselves. Unlike most people, Paul was not disgusted by these sights and smells. In many ways, he enjoyed them. He also knew that in the profession, a combination of improved fluids and hard-working air extractors resulted in less odour and particulates.

Tim Bluntstone was the sole proprietor of Bluntstone Funeral Directors Ltd in Sutton End's main shopping district towards the centre of town. He shared much of the overall workload with his wife and daughter, who divided up the admin and arrangement-making duties between them on a part-time basis. The embalming stage and care for the deceased was Tim's domain, procedures for which only he among them was trained. It was also an aspect of the business known to make both women uncomfortable. Paul was therefore confident of discovering Bluntstone alone that Tuesday afternoon.

Paul's information suggested the police had visited the man within the past twenty-four hours, and that during their meeting they provided him with a clear warning in respect of the danger posed to those suspected of killing Charles Baker. How seriously Bluntstone took their advice was anyone's guess, but he was not thought to be one of the two people to have requested protection. Given how easily Paul had gained entry into the high street shop by picking a single cheap and flimsy lock, his impression was that the funeral director did not believe he was in any imminent danger. All counsel banished from his thoughts, Bluntstone had lost himself in his work.

Unsure whether to be delighted or affronted by the lapse, Paul gradually made progress from room to room, inspecting each before moving on. As expected, there was nothing in the way of flamboyance. Sombre tones for sombre occasions. Entering a short passageway leading off to the far right corner of the building, Paul heard a radio or CD player offering up brass band music. He thought he detected a phrase from *The Gay Hussar*, but the genre took him out of his comfort zone and he could not be certain of the tune. Still, the sound pleased him, because it would obscure any noise created as he entered Bluntstone's dungeon of delights.

Such was the man's tall and slender frame, Paul had no need to check the photograph and description he carried with him. Bluntstone stood side on to him, eyes unblinking as he gazed at the face of a woman whose transformation was almost complete. Morticians worked to strict moral guidelines, which included covering the corpse's genital regions appropriately. In this instance, however, Bluntstone had not done so, or at least had not replaced the cover following the moisturising session. Paul did not care to dwell upon where the undertaker's fingers might have probed during this stage of the procedure, but as the lanky man bent double over the face to apply makeup, the woman's heavy breasts and groin remained fully exposed.

Paul slid his gun from its holster strapped to his waist. The sheath's leather was well-oiled and the cold steel slipping from it made a sound no louder than a faint whisper. Certainly it could not be heard above the combination of music and the wall-mounted aluminium air extraction system. He held the revolver at chest height as he approached, a brass band in the background having shifted to a surging version of *Jerusalem*. Bluntstone's long-fingered hands were gentle and skilful as he slowly made the woman appear human again, if not exactly beautiful. Only when the undertaker stood upright to survey his work did Paul make himself known.

'Nice job!' he called out.

At first the man's head twitched and his body stiffened, uncertain as to what – if anything – he had heard. His peripheral vision must then have caught something out of place, for he turned slowly to his left. His eyes latched onto the weapon pointing straight at him.

Paul set a cooler box down on the floor, then raised a finger to his lips. Shook his head. 'Not a word,' he cautioned. 'Not a single sound.'

Bluntstone nodded, unable to wrench his gaze from the dead black eye of the revolver.

The man was on the list. Therefore he existed as a name, not a person to Paul. A job to be completed, no more, no less. Six such victims had already met the desired end; the half a dozen heads sitting in his chest freezer behind the caravan bore testimony to his diligence. The only difference now was his curiosity. He knew all about the perils of being curious, but was no feline and always felt in charge of his own destiny. His task now was simply to pull the trigger three times, then use the tool he carried in the cooler box to detach the funeral director's head from his neck.

Only, this time he had questions. Unsure why, but seeking an advantage should he need one in the future. 'Which of you led the attack on Charles Baker?' he asked.

Bluntstone blinked rapidly, his mouth opening and closing again, with only a low strangled retching sound emerging from the back of his throat.

'I want to know who led the attack on Baker,' Paul reaffirmed, more forcefully this time. The gun in his hand stirred the air in small ever-decreasing circles. 'I can guess why. I just want you to tell me whose idea it was and who took charge on the night he was stabbed to death.'

Bluntstone shook his head. He wore thick-framed spectacles which perched precariously on the narrow bridge of a thin, pointed nose. His gaunt features appeared to shrink further still, the flesh drawn as tight as a drum skin across the skull.

'I had nothing to do with that,' Bluntstone protested. His voice was surprisingly deep, as if booming out from a considerable distance via a form of amplification. 'Nothing.'

Paul sighed. He took a look around the room. Many fascinating instruments lay alongside the stainless-steel bench and hung from hooks arranged along one wall. When his eyes alighted upon the centrifugal pump and the various tubes sprouting from it like some abhorrent arachnid whose transparency only lent it more menace, Paul smiled.

'This,' he said, waving the revolver in the air, 'is for later. How much later depends entirely on you, what you choose to tell me, and when. Before we begin, I will grant you one opportunity to make a choice. Embalming fluid pumped directly into your arteries, or a selection of shiny, sharp-toothed tools used upon your weak flesh. It's up to you, Tim.'

'What? Wh… what is? Choose for what purpose?'

Paul frowned and shook his head in disappointment. 'I would have thought that was obvious. I'm asking you to choose which method of torture you endure before I kill you.'

26

DS Short and the Lincolnshire RPU officer Barry Smyth had also come up dry with Jon McLaren, another of Baker's hired lackeys, and Bliss was starting to feel as if precious little had been achieved. Back in the task force meeting room discussing both the interviews and the protective watch on Jane Monkton and Brian Stout, the small team decided there were only three channels left open to them.

Smyth counted them off on his fingers as he laid it out. 'First, we hope he turns up at one of the two locations we have obs on, allowing us to snatch him up; second, we interview the Baker family and maybe catch a break there; third, and final as far as I can see, we track down those officers who are feeding information to the family or the killer, or both, and we flush out the name of our man that way.'

It was a dismal set of options in Bliss's opinion. The first relied on chance and a probable armed confrontation, the second required seasoned criminals to break their silence, whilst the third meant somehow weeding out bent coppers who had remained undetected for any number of years. None of the possibilities filled

Bliss with much enthusiasm, but neither he nor any of the other members of the task force team came up with anything more solid.

Eventually he said his piece. 'If nothing happens at either location tonight, we go mob-handed to Sutton End early tomorrow morning. We split up again and each couple takes one of Baker's offspring. We leave the wife to stew in her own juices a little, and the first pair finished with their interview bags her. Different teams this time, though. These interviews are unlike the others we've conducted so far, and I think it's important for each of us to be familiar with the way the other works in the room. So, Diane and Barry, you get Steven Baker, the eldest son. Penny and I will take his brother, Harry. Leaving Mia and Bish with the baby of the family, Charlotte.'

Bliss knew all about the best laid plans. No matter how much time went into formulating them, nor what strategies were used prior to or during, they had to remain fluid. Situations changed continuously. One answer to one specific question might alter the entire investigative process from that point on. He was prepared for any eventuality.

Which was just as well.

Bliss didn't think anything of it when DCI Warburton's phone chirped. Nor when she glanced at the screen and her eyebrows raised. But the immediate change in her demeanour once she started listening to whoever was on the other end of the line told him something was terribly wrong. He also thought he knew exactly what it might be. Warburton's words were resigned, curt. 'Yes. Thank you. Yes, I know where it is. As soon as.'

'Another one?' Bliss said as the DCI ended the connection.

Warburton nodded, her face seeming to crumple as she spoke. 'Funeral Director in the centre of Sutton End. Name of Tim Bluntstone.'

'Same MO I take it?'

'Yes and no. Not quite, seemingly. In addition to the three shots and the beheading we'd expect to find, Bluntstone appears to have also been tortured with a scalpel and his own embalming fluids.'

'Bloody hell,' Chandler breathed, screwing up her face in obvious distaste.

The room was completely silent for several seconds afterwards. Bliss shut his eyes to the horror of it all, but when he opened them again it was with renewed determination.

'We can't allow this to throw us off track,' he insisted. 'The protective details on Jane Monkton and Brian Stout must continue. Diane, Barry, it's your uniforms and firearms officers who are currently on location. If you can have them hold in place for a while longer, I'll make sure we have teams over there as soon as possible to replace them. I suspect we're going to be busy for a while.'

As each member of the task force team made preparations, Bliss pulled Chandler to one side. 'Is there anything, anything at all you can think of that I may have forgotten or neglected?' he asked.

His partner shook her head. 'Everything we could have done either has been or is. Bluntstone was warned. We could have protected him if he'd only agreed. You were right earlier, because none of those three options Barry outlined is ideal, but it's all we have at the moment. Another body probably isn't going to change our thinking too much.'

'I just feel this one is slipping away from me, Pen. Everything is coming at us thick and fast and we've had less opportunity to sit back and consider the nuances this time around.'

'That's how it goes sometimes. We might not like it, but we don't always get the rub of the green. Come on, you know this as well as I do. One day we're kicking our heels and cursing a lack of leads, another day we can't stop to draw breath. I know what you mean. It feels like we're reacting to events rather than being able to analyse every single aspect of the case first. But we go where it takes us, boss. You know who taught me that?'

'I have a horrible feeling I do.'

Chandler squinted at him. 'Then maybe for once listen to your own sound advice, eh?'

'You think that's likely?'

'Not in the slightest. But you should. No doubt this bastard has been one step ahead so far. Occasionally we run up against somebody who confounds us. This is one of those occasions.'

'Yeah, well I don't much like the state of affairs we find ourselves in, Pen. Our man is too slippery at the moment to get a firm grip of. I can't afford for anything more to go wrong on this one. If I do, then someone else dies.'

'Boss, it was you who recognised the tattoo. That alone got us as close as we are. It might not seem like it to you, but we're doing okay. Better than you realise or are willing to accept. I know you want to nail him, and nail him right now. We all do. But we've been at this for five minutes in realistic terms. Your legendary impatience and trying to force square pegs into round holes is not going to work for us this time.'

Bliss breathed out uneasily. He could not remember feeling this impotent when investigating a case before. He had operated under enormous professional and personal duress while working the Jade Coleman stalker murder back in June; an operation which gained its own momentum by following all of the usual protocols and procedures. This, however, was unlike any case he had ever previously investigated. It had thrown up no hooks to cling to, the crime scenes were as forensically clean as any shooting incident and subsequent decapitation could be. This time they even knew exactly who their victims were going to be, yet they were apparently helpless in preventing further atrocities. For the first time in many years, Bliss felt out of his depth.

'I guess we'll see where we are after visiting the fresh scene,' he said finally. 'That and speaking to the Baker family. Perhaps then we'll have a clearer idea of who is behind these killings, if not a line on the actual killer himself.'

'There is one thing, boss,' Chandler said.

Bliss sensed a little hesitance from his colleague. 'Go on.'

'Well, without wishing to appear crass and opportunistic, of the thirteen original people on our list of potential victims, only half a dozen are still alive. We already have a commitment to sitting on two of them. The only two who requested it. Is it really such a stretch for DCI Edwards or even the Super to now work with their Lincolnshire counterparts to jointly fund a watch on them all?'

Bliss thumbed the scar just above his brow. He dug his upper teeth into his bottom lip as if physically chewing over the notion. Chandler was right. In a world where budgets offered no constraints, they could safely secure every potential victim. That was not the case when it came to the reality of their current situation, however. The killer was inadvertently whittling down the costs for them, though Bliss felt appalled at thinking about such loss of life in those terms. He had no idea which way it might go, but he felt it was worth raising the prospect.

'Nice work,' he told Chandler. 'I should have thought of it myself. Well, in a way I suppose I did, but I dismissed it on the basis of everything the bosses have said so far. But you are absolutely right to point out that if we're currently protecting two, why not an additional four? It's nothing like the initial eleven we first had to consider.'

Bliss asked to speak with Warburton alone. He did not think it fair to place the DCI under any undue pressure by asking her in a crowded room to support the request he was about to make. Having worked so closely with the woman over the past couple of days, he had a sense that Warburton operated much as he did – in terms of a determined focus on each individual investigation, with no eye lingering on longer-term career objectives. On the other hand, neither did he want to back her into a corner she wanted no part of.

In the corridor running between the stairs and lifts, past the major crimes unit, and on towards the incident rooms, he laid it all out, admitting Chandler's common sense approach had won him over. Bliss felt relieved when the Lincs DCI gave a firm nod of approval. Her tumbling layers of wavy hair bobbed and coiled around her shoulders.

'Your idea is absolutely the best method of tackling this now,' Warburton said. 'On the way to the new SOC I'll call my own superintendent. You'll speak to Alicia and Marion yourself?'

Neither DCI Edwards nor Detective Superintendent Fletcher could ever be described as pushovers, but Bliss suspected both women were capable of looking beyond the finances, able to steer their thoughts towards the greater good achieved by putting secure observation and armed units on the remaining half a dozen suspects. There was the potential fallout to consider should they not do so once the full and gruesome details emerged, but he liked to think that they, too, would concentrate more on the saving of life and the arrest of a monster.

'I will,' Bliss replied. 'You and Barry get going. I'll have Mia and Bish follow you over. Penny and I will join you as soon as I've had words with the boss.'

Warburton maintained her gaze for a few seconds longer. She smiled warmly and her cheeks flushed a little. 'It's been a genuine pleasure getting to know you, Jimmy. And to work alongside you. I confess I was warned your attitude might be somewhat… abrasive at times. But you've made it an enjoyable experience for me, despite the awful circumstances.'

Bliss glanced down at his feet for a moment or two. 'I received no similar warnings,' he said. 'But right back atcha in terms of the pleasurable experience. You're not at all what I expected of a DCI.'

'Don't fool yourself with this one-off case, Jimmy. I'm not usually this proactive in the field. I'm as desk-bound as Alicia under normal circumstances – sorry, she is DCI Edwards to you, of course – but it didn't feel right somehow allowing anyone else to get their hands dirty on this particular tainted investigation.'

'Well, I'm glad you decided to venture out into the light, Diane.

Your experience has been extremely helpful. We needed an insight into these people, especially the Roma elders.'

'Not that I was able to help much there.'

'You helped by paving the way. I picked up a lot during my stint at the NCA, but each community operates a little differently from the other, so you got us in the door whereas I'd probably have had it slammed shut in my face.'

Now it was Warburton's turn to grin. 'Don't be too hard on yourself. If it helps, your super admires you enormously. As for your DCI, let me tell you she has warmed to your… particular brand of coppering.'

'You mean old school.'

'If I do, it's by no means a bad thing. We are both old school, Jimmy. Along with the warning I was given about you, I was also told you are a DCI in all but name. Although in my view they're wrong about that.'

'Oh?'

'Yes. I think you're a DS at heart, with the skill set and experience to have become a DCI.'

'If that was a compliment,' Bliss said, 'I'll take it.'

'It was. So please do.'

Sergeant Smyth came out into the corridor looking for them. 'We good to go?' he asked.

Warburton winked at him. 'We are, Barry. We'll talk during the drive up about what we hope happens next.'

Bliss said goodbye to them both and walked back into the meeting room. He gave the remaining team members his instructions and then headed upstairs to find DCI Edwards. She was not in her office, and Bliss discovered she was attending a conference at the county HQ in Hinchingbrooke. Undaunted, he walked further along the corridor and found the super's PA at her desk.

'Is the boss lady in?' he asked.

'She is,' came the stern response. The PA peered at him over the rim of her glasses. 'But she is also extremely busy.'

'I'll be very quick,' he pleaded.

'You won't let it drop will you, Inspector Bliss?'

'You know me too well, Janet.'

The woman's eyes flicked towards the door. She huffed but said, 'If you must. Five minutes, and then I will chase you out of there.'

Bliss winked. 'Four is all I'll need,' he said, with far more confidence than he felt.

Fletcher listened in silence to everything Bliss said. Only when he was done talking did she form a response. 'From what you tell me, this is unlikely to play out for any real length of time. Three premeditated murders have been carried out in as many days, so our exposure in terms of budget ought to be limited.'

'I'd say so, ma'am. He could well hit another tonight, but tomorrow for sure.'

'Unless this man has planned ahead and pauses long enough to see us retreat.'

'That's always a possibility,' Bliss agreed.

The super said, 'I want to do this. I mention finances only because I will be called upon to answer for our costs at some point. However, it seems to me that these remaining half a dozen individuals are in grave danger, and if we don't protect them, who will?'

'So we have your go-ahead?'

'You do. For the time being. And in a limited but functional way. By that I mean, do what you can but we can't afford to have dozens of officers tied up for lengthy periods. Hitman or not, there just isn't the money. Check back with me in forty-eight hours if our man hasn't taken the bait.'

'Thank you, ma'am.'

'We need this sick bastard off the streets, Bliss. I take it our colleagues from Lincolnshire are playing their part.'

'Absolutely. They've been a great help to the investigation. Not just local knowledge, but they bring their own expertise into the mix as well.'

Fletcher flashed a flickering smile. 'I'm pleased to hear it. The

DCI had only good things to say about you and your team. It's nice to see cross-county co-operation working for a change.'

Bliss rose from his chair. 'I'll be off, then, ma'am. Unless there was anything else?'

'How's the Short situation working out? Her temporary elevation to DI, I mean?'

'Mia hasn't really had the opportunity to prove herself yet. But she will. She's ready.'

'Your confidence in her is understandable. From what I've read in her annual reviews, Short is a first-rate detective. Nobody has a bad word to say about her.'

'Me included,' Bliss said, itching to leave but wanting Fletcher to be in no doubt as to where he stood on the issue of Short's promotion and her longer-term aims. 'I have the utmost faith in Mia's abilities. She'll make mistakes, as we all did and still do in some cases. But she will be a top-notch DI.'

The Super dipped her head in the direction of the door. 'You'd better be off. And, Bliss... be careful. Look after yourself and your team. I'm not happy about putting you in the direct path of a psychopath, so whatever you do, make sure the armed units back you up at every stage.'

Bliss smiled. 'I will do. Don't worry, this is one suspect I won't be taking for granted.'

27

The neglected old house was attached to dozens of acres of rich farmland, all of which appeared to be fertile and potentially prosperous. Paul wondered why the man who lived there laboured every day for a business selling plants rather than toiling his own soil. Not that it mattered in the scheme of things, but he hoped he got the opportunity to ask Alan Brewer about it before taking the man's life. As he would also enquire about the dilapidated condition of the dwelling, whose render was flaking and water-stained, wooden doors and window frames peeling and rotting. Paul did not understand owning property only to treat it with such inattention.

Having spent the past few hours circulating, Paul noticed much of what was going on in and around Sutton End during the afternoon. Because of the considerable effort he had put into doing his homework, he quickly became aware of the differences in the town. The police presence outside specific homes, including Brewer's, was not announced by liveried vehicles – even the local cops were brighter than that. However, shiny new cars parked up in driveways or out on the pavement, cars Paul had never seen anywhere near the same properties before, told him what was happening here.

As anticipated.

Then there were the other vehicles cruising the streets and lanes. Those with two, three, sometimes even four people – mostly men – on board. He noted their inquisitive eyes, sensed their coiled tension. Each reminded him of his diamond-backed beauty slithering around inside his caravan, all nervous energy masked by a casual expression. Armed response vehicles was Paul's guess, on the hunt and fully alert.

Not that they noticed him at all.

The Transit van he used came with almost perfect BT Openreach logos on all four doors, the psyche of which meant that nobody ever gave the driver a second glance.

He saw them clearly, though.

They remained oblivious to him.

An ideal combination.

Still, his job was now predictably much more difficult. His analysis of the homes belonging to the remaining six people on the list, suggested Alan Brewer's as being the one which might afford him the best opportunity of getting close enough to make a final hit before his tactical withdrawal. Taking a short break from his assignment was necessary if the authorities were going to provide these soon-to-be victims with round-the-clock security. Such close protection could not go on indefinitely, and Paul believed he could either wait them out or delay until lethargy set in, delaying the response times of those providing the first line of defence.

It was the close proximity of the fields to the property itself, delineated by tall hedgerow and a dense treeline, which interested Paul most of all. He believed the landscape provided him with his best chance of making one more successful hit. In his estimation, the two police officers assigned to each protective detail were unlikely to be armed. Their job, whether based inside or outside those homes, was to stay alert and to summon the firearms teams roving the countryside roads nearby. Even so, they were professionals, and taking them out first was essential.

Which left Brewer and his two children to handle.

Paul had no desire to harm either child, and their names did not appear on his list, but if they got in his way and prevented him from completing his mission, then removing them from the equation was no big deal. Should the opportunity present itself, he had other ideas in mind for them. He could put a few bullets in them before taking down Alan Brewer, but far better to make them watch as he took their father's head. Neither would ever forget witnessing such a thing, the face of the man who did it forever etched upon their souls.

The thought made Paul smile.

He parked the van up on the side of the road alongside an olive-green BT junction box. It was early evening, the sun continuing to provide warmth ahead of the promised rainfall. The Transit might attract suspicion if he kept it on the roads too much longer, but he intended on driving back to the caravan to swap it out for the next vehicle required for the plan he had formulated. It was a bold scheme, carrying far greater risk of capture than any of his previous hits. Yet the reward of taking another name off the list was tempting. Now was the right time and place in which to make up his mind if he was going to return later on under the cover of darkness, or instead begin his brief hiatus immediately.

Paul was not an impatient man, so the delay did not bother him in the slightest. Not even if it continued for days or a week or more. However, his preference was to shave the list down by one further victim before he withdrew. It was a move he believed the police were unlikely to suspect of him; the taking of two lives in a single day. The unexpected nature of this provided a genuine advantage, and he felt the pull of accepting it.

Paul gave it more thought before nodding to himself. Within thirty seconds he was rolling again. He selected roads running alongside the large fields abutting the Brewer home, identifying entry and exit points while daylight remained. As he drove carefully and within all speed limits, his thoughts flitted back to the property itself, the angled driveway, a quiet street on the outskirts of the town.

Paul smiled to himself.

Yes. Yes, there certainly was a way to get this done. Something they would surely never see coming.

2 8

The scene at Tim Bluntstone's place of business looked like something from the set of a Frankenstein movie. Various items of medical equipment, jars and tubes glistened beneath a bank of harsh white LED lights. The undertaker's pale headless corpse lay on the bloodstained embalming table, triggering a response in Bliss's gut that was more than mere revulsion. Another cadaver sat on the floor, its back propped up against a wall. Bliss assumed Bluntstone had been working on the body when he was disturbed.

The beheading was a gruesome enough detail to tolerate, but there is something completely nauseating about looking down at a victim of torture. No matter how much of a sickening violation decapitation clearly was, there was some consolation for the team in knowing that the head was severed only after the man was first shot to death. In Bluntstone's case, imagining the pain and suffering endured by this man in the last minutes of his life was completely overwhelming.

The killer had used a scalpel to slice flesh open on several areas of the body. A reddening around the wounds beneath the blood could be explained by the other aspect to the torture, Bliss thought; that of the tube running into a further gaping wound across the side of the neck, held in place with a pair of gleaming forceps. One end of the transparent plastic tubing had been plunged deep inside the body, while the other fed from a container of what appeared to be embalming solution located close to the pump. The clear bottle now contained only a small amount of fluid, the rest apparently forced into the undertaker's bloodstream whilst the man was still alive.

Bliss imagined the killer's initial approach might explain the other cuts, probably going on to pour the fluid into exposed open wounds as the blood bubbled out. Perhaps they had not elicited the required amount of agony, but whatever the impulse, the final flourish left no doubt as to the man's intentions. Given the devastation wrought upon Bluntstone, the three gunshots doubtless proved unnecessary, yet the shooting had been carried out nonetheless. Part of the ritual, Bliss assumed.

Although grateful to find the extractor fans still switched on, he spent less than thirty minutes with the fresh victim before deciding he had seen enough.

'Penny and I are having it on our toes,' he told Warburton. 'Staring at this poor bugger for another hour is not going to achieve anything.'

The Lincolnshire DCI grunted. 'It's bloody grim, isn't it?'

'It is. But remember he may yet be a killer himself,' Bliss reminded her.

'I know. But did he deserve this?'

'Does anybody?'

'It makes my skin crawl thinking about how much he must have suffered.'

Bliss nodded and screwed up his face. 'Me, too. To be honest, that's the main reason I'm not sticking around. I take it this horror show was discovered by a member of his family and that they confirmed the decap victim's identity?'

'His wife,' Warburton said. 'Surgery scar along his shin, and a birthmark. It's Bluntstone.'

He did not care to imagine what that experience must have been like for the poor woman. 'We're out of here,' he said. 'And not before time.'

'We'll be off soon ourselves. Mind you, I have to wonder why this escalated so badly.'

'The torture?'

A nod. 'You think he questioned Bluntstone about something? Or did he just get off on it?'

Murder was never easy on the eye, and the memory lingered for days, sometimes even weeks afterwards. There was a theory that after a while you got used to looking at the aftermath, but Bliss never bought into it. Often the only way to deal with such a graphic nightmare made real was to use the darkest kind of humour; sanitising the imagery inside your head by dismissing its impact. But in his experience they stayed with you anyway. All of them. And the effect was incremental. Murder scenes were also usually instructional, the one place you could learn the most about your perpetrator. However, Bliss found this particular crime scene confusing, the killer's impetus beyond him for the moment.

'I can't imagine what he might have needed to know that could possibly have prompted this. He must have all thirteen suspects; their names are not hard to find on the internet. What else is there?'

'Beats me. You off to see the middle Baker kid?'

'Yep. Not that I'm expecting to learn much from him. Any of them, for that matter.' He realised he sounded dejected, maybe even a little jaded. Because he was. Bliss could not recall the last time he had worked on a case in which so many people needed to be spoken to, yet all the while approaching each of them with such little expectation of the interviews achieving anything worthwhile. It left him feeling subdued and merely added to his exhaustion.

As he turned to leave, Bliss said, 'We'll meet up later, yes?'

Warburton seemed pleased by the suggestion. 'How about the Riverside Hotel in Surfleet?'

'That big old white place on the bank of the river Glen?'

'That's the one.'

'Sounds good to me.' Bliss raised a hand in mute farewell as he left, Chandler at his heels.

'I like her more every time I meet her,' she said as they got back into the car.

'Who, Diane?' Bliss thought about it and shrugged. 'For a DCI she's great. Could almost be one of us.'

'One of you, maybe. I'm a rung further down the ladder, remember.'

Bliss chuckled. 'That's your choice, Pen. No jealousy going on because Mia got made up to acting DI, is there?'

'I told you, I'm thrilled for her. And I don't want it. Not right now. All I meant was, Warburton acts more like an old school DI than someone of her current rank.'

'Probably because she still is. Deep down where it counts.'

'Have you asked about the rings on her finger yet?'

'Oh, do bugger off, Pen. I haven't, and I'm never going to.'

Chandler's shoulders rocked as she laughed. 'You want me to ask for you? Set you up on a date?'

He shook his head. 'You are incorrigible.'

His partner's jaw fell open in mock surprise. 'You know a five-syllable word? You really must be a DI.'

They settled into the short drive, heading west out of town. The further they drove the more distance there was between individual properties, and the bigger and grander the homes became.

Thirty-year-old Harry Baker lived with his much younger girl-friend in a sprawling detached house that seemed to be a mock version of every architectural style imaginable. A triumph of money over taste, was Bliss's first thought as he nosed his car into the driveway where the full horror of the clashing periods presented itself to them both.

179

'Wow!' was all Chandler could manage as she peered up out of the windscreen.

Bliss was unable to find any words at all. The four-vehicle garage appeared to have as much square footage as his entire house, but the very idea of swapping his humble abode for this abomination with its Tudor beams and gables, Georgian windows, and even a gothic tower, appalled him.

'You reckon he designed this himself?' Chandler asked, stepping out of the car.

Bliss peered at her over the Insignia's roof. 'Yeah. With a sketch he did with a pack of crayons when he was ten by the state of it.'

'I read in his file that he owns a Maserati GranTurismo. That's a cool hundred grand's worth. I'd love to take that for a spin.'

'Behave yourself. You can barely handle a Ford Focus.'

'Says the man who drove his car into a lake.'

Bliss shrugged. 'Fair point. Though it was for Queen and country at the time.'

Chandler looked back at the house and shook her head in dismay. 'What would you do if you had their money, Jimmy?'

'You mean in my spare time?'

'It could all be spare time if you wanted it to be.'

'I don't think so.' Bliss pursed his lips. 'I'd still work. Don't tell me you wouldn't, either. It's in the blood now, Pen. Shit, it *is* your blood. Same as it is mine.'

'Sadly, you're almost certainly right. Okay, so when you do eventually hang up the tattered warrant card, how do you see yourself living the rest of your life?'

'Same old simple pleasures,' he said without pause. 'Cold beer, decent Scotch, good music. Bit of sport. Maybe a season ticket at Stamford Bridge, the odd England game at Twickers.'

'You'd get sick of that all too soon.'

'I doubt it. Especially when I have my garden to look at as well. Sounds idyllic to me. But if I got fed up, I reckon I'd find my old boat, buy it back with an offer they can't refuse, and putter off into the sunset down the Nene.'

Chandler was grinning at him. 'What?' he asked.

'It really is all about the simple pleasures for you, isn't it? And when you gaze into your crystal ball do you see yourself alongside someone?'

'What, sunbathing out on the deck of *The Mourinho*? I don't know. Maybe. Sure, why not?'

'So who is she?' Chandler asked after just a moment's pause.

'Who's who?'

'Come on, Jimmy. Don't be coy with me. Who is the woman lying on your boat as you move on?'

Bliss cleared his throat. Glanced down at his feet. Back up again. 'Who do you think it's most likely to be?' he asked.

Wagging a finger at him, Chandler said, 'This is your vision of the future, Jimmy. You tell me.'

For a moment he made no reply. When he did, his voice was low and even to his own ears sounded distant. 'I actually don't know. I can't see her face. Just tanned legs gleaming in the last of the setting sun. Nice pair of pins, though. No Yorkshire pudding knees.'

Two security lights snapped on, bathing them in a ferocious glow. Happy to be spared any further grilling about his future, Bliss looked up at them and said, 'No more night games for my team, then. This bugger's nicked our floodlights.'

Shielding her eyes from the glare, Chandler said, 'They'd be able to see this place from the bloody moon right now.'

Bliss grunted. 'Come on, Pen. Let's see what planet this twat is from.'

181

29

B aker proved to be every bit as obnoxious as DCI Warburton had led them to believe. Immediately belligerent, the man proceeded to lambast the pair of detectives for having the sheer effrontery to harass him when they ought to be out turning over rocks searching for his father's murderers. The entire five-minute tongue-lashing took place on his doorstep, while Bliss and Chandler remained passive and mute.

Aware of a sudden silence, Bliss looked deep into Harry Baker's wild, round eyes.

'Are you done?' he asked. 'Do you feel better having got all that out of your system?'

'No, I fucking well don't!' the man screamed in his face. By this point, his girlfriend, who was still in her teens, had sidled up beside him, arms wrapped around his waist, her head resting against the side of his chest.

'Who's this, babe?' she asked him, her eyes hooded and dark. The haunting stuff of nightmares trailed up both arms in various coloured inks, failing to obscure obvious track marks from needle use. Intelligence gave her name as Tanya Muldoon.

'Just the filth. They'll be fucking off again in a sec.'

Bliss took it all in his stride. 'Mr Baker, if you don't calm down right now and allow us to speak with you inside, I'll have a couple of uniforms come back in the dead of night with a warrant for your arrest.'

'For what?!' Harry Baker was not a tall man, but he was solidly put together. Heavily muscled, arms also sleeved with ink, and numerous piercings dotting his ears and lower lip. His head seemed massive by comparison to the rest of his body, square and heavy as if he had a skull made of cast-iron. The look of astonishment on his face created bulges where before there had been rigid lines, contorted by more than fury, Bliss thought. He knew steroid abuse and 'roid rage' when he saw it.

'Believe me, I'll think of something,' Bliss assured him. 'Littering. Loitering. Bestiality. Being a brainless doughnut. Whatever it takes.'

'You what? You can't fuc–'

'On the other hand, we could have a chat here and now and save us all a great deal of time.' Bliss understood the type of person he was dealing with. Baker was busting for a fight, so Bliss's equanimity enraged the younger man all the more because it gave him no excuse to unleash his anger in the physical way he desired.

Baker stood there panting, veins bulging in his neck and pulsing in a vertical line running down the centre of his forehead. Meanwhile, Tanya stared malevolently at Bliss and Chandler while she squeezed her boyfriend tighter still.

The ensuing silence added weight to Bliss's reasonable offer. Eventually, Baker shrugged off the girl, turned on his heels and marched his way back into the depths of the house. She ran after him, bare feet slapping on the hardwood floor. Bliss took the open door as tacit acquiescence for him and his colleague to enter.

It came as no surprise at all to discover gold-coloured bannisters and trim all around the garish entrance hall. They found the pair in a vast living room, whose central feature was a huge media station supporting two large-screen TV sets, plus a variety of games consoles and other electronic equipment. One of the games had been paused, leaving the image of a western gunslinger frozen on screen. The floor in front of the unit was a rats' tails mess of cables and wires, handsets and controllers.

Uninvited, Bliss sat down in a deep armchair covered in cream leather so soft it felt like velvet. He indicated with a glance for Chandler to take a similar seat opposite, allowing the pair to flank the four-seater sofa on which Harry Baker sat rocking back and forth, while his girlfriend was curled up in a ball at the far end.

'As I started to inform you at the front door,' Bliss began, 'my colleague and I are from the major crimes unit in Peterborough, and are here to speak to you about a number of recent murders which took place both abroad and locally.'

'Yeah, and I said you should be looking into whoever killed my dad,' Baker growled, a deep sound emerging from the back of his throat.

'It's not part of my remit, so you'd best take up any complaints you might have with the Lincolnshire Constabulary. Now, then, the names of Florin Budescu, Constantin Benzar, and Tim Bluntstone are known to you. I am certain of this because they are all thought to have been involved in your father's murder. The three of them, in addition to four other Romanian nationals who were also suspects at the time, have themselves been murdered.'

'What?' The man's reaction, a mixture of confusion and joy, looked genuine to Bliss. 'You're telling me seven of those wankers who killed my dad are now dead?'

'I am, yes.'

Baker's initial response was swept away in an instant, replaced by one of unfettered elation. 'Fucking good job, too. Please come back and let me know when the others have gone the same way. I'll pop a bottle of champagne.'

'Mr Baker, I'm not sure you fully appreciate why we're here. I didn't drive all this way just to tell you these people are dead. Given what they are alleged to have done some nineteen months ago, it would be unreasonable if we did not meet with you and the rest of your family to discuss their murders.'

Baker's head jerked. 'The rest? You mean you're paying a visit to my brother and sister as well? My mum, too?'

'Sir, as we speak they are already being interviewed by our colleagues. With the exception of your mother, who will be spoken to later on this evening.'

The man leapt to his feet, his hands curling into tight fists. 'You leave my mother out of this!' he bellowed. He took a couple of deep breaths as his face grew florid. Then he jabbed a finger at Bliss. 'I mean it. You go anywhere near her and I'll… I'll…'

'You'll what?' Bliss prompted, unmoved by the looming physical presence. He prepared himself, though, ready to respond if Baker took a step towards Chandler. 'Empty threats are of no use here, Mr Baker. We have interview rooms waiting for you, your mother, brother and sister back at our nick in Peterborough. We can do them there, or in the comfort of your own homes. Makes no difference to us, but we will speak to all four of you. You might as well sit back down and just accept the fact.'

'It's not fucking right,' Baker complained, continuing to stand, his face twisted with rage.

'What you mean is, it's not right that the protection for which you pay some of my Lincolnshire colleagues appears not to be working in your favour tonight.' Bliss sniffed and dipped his head towards the western game still paused on the TV screen. 'Well, there's a new sheriff in town, Harry, she has a whole posse of deputies and we are going to start enforcing the law around here.'

Baker set his chin, but lost the edge off the rest of his features. Silently relenting, he slumped back down onto the sofa and glared at the two detectives instead.

Bliss nodded. 'Good. That's better. So, Harry, what can you tell me about these murders?'

'It's still Mr Baker to you, filth,' the man said with a sneer. 'And I can tell you fuck-all apart from offering the best of British to whoever did them. Taking out a bunch of Eastern Europeans does us all a fucking favour, and as for the rest of those lousy bastards they can all rot in hell for all I care.'

'Thanks for adding a hate crime to the possible list of charges,' Bliss said, following up with a wink when their eyes met across the ornate wooden coffee table standing between them. Its peaceful Oriental carvings were at odds with the brute who owned it.

'Fuck them. And fuck you, too.'

'Yeah, fuck you both,' his girlfriend said suddenly, raising her head to peer at them. Baker turned his glare upon her and she recoiled and clamped her mouth tight.

'This Mensa meeting really isn't getting us anywhere,' Chandler said on a deep sigh of obvious exasperation. 'I say we wrap this up, boss. Bring them both in. Verbal abuse of a police officer will do, and we can add resisting arrest even if they don't.'

'All right, all right,' Baker said, forcing himself deeper into the cushion behind him. 'Look, you asked what I knew about the murders. All I know is what I saw on the news and what me and my brother talked about when we met at lunchtime. It was two men as far as we were aware at the time, now you say there's seven of them dead. Either way, it's got fuck-all to do with us.'

'Then if not you, who?' Chandler pushed. 'I mean, who could possibly want revenge on the killers of Charlie Baker more than his own family?'

'Plenty of people, darling. My dad had loads on the payroll, loads who depended on him for a living.'

'But few who actually lost out after he died. It's not as if the Baker clan stopped running any of the businesses afterwards.'

'Maybe. But maybe we also do things differently now. Out with the old, in with the new, you know?'

'In which case they'd be more likely to take it out on you and your family,' Bliss pointed out.

Baker scoffed at the suggestion. 'You reckon, do you? Nobody we've ever done business with is going to be brave enough to take us on.'

'Are you sure about that? The way I hear it, you all got by on the back of your father's reputation, not your own.'

'Yeah, well his standing was based on how me, Stevie and Charlotte handled things for him.'

Bliss smiled. 'I see. So, those two are the brains and you are the brawn, eh?'

'Don't underestimate me. Others have found out the hard way not to take me lightly.'

'I imagine so. Your girlfriend certainly seems shit-scared of you, so kudos to you there, Baker.'

The man is a quick learner, Bliss thought. This time he did not rise to the bait. Either his drug-induced temper was dipping as the chemicals in his bloodstream diminished, or he had reeled it in in order to learn more whilst giving less away. Bliss decided to give Harry Baker another nudge. 'We've been asking around about you Bakers,' he said. 'Despite everything you tell me, what we're picking up on the street is a pretty common theme: you're all nothing without the figurehead your father came to be. Prime for the taking is what we hear.'

Baker shook his head and folded his arms across his enormous chest. 'I don't believe you for one minute. First, nobody in their right mind would say anything like that out loud, even if they did think it. But second, none of them is ever going to say something poisonous about us to you people.'

'Because we're the police or because they couldn't be certain which of us were in your pocket?' Chandler asked.

'Either. Both.' The man snapped off a rapid, shark-like grin. 'It don't matter. The Bakers aren't going anywhere soon. Understood?'

'Still sounds to me, then, as if you're also the only ones who really have a solid motive to take down these murder suspects one by one. What do you have to say to that, Baker?'

Harry looked down his nose at Chandler and instead turned his attention to Bliss. 'You allow her to take charge whenever she feels like it, do you? Get your woman under control, copper.'

Bliss stifled a laugh. 'You're really poking the bear there. Give her half a chance and my colleague here will suck you in and spit you out in bubbles. I guarantee she'll make you weep like a baby and beg for mercy inside twenty seconds.'

Having taken the wind out of the man's sails, Bliss continued, 'Look, this is not something you can bank on to go away. Sit there pumped up full of bravado all you like, but eventually you will have to talk to us properly. Your father was murdered. The police tried to nail those responsible, came up with a list of thirteen suspects to match the thirteen wounds individually made, and now seven of those suspects are dead. You must see why the focus has fallen upon you and your family.'

Though clearly still fuming, Baker took a deep breath before responding. 'I'm not stupid. Of course you're going to look at us for it. But none of us are murderers.'

'Nobody is suggesting you pulled the trigger yourselves.'

'Just stumped up the cash to pay for it, eh?'

'It's a reasonable assumption.'

'It may well be. But it's wrong, all the same.'

Bliss glanced over at Chandler, who shook her head when she caught his eye. Either his DS had nothing more to ask, or she was telling him they were getting nowhere. If it was the latter, Bliss agreed. Harry Baker was evidently a thug along the lines of his old man, using his name and his physical appearance to intimidate and bully, but if he or anyone else in his family was responsible for murder, he was not about to give it up. Also, the look of surprise when told about the other murders was hard to fake.

Back in the car a few minutes later, Bliss texted the rest of the task force:

Harry Baker done. Moving on to the mother now.

He sent the message and then turned in his seat to face his colleague.

'First impressions?' he asked.

Chandler let loose a steady sigh. 'I'm honestly not sure. If what he demonstrated back there was feigned annoyance and disbelief, then he was better at it than most.'

'I know.' Bliss scowled. 'If you strip away the chemically-induced outrage, beyond it there appeared to be a genuine anger at being suspected. And the shock also seemed sincere to me.'

'Is it possible that someone else in his family is responsible and he just doesn't know about it?'

'I reckon that's a discussion for when we're all back together. We'll pool our impressions and wring something out of it. But from my experience, the one person in any such family in similar circumstances to have genuine authority and also to possess the will to take revenge, is the spouse.'

As Bliss gunned the engine, Chandler said, 'Well, at least there's one piece of good news.'

'What's that?' he asked, turning out of the drive.

'Nothing in from our personal security observations teams. Looks as if our man might be taking the night off after all.'

30

A twelve-year veteran of the job, PC Brynn Cater had seen nothing like this during his tenure. Providing personal protection to a civilian was absent from his litany of experiences. DCI Warburton's order had been resolute: convince Alan Brewer to accept the offer and allow two officers to be stationed inside his home. If agreement proved to be impossible to negotiate, then the instruction was to maintain vigilant observation somewhere on or close to the property, even the street outside if necessary.

Brewer initially took some persuading, but Cater's sergeant, Elaine Ripley, eventually charmed the man into accepting the security detail. In a calm and methodical manner, Ripley explained why the team believed their presence was likely to be required for a maximum of thirty-six hours – probably a lot less – all of which amounted to a minor inconvenience compared to Brewer having to look anxiously over his shoulder for the rest of his life.

The man finally saw reason, making a further concession to the situation by allowing both his children to stay overnight with friends. According to Brewer, it had not crossed his mind to do something similar; to pack up and leave. This was his home, he reasoned. He would not be driven from it. Moving away was likely to only delay the inevitable, he insisted. And if someone wanted him badly enough, then he was prepared to face them down.

All bluff and bluster was Cater's first thought. It's easy to be brave when you have other people around you to offer protection, easier still to say rather than do.

While Brewer sat in the lounge watching TV with heavy curtains drawn and only a single lamp glowing, Cater and Ripley took refuge at the dining table in the other half of the open-plan room. The sparsely-furnished area contained time-worn pieces lacking in quality. A perfect match for the structure itself, in Cater's opinion. Cooling air sighed beneath doors and caused draughts in every dark and dreary room and passageway. He wondered how Brewer's children felt being raised in a home where style and comfort were both absent.

Throughout the early evening the two officers chatted amiably, but a nervous tension woven into every conversation made it feel forced and unnatural. Cater noticed his boss was on edge, and he found himself drawn more closely to her every tic and mannerism. Ripley was edgy and uncomfortable, her mind seemingly elsewhere.

Given her history, it was understandable. It was his good fortune never to have faced a suspect who wielded a firearm as casually as this killer apparently did, but his sergeant had been involved in a shooting incident in Birmingham where she was previously stationed. She never spoke about it, but the possibility of lingering PTSD issues raised concerns about how she might react if confronted by another armed man.

Just my rotten luck if he shows and she winks out on me, Cater thought.

No sooner had the notion flickered through his mind than he was mentally cursing himself for it. It was unworthy of both him and his sergeant. He liked Ripley. She was a pleasure to work with, and never shirked a duty or threw her rank around unnecessarily. Always the first to pile in if backup was required. Still, it wouldn't do to take anything for granted where she was concerned. If she froze, it could be disastrous for her and him, never mind the man they were supposed to be protecting.

'You think he'll show?' Cater asked in a low voice during a lull in the conversation. 'I mean, show up here?'

Ripley frowned at him and shook her head. 'What kind of question is that, Brynn? How the bloody hell should I know? I'd be surprised, given he's already carried out one atrocity today. But who knows what's going on inside his sick and twisted brain? As for where he strikes next, here is just as likely as any of the other homes I suppose.'

'Apart from the Roma camp. I heard they refused to let our team on site, so our mob are parked up on the verge at the end of the road trying to appear inconspicuous.'

'We were never going to get any co-operation there. The Roma people have their own ways of dealing with situations, which can be frustrating for us at times. On the other hand, I pity the gunman if he tries it on inside that place. They know how to look after their own.'

'Nothing will happen until the early hours anyway. This man is no mug. If I were him, I'd wait until we're all tiring, lacking in concentration, even dozing if he's lucky. That's when he'll strike.'

Ripley seemed to recoil at the idea. 'Let's just hope the firearms units are on the ball. Their response time needs to be double-speedy if it all goes off. Anyway, if you're right, by then you and I will be sound asleep in our own beds. All I can say is the second watch better be here bang on midnight.'

Cater made a cup of tea for Brewer and a coffee each for him and Ripley. There was no chance of taking forty winks in turns. They both needed to be wide awake until change of shift, which was still several hours away. Brewer was engrossed in whatever he was watching on the box. Other than chain-smoking, which appeared to be a way of life for him, the man was relaxed and silent, seemingly unperturbed. Cater hoped Brewer's confidence was justified.

Both officers sat quietly sipping from their mugs when Ripley jerked her head up. 'What was that?' she said, squinting towards the front windows as if doing so might allow her to see right through the thick material.

'What was what?' Cater asked.

'I thought I heard something.'

He shook his head. 'I didn't hear a thing. Maybe you're a bit jumpy.'

'Perhaps. Do me a favour, though, go pull the curtains back and take a look outside will you? Just to settle my nerves.'

With a heavy sigh, Cater got to his feet. He offered a thin smile and a nod to Brewer who barely seemed to notice him, stepped around the coffee table in the centre of the lounge and yanked the curtain aside.

Before he could press his nose to the glass, a dazzling bright light coming from outside illuminated the room. At the same moment, Cater heard an engine racing, screeching as its revolutions peaked, then suddenly the lights began to move closer, their brilliant glow ghosting across the walls.

'Secure Brewer!' Ripley cried, leaping to her feet and running hard for the front door. 'And call for the ARV! He's ramming a vehicle into the house!'

Cater reacted swiftly. He reached down and grabbed hold of the startled Alan Brewer with both hands, dragging him from the chair as if he were as light as a feather. A surge of adrenaline gave him a strength he was unaware he possessed. Stumbling away from the bay windows towards the dining area, removing their protectee from the most immediate source of danger, he heard the front door crash against the skirting as Ripley threw it open, her rubber-soled shoes thrashing on gravel out in the front yard. Cater steered the now terrified man beneath the table and then squatted down in front of him, creating a physical barrier with his own body.

When it came, the sound of something large and heavy smashing into the house, was not quite as devastating as Cater had imagined it in those few brief moments between seeing the headlights spring to life, and feeling the juddering vibration of steel striking brickwork and masonry. Whatever the vehicle was it did not have either the force or momentum necessary to break through into the lounge, nor even to damage the glass in the window, the surrounding stone structure having taken the impact incredibly well.

By now, Brewer was shouting out incoherently in a loud shrieking wail of terror, and Cater raised a hand to quieten the man. He depressed the transmit button on the Airwave device strapped to his chest. In a flurry of agitated words he summoned urgent assistance, but his own voice sounded foreign to him, and he wondered if those listening could make sense of his request.

For a moment afterwards there was silence. It seemed to scream in Cater's ears.

Then he heard the sound he feared hearing most of all.

It came in rapid bursts.

Crack-crack-crack.

Cater felt his face crumple like soggy cardboard. His stomach clenched and his veins chilled as if ice was flooding into them. A rushing sound, similar to that of a waterfall spilling down a cliffside, filled his ears. He knew what had happened out front. In not freezing up, and instead dashing outside to confront her own fears, Ripley might well have paid the ultimate price.

Now it was his turn to react, to secure Brewer and save his own skin at the same time. Only, to move anywhere else inside or outside the house, he and the man he was here to protect were going to have to either climb through the back window or step out into the narrow hallway.

The latter of which would put them right in line with the open front door.

'What the fuck is going on?' Brewer asked, his face so leeched of blood it was almost grey.

'Sit tight,' Cater told him, in a voice cracking under duress. Being involved in violent and aggressive encounters was an accepted part of the job, but he had experienced nothing like the sheer panic he now felt cramping muscles and clawing frantically at his insides.

Brewer was shaking his head and sobbing. 'Sit tight? Are you bloody mad? Get me the fuck out of here!'

Glowering at the man, Cater shot back, 'You stay put. I have to find out what happened to my colleague. She could be dying out there.'

'And we could be dying in here at any moment.'

'Funny you should say that,' came a voice from the doorway.

Cater snapped his head around. It was the last thing he ever did.

31

Inspector Eric Price was first through the door, his H&K semi-automatic rifle jammed against his shoulder, the sight magnifying everything to the point where it felt impossible to miss any target.

Upon arriving at the scene he first checked on the fallen officer lying in a crumpled and bloody heap across the driveway, while his colleagues cleared the vehicle and front garden. The body was Ripley's. Two of the three bullets fired at her had taken the sergeant in the face, and Price knew she was gone before he dropped to one knee to feel for a pulse that was not going to be there.

'Training kicked in,' he later told the gathered members of the task force, with a nod of professional recognition to Barry Smyth. 'There was nothing I could do for the downed officer. My focus immediately switched to those left inside the house. My team and I entered the premises and cleared it room by room, and we didn't take our time about it. Even so, we were too late for either our constable or Alan Brewer. It took us less than three minutes to get here after receiving the call, but somehow we still managed to miss the bastard.'

'There's a chance he could have still been inside the house when you turned up,' Bliss suggested.

He and Chandler had been about to enter Megan Baker's driveway when the news came in, resulting in them scrambling hurriedly back across town to the Brewer home, along with every other vehicle in the vicinity. 'One of your colleagues told us he found the back door in the kitchen hanging wide open when he first cleared the room, so our killer could easily have slipped out of there, moved beyond the treeline, and made across the fields to a motor parked up off road. None of our patrol vehicles or your ARV units encountered him if so. But I suspect that's the only way he avoided being seen leaving the immediate area.'

Price shook his head angrily. The task force gathered together on the dropped kerb leading into the drive, work going on in the background of the blue-lit scene to check the stability of the bay window structure into which the killer had propelled a small hatchback. It too was receiving attention from the forensics team.

'Either way, the cheeky prick still took time to remove the head and cart it away with him. Is he lucky, or just bloody good?'

'He's good,' Warburton conceded. 'But he is also lucky, and logic says it has to run out eventually. We're agreed that he wound up the little Renault, popped its automatic gearbox into drive, and released the handbrake as he clambered out. His intention was not to cause damage or gain entry, but rather to create a diversion and draw attention away from his true purpose. When Sergeant Ripley emerged through the front doorway, she must have been fully focussed on the motor. Meanwhile, our killer, having slipped off to the side of the front yard into the darkness, approached and took Ripley out with his trademark three shots. Then he headed into the house to finish off Constable Cater and Mr Brewer. It must have been tight here in terms of time, but clearly he planned ahead. One vehicle used for the diversion at the front, another to make his getaway at the rear. I agree with Inspector Bliss in that respect.'

'If he's as good as you say, then he knew what to expect. Knew he'd find a couple of officers inside plus us cruising the area close by.' Price let a hand slide off his H&K and used it to thump a clenched fist into his thigh. 'Dammit! We should have had more mobile firearms crews on duty.'

'I got as many as could be spared,' Bliss said softly, regretting now that he had not pushed harder for more resources. 'We couldn't leave our counties completely unprotected. If I could have secured one crew per home, I would have. But you're right, we should have had more. I screwed up.'

Price shook his head and lifted a hand. 'Woah. I wasn't laying blame at your door, Bliss. There are six of you in your task force plus there's me and my team, and also Barry's unit. None of us raised the issue of insufficient resources before the evening, and we all had the opportunity to do so. No, the simple fact is we're used to doing more with less, only this time it bit us on the arse.'

'And cost the lives of two fine officers,' Warburton reminded them. 'Not to mention their protectee.'

'I don't think any of us are about to forget that,' Price said. 'But I also know there's no way the bosses would have given approval to staff this the way it needed to be in order to make it fully secure, with an armed crew inside every house as well as mobile units in the area. We can't provide it twenty-four hours a day for six people in six different locations. And that's just a fact of life.'

Bliss was feeling as disconsolate as he had in several months. Accepting an occasional operational failure was part of the job. It left you with no choice but to readjust and move on. The urge to blame this particular debacle on limited resources alone was tempting, but the killer's decision to take out a second victim in the same day had also wrong-footed them. Given the underlying circumstances, Bliss was not sure what else they could have done, but three more bodies lay dead on the ground, and when this case was over, somebody would be called to account. It was then that something lying fallow in the back of his mind surged forward. 'I have a question,' he said. 'If our killer escaped in another vehicle, how did he get both of them here this evening?'

'That's an excellent thought,' Smyth said, nodding furiously. 'He must have left his getaway motor somewhere close to the fields out back and then driven the Renault here. But as Bliss says, how did he achieve this on his own?'

'He had help,' Warburton said. 'Must have had.'

'I'm not so sure.' Bliss shook his head. 'This man doesn't strike me as someone who works well with others. I suppose it's always possible that he stole the Renault from somewhere close by. He's not going to have dropped his escape vehicle off and cabbed it to wherever the Renault was, so nicking it locally makes some kind of sense.'

'I'll make it a priority to chase it up, boss,' Chandler said. 'But there's still a chance he worked it out with a partner.'

'Of course. I suspect it's something much simpler, though.'

'However he did it, the bastard is still at least one move ahead of us,' Price said, kicking out at a loose stone on the kerb.

'Nothing was in our favour here,' Bliss responded. 'Even if we'd persuaded every one of our remaining suspects to stay in a single safe residence and had them individually shadowed by firearms officers, it would only have driven our killer underground to wait us out. In a game of chicken with those parameters, we blink first because we are hamstrung by costs. The moment we ease off, up pops our man again. It's what we feared might happen, and with each victim it becomes more likely.'

'Because the fewer we have to protect the more protection we can offer them,' Chandler said bluntly.

'Precisely. We put two unarmed officers in here tonight. Their job was to alert the ARV units as soon as they sniffed out any danger. Which is exactly what they did, but the man we're up against is clearly no amateur. To be honest, even if we'd had a couple of firearms officers here tonight instead, I'm not confident it would have altered the eventual outcome. Our killer has the tactical advantage of deciding where, when and how to strike, which makes all the difference.'

The day had begun with a chill in the air and it was ending that way, too. There was no breeze, nor any cloud cover, the absence of either allowing the low temperature to settle over the flat terrain of the Lincolnshire Fens. The stars were bright and plentiful, and Bliss thought dawn might bring with it a light frost. He shivered, but not because he was cold.

'So what do we do now?' Warburton asked. 'If sheer volume of numbers is likely to send him running for cover, and lack of numbers leaves us vulnerable and puts our own people at risk, how do we overcome such a dilemma?'

'Although I don't like to suggest it, and in doing so I realise I'm going back on everything I said before, we now need to buy ourselves some time,' Bliss said. Resigned to the inevitable, his voice was dull and flat. 'I think we have to come down in favour of the safest option available to us at present. Even if it's only to allow us to regroup.'

'Which is?' Price asked.

'Pretty much what I said a minute or so ago. The very thing I'd rather not do. We gather up the remaining five suspects and hold them in a single location. We flood the area with armed officers, have them roaming the neighbouring streets as well, and we secure these people to the point where our man realises it's pointless even trying. That way we buy ourselves a couple of days, perhaps three or four. And during the lull it creates we find another way to nail this bastard while he's underground.'

'But how and where do we even begin to track him down?' Smyth asked. 'Him coming to us seemed like the only sure way of getting our hands on the man.'

'It may not be much, but we still have Charlie Baker's wife to talk to. Plus, we have the names of the prominent people Baker did business with, people who must have felt some impact at the man's loss. It doesn't matter who they are, what they do, or how prominent they might be. I want them spoken to. More than that, I want them grilled, harassed even. Same with officers potentially on the family payroll. I don't care about upset feelings right now, nor do I give a stuff about protocol. I want to shake the tree and see what falls loose. Maybe then we find the one rotten apple we need.'

Warburton whistled. 'Our bosses are not going to like that.'

'No,' Bliss agreed. 'But I think they may like further headless corpses and murdered police officers even less.'

32

Bliss arrived home in the dark moments during which Tuesday ticked slowly over into Wednesday. He threw himself down into his armchair, letting out a low groan as his body protested. Running a hand over his scalp and down to the back of his neck, he released a long sigh.

For thirteen years he had lived with Ménière's disease, a chronic ear condition which affected his equilibrium and his hearing. A better outcome than the brain tumour he and his doctor initially feared, but a life-changing illness nonetheless. Time and experience had allowed Bliss to manage the disorder, so while his episodes of vertigo were now rare, fatigue and imbalance remained as permanent reminders. Stress was a known trigger, and could often set off an attack. Hence his Zen garden, and the more relaxed and practical approach he tried to adopt to his work environment. It was not always successful, but without it he would not have been able to remain in a job whose very nature brought with it untold stressors in many guises.

The day had drained him, no question. The investigation weighed heavily on him, and each death now felt personal. These days, Bliss knew how to adapt, to embrace the unacceptable. What he needed was some relief from the jumble of thoughts cascading around inside his head, a period of relaxation, and a decent night's sleep. Considering the day he had experienced, he thought it unlikely any of those were coming his way soon.

It was only after vowing not to move again until the morning light edged across the fringes of his lawn, that Bliss realised he had not eaten since the night before. Moonlight crept in through the glass sliding doors leading to the garden, bathing the room in a stark silver glow, which cast long shadows over the walls and floor. Sunlight always filled the lounge with vigour and life, whereas a cold sterility now surrounded him. It seemed fitting.

He was hungry, but could not bring himself to cook or even rustle up a snack. He was thirsty, but he eschewed his usual chilled beer and lacked the energy to even make himself a cup of hot tea. With another long groan, Bliss finally wrestled himself up off the recliner and walked into the kitchen, where he fetched himself a glass of water from the tap. The cold, clear liquid slaked his thirst, yet at the same time caused his stomach to protest against its lack of sustenance.

Bliss caught and held his own thoughts, becoming angry with himself. Going without food or drink was nothing unusual for him once a fresh case had him locked firmly within its grasp. Given the pace at which this operation was moving, his lapse was all the more understandable. He had not once enquired as to the welfare of his colleagues, however. While they were big enough and ugly enough to take care of themselves, the task force was his responsibility and therefore it was part of his job to ensure they kept themselves fuelled, rested and ready to go. If his team were feeling anything like him, right now they would be shattered, lethargic, their minds woolly and off centre.

His fault, not theirs.

Ignoring them in the same way he disregarded himself, was unacceptably poor leadership. It was his responsibility to set the pace and have others follow. He should have ordered a lunch break at the very least. Oblivious, he had ploughed on, full steam ahead without thought or caution for anyone else.

As a consequence of events at Alan Brewer's home, the team had brushed aside their planned meal and drink at the Riverside Hotel. Instead, having first gathered to discuss the case outside the property, they then joined in with the search in surrounding fields, streets and lanes, checking on isolated structures that looked as if they might provide temporary shelter for a fugitive.

Bliss recalled the line from a movie in which Tommy Lee Jones's character orders the search of every warehouse, farmhouse, henhouse, outhouse and doghouse in the area. But even as he continued to search, Bliss knew their own quarry was long gone, somehow managing to slip away from the scene of crime carrying another victim's severed head in a container of some description, and that no manhunt – irrespective of how thorough it might be – was going to unearth him.

The question of how the killer had managed to get two vehicles to the scene continued to nag at Bliss. The information on the Renault left them none the wiser. It was listed as an MOT failure four years earlier. This detail matched that of the white Range Rover, yet did not preclude it from having been stolen from a nearby home. The owner was hardly going to report it missing.

Confounded by the fast-moving events of the past few days, Bliss could not recall the last time he had investigated a case of such headlong pace and forward momentum. The tension of it felt solid enough to wring out in two hands, and the nervous energy coursing through their blood was what kept the team going.

At the back of his mind, Bliss recognised the unpalatable aspects of the operation. The group he and his team sought to protect were, themselves, likely killers. Also, it never once escaped his attention that the single man murdered by those thirteen people, was a monster of a human being. The entanglement of right and wrong was not easy to unravel in this case, so Bliss made sure his team maintained a single specific victim: Kelly Gibson.

Kelly was the one incontrovertibly innocent person in all this prior to last night's shootings. Now Riley and Cater also lay in the morgue. Bliss had not known either of the two Lincolnshire officers, but their being murdered in the line of duty left its own mark. As a consequence, those involved busied themselves preparing for the inevitable media explosion. The bosses would find it almost impossible to resist the urge to reveal all, encouraging journalists to swarm over every single aspect of the investigation. It could only make the task force's job harder, which in turn could only damage their chances of a successful resolution.

If such a thing was even possible now.

Back in the living room and spread out in his chair, Bliss briefly considered putting on some music. He was in the mood for something smooth and melancholic, but decided his attention was too scattered to truly appreciate the indulgence. He also dismissed the idea of putting something mind-numbing on the TV.

Eyes darting around the room, his gaze fell upon one of the photos retrieved from a cardboard box a few months back. There was a time when simply looking at the two-dimensional landscape of Hazel's face sent him careering over the edge. But after yielding to Penny Chandler's constant nagging, he now realised that, far from causing him pain, the photographs gave him a small measure of comfort. Without them he could not be certain of remembering the precise contours of his wife's delicate features, and he missed catching unexpected glimpses of her beautiful smile.

The last time he and Chandler sat together in this room, she asked him what it was he missed most about his late wife. Initially unable to form a coherent response, he eventually considered the question and gave the truest answer he could think of.

'Oddly enough, our disagreements. Although few and far between, when they occurred they reminded us both just how complete we were as a couple. I spent much of our married life believing it might all disappear like smoke. There was an ethereal quality about it. It felt unnatural to be so happy. That's why, when we did argue, it made me realise our relationship was all too real and we were actually living that life together.'

In the darkness splintered only by moonlight, Bliss smiled to himself as a warm glow of contentment settled in his stomach. Hazel was here with him again. It was all he needed or wanted. Yet wrapped inside this small pleasure was a growing and unfurling disturbance: the investigation fighting its way out to demand his attention. He took a breath and gave in to its insistent demands.

It occurred to Bliss that there were several strategies he could put in place overnight which might turn things around in favour of the task force again. He knew he did not hold all of the authority needed to start putting everything in motion, but as DCI Edwards had indicated recently, Bliss also lived by the maxim that it was better to ask for forgiveness than permission.

He first fired up his laptop and signed into the secure police network. He opened up the mail application and flexed his fingers above the keyboard. Bliss composed a few words inside his head before he started typing.

Subject: CRISIS MEETING!
Body of mail: Detective Inspector Bliss calls for a crisis meeting prior to start of business this morning (Wednesday).
Attendees requested: all members of task force, plus DCI Edwards, Detective Superintendent Fletcher, Detective Superintendent Yates (Lincs).
Time and location: 7.30am, Mobile Command Centre, Sutton End. (Details to be sent later).
Purpose of meeting: Update; Media; Interviews.
DI Bliss requires full commitment and agreement on stalling the media and on interviews to be held throughout the day. These will include influential people and fellow police officers

and speed is of the essence, which is why DI
Bliss requests the presence of relevant deci-
sion-makers at this crisis meeting.

When he was done pecking at the keys, Bliss reclined to read the message through in full. As far as he was concerned, what needed to happen from this point could not rely on the usual working methods, where requests got passed up channels and responses later came back down them again.

He wanted the remaining five Baker murder suspects rounded up and secured away in a safe location, with armed guards inside and out. Then he required the names of local officers suspected of colluding with the Baker family, with each of them immediately pulled in for interview.

Finally, he needed every known influential member of Charlie Baker's inner circle questioned hard about who might be responsible for the eight murdered suspects, plus the two police officers and police civilian worker caught up in the slaughter. What's more, Bliss suspected the only method of achieving any of it was to have all of the players in the same room at the same time.

It was a big ask and a massive undertaking, but he regarded it as the best way forward. Perhaps the only way.

He had a solid reason for electing to communicate using this method. The dedicated mail system included a delivery mechanism capable of calling the recipients' numbers and automatically reading the message to them when they answered the phone. One click of the mouse was all it needed. Bliss took a deep breath, knowing he was about to wake two very senior officers, in addition to DCI Edwards, none of whom were likely to be best pleased with him. He weighed up the options one last time, decided this was the way he preferred it to be.

Bliss clicked the button, signed out of the system, and closed the laptop. Then he took out his phone and arranged for the mobile command centre to be readied and made available for first thing in the morning over at Sutton End.

Essentially, the MCC was a vast motorhome designed for the specific task of acting as a central mobile office from which senior officers could make command decisions and control all communications if necessary. When asked under whose authority and responsibility the vehicle should be allocated, Bliss gave Superintendent Fletcher's name and hoped she would forgive his impertinence when the time came to sign for it.

When he was finished making the calls, Bliss checked his messages. Two of them sat in his voicemail box. The first was from Lennie Kaplan enquiring as to whether Bliss was free for a few beers and a curry at some point over the weekend.

The moment he heard the voice on the second message, Bliss cursed aloud in the empty room.

'This is Jennifer Howey. You missed an appointment with me earlier on today. I need you to call me as soon as possible. As I'm sure you are aware, Inspector Bliss, I have to report this missed appointment. I'd be interested to know why you failed to attend. It would be especially useful if you let me know ahead of next week. Thank you.'

Bliss swore. Although his inherent distrust of psychologists – especially those who attempted to mess with his head – was genuine, Bliss had once confessed to Chandler that he found the mandatory sessions with the occupational health therapist to be of use. Unlike Howey, he did not believe he was suffering from mild post-traumatic stress disorder, yet he did admit to being unusually on edge, often for prolonged periods. At some point during the last days of an investigation he and his team wrapped up towards the middle of summer, Bliss began to feel better about this life than he had in many years. But not long afterwards the mood swings kicked in; flashfires Bliss started everywhere he went, no matter who he was with. Butting heads was his default position, but there were times when it went overboard. It took all of Jennifer Howey's skills and finesse to pull him out of his downward spiral.

'Is she young and getting your red blood pumping?' Chandler asked at one point, and not entirely as a joke.

It wasn't like that for him. Most of all it felt as if the therapist discovered sound common sense in the same places he was looking, and in unearthing it somehow managed to soothe him, calming his soul. Rather than the stark prism of myriad occurrences over which he believed he had no control, Bliss was shown the logical paths created around him which collided at certain points in his life. Events which, at the time, felt chaotic and unstructured, revealing themselves to be no more than the inevitable product of a lifetime of unstaged happenstance.

'You're talking about fate?' Bliss had asked the therapist.

'Of sorts.'

'But I don't believe in fate.'

'Then what do you believe in?'

'Life.'

'Then call it that instead.' He recalled her saying it with a smile.

The memory of their conversation to the forefront of his mind, Bliss replied to her message by leaving his own voicemail, 'Sorry, Jennifer. I wish I had a good reason. I was snowed under at work, and couldn't get away. I'll do better next time.'

Bliss left his phone switched on. He was expecting a few more calls before daylight.

33

B liss ensured he was the first to arrive. He had already made arrangements with Chandler for them to travel separately, and was on the road early that morning. He stopped off en route at a Tesco supermarket and bought groceries. The mobile command centre provided a small galley kitchen, which included a kettle, toaster, a built-in microwave oven and fridge, and Bliss felt obliged to lay on a light breakfast for those he had summoned to the meeting.

The vehicle itself was hugely impressive. White and liveried in blue and yellow, its resin frame was long and wide, the interior plush and tastefully elegant. With the closing of numerous area stations over the past decade, it had become increasingly more difficult to find suitable locations to use as command centres, resulting in the county striking a deal with the manufacturers which eventually saw the arrival of what came to be known as the White Whale towards the back end of the summer.

Inside, Bliss busied himself getting everything ready for the arrival of his colleagues, hoping nobody cried off. It was too important, and only required one missing link in the chain to weaken the entire plan.

Surprisingly, he had received only two calls overnight. The first was from Chandler, who told him she wanted to both check on his sanity and also wish him well with his eventual firing squad. Moments later it was DCI Edwards, although her mood was somewhat less sanguine. Whilst refraining from chewing him out entirely, Edwards made her feelings clear about receiving such a directive from someone a rung beneath her on the ranking ladder. Bliss had brushed his boss's irritation aside, and now awaited the main event.

He thought he had played it okay so far. He felt he had earned the support of those from his own city base, and he was also convinced that both DCI Warburton and RPU officer Smyth would back his stance. However, for the first time it was the Lincolnshire Superintendent, Jasper Yates, who held the balance of power. Any officers suspected of having a relationship with Baker worked under Yates's command. Any prominent members of the community about to be caught up in interviews were all likely to be from Yates's county, something that was bound to reflect poorly on him irrespective of their complicity. Bliss hoped the man was up to the task of making the right decisions for the right reasons.

Bishop and Short came through the door next, swiftly followed by Chandler. Bliss knew they each preferred coffee to start their day, so immediately set about making them each a drink, plus a tea for himself.

'You found it okay, then?' he said in the cheeriest tone he could muster.

'Your early morning text directions were spot on,' Bishop assured him.

Bliss noticed his colleagues looked drawn and weary. He felt a pang of guilt, but professional people accepted the disturbance to their lives during major crime investigations. It went with the territory, although he wondered if he was driving his team too hard this time.

The unit responsible for deploying the mobile command centre were experienced and entirely familiar with the problems associ-ated with siting such an imposing vehicle. Somehow, they had managed to procure the services of Sutton End's only secondary school academy. The mobile was now standing in the shadow of the building on the far side away from the main entrance, cordoned off by cones and tape from prying eyes and ears. Everyone involved had worked wonders, and Bliss made a mental note to find out which tipple they each preferred.

'Do we need a pre-briefing briefing, boss?' Short asked, sliding into one of ten deep and comfortable leather seats situated around a rectangular table in the centre of the meeting space.

Bliss shook his head. 'Not necessary. Just back me up if you will. Nothing I'm going to say will come as a surprise to any of you.'

'Ballsy move reaching out like that overnight,' Chandler told him. 'Let's hope it pays off.'

'Hope and even pray if that's your thing, Pen. But if any of them fails to show, or shows and then doesn't play ball, then we are all stuffed and I have no other direction for us to lean towards.'

'You don't have a reverse gear in there somewhere?'

'I do, but I refuse to use it.'

'Then Yates better be as amiable as Diane and Barry, or this enclosed space could get claustrophobic very quickly.'

The chance he had taken was not lost on Bliss. It was a signifi-cant step going against all protocol by virtually demanding senior officers over whom he had no authority attend this early morning meeting. Once they were all seated around the table, he intended on putting each of them under severe scrutiny, asking them to set aside internal politics and in some circumstances even external friendships or favours. Bliss realised he was placing under the microscope the kind of people who made it their job to avoid just such a precarious position. It was a risk, but one he was fully prepared to take.

Chandler asked him whether he had managed to grab any sleep.

Bliss grinned and pointed at his own face. 'What does this ugly mug tell you, Pen?'

She feigned close inspection before nodding. 'I see what you mean. Rough night, then?'

'Let's just say I'm hoping for an early one today. A quick result will be fine by me.'

'You sure you don't want to take a few minutes to spruce yourself up, boss? Diane will be here shortly.'

'What is your malfunction, Penny? Why can't you leave well alone?'

'Not in my nature, boss.'

'Then you should learn from your past mistakes and make it your nature. There's nothing there, so please don't waste your time.'

'Ooh, what's this?' Short asked. She flashed a wide grin and fluttered her eyelashes. 'Some juicy gossip I've somehow missed out on?'

'It's nothing,' Bliss snapped back. 'Really. Just Penny's oddball mind.'

Chandler fixed him with a tight glare. 'You know something, if it were possible I'd say you've become even grumpier in recent months.'

'If true, then look no further than yourself for the reason behind my low moods. You do my head in sometimes.'

'Sometimes? Is that all? Maybe I need to brush up on my dark arts.'

The vehicle filled quickly as the designated meeting time approached. Warburton and Smyth turned up with smiles on their faces and a nod of welcome to Bliss, gestures he appreciated as the weight of expectation began to add tension to his neck and shoulders.

Then it was the turn of Fletcher and Edwards to arrive together, their presence immediately heightening the charged atmosphere as each took their place around the table. Bliss handed over drink-making duties to Chandler while he studied a pad of notes he had written to himself first thing – prompts for if his mind seized up.

Finally, at seven-thirty on the dot, the door opened and a man Bliss had never seen before stepped up and into the command centre.

Detective Superintendent Jasper Yates stood tall and straight, with a military bearing to complement narrowed blue eyes which became immediately watchful and gleaming with curiosity. Bliss sensed that, having decided to attend, the boss from Lincolnshire had every intention of making his trip worthwhile. DCI Warburton got to her feet and shook the man's hand, while Yates and Smyth exchanged nods. Further introductions took place whilst Bliss hovered in the background, anxiety cramping his insides.

'And you must be DI Bliss,' Yates said eventually, holding out a hand across the table. He remained standing behind his chosen seat.

Bliss felt the man's steely grip, and was once again reminded of a military deportment. 'I am, sir. And thank you for coming.'

'Did I have a choice in the matter?' Yates asked, his eyes consuming every inch of Bliss.

'There are four of you in the room who chose to be here, sir. It's not my place to insist where you are all concerned.'

'Next best thing, perhaps?'

Bliss allowed himself a modest smile. 'As far as I felt able to push it,' he admitted. 'But the hard work starts now that I have you all here under one roof.'

Yates nodded, continuing to assess Bliss. Finally he sat down and said, 'Then I suggest we waste no time in getting on with it. The floor is yours.'

Bliss decided not to dwell on what he had got himself into. Any formal repercussions could wait until later in the day. This was his moment, and he had to make the most of it.

'Thank you all for coming. To begin with, I'll quickly cover old ground; everything we know leading up to my calling for this meeting. Afterwards, I am going to discuss what your media approach might be. Or, to be more accurate, how I prefer it to go. And finally, I'll tell you what I want myself and my team to be doing today, and I will outline exactly what I need from the most senior of you in order that we are able to do our work unencumbered and unhindered.'

Bliss glanced around the table, but did not pause long enough for anyone to ask questions. Instead he began describing the Baker's Dozen case, the four suspect murders and decapitations carried out abroad, plus all seven murders since Sunday evening, only four of which were part of the original planned hit list of thirteen. He then went on to insist that the only way to protect the remaining five suspects was to deny them any choice in the matter and remove them from their ordinary lives on a temporary basis.

'I'd like a suitable property designated immediately,' Bliss continued. 'A safe house in which we can secrete and secure five people, one of whom is a woman. We then have every spare firearms officer across our two counties guarding those five people and the property itself, both inside and out. I'm talking about a visible and obvious deterrent, the purpose of which is not just to keep these five suspects safe, but also to drive the killer underground for a day or two. A day or two we must use well. To find them rather than wait for them to resurface.

'How do we do that? First, we conclude the Baker family interviews by pulling in Megan Baker, wife of Charlie. Second, we grill every member of Baker's Masonic lodge, without fear or favour. We treat them like any other person because we don't have time for the niceties of life they might otherwise expect. Third, we pull off the street or out of the station or back from leave every single police officer believed to have worked for Baker or his rotten family. My bet is one of them, perhaps even more than one, knows why this is happening and probably who is carrying out these murders. If those thirteen suspects are on a hit list, then it must surely be out of revenge for Charlie Baker's murder. It's our duty to speak to everybody connected with Baker, and that has to include those I have just mentioned.

'Most of all, I not only want the go-ahead and the wherewithal to do all of this, I want to do it immediately. I need to, without wasting time being second-guessed or delays in the decision-making process. It's why I asked you all here, paving the way for us to get decisions made here and now. To be blunt, I need to be firing off orders from the second I leave this command centre.'

After a long moment of silence, it was his own superintendent who broke it. 'Now I fully appreciate why you asked us all here in the manner you did, DI Bliss. You want actions which rely on getting the right response from myself and Superintendent Yates, and you don't want the kind of delay so often encountered when dealing across county lines.'

'Sometimes even within our own,' Bliss said, knowing he was chancing his arm but beyond caring about how he might appear to those who were not familiar with his methods.

'Point taken. At the same time, although these are relatively easy requests for me to go along with, it is my counterpart from Lincolnshire who has the weightier decisions to make.'

For a few seconds, Yates seemed to look both inward and out at those seated around him at the table. He used a thumb and fore-finger to briefly pinch the flesh of his bottom lip, eyes flickering as his thoughts unravelled themselves inside his head. A tall, needle-thin man, who wore glasses and whose grey hair was receding fast, Yates nonetheless gave the impression of having enormous inner resources of strength and depth of character. His gaze switched back to Bliss alone.

'If I'm understanding this correctly,' he said. 'You want to secure the remaining five suspects and thereby force the killer to take a step backwards. Make him pause long enough for you to get a handle on him and track him down. Is that about right, Bliss?'

'It is, sir. Whilst at the same time being prepared for another attack should he deviate from the expected pattern of behaviour.'

'So you don't believe it's possible for us to prevail if we lure this man out again?'

'I have no confidence in being able to do so, no. I certainly have no intention of taking such a risk. Two lives yesterday were more than enough losses for me, sir. The man is an obvious professional. To lure him back out we'd need to leave open a window of opportunity, and that will only end up costing us more of our own people.'

'But you believe it's possible to place these suspects out of harm's way?'

'Provided they agree to it, that's the easy part. Given the right amount of manpower and weapons we are absolutely capable of ensuring their safety for as long as it can be afforded. The problem being it gets us no closer to our killer, and he will know we can only secure them for a limited period due to the overwhelming cost. Which is why we need the approach I have suggested.'

'It's your belief that someone, perhaps even several people, from the family, their friends, or those on their payroll, have paid this killer to exact revenge on behalf of Charles Baker.'

'If revenge is the motive here, then who else?'

'And if revenge is not the motive?'

Bliss shrugged. 'Then we're left chasing our tails, because nobody has yet come up with an alternative theory, sir. It has been our sole focus since we discovered what was going on.'

Yates glanced across the table, where Warburton held his eyes and acknowledged the unasked question. The man turned back to Bliss and said, 'They are powerful people, these friends of the Baker family. Are you prepared to take them on, Inspector Bliss?'

'We are.'

'And what of our paid-off colleagues? Are you also ready to face not only their wrath but that of their fellow suits and uniforms?'

'To be brutally honest, their anger is of no consequence to me if they are guilty. Those who stick by them even if they are bought and paid for by the likes of Baker, will just have to get over themselves. We have to take this man down. We've tried one way, now we have to try something different. Something that won't cost the lives of more innocent officers.'

Yates cleared his throat and seemed to reach a decision, at which point he turned to look directly at Warburton.

'Chief Inspector, given you worked on the Baker investigation, do you already have a complete list of known or suspected Charlie Baker sympathisers from within our own ranks?'

'I do, sir.' She gave a stiff nod, as if accepting this statement carried an unspoken burden with it. 'However, hard evidence against them is in such short supply as to be virtually non-existent.'

'That may well be the case, but forward the list to me anyway and I'll take care of it myself. I won't have fingers pointing in your direction afterwards. If there is a reaction from fellow officers, let them face me down.' Yates turned to Bliss. 'Inspector, you will have our officers interviewed however you want them. I guarantee it. I'll take the heat from our local heavyweights and, legal teams allowing, I will also deliver those people to you today as well. I extend our full co-operation to you and your task force.'

Bliss was both delighted and surprised at how easily the man accepted the situation they now found themselves in. That he had also taken it upon himself to be the focal point for the inevitable ire resulting from the decisions was a testimony to Yates's authority and approach.

'Thank you, sir. I must say that comes as a great relief.'

Yates waved it aside. 'As for the safe house and security, I'm happy to split the costs and physical resources with Cambridgeshire. Order whatever you need.'

'Do I have everyone's agreement?' Bliss asked, glancing around the table. 'Be in no doubt, this will stretch us to the limit. We are going to be fighting legal battles throughout, and the five people we're going to be protecting may well be guilty of murder themselves. I need to know we speak with one voice here.'

After nods all round, Fletcher was the first to respond directly.

'Inspector, while these are decidedly unusual circumstances, and this meeting itself is extraordinary, the job is still about protecting life and limb, while at the same time putting together a manhunt. If toes need treading on, then do so with care but don't let them stop you moving forward. I hope I speak for everyone here at this table when I say we are fully supportive of any methods that will put a stop to this, especially one that prevents us from having to attend any more than three funerals in the coming weeks.'

It was a sober reminder of the death of three colleagues. Bliss thanked his super and everyone else in attendance. 'I'm ready to go ahead with this immediately,' he said. 'But in presenting my case to you I wandered off course slightly. There is one final difficulty we face: the media. None of you are going to appreciate my next suggestion, but what I'm asking for here is as close to a blackout as we can possibly achieve.'

'Why is this the best way to go?' DCI Edwards asked. There was no emotion in either her voice or her countenance, but as someone who enjoyed being in the city spotlight, the DCI was bound to fight this request.

'Simply because I believe the fewer people who know what we're doing here the better it will be. This is not something we want the media trampling all over, nor do we want them running their own investigative lines of enquiry. You know these people, they'll pick it apart bit by bit and decide upon the most negative way to report on what we're doing. If they do that afterwards, when it's all over, well then so be it. But not while it's ongoing. Not at this critical juncture.'

'But we must talk to them, Bliss. We have to have something for them, or our silence will only encourage them to do their own digging. That's the very opposite of what you're looking to achieve.'

Edwards had a point, Bliss acknowledged. 'Which is why I didn't ask for a full blackout,' he said. 'We first of all let them know our investigations are continuing, and then we tell them a full briefing will be provided at around five this afternoon. By which time we'll have figured out a decent cover story close enough to the truth that they'll have few complaints afterwards, but not so close that it raises flags with them.'

'What about your own contact at the local paper?'

'Sandra Bannister? I've already fended her off. She knows not to try obtaining ongoing case details from me. If she calls again – and I suspect she will – then I'll point her in the direction of the briefing. If I ask her to come back to me with any information she digs up on her own, the cost of doing so may be a head start on the rest of the media. If she does turn up anything it'll probably be worthwhile, so it's something to keep in mind.'

'I think we're good to go,' Yates said, getting to his feet. 'I'll have a quick word with my own officers, then I have perhaps a further thirty minutes or so before I have to leave.'

'We can catch up,' Fletcher suggested. Her glance flitted across to Bliss, and she smiled at him and gave a single nod. He returned both.

Bliss was not entirely happy with the situation, but the meeting had gone better than anticipated, and now he and the other members of the task force team could begin to make progress in stripping away the thick veneer of dishonesty erected around Charlie Baker's memory. Bliss knew that all they had to do was peel away one corner, leaving the ugly truth beneath exposed for all to see.

The interview with Megan Baker went about as well as Bliss could have expected. The once attractive woman, now bloated and ravaged by whatever consumption of alcohol and pharmaceuticals she enjoyed – ably backed up by her daughter, Charlotte, who was visiting – stonewalled the two detectives to the point where even Chandler became irritated with the pair.

To a certain extent, Bliss understood why none of the Baker family were bending over backwards to be of help. After all, the people on the hit list had most likely killed Charlie Baker, so they might regard it as a fitting end for all thirteen suspects. This was true even if the Baker family happened to be uninvolved with the shootings and beheadings. If any of them were responsible, then they had all the more reason to blank the police.

Bliss believed he and Chandler had drawn the toughest group of people to speak with. After forty frustrating minutes with Megan Baker and her sneering female offspring, they headed to Boston to catch up with ex-Euro MP Simon Thaw.

A one-time UKIP representative, Thaw now led a local party whose narrative was pro-Brexit and anti-immigration. In a county which had seen a huge increase in the Eastern European population over the past decade, the independent ticket Thaw ran on was an easy sell to many people with roots in the community going back hundreds of years. Having no particular political leanings himself, Bliss was looking forward to Thaw rubbing Chandler up the wrong way. He sensed fireworks ahead.

The minor party's headquarters was a small shop front on a side street off Boston's busy Wide Bargate shopping district. Once a flourishing travel agency before the internet provided greater convenience and choice without the purchaser having to leave home, the windows still bore several posters advertising flights to a number of tourist destinations. At the far end of the lower floor was a single office commandeered by Simon Thaw. Other than the man himself, the only other member of staff appeared to be a woman who sat behind a computer monitor filing her nails with keen interest. Certainly more than she paid Bliss and Chandler as they entered and brushed by her desk.

Thaw proved to be a big man with a long-established large belly. Unlike most overweight people, he looked comfortable in his own skin, and his suit jacket provided the good fit of a decent tailor. Though instantly abrasive and irritated at having to speak with the police, Bliss found the political outcast relatively easy to talk to.

Thaw was a small-time politician with many opinions. He enjoyed sharing those views with others, often in a loud voice full of piss and vinegar. He made himself plain to the two detectives, leaving both of them in no doubt as to Thaw's friendship with Charlie Baker.

'What did you make of the claims against Baker?' Bliss asked. 'By that I mean allegations of bullying, a criminal who made the lives of others a misery, and also a rapist.'

'What constitutes a bully these days?' Thaw clasped both hands together around his extended waistline. 'This snowflake generation make all kinds of claims, most of which we would have laughed off years ago.'

'The good old days, eh?'

'Precisely. Too many hand-wringing malcontents now. Don't know what genuine hardship is.'

'Unlike you, of course. Your parents must have been down to their last Rolls Royce at the end. Perhaps just the two annual trips to the Caribbean, and a threadbare choice of homes once the estate in the south of France was sold up.'

'You've done your homework on me. Well, mock all you like. My father worked bloody hard for everything we had. One doesn't have to live in poverty to know what poverty is. These days people leave their food banks with a few meagre groceries and then on their way home buy their cigarettes, top up their mobile phones, collect a takeaway, a few cans of beer and a bottle of wine, before choosing which of their devices to play games on, after which they spend the rest of the day watching Netflix on cable. How dire an existence it must be for them.'

Bliss decided not to get into it with the man, steering the conversation back to the reason behind their visit. 'Charlie Baker had a good life, though. Seemingly way above anything his genuine business could afford. Almost as if he benefitted from another, hidden, source of income.'

'I know nothing about that.'

'Of course not. Wouldn't do to have a local politician mingling with the criminal element, would it? Yet that is exactly what the police believed him to be.'

Thaw grinned. 'Yes. And what is the legal definition there? Nobody ever found Charlie guilty of anything.'

'Which is where intimidation came in,' Chandler said. 'Those who opposed Baker, who tried to stand up to the man, were slapped back down. Often viciously.'

'That was certainly the allegation, yes. Of course, it was also another charge never proven against him.'

Chandler scoffed. 'I suppose you have to remain supportive of a man who made such a contribution to you over the years. I expect you hope Megan Baker will continue to write the cheques for as long as you stay in politics. Not that I'm absolutely sure what it is you do these days for the people of Boston.'

'It's difficult to do anything when you're not in power.'

'Oh, that's right. In your case, the contributions come in, you take your salary, and you oppose those who hold office. Hard to see what Baker was paying for.'

For the first time, the man bristled. He leaned forward until his stomach wedged against the desk. Jabbing a finger at Chandler he said, 'You make your snidey insinuations, officer. I'm an easy target, especially for the liberal left as I assume you are. But the fact remains I want only the best for my people. Charlie Baker felt the same way. Believe me, our day is coming. Leaving Europe and taking back our borders is only the beginning.'

'Calm down, Mr Thaw,' Bliss said. 'Your hard edges are show-ing. I think we've established just how much you liked Baker, and of course to what extent you relied upon him. Seeing those thir-teen suspects walking free must really have bored its way beneath your skin. Well, it's not thirteen walking about now, is it, DS Chandler?'

'No, boss.'

'What are we down to now?'

'Just the five, boss.'

'Somebody got angry with them, that's for sure. How about you, sir?' Bliss drilled his gaze into Thaw. 'How angry were you?'

It was the question that shut down the interview. Thaw's reac-tion was to rant and rage against a system that pointed fingers at people like him because they were anti-establishment, because they chose to oppose an open-door immigration policy, unafraid of speaking out in the face of stern opposition. When it came to the murders of eight of the Baker killing suspects, his denial was vehement.

Bliss's natural inclination was to disbelieve everything the man told them. Unfortunately, every word he uttered seemed genuine. Experienced detectives learned to look beyond initial appearances, however, and neither Bliss nor Chandler were entirely convinced of the man's innocence.

'He's a pig, a bully, and a racist prick,' Chandler said to Bliss as they exited the premises. She glanced back over her shoulder to glare through the grubby window. 'On the other hand, he's a wide-open book and although his views are offensive, he doesn't appear to be hiding anything.'

Bliss could only agree. For the most part. To his sergeant it was black and white: if you railed against mass immigration then you were a racist. Bliss thought her perspective was a little naïve and self-defeating, that at times the situation contained more grey areas. He considered Thaw's opinions to be more nuanced than Chandler claimed. But he did share her view that the man had said nothing incriminating in regard to the hired killer.

Is that because he was a genuinely honest man, or did we not ask the right questions?

Bliss spent a few minutes pondering the question. He had held back from directly asking Thaw if he knew anything about a hit man contracted to kill all thirteen Baker's Dozen suspects. They needed more than yes or no responses. Still, Bliss drove away contemplating a second conversation with Thaw, perhaps under caution and taking place in the worst of the five interview rooms back at Thorpe Wood police station.

He could not be certain of Thaw's innate racialism or xenophobia, but he did not trust the man either way. It was not so much what he said, rather the conversations he steered clear of. Thaw had clammed up towards the end and that was a sure sign that Bliss had moved beyond the politician's comfort zone. Whether that amounted to guilt or not, Bliss could not tell. Certainly there was a reluctance, almost as if the man had reached the limits of his endurance. It was something to ponder over.

Standing on the bank of the river Witham, the Boston police station comprised a series of buildings built from red brick and grey, water-stained concrete. It was here that Bliss had chosen to speak with Sergeant Lewis Waring. Having managed to wedge the car into what looked to be the only available space out in the visitors' car park, Bliss announced himself and Chandler at the front desk. After a wait of less than five minutes, the two were shown into an interview room clearly designed for witnesses rather than suspects; it was larger than any at HQ, painted in neutral tones, with comfortable and sturdy chairs as opposed to the old plastic bucket type.

While they waited, a uniformed female officer entered the room carrying two steaming mugs, setting them down on the room's only table. She smiled at them both, saying, 'Thought you might like a cuppa while you're waiting.'

'Thank you so much,' Chandler replied, raising her own broad smile. 'I'm actually gagging.'

'No problem. If I can find some biscuits I'll pop them in.'

The officer flashed them both another cheery grin as she left. Chandler immediately picked up her mug and raised it to her lips. Bliss shook his head and stuck out a hand to prevent his colleague from drinking from it.

'Don't be so bloody naïve,' he said, though a grin softened the rebuke.

'What do you mean?'

'When was the last time you went to another nick and were even so much as offered a drink, let alone had one brought to you unasked?'

Chandler placed the mug back down on the table. 'Perhaps she was just being thoughtful.'

Bliss shrugged. 'Do what you want, Pen. But there's no way I'm taking a chance on drinking mine.'

'What do you imagine is wrong with it?'

'All I know, Pen, is we have arrived at a station at which we are an unknown quantity, here to interview one of their own. So what I reckon is that at least two or three of the sergeant's colleagues, including the pleasant woman who brought the drinks to us, probably gobbed in our mugs when the tea was made.'

Chandler recoiled and twisted her mouth. 'Ugh! That's disgusting.'

'It is. And I guarantee that's what's mixed into our lovely hot drink right now. No sugars, but a couple of lumps of hawked-up phlegm.'

His partner's entire face creased up. 'Oh, don't. I might be sick.'

He laughed. 'They do it to solicitors' drinks all the time. Which is why you'll find the savvy ones getting their own from vending machines.'

'Well, I've never spat in anyone's drink.'

'Me neither. Doesn't mean to say it doesn't happen.'

The interview room door opened and a tall, rangy figure stepped inside. Sergeant Waring carried his own mug of tea. He looked at them both as he joined them at the table, and gave an assertive nod. 'Good morning, detectives. Enjoying your brew?'

'We were just discussing the distinct flavour,' Bliss said. He held the man's gaze.

'Not unique. But something we're proud of here in Boston.'

'I'm sure you are.'

Waring's dark curls were expensively trimmed if Bliss's eye was correct. The officer's white shirt appeared crease-free, its collar starched. Neither his uniform nor tie contained a speck of lint as far as Bliss could tell on a single appraisal. He looked well rested, with tight soft skin, and a light undercurrent of citrus emanating from his body. *The man is vain,* Bliss thought immediately, uncertain if the trait was suggestive of anything else about him.

The sergeant huffed a sigh and sprawled back in his chair. Bliss understood Waring was displaying his contempt for their visit, attempting to demonstrate a lack of interest in the proceedings.

'Let's get on with it, shall we?' Bliss suggested. He shoved his mug aside and leaned both elbows on the table. 'Sergeant Waring, we are not here today to discuss any involvement you may or may not have with the Baker family or their friends. That's a conversation you will be having at a later date, with some very different people, especially in light of the loss of two colleagues from this county constabulary. However, what I can say is if you played any part in what happened, if you leaked any information at all, then getting ahead of things now is the right thing to do.'

Waring nodded and raised his eyebrows. 'Wow. Very impressive. It's almost as if I've never heard a detective attempting to persuade a villain to give it up before.'

'Interesting that you see yourself in the role of villain, Sergeant Waring. Nonetheless, if you have something to confess, then doing so may just lessen the punishment you are likely to receive in relation to the murder of your colleagues. The finer points will be down to others to discuss with you, but if you provide me with information today which leads us to our killer, or even a step or two closer, then you can only gain from it.'

'Is that so? Well, tell me how you think I can help you, Inspector Bliss.'

'As you are fully aware, the thirteen people suspected of murdering Charlie Baker are, themselves, being picked off one by one. The problem for whoever instigated this revenge attack is in having two serving police officers and a civilian police worker caught up in it all. Innocent victims. Colleagues of ours. That makes the penalty for aiding and abetting so much harsher than it otherwise might be. However, if information came our way, such as who our revenge killer is or who might have hired him, then we can probably make a deal.'

'And why are you convinced I somehow have this information to offer you?'

'We don't know what you have,' Chandler said, drawing his attention. 'What we do know is that a list was drawn up of police officers suspected of being on the Baker family payroll. Your name is on the list. So if you have anything to say in your defence, anything at all that might help us catch a killer before he shoots someone else, then do yourself a favour and tell us.'

'What puts me on this list of yours? What intelligence do you have implicating me in working for or having worked for the Baker family?'

Chandler shook her head. 'I don't have those details. Only the list. The why is not an important factor to us. That you are on it, clearly is. Look, you can sit there and deny your involvement and when you're later found to be lying then you can pay for it in full. That's entirely your choice. Anyone proven to have worked for Baker will be arrested, charged, and the punishment when convicted is going to be severe. But as coppers we can also agree that the right words in the right ear can lessen any sentence. If we so choose. If we receive the right information from the right person. Right?'

'I'd be bloody crazy to admit to working for Baker without you showing any evidence of my guilt, wouldn't I?'

'Perhaps,' Bliss conceded. 'But perhaps not quite as crazy if you are guilty and know that we will eventually prove it, and all the while you did nothing to help yourself.'

For a few seconds, Waring was quiet. Neither Bliss nor Chandler spoke, either. They allowed the silence to work in their favour. After a while, the sergeant relaxed his shoulders and sat forward, leaning in towards them.

'Let me just say this,' Waring said. 'Hypothetically, if I earned from providing the Baker family with information, it must have made me a high card in their pack. Now, to my way of thinking, if I'm a high card then I'm going to be included in high-level decisions. Especially something as high-level as hiring someone to take revenge on Mr Baker's killers. Agreed?'

Bliss nodded. 'Sounds about right, yes.'

'Right. Trouble is, I wasn't told anything. I didn't overhear anything. Nobody said anything about it to me. I don't know a thing. And if I'm as bent as you say I am, I'd know everything, believe me.'

'Maybe you're just not as high a card as you reckon yourself to be.'

'If I'm a part of it, then I'm a high card, believe you me. That's a given. So maybe the only reason I'm not in the loop on this is because there's no loop to be in.'

'So you are telling us the Baker family had nothing to do with these revenge killings.'

Waring nodded. 'That's precisely what I'd be telling you if I was as involved as you insist I must be. They have nothing whatsoever to do with it.'

'But then you would say that, wouldn't you?' Chandler prompted.

Waring shrugged and flapped a dismissive hand. 'Have it your own way. You want to spend all your time looking at the wrong people, be my guest. You want to come after me, I'm ready for you because I know all your best moves. It changes nothing. If I am who you think I am then it stands to reason I'd know the truth. And the fact of the matter is, in a game of hot and cold, you lot are bloody freezing.'

With that, Waring got to his feet and left the room without another word or a backward glance. His parting shot ringing in their ears, the two detectives followed shortly afterwards.

Settled in the car and nudging their way back out of Boston, Chandler turned to Bliss with an excited smile playing across her lips. 'I forgot to mention earlier, but there was a letter waiting for me when I got home last night.'

'Ah, that plastic surgeon finally got in touch, did he?'

He got the look before his partner continued. 'It was from the Foreign Office. Jimmy, I got the official nod. Arrangements are in the process of being made. Mehmet has agreed, Hannah has agreed, and the local police have also agreed to act as go-between.' Chandler gave him a gentle punch on the shoulder, her face radiating joy. 'It's happening. It's really happening.'

Bliss could not have been more delighted. 'And about bloody time,' he said. 'I can't imagine how you feel right now.'

'To a certain degree it's probably not fully sunk in yet. Each tiny step forward feels like such a huge leap. But this is the big one. This is the FO telling me it's done. All we have to do now is settle on a date and time.'

'I'm so happy for you, Pen. For you both. Drink tonight to celebrate?'

Chandler nodded. 'Too bloody right.'

'I'm in the chair. Just don't get too rat-arsed. We both know how soppy you can be when you're pissed.'

On their way back to the command centre, Bliss said little more. His mind was now spiralling and sucking thoughts down like a whirlpool. A trio of odious characters had given them nothing, other than the notion they were barking up the wrong tree. As they neared Sutton End, Bliss eventually turned to his partner. 'Did you believe him?' he asked. 'Sergeant Waring, I mean.'

After a slight pause, Chandler answered, 'I believed in some of the things he said. But he was being very precise, exact in every response. Almost as if what he didn't say was of equal importance. I'm not as convinced as he is that he's such a big deal in their organisation. Frankly, boss, although Waring might well be working for the Baker family, there's no way they are going to tell a serving police officer of their intentions to carry out mass murder.'

Bliss scratched the scar on his forehead. 'I think you're right. It doesn't seem likely that they'd share such information with us cops, no matter how bent. Too great a risk. On the other hand, that doesn't make him wrong about the Bakers not being involved. They might not tell him directly, but it's the kind of thing that would eventually find its way to his ear.'

'So what are you saying?' Chandler asked him.

'I'm not at all certain. Not yet, and not about any of them, either.

My problem is I believed them, but I couldn't bring myself to trust them. None of them are responsible for killing those suspects out of revenge for what they did to Charlie Baker. I'm convinced of that now. But I am wondering if we have been wearing blinkers on this one. Following only one avenue.'

'So if not the Bakers or their supporters, then who?'

Nodding, Bliss turned to look at Chandler. 'That's precisely what we must ask ourselves next. But also, I have to wonder if we've been asking the right questions at all this whole time.'

There is a lot to admire about an adder, Paul thought. *They are venomous, but not aggressive.* He knew that adders can detect ground vibrations and use this as an early-warning system, allowing them time in which to find shelter from whatever creature may be approaching them. Britain's only indigenous poisonous snake, the species is protected by law, by its camouflage, and by its own innate passiveness when it comes to confrontation. Paul liked that about them. Adders bite humans infrequently, usually when being deliberately handled, accidentally stood upon, or when feeling threatened in some obvious way.

Confident that a bite was not going to kill him, but equally sure he would become quite ill afterwards if he was bitten, Paul understood and accepted the risks he took by having his little beauty living out of her glass tank. His faith in the reptile not striking at him, even while he dangled food in front of her, was based on a simple gut feeling. He had no idea whether she was able to recognise his shape, form, colour, or scent, and no clue if his familiarity played any part in the beautiful creature's decision-making process when it came to sinking her fangs and injecting her venom. All he possessed was his instinct, and for Paul this was more than enough;

it had served him well down the years, his mere existence providing ample evidence of that.

He needed his little amusements more so now than ever. He knew he was going to have to lie low for a few days, perhaps even longer. The last hit had been too tight for comfort, despite the plan unfolding exactly as predicted.

His belief from the outset was that the full-on frontal attack by the vehicle would draw out one of two officers he assumed were deployed inside the house. Having stepped outside the car, he made just enough noise to draw attention. The moment he saw the curtain first twitch and then glide back, he leaned in through the open car door and switched the lights on full beam. After gunning the engine and releasing the brake, the automatic gearbox did the rest of the work for him.

By the time the police officer had rushed out of the front door, Paul was standing in the darker reaches of gloom away to the officer's left. As she raced across the gravel path to approach the vehicle, he stepped out and shot the woman three times. The first spun her around toward him, resulting in her taking the following two bullets in the face. He did not pause to check for a pulse once she went down.

Unarmed and ill-prepared, the second cop put up no fight at all. Three shots dispatched him before he had even risen to his feet. Sheltering beneath the table and behind the cop, Alan Brewer wept and begged for mercy. Paul dragged the hyperventilating man out by his ankles, Brewer screaming and kicking as his face bumped along the timber-boarded floor. Three rapid bursts subsequently ended any lingering resolve. This time, Paul carried the saw clipped to a belt around his waist. When he was finished with it, he withdrew a large freezer bag out of his jacket pocket, which he proceeded to unfold. With the bag fully expanded, he puffed out the opening, slipped the head inside and slid the ziplock across the seal to secure his prize.

While he worked, he listened intently for sirens, but what Paul heard was a racing engine coming hard and fast. If he had not planned ahead, he would have had to fight against armed officers out of his main egress route. A skirmish, he believed, he would ultimately win, but one which was needless and carried with it danger and the opportunity for chance occurrence. Instead, he slipped out of the back door. By the time the firearms unit began scouring the inside of Brewer's property, he had made his way through the line of trees, heading toward the spot where he had parked the van.

He drove a pre-selected route away from the scene, suspecting he would not encounter a single vehicle along the way. He was right about that. Emerging onto the London Road which ran parallel to the A16, Paul circled around and eventually made his way back to the caravan. He took all necessary precautions, but his journey was unhindered.

Thinking about the incident afterwards, Paul felt elated. It had been a risk removing another name from the list on the same day as the undertaker, but at the time he believed he had only one more opportunity before the police found a way to secure the remaining murderers inside some sort of safe house.

Having received word earlier that the cops running the investigation had acted exactly as predicted, Paul accepted he would have to be patient for a while. For as long as it took. He had more time to waste than they did. Eventually the security would be pulled, allowing the four men and one woman to return to their homes – that is if the police were able to convince Nicolai Stoian to leave the Roma enclave in the first place.

Paul needed to find out more about the situation, because despite the notorious reputation enjoyed by the Roma community, especially inside one of their own campsites, if Stoian remained *in situ* then Paul believed he was capable of getting to the man at his leisure. Not that there was any rush. He was going to have to wait for things to quieten down anyway, so he was not about to take any unwarranted chances.

On the previous day, the undertaker's response to questioning had been interesting. Bluntstone had shown no bravery, nor was he irrationally loyal in the face of torture. He genuinely seemed puzzled as to who had been responsible for provoking Baker's murder. He eventually admitted his own involvement – at the point where the man realised Paul was capable of inflicting far greater pain and devastation than anyone else who might prefer his silence on the matter – but could draw on only confused memories when it came to the hours prior to the stabbings. Realising Tim Bluntstone could offer him no further insight, Paul finally put the man out of his misery. The eyes of the undertaker had been grateful for that at the end.

Paul thought of himself as the adder, the beautiful reptile who fed on mice to the point of satiation. He, too, had dined well on his kills. Figuratively, at least. He was no cannibal. Eight heads in his outdoor freezer had so far earned him £40,000. Not his usual going rate, though more than enough to buy him many further trips to the coast, and plenty of fish and chip dinners. But he had given his promise. There were six further heads to claim, £30,000 more to fund his future pleasures and whims.

Biding his time was no bad thing. It gave him scope to engage his hunger once more. Meanwhile, he had his little beauty, his music, his booze. What more could he possibly want? After all, he was completely safe. Because the police were never going to work out who he was or where they might find him.

B liss was unhappy. Mostly with himself. Like everyone else involved, he had become too fixated on the Baker family and members of their cabal. It was easy enough to believe that one or more of them was responsible for hiring somebody to kill thirteen people in order to avenge the murder of Charlie Baker. So easy, neither he nor his team had considered any other reasonable alternatives.

By now the mobile command centre was heaving, with everyone from the task force in place plus the firearms officer from Huntingdon, Inspector Eric Price, in addition to DCI Edwards. As each pairing returned to the trailer, they related their experiences to the rest of the group. When Bliss mentioned the hot drinks they were given in Boston, there was a release of much-needed laughter.

'Oh, no question they spat in it,' DCI Warburton confirmed, wincing at the thought.

'If not worse,' Smyth offered in his dour, low growl.

Bliss did not want to imagine what the "worse" might consist of.

The interviews had so far revealed a single common thread emerging from the two main groups of people questioned. From Baker's acolytes came ringing endorsements of the man, with only a couple of his fellow Freemasons confiding otherwise. It was to be expected – these men and women held powerful positions within the community, both willing and fully capable of doing absolutely anything to distance themselves from the mire in which Charlie Baker was known to have been buried up to his neck.

One woman, a television presenter working for a regional BBC news team, told Short and Bishop she regarded Baker as a bully and a misogynist who fought a determined but ultimately futile campaign against her joining the lodge. The lodge was not part of the Grand Lodge fraternity so she was allowed to join the local ranks before Baker managed to take a firm hold of proceedings, by which time they had also voted in a second female applicant.

The TV presenter – who was desperate to keep her name out of the investigation – freely admitted to Baker often using the lodge associates to turn against other members of the community whose business or ideals happened not to coincide with those of the Baker family. According to DS Short, the woman never came straight out and said she believed in the man's volatile and criminal reputation, but did confide to both her and Bishop that she was surprised by nothing of which the man was accused.

The other outspoken lodge affiliate was a businessman, who had stood on behalf of the Liberal Democrats in the last general election and who now served on the county council. His thoughts on Baker were that the world was a better place without the man in it, and while his fellow Masons suspected Baker to be guilty of many things, none of them ever provided firm evidence to back up their opinions. He did query a senior police officer's role, but the superintendent batted away each of their questions with one of his own and the interview eventually stumbled to an unsatisfying halt.

Every Lincolnshire police officer questioned appeared to speak with a single voice. They knew nothing about the allegations against them, less still about the inner workings of the Charles Baker fiefdom. It was not what Bliss had hoped for, but neither were the responses entirely unexpected. Nobody was going to admit to being aware of any revenge plans made by the Baker family until verifiable evidence against them was presented, and perhaps not even then. It was one thing to be suspected and charged with being on the take from a known local villain, quite another to have it proven against you.

This aspect of the case reminded Bliss of everything he had experienced just a few months earlier. He felt for any of the officers currently under investigation if they were as innocent as they claimed to be. In his own case, he had, for a second time, been suspected of murdering his own wife some seventeen years ago. He knew the truth, but the false evidence stacked against him was daunting. That was a situation he managed to extricate himself from, but the week or so during which that cold shadow threatened to engulf him was one of the worst he had endured since the loss of his wife.

Were there officers out there now sitting at home with a drink in their hands dreading the dawn of each new day?

Bliss knew better than most that just because people suspected you of wrongdoing did not make you guilty of anything. He felt a stab of remorse at the possibility of his actions causing the same kind of strain and worry for innocent colleagues. Yet the process of interviewing them had been as unavoidable as it was unpleasant.

Time and again his thoughts turned to the prospect of he and his team being mistaken. With all of their stories told and the meeting becoming negative and doleful, Bliss decided to raise the notion of the task force being on entirely the wrong path.

'Sergeant Lewis Waring is, to my mind at least, an officer who spent quite some time providing Charlie Baker and his family with information. I don't necessarily agree with his assertion that, as a high card in the Baker deck, he would have known if the Bakers had taken out a contract on the thirteen suspects. But I do have to ask a question arising from the interview: what if our basic premise is incorrect? Is it possible for there to be a reason for the murder of these people other than revenge? If so, what is it? I think we need to address this as a matter of urgency, because if we do, it may lead us to a whole new pool of suspects, and I for one believe this is the perfect opportunity for us to digress.'

Warburton, who sat between Barry Smyth and DCI Edwards, nodded and tapped the table with a perfectly manicured fingernail. 'I second that. I realise I am partially, perhaps even largely, responsible for the task force taking this particular path. It's the bloody Occam's Razor theory that the most obvious solution is likely to be the correct one. Thirteen people from within the local community at the time took it upon themselves to murder Charles Baker – at least that's what we believe to be true. When a number of those thirteen suspects are not only shot but also beheaded, it smacks of being personal, and the most logical people to start looking at were the Baker family and their friends, including our colleagues who helped them out in exchange for a nice backhander. But Inspector Bliss is absolutely right to question whether, in this case, the most likely answer is perhaps the wrong one.'

'Are you saying you now doubt your entire case strategy?' Edwards asked, looking askance at her fellow DCI.

'To be accurate, boss, it's *my* case strategy,' Bliss said. 'Yes, I leaned heavily on everything both DCI Warburton and Sergeant Smyth told me, but I agreed with them in respect of the Baker family being firmly in the frame. I'd argue that a case strategy can sometimes take a positive from a negative, and in this case having investigated and interviewed relevant people, the perceived negative of this murder spree not being anything to do with the Bakers actually becomes a positive lead. It's our job now to ask ourselves what our shiny new lead might be.'

Edwards cleared her throat. 'That's a healthy spin to put on it, Bliss. But it does leave us rather in limbo all the same. The supers and I did as you asked and stalled the media until later on this afternoon. But at the briefing they will be foaming at the mouth and we need to feed them something tasty. Something they can get their teeth into. Something I am not hearing as yet.'

'Because we are only now discussing it. We've been busy running down leads and interviewing witnesses. Standard procedure. With none of them panning out, we have to turn our attentions elsewhere. Again, this is nothing unusual. We take our theories as far as they will go, and when we come up short we start looking in other directions. Which is what we're about to do, and I'll gladly open the floor to all of you at this point.'

'Well, I still can't see beyond the obvious,' Bishop admitted with a languid shrug of those massive shoulders. 'Who else could have a grudge against those thirteen people? From what I hear, the outcome delighted many local families.'

'So maybe it's not locals at all,' Chandler offered. 'If Baker was involved with organised crime in some way, then perhaps one of his national connections didn't take kindly to a valuable asset being taken off the map.'

Bliss liked where that idea was heading, and expanded upon it. 'I made a call to a contact at the NCA on Monday. I also followed it up. Charlie Baker never appeared on their radar, which doesn't necessarily mean he's not connected.'

'Even so, is an OC boss likely to order such a hit?' Warburton asked, looking around the room. 'Killing thirteen people seems to me like an extreme reaction. Their deaths achieve little, and is high risk because of the attention it draws.'

Bliss understood the logic. He had no intention of dismissing the idea entirely, although the DCI's argument poured cold water all over the flames Chandler's suggestion had ignited beneath him. He shook his head in despair.

'So where does all of this leave us?' he asked. 'Right where we started. And if that's where we are, then we have no choice but to go back even further, all the way to basics. Which means we start with motive. As far as I can tell, nobody stands to gain from these murders. Which is why we went for revenge last time around. And it's still the most obvious motivation we have, in my view.'

Acting DI Short said, 'For eight carefully planned murders, each of which so far has included decapitation, we have to be looking at something personal. So, yes, revenge remains high on the list of motives in my estimation.'

'Which means we're back to the Baker family. There's no way we should be clearing them yet. Just because we got nowhere in our interviews with them, and don't seem to have any specific feelings about them one way or another, doesn't exclude them from further investigation.'

'Other motives?' Edwards queried. 'Do we have any?'

The room fell silent. Bliss felt one or two eyes turned his way, as if expecting him to pull a rabbit out of a hat he did not possess. His mind was swirling as he tried moving his thoughts away from the act of revenge. Each time he set them loose they funnelled back, insisting he and his team were on the right track. And yet, Bliss remained unconvinced. Yes, it still seemed the most likely path to follow, but so far the task force had drawn blanks. Applying further pressure to the Baker family looked to be the next positive move, but Bliss knew there was no clear evidence with which to argue for arrests.

One thought became ensnared for a second or two as it swam past him amidst the torrent caught up in the maelstrom. A single notion refusing to be ignored. The next time it came around, Bliss latched on and held it firm. It was only the germ of an idea, really. But as the team had nothing new to work with, and nobody seated at the table had any suggestions, Bliss figured he had little to lose by exploring the possibility.

'So what if we *are* looking at this completely wrong?' he said. He forced himself to keep both hands away from the scar on his brow. He looked up and met the eager gazes of those who sat with him at the table.

'In what way, Bliss?' Edwards asked.

'I wonder if it's the sheer volume of murders putting us off our game here. Reduce it to a single murder in your mind. A single contract. Let's start with the murder of Charlie Baker, because that's where all of this began in the first place.

'I don't see thirteen people coming together at a meeting all with exactly the same thought in mind: to share the killing of Baker between them, one stab each, none of them knowing which of them held the knife that ended the man's life, but each of them with something to lose if they gave it up. Somebody had to be the first to say it out loud, even if the grumblings from others laid the groundwork.'

'But what does that have to do with those thirteen later being put on a hit list?' RPU officer Smyth asked.

'I think I know where Bliss is taking this,' Price said. The Cambs firearms officer stared hard at him. 'You're thinking somebody built on their own frustrations and anger, got the rest of the community riled up, to the point where suggesting a single stab each was no big deal, with none of them needing to feel any guilt because they could never be certain which of the blows was fatal.'

'I am.'

'And by extension, you're asking whether this same individual is now getting rid of them one by one so that they can never tell anybody outside of the group who stirred them up.'

Bliss nodded. 'That's what I'm wondering, yes. Something along those lines.'

'Except for one small detail. All thirteen are in the clear,' Bishop pointed out. 'The CPS decided not to file charges.'

'For now,' Bliss said, nodding. 'Doesn't mean it was never going to happen, that the police were never going to get one of the thirteen to crack. Fissures behind the scenes may have started to show. It's a bloody hard secret to keep, after all. Brings a lot of pressure to bear. Something might have been said, or perhaps occurred, to cause whoever stoked them up to take drastic action. To hire somebody to do their dirty work.'

'Are we saying it's someone inside the thirteen?' Short asked.

'Doesn't it have to be?' Chandler argued. 'Surely you couldn't have a situation where somebody got those thirteen people so enraged they followed this person's initiative but then allowed that very same person to sit it out? Could that possibly ever work?'

'I don't see it happening, either,' Warburton said. 'But I am intrigued by the idea Inspector Bliss has posed. We're looking for alternative theories, beyond the Baker family and revenge. As the inspector suggested, if we dismiss the thirteen people and think of just a single hit, then it's not so absurd to imagine somebody putting down a minion who did a job for them. Extrapolate that to include thirteen people and the theory still holds together.'

DCI Edwards shifted in her seat, clasped both hands on the table and said, 'Except it's not thirteen, is it? Aren't we now saying it's feasible for one of them to be behind the whole thing? And presumably the killings are continuing because the person behind them is still alive, which means it has to be one of the five suspects left on the list.'

Bliss held up a hand to forestall any further conversation. 'In essence you're correct, boss. *If* the instigator was indeed one of the thirteen. And while I'm not dismissing the idea of him or her being among them, I think it's just as likely to have been suggested by someone who was part of a much wider audience, from which thirteen of them volunteered amidst a frenzy of mass hysteria.'

'Which doesn't narrow things down for us at all,' Chandler said. 'Because we have no idea when such a meeting might have taken place, nor who attended.'

'You're right. On the other hand, the five people currently under our protection were almost certainly there at the time. Now that they know we were telling the truth about them being on a hit list, they may be more inclined to talk to us. If necessary we could make it clear that at no point are we going to query them about their role in the murder of Charlie Baker, only their attendance at a meeting during which it was discussed.'

'Can that possibly work?' Edwards asked.

Bliss took a breath and said, 'There's only one way to find out.'

The designated safe house was a converted barn on farmland located to the southern edge of Kirton Holme. The farm, including all of its associated properties, structures, equipment and land, was owned by the Richard Kenwright Estate, Kenwright having been a chief constable in the county of Lincolnshire throughout the seventies. Although the man himself passed away shortly after the turn of the millennium, his family remained great supporters of the police, who previously used the property to secure a major drug dealer turned supergrass.

At its hefty oak dining table sat Brian Stout and Jane Monkton, the two Sutton End residents who had opted for protection from the outset. Bradley Harris and Liam Storey, who made up the quartet of protectees secured away inside the barn, joined them. The safe house manager had allocated each of the suspects a bedroom of their own, leaving the other two beds available for use by officers on a shift basis. Nicolai Stoian had once again declined any form of outside security – according to Tudor Chipcui, that was.

Unhappy at being blanked by the Roma elder, Bliss had discussed the issue with his team as well as a GRT liaison from

Peterborough City Council. After listening to advice, he made the decision to keep an eye on the site, but not to attempt forced entry into Stoian's home. As irritated as he was by Chipcui's stance, the feeling of being powerless to act angered Bliss even more.

He and Chandler sat with the suspects, the remaining four task force members observing from two sofas placed either side of the rectangular table in the centre of the enormous dining area. The barn conversion was tasteful and spacious, its austere décor much to Bliss's taste.

Despite the foursome having spent only a few hours together so far, tension cut through the atmosphere in the room like a sharp serrated blade through tender steak, setting everybody on edge. Inside the house, six members of the firearms unit stood on full alert. Eight additional gun-toting officers patrolled the immediate grounds, while four armed response vehicles cruised the streets surrounding the property, each containing two firearms experts. All twenty-two armed officers communicated via a single control centre, switched to a secure bandwidth known only to them and their command base.

Bliss refused to consider separate interviews, which was why all of the protectees sat around the dining table together. He put a great deal of stock in being able to assess the reactions of people, and he was interested to see how these four interacted during pressure-point questioning.

Following brief introductions, Bliss got straight into it.

'We are not gathered here to discuss the murder of Charles Baker,' he said. 'Not directly, at any rate. Neither are we here to talk about your current situation. What we are interested in is what I've come to think of as ground zero for this entire awful series of events.

'See, we have learned that on several occasions, members of the public from Sutton End and the surrounding region met in the church hall to discuss the levels of intimidation and criminality relating to Baker and his cronies. It is now our suspicion that at some point, fuelled by justifiable anger and righteous indignation, the people attending those meetings rallied together in order to take matters into their own hands. After all, if the police weren't going to do anything, then who did that leave to take action?

'The way I see it, somebody ladled chum into the water and waited for the sharks to arrive. Then, as the waters churned, the predators let loose on a feeding frenzy in the shape of Charles Baker, who was used as fresh bait. What I don't see happening is thirteen people separately coming to the same conclusion regarding Baker's imminent demise, and in such a way as to leave nobody clear about who actually killed the man. No, we reckon that idea, and the subsequent stirring-up of the crowd, came from a single source. We're convinced of it. And we want to know who the source was.'

'You think it must be one of us,' Jane Monkton said, folding her arms across her chest. She had cleaned herself up considerably, and looked all the better for wearing fresh, smart clothing. 'One of the remaining suspects. That's what this is all about, really. Once again the police have decided to blame us for something we didn't do.'

Bliss shook his head. 'Not necessarily, no. I won't lie and tell you we've cleared you all of suspicion, but our feeling is there were more than thirteen people involved at these meetings and the person who stirred it all up need not have taken part in the murder itself.'

He was intent on the faces of all four suspects. First of all, he searched their expressions for signs of guilt. If none registered, then he at least wanted to see in whose direction their gaze slipped; especially if three of them focussed on a single individual. Bliss also looked for any obvious sign of culpability. Not in respect of the murder of Charlie Baker, but specifically in regard to their attending the meetings he described. He knew Chandler would be doing much the same from her position alongside him.

What Bliss saw disappointed him. If guilt existed at all here, it was greatly suppressed and restricted to involvement in the murder itself, not for whipping up the kind of mob mentality required to convince twelve other people to become murderers. It occurred to him then that any form of brainwashing of such depth and detail could last only so long, and a thought winked into life.

'I think it's quite likely there was a meeting on the night Baker was stabbed to death,' Bliss said then, taking a chance. 'I believe it was suggested at a previous meeting that some kind of action be taken against the man, but on that particular evening those attending became caught up in the moment, its impetus inspired by somebody who wanted Baker dead but did not want to get their own hands dirty. Sound familiar?'

Brian Stout, who appeared timid and fearful on the surface, yet with a strong conviction when he spoke, said, 'Tudor Chipcui.' Stout nodded a couple of times as if to reaffirm the suggestion to himself. 'He was there that night. It was only his second meeting as far as I'm aware, but his fellow Roma associates had been getting the rest of us agitated. They claimed to be ready and willing to tackle Baker themselves, but demanded to know why we were all talk and no action. Chipcui dug deeper with that accusation, and really got the crowd wound up. They questioned our desire to act in order to improve our lives. It was like some kind of spiritual thing, only we were being driven on to do something bad rather than good.'

'What the fuck, Brian?' This from Bradley Harris, who glared at Stout. The knuckles of his fingers turned white as they splayed wide on the table. 'Why are you telling them that?'

'Why are you telling them *anything*?' Liam Storey demanded.

But Monkton was shaking her head. 'No, no, it's okay. Brian is only admitting to being at meetings, isn't that right, Bri?'

Stout nodded furiously. 'Yes. Of course. Nothing anyone can do about people attending a meeting at a church hall.'

'Nothing at all,' Bliss confirmed. 'In fact, when you have someone like Baker ruining things for you in a small community, it would be odd if the locals didn't want to do something about it.

Like Jane and Brian say, there's nothing illegal about being at a meeting, no matter what was discussed and agreed upon during the session. Bearing that in mind, do the three of you remember that night the way Brian does? Was Tudor Chipcui leading the sabre-rattling call to arms?'

Monkton blew out a long breath and nodded. 'That's exactly how I remember it, too. It got loud and aggressive inside the hall. You could hardly hear yourself think.'

With obvious reluctance, both Harris and Storey admitted to being at the meeting. They also agreed that the Roma elder had enjoyed pumping everyone up, calling for action against Baker, for the people of Sutton End to take back their town and regain some pride.

'But that's all you get from me,' Storey added. Bliss knew the man was forty, but the manual labour he did working a large farm gave him the sinewy muscle tone of a thirty-year-old and the ravaged complexion of a quinquagenarian. 'I was there. We all were. But that's where it ended for us. That's all I will say about that night.'

The three other suspects nodded their agreement. Happy to admit to attending a meeting at which somebody other than them stirred up the trouble, but not to being wound up enough to commit murder as a consequence.

Which was fine by Bliss. Though he was troubled at the thought of Tudor Chipcui being at the root of Baker's death. On the one hand it made sense. The Roma community had probably suffered badly at Baker's hands, leading to a loss of income as well as face. In addition, the young woman allegedly raped by Baker was from the same Roma camp. And who better to be able to trace the four Romanians who returned home only to be murdered there?

Yet at the same time, Bliss sensed it didn't quite fit. Why would Chipcui allow seven of his fellow Romas to take part in the murder of Charlie Baker, only to then have them killed along with the other six members of the community who stabbed Baker to death? That aspect made no sense at all to Bliss.

Nonetheless, he called a halt to the discussion and gathered the task force around him outside the barn to confer about what they had learned.

'I have to say, none of what I just heard sounded rehearsed,' DCI Warburton said. 'I think the other three are reluctant to admit to being there on the night in question, at the meeting itself, but I believed Brian Stout when he told us how it went down.'

'I have to agree,' Chandler said. 'He seemed completely genuine to me. I have no doubt they were all involved in the murder of Baker, but as that's not what we're here for at this precise moment, I think what we got from them draws us closer to the man who may well have inspired it.'

'But then also decided to wipe them all out, including seven of his own men?'

The reservation in Smyth's voice echoed Bliss's own doubts, which he expressed next.

'There's a chain of logic here which to my mind is missing a few links,' he said. 'I think we can agree that our four suspects are probably telling us the truth, at least in respect of Tudor Chipcui beating the drum for some form of reprisal against Charlie Baker. As a result, he gets bumped up to the top of our list of people to interview. And while we're there, we can also speak to Stoian again if possible, given he remains on the hitman's list. As for the elder having anything to do with our assassin, I've yet to be convinced.'

The six of them debated for a further twenty minutes, going back and forth on the main bones of contention. By the end, the only decision left to agree upon was who should pay the Roma camp a visit.

Bliss had known immediately that the unenviable chore of interviewing the Roma elder would come down to him and DCI Warburton. For any number of reasons it was the right call. The remaining four members of the task force team did not remain at the safe house, nor did they return to the command centre. Instead they parked up in two vehicles on either side of the road leading into the site. If somebody decided to make a break for it, they were ready to take them down.

For a second time it was Warburton who made the initial approach, although on this occasion Bliss accompanied the DCI and stood a step behind her when she knocked on the door to Tudor Chipcui's home. If things became physical, Bliss wanted to be on hand. The two detectives had decided their initial approach should be to try to persuade Chipcui and Stoian to accompany them back to the mobile command centre in which a formal interview would then take place. The intention was not to add pressure to the Roma men, rather to remove them from their comfort zone. However, the Roma elder was far too streetwise to agree to any such suggestion.

'Warrant,' he said bluntly, holding out a hand palm upwards.

'I'm not arresting you, Mr Chipcui,' Warburton explained, shaking her head. 'We simply have further questions for you and Mr Stoian. We need not even ask them under caution unless we all feel it wise to do so for your own protection. We'd happily have spoken to Mr Stoian with the other remaining suspects if he'd agreed to us protecting him.'

'Stoian protected here,' Chipcui said.

'I'm sure you and the rest of the community are fully committed to that objective, sir, but I can assure you the protection we offer is guaranteed to be effective.'

'Mr Brewer might not agree, I think.'

Bliss noted Warburton's cheek pulse at the jibe. Her manner when she responded remained civil and courteous. 'That was extremely unfortunate. This is a different level of protection altogether. A different type of guarantee.'

'Guarantee here.' The man nodded, his hooded eyes giving nothing away.

'Will you answer a few questions here, then, Mr Chipcui? Perhaps we could use the same facility as last time, and Mr Stoian can then join us.'

'Ask now. Here. No Stoian.'

Warburton sighed and turned to look at Bliss. He had to make an instant decision. He wondered why Stoian was now being kept out of reach, and the thought that maybe the man might no longer be available on a permanent basis wriggled across his mind. What he did not want to do was leave without gaining any impression at all from the elder. He gave the DCI a nod and switched his attention back to the short and wide man standing on the threshold.

Warburton also turned, and requested co-operation one last time. Chipcui's stubborn refusal caused her to shake her head in exasperation. 'Very well, then. Mr Chipcui, we understand that several men from your community attended meetings at the Sutton End church hall last year. Those meetings were devoted to complaints about Charles Baker.'

'Baker is bad man,' Chipcui growled, waving a dismissive hand.

'Quite. Hence the meetings. Now, in addition to those men I just mentioned, of whom Nicolai Stoian was one, we have information suggesting you also attended two of those meetings.'

The Romanian stared back at the DCI. Not once did he switch his gaze to Bliss.

'Mr Chipcui?' Warburton prompted. 'Did you attend meetings at the church hall? Meetings at which Charles Baker was the topic of discussion. And please remember that we can easily obtain verification from others, so don't bother to lie.'

'Yes.'

'And did those meetings concern the behaviour of Charles Baker?'

'Yes.'

'In which case, what was your response, sir?'

'To what?'

'To those concerns? To what you heard at those meetings?'

'No response.' Chipcui shrugged. 'No response.'

'So you did not urge others to stand up to Mr Baker? You did not suggest they find a way to end the issues each of them had with him?'

'I say already. No response.'

'How about you, Mr Chipcui?' Bliss interrupted. 'Did you have any issues with Mr Baker directly?'

The man huffed and shook his head. 'I tell you this twice now.'

'No, sir. Those answers were responses to a different question entirely, about what took place in the church hall. I am asking if you personally had issues with Charles Baker. Issues perhaps affecting your businesses?'

The Roma elder glowered at Bliss, his head seeming to shrink back into the neck as if seeking to hide itself away within the fleshy folds. He raised a hand and jabbed a thick finger at Bliss. 'No. This is my response,' he said. Then turned on his heels and slammed the door shut with him on the other side of it.

Warburton turned to look at Bliss, arching her eyebrows. 'That was a roaring success,' she said.

Bliss grinned. 'What were you expecting? A signed and sealed confession.'

'Not exactly. Do you find him refusing to let us speak with Nicolai Stoian at all odd?'

They started walking back down the narrow path to where Bliss had left the Insignia. He shook his head. 'Not really. I have a hunch Stoian, if he is still above ground, is a good fifteen hundred miles east of here right now.'

Settling into their seats, Warburton asked Bliss if he believed Chipcui's version of events. He started the engine and let it idle. Gave the question some thought before responding, 'I wouldn't trust the man as far as I can throw him, which is not a long way at all given his physical stamp. It's not a stretch to imagine him being involved in Baker's murder, just as easy to believe he was behind the incitement that resulted in Baker's death. What I am still having trouble with is believing he would then put seven of his own people on the hit list. Or if I could even begin to believe in that story, that he'd leave Stoian alive until now. Only part of it adds up for me.'

Warburton was nodding. 'I agree with you entirely. Judging by the look on his face and his behaviour this time around, I'd say the man is angry. Either at being given up and betrayed, or perhaps being in the frame at all. Beyond that, I really couldn't tell.'

'So, not the full picture?'

'No. Definitely not. I think our four musketeers were right to say he was in the mix when it came to stirring up trouble. But I also agree with you when you say he's unlikely to be in the frame for the current spate of killings.'

Bliss blew out a troubled sigh. 'Not much to take back to DCI Edwards for her media briefing, is it? More questions than answers.'

'If you'd like me to, Jimmy, I'll have a word. DCI to DCI. I don't want to go around you or over you, but Alicia might listen to me without judgement. I'm from a different county, I'm of the same rank, and, whether it counts or not, we are both female.'

Bliss shook his head. 'Thank you, Diane. I appreciate it. Really I do. But I was given the reins on this, so I can't just shrug them off when it suits me. If you fancy being in the room as backup, I won't say no. I genuinely believe we've done everything possible up to this point. But some things you have to do yourself. And taking a bollocking from DCI Edwards is one of them in my case.'

By the time they got back to the command centre, DCI Edwards had returned to Thorpe Wood to prepare for the media. Bliss remembered to ask his team if they had managed to grab lunch while he and Warburton were visiting the Roma site. Pleased to receive an affirmative response, Bliss insisted the DCI take a break and do the same.

'What about you, boss?' Chandler asked. 'You not taking a break today?'

'I have an errand to run, so I'll pick something up while I'm gone. You, Bish and Mia can meet me back at HQ in time for the briefing.'

'What about our meeting with DCI Edwards?' Warburton asked Bliss before he stepped outside.

'That was when I thought she'd still be here. There's no point in you traipsing all the way over to Peterborough.'

'But we agreed I should be in on the discussion.'

'True. But only to add weight to my argument. Seems pointless now. I'll cope with whatever the DCI tosses my way.'

What he did not mention was the plan that had come to him as they were driving away from the Roma camp. Outside in the school car park he placed a call and then pushed hard back to the city. He found a parking space at the back of the Rivergate Shopping arcade, then made his way inside, taking the route toward the courthouse. Before the exit, Bliss ducked into a little Italian bistro. The person he had arranged to see was already sitting at a table waiting for him.

Sandra Bannister waved a hand, a broad smile plastered across her face. Not for the first time, Bliss wondered what cost this devil might place on his soul for conspiring with her, though in truth he trusted Bannister more than he had her predecessors.

The woman stood to greet him. She was tall – close to six foot in what looked like high heels – and slender, with a narrow waist and long brown hair pulled around the back of her neck to drape down over her right shoulder. It was a fashionable look, and it suited her. From her newspaper's online bio, Bliss knew the journalist was forty-one, but she could easily have passed for someone a decade younger.

'It's good to meet you formally at long last,' Bannister told him, as they sat down at the table for two.

'You, too. Though we would have met soon enough anyway for our interviews.'

'Of course. Which was why I was so intrigued by your call, and could not resist your offer to buy me a coffee.'

She had waited for him to arrive before ordering. When the waiter sidled up to their table, it was just a large latte for her. Bliss was hungry, and so went with a black coffee and a serving of arancini.

'What on earth is arancini?' Bannister asked as the waiter scooted away.

'Stuffed rice balls, coated with deep-fried breadcrumbs. The rice is usually mixed with ragu, mozzarella and peas. They make them in the shape of an egg here rather than a ball, but they are still delicious.'

'So you're a foodie?' Bannister appeared surprised by this revelation.

Bliss laughed at the suggestion. 'Unless I order a takeaway or eat pub grub, my meals at home usually consist of dry cereal, tins of rice pudding, cheese toasties, or peanut butter on bread. That's not to say I don't enjoy a decent meal, I just rarely have time to treat myself.'

Bannister flashed her brown eyes. 'Wow! I've already got more background material out of you than I ever expected.'

'Yeah, well, make the most of it. My history with you people is not very good.'

'Do you mean journalists or brown-haired white women?'

Bliss raised his eyebrows. 'Ah, excellent comeback on the "you people" jibe. I'm going to have to watch myself around you, Ms Bannister.'

The reporter sighed. 'Even now, here in this quiet and relaxed setting and just the two of us sitting together, you still won't call me Sandra?'

'Familiarity can breed contempt. Either way. I suffered some misfortune with those who came before you. During my first posting here, Sheryl Craig gave me a bit of a pasting in what was then the pages of the *Evening Telegraph*. At the back end of last year, it was Evette Jordan's turn to get on my case. Mind you, it was my issue with her that forced my DCI to stop me from running media briefings, so her aggressiveness may have actually done me a favour.'

Bannister grinned. 'Evette is still with us, just moved to the editorial team.'

'Well, you've been fair with me so far, so I take as I find.'

'Me, too. At my core I am looking for stories, but I have no interest in sensationalism for the sake of it. Take these planned interviews, for example. Yes, I'll be looking for some deep back-ground, because that's part of who you are, and who you are almost brought down the entire police service here in the city. I don't want my book to dwell on your personal life, but it wouldn't be much of a book if it didn't touch on it at least.'

'And of course, the delay in my fulfilling that promise to you hasn't hurt, because now my back story has an ending.'

'You're referring to the events of the summer.'

'I am.'

'In all honesty, I'm rather looking forward to exploring what happened in more detail with you. Though I expect there's a great deal you can't tell me, particularly concerning the IOPC interest.'

'In that you are correct.' Bliss nodded, recalling the embarrassment he had caused the Independent Office for Police Conduct, none of which had so far been made public. Bliss was still awaiting a legal decision on the issue.

'In which case, let me just say how glad I was at the eventual outcome. I'm sure you won't be surprised to learn that I have a better relationship with one or two of your colleagues, but none of them have proven to be anywhere near as interesting a person as you are.'

Bliss sensed the journalist's sincerity. Their drinks arrived, along with the plate of two large and golden Arancini, heat coming off them in waves. Bliss caught Bannister regarding the dish with fascination. He pulled her side plate across and forked one of the two oval rice balls onto it. Nudging it back in the journalist's direction, Bliss said, 'Here, try one. I promise you it'll be the best thing you eat all week.'

Bannister thanked him, and again when he warned her to leave it for a few moments as the filling inside was molten. 'Make a cut in it and allow the steam to pour out,' Bliss advised, demonstrating the technique on his own egg-shaped snack. The resulting aroma was wonderful.

'So tell me why we're here,' she said a moment later, looking into his wide-open gaze.

'Because I need your help. Simple as that, really.'

'Hmm. The word "need" covers so many possibilities and permutations. I take it there's something in it for me.'

'For both of us. Let's just say it will take the heat off me, and will put you in the good books of your employers.'

'I'm always in their good books.'

'Then you can bank it for the day that changes. As we both know it eventually will.'

Bannister gave him a curious look. He could not tell what it meant, but he saw he had piqued her interest. He decided to push on.

'I take it you're intending going to HQ later on for the formal media briefing?'

'HQ? So that's what you call Thorpe Wood police station? How interesting. I'll store that little flash of colour away for a rainy day. But in answer to your question, yes I am going. Is there a reason why I shouldn't?'

Bliss thought for a moment. 'More a perfectly good reason why you won't need to,' he said. 'Not if you go along with my request.'

'There's that word again.'

'Yes. I used it deliberately this time.'

'Okay, so now tell me what you *need* from me.'

Bliss sipped some of his coffee, which was strong and tasty. He dipped his head toward the plate sitting before her. 'Let's eat first. It'll be just about right by now.'

They ate their food, which Bannister could not stop enthusing over afterwards. Bliss was less than satiated after consuming only one ball, but happy to have shared the experience with the reporter. He found himself enjoying her company, and he liked the woman even more in person.

Bliss wiped his mouth with a serviette, leaned both elbows on the table and told Bannister what was on his mind.

'The shootings are what we are here about, obviously. The first exclusive I'm giving you is that, whilst the murder of our admin worker, Kelly Gibson, is connected, it is also incidental to the main batch of murders.'

'Which confirms our own theory,' the woman told him, around the rim of her coffee cup. 'We've already sussed out for ourselves that somebody is working their way through the Baker's Dozen suspects, and Gibson did not fit the pattern.'

'You knew about the case? I'd never heard of it before.'

'Me neither. Not until someone came up with it at a staff meeting. Background checks into the two Romanian men murdered stirred somebody's memory, but then Tim Bluntstone was the name that slotted it all together. Now Alan Brewer, plus two of your own officers, I'm sorry to say.'

Bliss found her comment interesting. 'You're not sorry about Bluntstone or Brewer?' he asked. 'Or the rest of them?'

'Less so. They were killers in their own right, let's not forget.'

'Allegedly. We prosecuted none of them, so technically they were innocent men.'

'Technically. Which is not the same as actually.'

'You do surprise me. I had you down as someone who firmly believed in the maxim that people are innocent until proven guilty in a court of law.'

'I'm very much of my own mind, Inspector Bliss. I see the way the wind blows, and I tend to lean with it rather than push against it.'

'A woman after my own heart,' Bliss said approvingly. Bannister's red lipstick was several shades darker than Bliss preferred, but the colour certainly drew attention to her mouth.

'Well, let's not go too far. Not yet. You said that was the first exclusive. How many are there?'

'Two more. First of all, you said two Romanian men had been murdered. In fact, the total currently stands at six. Four of them returned to their homeland, where they were assassinated in the same way.'

'Shot three times.'

Bliss took a breath. This was the point of no return. He believed that what he was about to do was for the benefit of everyone concerned, although if his team or bosses found out they might have different opinions. But he was convinced that if the truth emerged, it would not only make the planned media briefing almost moot, but also compel Edwards to either deny or agree with the story Bannister was about to write and publish online. Bliss was certain that releasing his own news in no way jeopardised the ongoing case, and his hope and partial reason for telling the journalist was a genuine expectation of it having the opposite effect.

'Shot three times is only part of the story,' Bliss said eventually. 'What we have yet to release is the horrifying aspect that each of the Baker's Dozen suspects was also decapitated and their head removed from the scene.'

Whatever else she might be, Sandra Bannister was not a gasper. There was no sudden blur of motion as a hand shot to her mouth, no stifled cry of horror. The journalist simply sat still, staring at him unblinkingly, her chest heaving as she took in the fresh revelation. Bannister understood the significance of what she had just been told, and was taking it in slowly.

'Why are you giving me this?' she asked finally.

'Because I need you to write the story, and I need you to put it up on the *Telegraph* pages online before the briefing. The quicker you get it done the better all round. Maybe even a small *breaking news* place holder, with the highlights, if you need more time to write the piece properly.'

'Okay, but again, I have to ask why. What's the purpose from your side?'

'I'm due to meet with my DCI. At which point I have to tell her the only positive news I have for her is that we are starting afresh, going in a new direction. None of which is what she wants to hear, nor is it what she wants to tell you lot. So at the subsequent briefing I'm expecting her to vomit up some bullshit that will say plenty without telling you anything at all, and it may hurt us if she does that. In my opinion, and despite the fact that I actually advised against it earlier today, I now believe that getting the truth out there will help us with this phase of our investigation.'

Bliss was unnerved by how rapidly his mind had changed on any number of things over the course of the past few days. The only certainty seemed to be confusion.

'So, you're looking to rattle some cages. Make a few people think about this in a way they haven't done before.'

'Yes.'

'And you want to use me to do it for you?'

'Yes.'

'So, then you'll owe me all over again?'

'No.'

'No?'

'Correct. I'm giving you a huge exclusive. Which makes us even at worst, and may leave you owing me.'

Bannister blew out her cheeks. 'Do you have anything else to go with this? A suspect? A name? A motive?'

'No, no and no again. But we're working on it, believe me.'

'And what about the remaining Baker's Dozen suspects? Rumour has it you've rounded them up and have them squirrelled away under lock and key somewhere.'

'Then rumour has it slightly wrong, but I'm not giving you anything along those lines. Not yet.'

One thing he liked about Bannister was that she knew when to stop pushing. 'I'd better scoot,' the journalist said, getting to her feet. 'I'm going to need all the time I can spare putting this together.'

'I only need the salient points out there before the briefing,' Bliss reminded her. 'The real meat can come later on if you prefer. I just need your story to be the thing everyone else at the media briefing wants to discuss.'

'Don't worry about that. I'll get it done. I don't look gift horses this good in the mouth.'

'Thank you. Now I can focus on catching the bad guys.'

'Plural? You mean there's more than one?'

Bliss smiled and nodded. 'There always is, Ms Bannister,' he said. 'There always is.'

40

'Hello, stranger,' Chandler said to Bliss as he emerged from DCI Edwards' office on the third floor of the Thorpe Wood building.

Bliss grinned. It had felt strange working alongside someone else, even though Diane Warburton was a charming and beguiling companion. For all her positives – and there were many – she was not Chandler. His regular partner somehow always managed to sense his moods and instincts, knew when he wanted to discuss something and when to leave him alone. Here she was now, on a floor where she had no reason to be, at the very moment he needed to talk.

'Make the most of it,' Bliss told her. 'We'll be side-by-side again before you know it. The dynamic duo back in tandem.'

'Just so long as it's not actually *on* a tandem, that's fine with me, boss.'

He laughed. 'How's Mia working out for you during my absences?'

Chandler nodded enthusiastically. 'Very well, as it happens. I've no idea how someone of her stature can be so commanding, but she is. It's as if size doesn't enter into it. When she speaks you listen. Simple as that.'

'Some people are born to lead, Pen. Mia is most definitely one of them.'

'Indeed she is.'

'She's living proof that size doesn't matter, just as we men have always insisted.'

Chandler groaned. 'I haven't missed your archaic sense of humour, I'll tell you that for nothing.'

'Hey, that's my best material.'

'I don't doubt it. Boss, I hope you don't mind my mentioning this, but you seem to be hitting this at full throttle.'

'Is there any other way?'

'Perhaps not. Only you're supposed to be easing yourself back into the job after what you went through in the summer. Remember all that talk about nursing your health? I don't think this is what your doctors had in mind.'

Having anticipated his partner's concern, Bliss said, 'I'm not sure any of us were prepared for this case, Pen. We don't get to pick and choose, and we especially don't get to dictate the pace at which the person we're hunting operates.'

To his relief, Chandler let it go. She pulled a face and gave a long, drawn-out sigh of frustration. He was in no doubt that she would come back at him about it if the investigation was still running flat out twenty-four hours down the line, but he felt that was unlikely.

'So what did the DCI have to say?' she asked him.

It had been an awkward meeting. Fifteen minutes earlier, the article written by Sandra Bannister had hit the *Peterborough Telegraph* website. It took less than five minutes more for Edwards to receive a link to the page from the media manager. This much Bliss learned from Edwards before taking his seat. From that point on, the DCI spoke about damage limitation. So focussed was she on the leak that his update regarding the team's progress made little impression on her.

Bliss told Chandler everything as they walked back down to the major crimes area on the floor below. 'Does the leak help or hinder our investigation?' she asked.

'Neither, probably. But if it happened to lean one way or the other, I'd say it will be in our favour.'

'How d'you make that out?'

'Because whoever is behind this has been sitting comfortably so far. Now they'll be wary, wondering what else we might know but are not yet saying. Basically, Bannister's article reveals we have been squashing pretty powerful information since Sunday evening. Three days of keeping things to ourselves. My hope is this will stir it all up a little, put some doubt in the mind of the person responsible for letting a killer loose on our streets.'

'If they are brazen enough to hire a hitman, they're not likely to be overly rattled by a news item telling everyone only what has actually happened,' Chandler argued.

Bliss licked his lips. 'On the contrary. The tiniest seed of doubt can work wonders on someone's psyche. Even someone as bold as whoever this person is. They'll want the job finished sharpish, and they might just urge our killer back out there before he's ready. While we're still set up for him. Either that, or it could force them into making a mistake.'

Chandler frowned at him as they took seats on opposite sides of a double-width desk made from two singles. The area was clear, with task force members still tucked away in the small office, other detectives and assigned uniforms working in the incident room looking into securing evidence on the Kelly Gibson slaying.

'Which was precisely what you were looking to avoid, wasn't it?' she asked him. 'The whole purpose behind securing the suspects was to drive the killer underground while we found a way to track him. Now you're saying you want him out there again.' Chandler shook her head. 'I don't understand this at all.'

'Pen, I wanted him underground because he was in control and needed to be put on the back foot. That's still the case at the moment. If we manage to locate him, then great. But even if we only force him to raise his head before he's ready, then he's much more prone to error. Which gives us two chances at him. One to find him if he stays under, one to snatch him up if he pops up unprepared.'

'Uh-huh. So, in that case, we ought to be grateful to whoever leaked this story. Is that what you're saying?'

'Not in so many words. Only that it may work in our favour, so there are no complaints from me this time.'

'It's odd, though. I thought you were Bannister's go-to man here.'

'Not for leaks, I'm not.'

Chandler squinted at him, as if weighing his statements against his demeanour. After a moment she nodded. 'So, back to whoever is behind this dreadful series of murders. Are you ruling out this Chipcui bloke from the Roma camp?'

'Not at all. Neither in nor out. I'm keeping him in mind, only he's further back than I'd prefer.'

'You sound almost as if you'd like it to be him?'

'Things might be a little easier that way.'

'A Roma elder?'

'I'd rather know who was responsible. Roma elder or not. Thing is, despite those fingers pointing his way, I'm not sure it's him.'

'But you still think the person we're after is the person who got those thirteen people fired up enough to kill? You no longer believe it's a revenge killing?'

Bliss sighed and shook his head. 'I wish it were that simple. I'm open to it being either. The important point is not being solely focussed on one agenda. Now we have a second, which I regard as a positive step because it allows us to explore many more leads. We were getting bogged down before.'

'So if not Chipcui, then who?'

'That I don't know. In all honesty, I'm really struggling on this one. We seem to be gaining no traction whatsoever, which frustrates me so much. My only thought is it has to be someone influential. I'm thinking of taking another crack at the four musketeers back in the safe house. Between them, they may be able to supply us with a comprehensive list of who attended those meetings.'

'Are you sure it's not one of the four?' Chandler asked. 'I mean not quite a case of last man standing, but it's not far off. We should dig deeper into Monkton, Stout, Harris and Storey. Stoian is gone, I reckon. One way or another.'

'I think you're right about that last part. As for the others, again I've not closed my mind to them completely. It's just... none of them exactly strikes me as the next brain of Britain.'

'You mean they're all too dumb to have concocted this entire thing?' Chandler's smile curled the corners of her mouth.

'A little. More that I don't see how they wield any kind of influence over others, nor how they happen to know a top-notch hitman, let alone afford one.'

'That's an excellent point, actually.' Chandler wagged a finger at him. 'Who does have that level of influence and finances?'

'Tudor Chipcui, for starters. But none of the four suspects from what I can tell.'

'So somebody else, then. Someone who was maybe playing both sides of the fence.'

Bliss regarded Chandler with interest. 'You mean one of Baker's pals. Maybe even a fellow Freemason. Influence and money to a man – or woman.' He gave an excited nod. 'Let's go have that word with the musketeers right now. I really want to know who might have been playing the field.'

41

Jane Monkton was the first to respond after Bliss put the question to them. She wedged herself back in her chair as the cogs turned, but a moment later she was all nods and grins. 'I can think of a few names right away,' she told them. 'But what's in it for me?'

'You get to live,' Bliss said abruptly, a hard edge to his voice. He was sick of the attitude and did not mind showing it. 'Let me remind you about a couple of things: earlier today you threw Tudor Chipcui under the bus, and seemed perfectly happy to do so. Now you seem excited because you're about to be putting someone else in the frame. But let me make it clear to all four of you, if our hitman has not resurfaced in another day or two, we'll be taking you home again because we can't afford to secure you indefinitely. It's a sad fact, but in doing so we might as well be pinning targets to your back. So, if you are screwing with us, the only people you're hurting are yourselves. On the other hand, if we can track him down before he comes looking for you…'

Bliss let it hang in the air unspoken. It was enough to give Monkton the required nudge.

'Simon Thaw was there.'

'You mean Simon Thaw the ex-Euro MP?'

'Is there another?'

'What was he doing there?'

'Supporting the rest of us, and weighing in with his own griev-ances. He was pissed off with Baker ruling the roost and calling all the shots in and around town. To tell the truth, I think it was more a case of him wanting Baker out so's he could step into his shoes, but he was extremely vocal about his dislike of Charlie Baker and his whole rotten clan.'

Bliss thought back to his meeting with Thaw. This was not the relationship Thaw had described, but then Bliss recalled his doubts concerning the man's honesty. The politician had made his skin crawl, but on leaving his office, Bliss's villain antennae wasn't twitching enough to have marked him down as a murderer. A person capable of misdeeds, yes. Socially repugnant, absolutely. But someone who first cajoled thirteen people into stabbing Baker to death and then paid a contract killer to shoot and behead those same thirteen people? Bliss had not seen that in him at all.

'Anyone else?' he asked, glancing around the table.

'Come on,' Chandler urged them. She took a spiral-bound note-book from her bag, uncapped a pen and tossed both onto the table. 'Jane, you start a list. All of you call out names, other than the thir-teen of you who became suspects. We came back here to find out who attended these meetings, especially on the night Baker was killed.'

'But admitting we were at the meeting is not the same as owning up to anything else that happened later, right?' Brian Stout's beady eyes shifted between the two detectives as he asked the question.

'That's correct,' Bliss assured him. 'Two entirely unrelated events.'

Over the course of the next ten minutes, the group did their level best to recall the attendees. A couple of new names popped up, and Bliss felt his heartbeat quicken. When they were done here, he and his team would run thorough background checks on these people, hoping to find just one with the means, motive and opportunity.

'This has to go in our favour,' Bliss said quietly to his partner. 'One of these names has to be the person we're looking for.'

'You don't think Thaw is responsible?'

'Not alone. If at all, but definitely not on his own.'

'And if another name doesn't pop?'

He let out a deep sigh. 'I don't even want to think about it. What that might mean.'

'Have we done enough to find the killer ourselves?' Chandler asked. 'Can we honestly say that?'

'We have calls being made to all hotels, pubs, bed and breakfast places, hostels and camping grounds. If he's registered somewhere locally, then we'll find him. But what are the chances? We've located no vehicle, and the forensics we have are not worth a damn at this stage. Traffic stops have produced no further information, and the only apparent witness was also shot dead.'

'Well, that fills me full of hope.'

'I know it sucks, but the man's a ghost, Pen. The Operation Observer team is working tirelessly under the guise of looking for Kelly Gibson's killer, but they are running into blind alleys at every turn. If we find him and he still has the same weapon, then we'll nail him. If he has the saw he's been using, we'll nail him. As for tracking down his whereabouts in the first place, yes we're doing everything, but still coming up short.'

'So if we're doing all we can, don't give up on it yet. Something could break in our favour at any moment.'

Bliss knew he was being given one of Chandler's famous pep talks, but he nodded anyway. 'Of course. You're right. We have to go through the motions.'

'So what about Thaw? Why couldn't it be him?'

'I suppose it could.'

'You didn't seem too keen when his name cropped up.'

'Because for me it doesn't quite fit. I can see him providing the finance and being the man in the background egging others on. I can imagine him being behind the Baker murder, though purely on the periphery. As for killing the suspects, I'm just not buying that aspect so readily.'

'And yet he was at the meeting.'

'He was. Which keeps him in the frame.'

'So if he's involved, he's not working alone. That's what you now believe.'

Bliss shrugged. 'I am. I can visualise him providing the capital and the provocation, but the image gets fuzzy when I try seeing him as a criminal mastermind doing deals with a contract killer.'

Chandler nodded and went quiet. At about the same time, the four suspects slid the notepad back across the table.

'That's about it,' Brian Stout said.

'About it, or it?' Bliss snapped, irritated now by the thought that something had passed him by during the investigation.

'All the names we could remember.'

Chandler picked up the pad and read the list. She turned to Bliss. 'There are some familiar names here. People we might expect to have been angered by the antics of Baker and his lot. Our Roma elder is one of them, as is Thaw. But nobody else whose presence there raises flags.'

Bliss read the list for himself. Several names he had heard mentioned before, but with only good words to say about them. Concerned citizens, terrified to live in their own town, but perhaps without the means to move away.

'Maybe we should speak to them all anyway. If they stepped back from the thirteen who went on to murder Baker, they might still recall who got the crowd whipped up that night.'

'Good idea. What do we have to lose? Besides, none of these four are going to admit to it.' Chandler turned to face down the suspects seated across the table. They stared back at her.

Then Monkton shook her head. 'We want to help you as much

as we can,' she said. 'But if we're guilty of something, we'd not be stupid enough to drop ourselves in it.'

'Not even at the cost of your own lives?' Chandler asked, raising her voice a little.

'We've not reached that point yet.'

'So will you suddenly become more helpful if we kick you all out of here?'

'Who knows? Maybe. What you don't seem to grasp, detective, is that should you get your man and we walk out of this house, we still have to live in Sutton End. It's one thing being suspected of murder, quite another if there's a price on your head because you admitted to it.'

'But you're already in that situation. There's a madman out there gunning for you because somebody has paid him good money for your heads. Literally.'

'Yeah. But while we're here we're safe. You catch him, we get to leave. But what do we walk into if the Bakers find out what we know? We talk to you now, start pointing fingers, I doubt whether anyone is going to ask which of us blabbed.'

Bliss felt his anger rising, a flush creeping into his cheeks. 'So you know, don't you? You know who it was who wound you up and pointed you in the direction of Baker. It was no subtle brainwashing, no mob mentality that got you baying for blood without even being conscious of it. This wasn't something you woke up the next day not remembering. You could tell us right now who is actually responsible, but you fear the repercussions if you do.'

'Damn straight we do!' Liam Storey cried, rising from the table and sending his chair back with a heavy clatter.

One of the firearms officers stepped into the room, alert and eager to go about his business. 'We're okay,' Bliss told him. 'Just a heated disagreement is all.'

'Yeah,' Storey said, remaining on his feet, his eyes shifting from side to side as all kinds of thoughts drifted across his mind. 'But that's the last of them. You've got your list. So go. And take it with you.'

'The person we want is named here?' Bliss asked quietly.

'Yes. You already know who it is yourself.'

'And there's nobody else? No one at all who was both involved and at those same meetings?'

'No. I mean, I'm assuming you don't need to know which of your own people were there?'

'Which of our… you mean there was a police presence?'

'Of course,' Bradley Harris said, a deep frown creasing his fore-head. 'Thick as thieves they were, too. Especially with the man you're interested in.'

'Who?' Bliss demanded. 'Who were they, these police officers?'

Harris shook his head. 'No idea. Never did know their names. Though I understand one of them was a sergeant from Boston.'

4 2

Bliss was on the phone to acting DI Short before he'd even reached the car. He first outlined the situation, providing salient points in relation to everything he and Chandler had learned, and then explained to Short what he wanted her to arrange before the pair of them got back to HQ.

'Drill deep into Simon Thaw. His past, his present, and any plans he has for the future. See if there are any ongoing or planned business crossovers between Thaw and Baker. And tell whoever does the drilling that I am particularly keen to know whether Baker and Thaw were close and then fell out, or if this was a long con by Thaw.'

'Will do, boss.' Bliss could imagine Short tapping at her notebook with her pen. 'And what happens if we bump up against the political arena. His stint as a Euro MP is bound to be an iceberg in our way at some point.'

'Use as much of your new authority as you can to open up closed doors, Mia. Anything you can't prise ajar, send back to me and I'll have words with the super.'

'Sure. Is that it?'

'No,' Bliss said in a flat, pensive tone. 'That was the easy bit.

Please also arrange for Sergeant Lewis Waring from Boston to be brought in to Thorpe Wood. And one last thing, I'd also like you to shift the time and space continuum around and get him there yesterday if you can.'

'I'll do my best, boss.'

Bliss nosed the car back towards Peterborough. 'Mia's right about the iceberg,' he said to Chandler, who sat in contemplative silence. 'With these political characters, what we get to see in public is really only the tip. We are shielded from so much of what goes on beneath the surface.'

'If it were you, boss, I'm betting you'd act like an icebreaker and try smashing straight through the middle. Whereas Mia will negotiate her way around it.'

Bliss chuckled. 'You may be right about that, Pen. But you know what, you don't get to squeeze all the dirt out unless you're willing to get your hands dirty in the first place. There are times when talking doesn't work, leaving you with no choice but to break through an obstacle. Sometimes if you skirt it, you miss something valuable.'

Chandler gave him a querulous sidelong glance. 'This is me, Jimmy. Save the platitudes for the bosses in the fancy suits. We both know you're just too boneheaded to go around anything.'

This time he laughed. But the laughter froze on his lips when his mind turned once more to the Boston officer, Lewis Waring. Now there was a man he did intend smashing straight through in order to get the information he wanted. Because if Waring was in league with Thaw, if the two had put this whole thing together to gain status, money, and notoriety within their community, then Bliss was going to make them both pay.

To his mind, Waring deserved a harsher punishment because it was his job to uphold the law. Clearly the murder of Kelly Gibson was a by-product of one of the hits, something the police sergeant could not have anticipated. But Bliss found his thoughts drawn to officers Ripley and Cater, murdered whilst trying to protect Alan

Brewer. Waring must have known his colleagues faced great danger that evening, yet he had done nothing to prevent the hit from taking place.

If he was part of it.

And that was the crucial element here.

Bliss wondered if Waring had simply attended the town meetings in order to keep an eye on a potentially corrosive situation. It was certainly feasible, although his presence could also indicate possible collusion. He was, after all, taking money from Baker, though that in itself did not imply any form of loyalty to the man.

Then there was the part – if any – that Tudor Chipcui had played in the whole sorry mess. Silence and misdirection born of closely-guarded secrets had so far blurred the edges of this investigation, and Bliss was determined to bring it all into sharp focus and get to the truth.

'We have to nail these bastards, Pen,' Bliss said softly. 'Irrespective of who they are or what position they hold.'

'I couldn't agree more,' Chandler responded. 'But for once, be careful, Jimmy. Neither of these men are going to play ball, whether they're guilty or not. But if they are, they'll dig their heels in.'

'Then I'll have to push harder to topple them.'

'That's precisely what I'm afraid of. The more they stand firm, the more you're liable to do something stupid.'

'Thanks for the vote of confidence.'

'I don't mean it like that. Just… well, I know how you get when we're close to solving a puzzle and somebody stands in your way. It's the whole unstoppable force meets immoveable object paradox.'

'I see. And which of the two am I?'

'Either, depending on context. But whichever you are, you won't back down. Only, these are clearly dangerous men, with a long reach.'

'And I accept that. I'm not blind to the dangers, Pen. But if they are guilty then we have to wring that information out of them one way or another.'

'We don't need everything, boss. We just need enough.'

Bliss turned to look at his partner. 'What do you mean?

'I mean, all we want to know right now is the whereabouts of our contract killer – if that's even what he is. He's the one we have to take off the map immediately. Thaw and Waring are going nowhere. For the time being, all we need from them is information. The rest can wait.'

Warburton and Smyth were fetching Sergeant Waring themselves. According to Short, the DCI had been extremely eager to volunteer. Bliss stamped on his growing impatience while they waited. There was no point steaming into an interview irritated and hot under the collar. He had to at least give the appearance of control, especially with a fellow police officer.

'Can I ask you something, boss?' Short said, stepping into his office where he had been kicking his heels for the past few minutes.

'Of course.' Bliss noticed the look of concern on his acting DI's face. 'What's up, Mia?'

'Boss, I hate to even think this, let alone say it out loud, but are we absolutely certain there is no stink attached to DCI Warburton?'

'You mean in terms of being in Charlie Baker's pocket?'

Short nodded. 'Don't get me wrong. From what I've seen she is a first-rate detective and a thoroughly pleasant person to be around. But what do we actually know about her?'

Bliss realised his colleague was right. Police officers were known to be on the take during Baker's reign, and some had undoubtedly carried on feeding from the trough. One of the reasons for creating a task force was to prevent leaks from escaping. Only that did not appear to have happened. Not entirely.

'I can't believe I'm saying this, but have her checked out, Mia. Smyth, too, for that matter. Quietly, though. And I do mean way below the radar.'

'I thought you'd be mad at me for suggesting it.'

'Not at all. Look, for what it's worth, I trust DCI Warburton implicitly. I've seen nothing in her behaviour to suggest she might be involved. But you're raising a question I should have raised from the very beginning. We're being told there are bent coppers in a specific part of Lincolnshire, so we'd be pretty foolish not to be concerned about the background of the person doing the telling.'

'I don't want it to be her, boss.'

'Me, neither. It would certainly call into question my judgement. But I don't believe Warburton is involved. As for the leak, well with everything that's happened the past few days, keeping a lid on things has been impossible. Operation details have been known far outside the task force ever since we pulled in security measures from both counties. Still, you do whatever you need to do, and we'll worry about the results if they turn up anything suspicious. Meanwhile, walk with me. It's time for me to start running the show again.'

Bliss gathered everyone attached to the case in the incident room this time, the task force team extended by the presence of Hunt, Ansari and Gratton. Each of whom had been busy during the fifty minutes it took Bliss and Chandler to journey back to HQ.

'What do you have for me on Simon Thaw?' he asked.

'Thaw's background is unspectacular,' Short told them, reading from a sheet of A4 paper still warm from the laser printer. 'His parents called themselves farmers, but the truth is they were wealthy landowners. He started out in the family business after leaving school – no university. When the reins were handed over to him following his father's stroke, Thaw began expanding the empire. Made a name and some money for himself. He moved into local politics, then went for the Euro MP spot and was successful. Endured a bit of a scandal over expenses and lost his seat shortly afterwards. The minor independent party he now fronts looks to be a façade to keep himself in with the locals and his face in the news.'

'But it's those business dealings and his plans for the local community we're most interested in,' Bishop said. The big man leaned back in his chair, reading glasses perched on his nose as he, too, read from a sheet of paper. 'Thaw and Baker seem to have been orbiting each other for quite a while, before starting to do business a few years back. By this time, Thaw was selling sand and gravel for building developments, which covered everything including foundations, structures and roadways. He actually bought up an old gravel pit at one stage, but it didn't produce a great deal so he took as much out of the place as he could before closing it down. Apparently it's now used as a bit of a dumping ground.

'Anyhow, he and Baker were tight until Thaw decided to expand his empire once more. This time his move was into housing developments, thereby trampling all over Baker's territory. We managed to pick up some intelligence suggesting that whenever Thaw submitted plans for a new development, Baker initiated a campaign against it. In response, Thaw attempted to strong-arm local government planners, and evidently it started to get very messy indeed.'

Bliss nodded with no small measure of satisfaction. 'So, we not only have a crossover between Baker and Thaw which began their friendship, we also have the source of the eventual feud between them which ended it. Any sense of whether the initial relationship was genuine on Thaw's part?'

Short shook her head and said, 'Pretty much everything we're getting back suggests Thaw is a chameleon. His public and private personae are entirely different. He becomes whatever he needs to be in order to suit the situation he's in. Thaw was once connected to UKIP and now heads a similar movement, but there are some thoughts that he is not even particularly right-wing. He's just exploiting the current level of unrest.'

The notion intrigued Bliss. He wondered if the man had managed to sound so convincing during their first interview because he was able to change on a whim; metamorphosing into the person he needed to be at the time. But Bliss also recalled how specific Thaw's responses had been to the issues put to him. Perhaps he had sounded sincere because he was speaking the truth at that point, but only in terms of revenge not being the motive. Any limitations lay in the questions, not the replies.

DCI Warburton pushed open the door to the incident room. She caught Bliss's eye before ducking outside again. Bliss took a deep breath before getting up from the table. 'This is terrific stuff, people,' he said, puffing out his lips and glancing around at every face. 'No more than I've come to expect, because you always deliver your very best. But great work all the same. I don't know about you lot, but I think we've taken a massive step forward this afternoon. Thank you all for your perseverance. Assume tomorrow will be an even busier day, but hopefully also more productive. Oh, and Mia, before you do anything else, please attend to the issue we discussed.'

As the team broke apart and dispersed, Bliss looked across at Chandler. 'You ready for this?' he asked.

She gave him a quizzical look. 'You want me in there with you?'

'Who else?'

'I thought perhaps your new girlfriend.'

'If you mean DCI Warburton, then first of all, grow up. Second of all, while she is good at her job, even very good, you and I have a chemistry in the room, an invaluable shorthand.'

Chandler grinned. 'Why don't you admit you need me?'

'You want me to lie to you?'

'Go on. Say it. You know you want to.'

'I really don't.' He shook his head.

'And yet we both know you really do. Go on, rip it off like a plaster. One quick tug and it's all over.'

'Now you're sounding like a bad porn movie.'

But Chandler refused to be deflected. 'Tell me you need me in there with you.'

Bliss shrugged. 'Okay. I need you. In there. With me.'

He received a roll of the eyes by way of a reply. 'That wasn't so hard, was it?'

'And we're back to the bad porn again.'

'I'm guessing you'd know, boss. Now, any chance of you getting your mind off filth so's we can do this interview?'

'Just one thing,' Bliss said as they started towards the door. 'If I do go off on one, don't try holding me back. I'm really up for this.' He thought about the references to porn, and carried the resulting smile with him into the room.

43

Sergeant Lewis Waring sat in the smallest available interview room Thorpe Wood had to offer. Windowless, walls clad in their original soundproof tiles, now screwed into place to prevent them slipping off and tumbling to the floor. Many betrayed signs of damage, discolouration applying an overall beige wash. It all reeked of the late 1970s, with an undertone of bygone smoke and cleaning fluid. The chair Waring occupied was undersized and fragile, leaning to one side on its buckled frame. The chairs taken by Bliss and Chandler felt sturdy and comfortable by comparison.

Boston station provided the better chairs, but the lumpier tea.

Bliss said nothing at first. The folder of notes he had rapidly studied out in the corridor now sat unopened before him on the desk in the centre of the room. He had no interest in them anymore. Instead, he sat and stared hard at Waring, unblinking, his features betraying no emotion. Alongside him, Chandler acted as if the man seated before them was just some seedy little villain of no consequence. At one point she even sniffed her disdain, causing Bliss to smile.

'This is quite the routine you've got going here,' Waring said after a while. His arms folded beneath his chest as he slowly surveyed the room before allowing his gaze to fall upon Bliss once more. 'Never seen it done this way before. Much.'

Still Bliss said nothing. Chandler cleared her throat and continued to feign disinterest.

'I'm a copper with more than twenty years behind me,' Waring boasted. 'There's nothing you two can do that I haven't seen, nothing you can say I haven't heard. I've experienced the silent treatment, too. Used it myself on more than one occasion. So whatever this is about, get on with it. I'm missing dinner at home with my wife and kids.'

'That's not true though, is it?' Bliss said, cocking his head to one side. 'You no longer reside at home. You rent a flat, in which you live on your own.'

The silence had been a ploy, but not in the way Waring suspected. A silent room is uncomfortable when more than a single person occupies it. One or more of those people usually tries to fill it, even with meaningless, banal conversation. Bliss wanted Waring to be that person.

The uniformed sergeant pulled back, all the better to appraise his interrogator. 'You have been busy. Only a few people are aware of my… current situation.'

'One of them being your wife.'

The officer snorted, twisting his mouth into a cruel pucker. 'I wouldn't believe a single word coming out of that cow's gob.'

'We're not here to discuss your wife or your living arrangements. To be frank with you, one of the things I wanted from this interview was to look into the eyes of the man who allowed two of his own colleagues to be slaughtered. I wondered what kind of man could be capable of such an act. Now I see.'

'You see!' Waring huffed his contempt. 'You see what? You think I'm involved with all that nonsense? I thought we were here about Charlie Baker again.'

'In a way, we are,' Chandler said, nodding. 'Because that's where your sordid part in this began. First of all it was slipping Baker information, or something along those lines, then it was helping him by resolving situations as they arose in and around town. Not exactly the big time, but it was noticed.'

'Yeah, by who?'

'Does the name Simon Thaw mean anything to you, Waring?'

The sergeant's mouth worked as if he were chewing cud, but he made no reply.

'The word you're struggling for, is "yes". And the fact that you avoided admitting it tells us a whole lot more about you.'

'I don't know what the hell you're talking about,' Waring declared, reshaping his posture into that of a determined police officer in full control of himself.

'Then let's talk a language you do understand,' Bliss said. He squared himself in the chair. 'Right now, Simon Thaw is also being driven here for interview. We believe that one, or maybe both of you, incited the murder of Charles Baker, and then later hired a contract killer to keep those thirteen murderers silent.'

Waring shook his head and snorted. 'I've put up with all I'm prepared to,' he said, hugging himself tighter still. 'This is a fantasy and you're in dreamland, Bliss. I want my rep before I say another word.'

'Certainly. As is your right. But you should know that Mr Thaw is coming here without demanding legal representation. Which tells me something, and I'm sure you understand what I mean. You with all your two decades of experience.'

'Rep.'

'It means Thaw is open to the idea of making a deal. I'm quite certain you remember the days of the little brown envelopes and their contents, terms and conditions of a deal written up and handed across tables. Today it's all done via a computer, but essentially it's the same thing. As you mentioned earlier, you played the game yourself and you understand how it pans out from here, so I will be straight with you. Whoever opens up first gets the only deal I'm willing to offer.'

'I've asked for my rep,' Waring said, nostrils flaring. 'And you can't ask me any more questions until he arrives.'

'True enough.' Bliss nodded and smiled. 'But then, I'm not asking questions right now. I'm just talking and thinking out loud about the problem you have. See, I can't help but wonder how much you really trust Simon Thaw. How confident you are that he won't drop you in it as soon as a deal is offered to him. I reckon you must be asking yourself why he's not coming here with his brief and why he's not even asked for one. If you had complete faith in him beforehand, I suspect that little nugget of information has put at least a chink in your armour of certainty.'

'Don't flatter yourself, Bliss. The truth is, I don't believe you. I don't believe Thaw is coming here without his solicitor. I just don't.'

'That's a shame,' Chandler said, eyeing the man with disdain. 'Because now you won't get the opportunity to plead for some form of clemency regarding the murders of Sergeant Elaine Ripley, and Constable Brynn Cater. Instead, you'll be nailed for conspiring to murder them both, along with all the others, of course. Including Kelly Gibson.

'Bumping off a bunch of fellow murderers is one thing. A remorseless cop killer is something else entirely. On the one hand, your fellow inmates may treat you like royalty, but I wouldn't expect the same from the screws if I were you. I hear they regard cop killers exactly the same way I do.'

Waring was silent. Bliss watched as a single bead of sweat ran down from the man's high hairline, his nostrils flaring as his breathing became more ragged. Chandler had found a weak spot, yet Bliss doubted whether they could exploit it. Waring did not strike him as the kind of man likely to offer a confession, not without being absolutely certain of being dropped in it by someone else. Using Thaw against him was not working as well as Bliss had hoped. It was time to take a chance.

'Just give me the hitman,' he said to Waring, offering a shrug to suggest he was asking for something of little consequence. 'Nothing else for now. No apology. No confession. Just a name and a location where we might find him. That's all you have to admit to knowing if you like. Those two scraps of information won't save your career, but they could buy you a future outside of prison walls at some point. It's the only way you'll breathe free air again.'

The man looked up into Bliss's eyes. He tilted his head one way and then the other. Before finally, he leaned back, unfolded his arms, smiled and said, 'Rep.'

Bliss exhaled long and hard. 'Really? That's really the way you want to go?' He turned to his partner. 'Pen, before we switch on the audio and get the sergeant's refusal to co-operate on tape for our records, why don't you fetch us all a drink. Take your time about it. There's no rush.'

Chandler narrowed her eyes. 'I think it may be better if I stayed right here with you, boss.'

'I'm thirsty, though. I could really do with that drink, Pen.'

'And I say let's get the official statement out of the way first. Then we can concentrate on the rep.'

'What the fuck is this?' Waring said, looking between them. 'Please tell me you're not trying to pull the old good cop and bad cop routine on me.'

'Don't be a prick all your life,' Chandler snarled at him. Her gaze shifted his way. 'I'm doing you a favour here, you ignoramus. You really think this is a routine? Believe me, because of what you allowed to happen to two of your colleagues, I'd like nothing better than to beat the truth out of you myself. Only I know my boss here will get it done quicker and with far greater brutality than I can muster.'

The man laughed, though he seemed uncertain. 'Don't try pulling this shit,' he said. 'There's no way either of you are going to lay your hands on me.'

'DS Chandler would like to, but she won't,' Bliss assured him. 'She's too good a cop to resort to such a tactic. It's cheap and it's tawdry and it's just not the done thing these days. But that's where I come in, Waring. See, I am cheap, I am tawdry, and I am not the done thing these days by a long way. But I get results. And if I get one here, you think anyone will care about how you acquired your lumps?'

'I don't believe you.'

'No? So tell my sergeant here how you like your tea and she'll go fetch you a cup. Fifteen minutes ought to be enough. If you reckon I'm bluffing, then all you have to do is ask.'

The room was silent for several seconds. Bliss saw Waring's jaw shift as he physically chewed it over. A tic pulsed above his left cheekbone. When the man broke eye contact, Bliss knew fresh ground had been broken.

'Go fetch him a cuppa please, Pen,' he said. 'Try and find one of those special Boston brews for him.' He winked at her and grinned. 'We'll be fine. No fisticuffs.'

'Get your statement done,' Waring growled as Chandler left the room. 'Then get me my rep.'

Bliss shook his head and snorted. 'So you're perfectly happy to take the entire hit and see Thaw receiving consideration on sentence? That makes no sense to me. Waring, your trusted political ally is going to hang you out to dry. Surely there's a piece of you that wants to stick it to him first. Even a little.'

He saw a shift in the sergeant's eyes. If he hadn't been watching so closely he might have missed it. But there was a definite flicker of interest. The man was considering something. Churning it over, slowly reaching a decision. Bliss felt his gut clench and his breath stall. Each passing moment felt like a lifetime of misery. He wanted to climb over the table and beat the truth out of the man as Chandler had threatened he would do, but he also suspected this was the very moment their case was going to break wide open for them. One last push was all it required.

'Seriously,' Bliss said. 'You're absolutely right. Those old school copper interview techniques won't work with you. Not the good and bad routine, nor the threats of a sound hiding. You've lived and breathed it over many years. Of course you won't fall for it. But there's something you've forgotten.'

'Really? And what's that?'

'Simon Thaw is not a cop. He's a civilian who has never played the game before from either side of the table. He'll break. I make those same threats to him, he'll collapse like a straw man. And if he does before you do, Waring, then he's the one walking out of here on bail. I guarantee you that.'

This time the flicker in the man's eyes became a bright flare. 'I'll tell you this much and no more before the audio goes back on,' Waring said after a minute of brooding silence. 'Thaw reckons himself to be an astute businessman. That's something you might consider looking into.'

Bliss blinked. 'What does that mean?' he asked. 'What are you telling us?'

'If you're even a half decent detective, Bliss, you'll work it out. Just like I said. It's not everything you wanted, but it's enough. It's what you were willing to settle for. But before you toddle off, tell me something. Would you really have hit me?'

Rising from his chair, Bliss shook his head. 'Of course not.'

He held out a hand. Waring stood and begrudgingly reached out his own. Bliss grasped it, yanked the man a step forward and butted him squarely on the nose with his forehead. The Boston man reared back with a yelp of pain, clutching his face as his legs gave way. Waring slumped down onto the table and then fell to the floor, sending his chair skittering across the linoleum surface. Blood pumped from a nose Bliss knew was probably broken.

'I'll have you for that, you bastard!' Waring shrieked, raising up on one elbow.

'Have me for what?' Bliss said. 'You must have got your legs caught up in the chair and tripped. I told you I wouldn't hit you. I didn't say anything about nutting you, though.'

44

As Short navigated her way along the narrow, twisting road towards Wisbech St Mary, her thoughts drifted between DI Bliss and the job in hand. The boss had been torn between staying behind at Thorpe Wood to interview Simon Thaw, and following up on an idea given to him by something Waring had mentioned right at the end of their session.

'He refused to tell us anything outright, but what he dropped in before clamming up again was a lead. At least that's the way he thought of it,' Bliss told them. The four major crimes detectives had gathered together in the task force office after Waring had been taken away to the medical bay. Warburton and Smyth had gone to meet the car bringing Thaw down to Peterborough.

'About the man's businesses?' Bishop responded doubtfully.

Bliss nodded. 'Yes. It came across as a generalisation, but seemed far more specific to me. There was no point in referencing it otherwise. He mocked Thaw's astuteness as a businessman. From what I understand, Thaw has the Midas touch when it comes to his entrepreneurial instincts. However, the one business I know to be no longer functioning is his quarry. Seems these days he uses it more as a dumping ground, having taken everything out of the deposit that he could mine. The way I hear it, Thaw originally had notions of providing raw materials for his building company for years to come, so the quarry ended up being a bit of a lemon. That could be what Waring was hinting at.'

'But why?' Short asked. 'To what end?'

By now she knew the entire repertoire of her boss's expressions. There was not an extensive range from which to decipher, and he could often be a closed book. But when realisation came to him it was as if he were seeing the stairway to heaven itself. Which was the precise expression he wore when he spoke next.

'Think about it. Waring said it was what I'd settled for. I believe he meant the location of our contract killer. We've not been able to trace where our hitman is hiding out. Which may be because whoever hired him is also putting him up. Away from prying eyes. Away from the inquisitive. You could park a trailer on the site of a disused quarry and nobody would ever know it was there. Some of the buildings might also be still in use. That's my bet, anyway. I asked for the hitman's whereabouts. I think Waring may well have given them to me.'

It was at this point where Bliss had expressed his anxiety over what to do next, unable to decide which of the two leads should be his priority. Thaw was all untapped potential and only minutes away from interrogation, and it was Short's guess that her boss would crack him quickly and with the minimum of fuss. Equally, though, it was possible for the contract killer to be hiding out at Thaw's abandoned quarry; Waring could just as easily be sending them on a wild goose chase to eat up time and hope, giving him a good laugh at their expense.

'Let me go,' she suggested, recognising how desperately torn her DI was. 'You and Penny carry on as planned and interview Thaw when he arrives. You're much more likely to get the bigger picture from him. Me and Bish can check out this gravel pit. If Thaw spills his guts and confirms your theory, then you can join us with the rest of the troops.'

Bliss was clearly reluctant, but he could not refute the logic in Short's proposal. He was not able to be in two places at the same time. His natural instinct was to rush headlong towards danger, in the form of the man who killed without mercy. The only thing preventing him from doing so was uncertainty over whether their target was even at the quarry. Short, stepping up to her new role as acting DI, tried to make the decision easier on him.

'Boss, all Bish and I will do is recce the place. If we spot a trailer or a hut or cabin and see any sign of recent life or activity, we'll call it in and wait for backup. We could go all that way and find zilch. Better for you to get what you can from Thaw, in my opinion.'

It had worked.

'You two go ahead,' Bliss told them. 'But, I'm also sending in an ARV team to provide armed support. If you arrive at the quarry before them, you wait outside the perimeter until they turn up. You understand me?'

'Of course, boss.'

'I mean it, Mia, Bish. No steaming in there on your own. No heroics. This man is armed and about as dangerous as it gets. You do not approach him without armed backup. Are we clear on that?'

'Yes, boss,' Short and Bishop had said at the same time.

Bliss took a beat before summoning her outside where they could talk alone. She had never seen him acting quite as nervously around her before, and she knew precisely what was running through his head.

'You're thinking about the baby,' she'd said. 'You want to flag it as a reason why I should stay behind, but you also know that's no good reason to prevent me from going. Am I close, boss?'

He cleared his throat before nodding. 'I'm in a bind here, Mia. I'm the only one who knows about your pregnancy. So, yes, of course that adds to my concerns. I know it shouldn't. I'm supposed to ignore it. You're on duty so I should let you get on with it. But… I can't help being worried. I'm wired that way.'

'I understand that, boss. I do, and I'm touched by your concern.

But you needn't worry. It's not as if I'm six months in or anything and carrying around a big belly. My being pregnant, especially at this stage, isn't going to hamper my ability to do the job. You trusted me enough to put me up for this role. Trust me now to do it properly.'

She could tell he was still unhappy, but he also had a lot on his plate and was keen to get on with it. He wrestled with it for a few seconds longer before agreeing with a heavy sigh.

With the land now unused, no security lights warned them of the quarry's presence in advance, but Bishop was using his phone to plot the way ahead for Short like the good navigator he was. The site was fairly small for a quarry, and stuck out on the southern edge of Wisbech St Mary, a tiny village two miles west of Wisbech itself.

There was a time when it had been farmland here as far as the eye could see, but when the job of working the fields became more difficult, the owner leaned on a commissioned report regarding the soil beneath them. The notion of digging up and exploiting rather than nourishing and growing did not sit well with the local farming community, but land was land and open to many interpretations of its usefulness.

As they drew closer, Bishop told her the entrance was coming up on their right. Short switched to side lights only as she made the turn and then put her foot on the brake. She turned to her colleague and said, 'No ARV as yet. You and I both know that unless one happened to be nearby when the call went out, we could be waiting twenty or thirty minutes for them to get here.'

Bishop hitched his shoulders. 'It's what the boss told us to do.'

'Yes, and of course that's exactly what he'd do if he was here right now. Not. Look, Bish, I don't know about you, but I'm all for spending the next half an hour usefully. I don't mean busting in like the Sweeney, but it can't hurt to take a look around, right?'

'I suppose not.'

'I mean, we're two highly experienced detectives. We know what we're doing. We sneak in, see what we see, and sneak back out again. No confrontation. No fuss. You in?'

Short did not have to ask Bishop twice.

There was a good quarter mile drive around to the quarry itself, but the rutted lane was bumpy and Short kept her speed down to less than 10 mph. Bordered on both sides by hedgerow which had encroached over time and through lack of use, the narrow passage eventually started to widen and clear. Short killed the lights altogether and slowed the vehicle to a gentle crawl. As they slipped out into an open clearing overlooking the deep black pit of the quarry, the acting DI brought her car to a halt and sat there in the idling vehicle allowing her eyes to adjust.

'What do you see?' she asked Bishop, who had released his seatbelt and was squinting through the windscreen, his chest pressed against the dashboard.

'Not a lot. There's enough light in the sky to guide us. Just. But you'd have to take it very slow.'

'Or we get out here and walk.'

He nodded. 'I'd feel safer on foot.'

Short switched off her car's engine, and the pair exited as quietly as possible. The silence enveloped them like a physical presence. She pointed out the way ahead, and started following the powdery dirt and gravel track leading into the heart of the quarry's basin. In the darkness they made their way shoulder-to-shoulder along the track, each step a careful exploration of what might lie beneath their feet. It was painfully slow progress, but necessarily so. Short soon began to feel the difference in gradient in her calves, having to adjust both her gait and length of stride.

'You feeling that?' she whispered.

'We're going downhill.'

The next section was steeper still, and Short felt as if the land to her right was thrusting itself up towards the sky. She realised they were on the initial stage of the spiral track encircling the quarry, the first outer ring around the deep pit below. They carried on walking, stone dust puffing up in their wake. A couple of minutes later, Short put a hand across her partner's chest, forcing him to halt his progress.

'You see that up ahead and to the right?'

She felt more than saw Bishop's nod in response. 'Looks like a Portakabin. Offices once, I expect.'

The pair started edging their way towards it. The building was long and narrow, decrepit and crumbling. Broken wooden steps led up to its only door, jagged chunks of timber jutting angrily like sharpened teeth. There was no solid light emitting from inside, nor any flickering glow from a TV screen. The hut had the anticipated air of neglect about it.

'Nobody's been here in a while,' Bishop said.

Short agreed with him. The abandonment felt complete, and her gut began to insist they had been led astray. Either by Waring, or the boss's interpretation of the Boston officer's final words. Even so, Short decided to continue on. They approached the Portakabin with caution, peering in through dust-caked bare windows and finding nothing worthy of their attention within. As they slipped around the other side of the ramshackle structure, it was Bishop this time who reacted to the unexpected.

'Are you hearing what I'm hearing?' he whispered, lowering his mouth towards his partner's ear.

Short strained to listen. There was something in the air. Nothing she could put a finger on, only that it was incongruous. It had no place out here in this desolate location. Then she scrunched up her face as the distant noise became more recognisable.

'Music,' she said beneath her breath.

Bishop pointed ahead to where the trail used by vehicles to travel around the quarry curled around to the left, leaving a small cut of land between the bend and the path they travelled. In the centre of that wedge was a caravan. No more than sixteen feet in length. A Toyota flatbed truck was parked up alongside it. A blueish glow emitted from behind the thin strip of curtain up at the caravan windows. Soft music drifted in the wind towards the two detectives. Beyond the truck and the caravan, a long line of vehicles stood like silent sentinels. If anything, their stillness made them appear more menacing.

'This place is rather busy for an abandoned quarry, don't you reckon?' Bishop said.

Short agreed. 'That's exactly what I was thinking.'

'You want to take a closer look?'

'Maybe. It has to be him, though, right?'

'I can't imagine why anyone else would be out here.'

'Could be travellers.'

'I suppose there's always that possibility.'

'Do we need to make sure he's in there? I mean, just because there are vehicles parked up outside and music is coming from inside, doesn't mean anybody is in there at the moment. Before we call in the cavalry, oughtn't we confirm our man as being present?'

Now that she was here and confronted by the very real possibility of their killer being only a hundred feet or so away, Short was undecided how to proceed. If she called it in, got everyone out there and the tactical teams stormed inside the caravan, she was going to look pretty foolish if they came up empty. However, if she and Bishop eased their way closer, they might see or overhear something conclusive. With the ARV crew due at any moment, in her mind the best thing she and Bish could do was confirm what they had or did not have.

She glanced over at Bishop and said, 'You check the truck by the door, I'll get closer to the far window. See if the bonnet is warm. It might give us a clue as to when it was last used. You hear that other sound, Bish? Like a low constant hum.'

'Generator?' Bishop asked.

Short nodded. 'Has to be. Okay, let's go. And be careful.'

Without another word, the two inched their way closer, taking their time on the uneven surface, although there seemed little of consequence on the ground to give them away if they happened to tread on it. The path remained mostly powdery and soft, tiny nuggets of hardened dust destroyed by every footfall, gravel pushed deeper into the soil. As Short drew close and crouched down into a crab-like stance, her left ear turned towards the caravan, Bishop crept across to the Toyota, touched a hand to the long bonnet, before tiptoeing back to her side. He shook his head.

'It's cold,' he said so quietly she had to strain to hear him. For a large man he could be light on his feet and softly spoken. 'Which means nothing. Only that it's not been used in maybe the last hour. If our man is lying low, then it figures he wouldn't have been out and about in his truck today.'

Short gave it some thought as the night wrapped around them like a heavy shroud. The air was a little chilly now, but there was no breeze to speak of. Whatever cloud cover had sat overhead was gone, and the black sky teemed with glittering stars.

'I'm not seeing any movement at all,' Short said. 'The music is still playing, and I think he has the TV on. Could be he's just sitting there watching and listening, perhaps even dozed off. Mind you, I'd really like to know if he's in there for sure before I make the call.'

'I'm not,' came a voice from behind them.

Bishop whirled. Short did the same as she sprang to her feet from the low crouch.

Less than four yards away, a man stood facing them. His stance was solid, legs spread apart. In his hands he held a shotgun. It was pointing their way.

'You two are not very good,' he said, as if disappointed in them. 'I heard you coming from a long way off. Saw you kill your lights. You thought you were hunting for me when you came down here.' The man laughed, jerked the weapon twice and said, 'When all the time I was hunting for you.'

B liss didn't appreciate having his interviews interrupted, especially when it was with someone as loathsome as Simon Thaw. But when DC Ansari yanked open the interview room door and Bliss looked up to see the tightness in her body and the fear in her hollowed-out eyes, he knew at once that something had gone badly wrong.

'Is it Short and Bishop?' he demanded as he stepped out into the corridor.

Ansari nodded. 'Boss, we can't reach them. The ARV you ordered arrived and waited on the perimeter as requested. They gave it a few minutes, but grew concerned that DS Short and DS Bishop might have entered the grounds ahead of them. They went dark and carried out a silent approach, came upon Mia's car but found it empty. They contacted our control desk immediately. We tried calling their mobiles, and also raising them on the Airwave. But we're getting no response, and there's no sign of them.'

Bliss felt dread slip around him like a coat made of razor blades. A shudder ripped through his body, causing a muscle spasm in the pit of his back. Tension took a fierce grip on him and he wanted to scream. He should never have allowed Short and Bishop to go to the quarry on their own. Theirs was supposed to be a reconnaissance visit only, but even so it was one he should have made himself. The damned therapy he'd received had caused him to question his tactics, messing with his natural instincts.

Upstairs, the incident room was buzzing with activity. 'Dammit!' Bliss said as he walked through the door and laid eyes on a whiteboard which now held the names of his two colleagues. 'Why didn't I wait for a firearms unit to travel with them?'

'To be fair, boss,' DC Hunt said, matching Bliss's pained expression, 'they're all struggling as it is to protect those four suspects in the safe house. You couldn't have drawn a team away from them. Not before you'd confirmed our man's presence on site. And you did request an ARV as well as order Bish and Mia to wait for their arrival before making any approach. I'm not sure what else you could have done in the circumstances.'

Bliss knew Hunt was right. It was all perfectly logical and reasonable. You established the existence of a gunman before you sent in the firearms team, especially when doing so would lure those armed officers away from their current protectees. Only it didn't feel like the correct decision in retrospect. Because now Short and Bishop were out of contact, and to Bliss that meant only one thing.

'John, you come with me and Penny.' Bliss snapped his head round to face Ansari. 'Gul, get hold of everybody else on the command list, including DCI Warburton and her RPU man, Smyth. Before you do that, contact Eric Price. Tell him we need however many spare firearms officers he has over at Hinchingbrooke to get over to the quarry. Ask him to bring two further units from the safe house. I want them at the quarry as well.'

'Yes, boss. You're not going there now on your own, are you?'

'No. Chandler and Hunt will be with me.'

'I meant you're not going without further armed protection, are you?'

'Yes, I am, Gul. And I knew what you meant. Don't worry, we'll hang back with the ARV team already on site. I just want to make sure I'm there when Eric Price arrives.'

It was a thirty-minute drive, mostly on good road. Bliss did it in twenty. By the time he and his two colleagues reached the entrance to the site, Bliss was feeling less gung-ho than he had when leaving HQ in his rear-view mirror. Even so, the overwhelming sense of guilt and concern for Short and Bishop made him want to race into the quarry with headlights blazing in a full-frontal attack.

Bliss knew there had to be a better way to approach a problem now pitting them against a highly accomplished contract killer. Almost certainly ex-military, possibly a mercenary. A man entirely at home in such circumstances. Armed and extremely dangerous. As Bliss had known when he sent Short and Bishop ahead.

Nursing the Insignia along the same rutted lane and dirt track his colleagues must have taken earlier – given there appeared to be only the one way in or out – Bliss breathed a sigh of relief at spotting the two firearms officers waiting alongside their ARV which was parked up alongside Short's hatchback. His reassurance was short lived when he failed to spot either of his unit members standing there with them. His hope during the past twenty minutes was that the quarry happened to be in a blind spot for mobile phone signals, and that neither Short nor Bishop had remembered to bring the Airwave with them from the car.

He nudged his door closed upon exiting, Chandler and Hunt doing the same behind him. Making his way quietly across to the ARV crew, Bliss held out his warrant card for inspection.

'Any sign of my two detectives?' Bliss asked.

The taller of the two men shook his head. 'No, sir. We've not strayed beyond the immediate area, however. I radioed in and was ordered to hold our place here, wait for command to arrive. Would that be you, sir?'

'Possibly. Price is on his way, but I may need you before he's able to get here.'

'Sir, if we have no formal directive to approach our subject, our orders are to maintain a position here. That directive has to come from a senior firearms officer.'

Bliss was aware of the chain of command. 'I understand. You have greater responsibility by having those weapons. If you come with me into the quarry and you end up discharging them, your jobs may be on the line.'

'That's correct.'

'Still, you understand two of my team are down there somewhere. Most probably being held by a man who has already murdered several people, including two police officers.'

'I understand that, sir. I do. But we have to wait for the proper authority. You said it yourself: we have greater responsibility because we carry these weapons.'

'Fair enough. I accept what you say. But I'm going down there right now. I'll leave the rest of my team here, because I'm not adding them to my list of mistakes made today.'

'Sir, with all due respect, you really ought to remain here with us until command arrive. We have no idea what kind of situation we might be facing. You talk about a single armed man, but for all we know there could be others out there.'

Bliss nodded. 'You're right. I hadn't even considered the possibility. What I do know is that two members of my team are almost certainly there already, most likely in great and imminent danger. So, I'm not about to leave them facing such a situation alone. I'd prefer it if one of you remained here with my colleagues while the other joined me. But I won't ask you to. That's for you two to decide.'

He turned sharply and strode briskly back to where Chandler and Hunt waited. Impatiently so, if he was any judge of their expressions.

'So?' Chandler asked. 'Are we going in?'

'You're going nowhere at this point,' Bliss told her, shaking his head. He switched his gaze to Hunt. 'You neither, John. You two are to wait here with the ARV crew until backup arrives. When firearms command are on site, if they allow you any further in then so be it.'

'Boss, you can't be serious!' Hunt exploded. 'Mia and Bish are my colleagues, too, you know.'

Chandler folded her arms across her chest. 'Say what you like,' she told Bliss. 'I'm coming with you.'

'No, you're not.'

'Yes, I am.'

Bliss tightened his gaze. 'DS Chandler. This is one of those rare occasions when I will insist you respect my rank. I am ordering you to remain here with these two firearms officers. Tell me you understand my order and that you will obey it. Because if you don't, I'll have one of those two men physically detain you. And they *will* follow my instruction.'

Chandler set her jaw and made no reply.

'DS Chandler. I'm giving you one last chance. Do you understand my order?'

'Yes. Sir.'

'And will you obey that order?'

'Yes. Sir.'

It pained him greatly to have to take matters so far, mainly because Bliss understood Chandler's reaction. In her position he would have done the same. But he already had two colleagues in trouble, and did not want to be distracted by having either Chandler or Hunt alongside him as he sought to find the others.

Bliss waved over the ARV pair. 'We were using our outdoor voices,' he said. 'You overheard us, I take it?'

Both men nodded. 'Yes, sir. Clearly.' This time it was the shorter of the two who replied.

'Then you know what's required.'

'We do.'

The taller officer took a step forward. 'I'm going with you, sir.'

'Are you sure?'

'Yes, sir. We tossed a coin.'

'Did you win or lose?'

He grinned. 'I won, sir.'

Bliss patted him on the upper arm. 'Good man.'

He turned back to his two team members, almost able to smell the anger seeping out of their pores. 'I'm sorry,' he told them. 'It was a tough call, but one I had to make.'

With that he spun around and headed into the quarry.

46

They took their time making their way forward, beginning the slow decline deeper into the gravel pit, whose craggy and pitted sides seemed to swallow them up. Bliss figured the remaining Hinchingbrooke firearms units could easily take ten minutes to mobilise, plus a further hour to make the drive north and then north-east.

Too long.

His fervent hope was that additional ARVs had been cruising the area closer by, because Eric Price and whoever else he chose to join him here would not arrive any sooner than the rest of his team.

Bliss felt bolstered by the proximity of the one firearms officer at his side, whose name he had learned was Fraser Hamilton, but if they were going to avoid further loss of life then a greater armed presence was required.

They came upon the Portakabin which rose up out of the gloom as if gradually emerging from the earth itself. Bliss instructed Hamilton to hold back while he checked it out. If their killer was lying in wait, he wanted to present only a single target. With the firearms officer off safety and on scope behind him, it took Bliss less than a minute to satisfy himself that the building was empty.

Hamilton rejoined him the moment Bliss signalled the all-clear, and together they started towards the point where the track curved away to the left.

'With all due respect, sir,' the armed cop said. 'Next time, you let me go ahead and check things out. I am the one with the weapon.'

'And as I said to my DS,' Bliss replied, shaking his head, 'I'm the one with the rank. You let me worry about who goes ahead of who, all right?'

'If you say so.'

His reluctance was obvious, and Bliss knew Hamilton was right. But the thought that Short and Bishop might be lying dead deeper into the quarry had the effect of making Bliss both more cautious on behalf of others whilst at the same time more reckless when it came to himself.

A dozen paces further along, Bliss raised a hand. The caravan shimmered in whatever starlight spilled from the sky, its exterior appearing to glow in the dark. But then Bliss saw he was partially wrong. Much of the light was coming from inside the caravan itself. Sound as well, in the form of orchestral music. Beneath the insistent brass and string tones there was a deep hum. An unseen generator, was Bliss's first thought.

Taking a deep breath, he turned a full 360 degrees. There was nothing else apart from the caravan, a truck parked to its left, and beyond them both a haphazard line of vehicles which disappeared out of view, but which Bliss suspected included a white Range Rover. When his eyes came to rest on a flatbed tow truck, Bliss knew it was the vehicle their man had used the night he had taken out Alan Brewer, having transported the little Renault to the location on its back.

This was the place all right.

This was where their killer was hiding out.

The question now was, where were Short and Bishop?

And were either or both of them still alive?

As the thought came to him, so the night erupted in a burst of sound and flashing colour which illuminated the night sky around the quarry. When a firearms unit approaches an emergency situation, it often does so at speed, full blues-and-twos, and both Bliss and Hamilton heard their approach long before they saw the vehicles appear in the distance and screech to a halt alongside the lone ARV back up on the plateau.

In one way, Bliss was relieved, and he puffed out a fog of pent-up air. But he was also vaguely disappointed at the sharp and obtrusive announcement. The sound and lights told them backup was here, that they could breathe a little easier. But what was it telling their killer?

The answer came to Bliss less than thirty seconds later.

His phone chimed to tell him a text had come in. He took out the mobile and checked the screen. 'Shit!' he said, stamping down on the rough surface of the track. A cloud of dust took to the air around his heel. He shook his head at Hamilton and showed the armed officer the message.

DO NOT APPROACH.
IF YOU TRY STORMING THE CARAVAN WE WILL BE KILLED.
HE HAS A SHOTGUN POINTED AT MY HEAD. HE SAID HE WILL TAKE US BOTH OUT. THEN HE WILL USE HIS AUTOMATIC WEAPONS ON ALL OF YOU.
HE IS SERIOUS, BOSS.

His mind screaming, both ears muffled by a high-pitched whistle, Bliss reacted swiftly despite the tight ball of terror forming in the depths of his stomach. He typed a reply and hit 'Send'.

Will he communicate directly with us?

There was no response. Bliss allowed enough time for a quick-fire discussion inside the caravan, before composing another message and sending it on as well.

If not, will he allow you or Mia to communicate with us?

Again nothing came back. A further wail of sirens echoed off the basin formed by the quarrying, and Bliss could also see flashing lights causing shadows to dance across the quarry walls. At least one of the newly arrived vehicles was edging closer to take up a forward position. His mind turned to the hostage negotiation and rescue situation they now faced. Concerned by all the possible permutations, Bliss made a call to Chandler.

'I know you're angry with me, Pen, but let it go for now. Bish just sent me a text. Our man has him and Mia trapped inside a caravan with him. He's armed with a shotgun this time, and claims to have access to more aggressive weapons. I want you to give HQ a bell. Explain the situation to them, make sure they understand it completely. Ask them if they have any hostage negotiation specialists nearby, someone capable of getting here in under an hour. We have to get a dialogue going right away, or this could spiral out of control before we manage to get a grip on it.'

Without rancour, Chandler said, 'I'll make the call. Meanwhile, do what you can, boss. I've heard how you talk to bastards like him. You'll find a way to engage the man while we're waiting.'

Bliss managed to dredge up a weak reply of appreciation, though in truth he already understood he was the wrong man for the job. Entirely out of his depth in this specific situation. When he spoke with suspects he was always in control, which gave him all the advantage he needed. Right now he couldn't have less control if he tried. He dialled another number, which was answered just before the voicemail cut in.

'Bliss?'

'Yes, ma'am.'

'Thank goodness you called in. I was on the point of contacting you directly. But why are you speaking to me and not DCI Edwards? And what the hell is going on?!'

Bliss had hit Superintendent Fletcher's speed-dial number for one reason only. He made his play. 'Because the DCI can't do what I need doing, ma'am. And with the greatest respect, I don't have time to fill you in on every detail. DS Short and DS Bishop are being held by the gunman. Those are the broad strokes. But here's why I called you: by now, Sergeant Waring from Boston will have seen the doctor after his unfortunate accident and should be back in interview room five. He's not given us a great deal, but what he did give up led us here. He knows more, ma'am. Much more. I'm convinced Thaw does as well, but perhaps not the full details. That's why I need you to get me something from Waring, ma'am. Just the killer's name for now, so's I have a point of reference. You can feed me his background when you've dug it up.'

'The name of the contract killer. You'd like it before starting negotiations, right?'

'That's correct. Bishop texted a warning, which was clearly under instruction from the gunman. But nothing since. I'll try again, then I'll call. But that name could be crucial, ma'am.'

'Leave it with me, Bliss.'

There was a swift rush of unexpected movement around him. Hamilton stepped to one side as his shorter colleague joined them, swiftly followed by Chandler and Hunt, both of whom now appeared more anxious than angry. Behind them stood two more armed officers, their expressions sober and concentrated.

'Boss, I spoke to Gul,' Chandler said. 'It seems DCI Warburton is a trained negotiator and is less than twenty minutes out.'

Bliss turned to the firearms crew. 'Let me tell you what I know. The man inside that caravan is holding two members of my team. He is armed with a shotgun, claims to also have automatic weapons on hand, and he carries at least one revolver. He has shot and killed several people already, including police officers. I don't doubt that he will pull the trigger on our own colleagues again if he feels threatened. Other armed units are on their way, including Inspector Price, but for now I want a couple of you to try and find an elevated spot from which you can see the interior of the caravan. Get eyes on with our gunman and report back what you see.'

One of the two new arrivals nodded, patted his colleague on the shoulder. Both men scuttled away into the enveloping darkness, disappearing from view beyond the truck. To Hamilton and the shorter officer, Bliss said, 'Stick with us for now. When everyone else gets here then Price can take command of the scene, and a DCI out of Lincolnshire will negotiate. Until then, we're all we've got.'

'Yes, sir,' both armed men snapped back.

Facing the caravan once more, Bliss could no longer see the other two ARV crew members, who by now had merged with the night so completely they might not have existed at all. He drew comfort from that, desperately wondering if there was anything else he could do before Warburton arrived. There was still the phone to consider, which prompted an idea. He quickly sent another text.

I assume you are seeing this – whoever you are. Please communicate with me before this escalates. We want all three of you to come walking out of there alive and unharmed. We just have to find a way to arrange that.

'At least we know they're alive at the moment, boss,' Hunt said, his face creased with concern.

Bliss understood the constable had said it as much for himself as his colleagues, so although he disagreed he made no reply. The message could have been written by anybody, though the fact that it was sent to his phone and the term "Boss" had been included, suggested it was sent by either Bishop or Short. That did not necessarily mean the other detective was alive.

Bliss turned to one of the officers hugging an H&K. 'You are all on secure comms together, yes?' he asked.

'Yes, sir.'

'Good. As soon as the others report back confirming they have eyes on the suspect, ask them what else they can see from their position. Are my two team members okay? Is there any sign of the other weapons he claims to have? And is there anything they have observed so far that will help us right now?'

While the firearms officer started talking to his colleagues, Bliss refocussed on his mobile. There was still no reply. The killer had said his piece, now he was apparently no longer interested in communicating. Bliss suspected the man was simply trying to figure a way out of the situation he was in. Taking his time to formulate a plan.

Bliss checked the time on his phone.

Approximately twelve minutes until both Warburton and the other firearms teams arrived.

Too long, Bliss thought. *Way too long.*

47

Those minutes spent waiting that evening were among the longest of his entire career, Bliss reflected shortly after the various teams had rolled up. Minutes during which he felt both impotent and incompetent.

At the point at which he'd decided Short and Bishop should carry out a recce at the quarry, a lot was happening at once. With all manner of tensions building around the case, he and his team were working under impossibly stressful conditions. But the question Bliss kept returning to was whether, given the exact same circumstances, he would make the same decision again.

Bliss realised it was ultimately futile to query himself. What was done was done, and he could neither turn back the clock, nor save and reset as if life were a video game. It was unlikely that he would even learn from the experience, because such situations occurred so infrequently in the career of a major crimes DI that he might well never face anything remotely similar again. Still, that did not prevent him from taking the full weight of responsibility and blame upon his own shoulders. It was his default position whenever something went so drastically wrong: his fault unless proven otherwise.

Following the lengthy wait, a lot happened within a short space of time. Warburton arrived with Smyth. Price turned up with three other members of his firearms unit. An SUV packed with four more armed officers blew in from Hinchingbrooke. As Bliss had predicted earlier, Price immediately took charge of the entire company of armed officers, huddling up with them then sending them out to take up different positions across the surrounding area. At the same time, DCI Warburton discussed the situation with what remained of the task force team. Bliss handed over his mobile, allowing Warburton to read the exchange of text messages. When she passed back the phone, the Lincolnshire DCI nodded at him.

'You did well, Bliss. You gave it a great shot. And thank you for getting the name out of Waring. I don't know how much further it will take us, but it can only help.'

'That was Superintendent Fletcher's work.'

'Of course. But you thought to ask her, and it was a good catch. It's always useful having a name to use. Plus, now we're able to delve into the man's background, find out more about him.'

'It seemed like the logical thing to do.'

'And I'm glad you did. Your super is still interviewing Waring. DCI Edwards and DC Ansari are working on Thaw, who has started to talk more since learning that we have Pavle Savic.'

'We do?' Bliss shook his head and turned to face the caravan. The situation had improved, but they were far from having their man.

'We will.' Warburton laid a hand on his arm as she corrected herself. 'Don't worry, Jimmy. We'll see your colleagues home.'

Behind the scenes, dozens of people worked separately and together at gaining as much intelligence on Savic as possible, but the best information was more likely to come from either Waring or Thaw. Bliss, however, thought they already knew the most critical thing about the man holding Short and Bishop hostage.

He had killed before.

He would not be afraid to kill again.

Pavle Savic was not the kind of man who panicked easily. His years with the *specijalne jedinice* assigned to the Serbian Ministry of Internal Affairs – the Special Forces equivalent of SEALs or SAS in his own country – then as a mercenary working in warzones in Africa, the Middle East and Central America, had provided him with the necessary skillset and experience required to both assess and take charge of any given situation. Yet while all that training and battlefield action lent him composure and the ability to think clearly when under duress, fear was also a constant companion.

True warriors, he understood, were not fearless. If you did not fear then you did not consider consequences, and if you did not consider consequences then you put yourself and others at risk. To be the best, you had to both recognise the fear and conquer it, because it raised your levels of awareness and made all the difference between a brave dead soldier and a brilliant living man of war.

Yet try as he might, it was hard to see a positive conclusion to the situation he was now in. His paymaster had promised him seclusion and isolation among other things, but still somehow his location had been compromised. Somebody had talked. Pavle –

who went by the name of Paul when in the United Kingdom – made a promise to himself that if he was fortunate enough to evade capture on this night, the person who had given him up would eventually be found with three bullet wounds in their body, and minus their head.

But that was for later.

First he had to take stock and approach the next few minutes and perhaps hours with clarity of thought and a realistic outlook. As things stood, there was one thing in his favour: the hostages. Everything else – absolutely everything – was against him. By now he was surrounded, most certainly by armed police officers. He knew these men, though not battle hardened, were highly trained and highly skilled. It did not matter how many weapons and how much ammunition he had available to him, the most he could hope for in a situation like this was to hold them at bay for a limited amount of time. It was a fight he could not win.

But it was also a fight he felt certain would not begin while he held onto his two ace cards.

49

Mia Short knelt alongside her colleague on the floor by the caravan door. Their captor had her and Bishop facing him as he stood with legs braced apart towards the centre of the living room area. She had never seen the business end of a shotgun close up from this position before, and she was certain her mind had created an image in which its gaping twin barrels were as large as the exhaust pipes on an articulated lorry. Short was acutely aware of the devastation one of these weapons could cause, especially at such close range.

Inevitably, her thoughts turned to her husband and twins back home. Not to mention the child she carried inside her. Short fought against these thoughts, casting them aside. Thinking of her loved ones now did no good whatsoever. Her mind needed to remain uncluttered.

She and Bishop remained in position with their wrists bound together. Same deal with their ankles. Any sudden movement towards the gunman would be their last. Other than the simple dread of being blasted by the shotgun, Short's overwhelming emotion was one of remorse. Her actions had led Bishop into the clutches of this psychopath, and she could not bear the thought of him coming to harm because of it.

After binding them, the man holding them at gunpoint asked them both questions. Short was eventually able to convince him she and Bishop had come alone to the quarry, but after insisting she was unaware of any other units heading their way, the man accused her of lying. He shifted the shotgun slightly to her left, aiming it at Bishop's head. He then told her he did not believe in second chances, that if she lied to him again he was going to pull the trigger. Fearing for her partner's life, and hearing the sincerity and complete lack of emotion in the gunman's voice, Short nodded and admitted she was expecting an ARV on scene.

The man spent the next few minutes pacing the room, his cold eyes remaining fixed upon them. Then something completely surreal happened. He began looking around the caravan's interior, muttering to himself, crouching low to the ground and talking about his 'little beauty'. Short wondered if the man kept a cat or a small dog as a pet, but she saw nothing move, and no sounds gave away the presence of any animal, nor were there any bowls of food or drink sitting on the scuffed linoleum floor of the galley-style kitchen area.

Eventually the gunman stood erect once more, turning his piercing gaze towards the door.

'Your people are here,' he said. 'They have stealth. Those who follow... not so much.'

His face broke out into a wide grin, and that was when Short heard the sirens in the distance. She turned to catch her partner's eye. 'I'm sorry, Bish,' she said softly. 'I'm so sorry.'

'Quiet!' the man roared, his voice booming in the small space. His mouth formed a jagged sneer. He shook his head at Short, then switched his attention to Bishop. 'You. You have a mobile phone, yes?'

Bishop nodded but made no reply.

'Good. I will get it for you and then you will send a message. You know who is out there in the dark, yes?'

'I have an idea who it is. But if you want me to do anything you'll have to free my hands.'

'Of course. Then I will tie them together again at the wrists. But first, you tell this person outside exactly what I tell you. That and no more. You understand.'

'I think so.'

The man took a stride closer. 'Then know so. Or we have a problem.'

After sending the text, the man kept hold of Bishop's phone, and when a reply and then further messages came in, he read them but made no attempt at a response. Short watched him closely, searching for signs of anger, irritation, or more hopefully fear. The man proved to be impossible to predict.

Short glanced sidelong at Bishop. He caught the movement. Nodded. Smiled. She closed her eyes as a tear escaped from one of them.

50

Bliss huddled together with DCI Warburton and Inspector Price. The firearms officer confirmed he had all units waiting in place. Savic was under observation from two snipers. They could see Short and Bishop only from the rear, but both were moving and appeared unharmed. The relief at hearing this drew a long, tired breath from Bliss. Price patted him on the back.

'They're okay,' he said. 'I know how you feel. I've had colleagues in similar situations before.'

'You get them out?' Bliss asked, squinting at the man.

'Each time.'

Bliss nodded, his lips thinning. Warburton was less ebullient. Her attempts at contacting Savic met with no response. She had texted Bishop's phone. Made three calls, leaving three messages. She had also called out to Savic, using his name and asking him to talk. All to no avail. Establishing a rapport was essential for any successful negotiation, but if the hostage taker refused to respond then your options were limited.

'He's good at this,' she told them. 'He relayed his one message at the very beginning. Since then, no reply to any of our requests. No contact means he cannot say or do the wrong thing, he cannot be lulled or convinced by anything said. That's clever on his part, and I assume it comes from military training. If he communicates with us at all, it will be only when he decides the time is right. For him. At which point he will make his demands.'

'What if he doesn't have any?' Chandler asked.

'I don't even want to think about that scenario.'

'So what, we do nothing?' Bliss said, throwing up his arms in frustration.

'For now I keep on trying. It really is all I can do. Meanwhile, we're starting to get some intelligence on the man. We'll look through it all and try to find a way to puncture his silence. We'll monitor and assess. He will know there's no escape unless he surrenders.'

'Or kills himself.'

Warburton dipped her head in acknowledgement. Neither of them felt like putting voice to what they both knew such an act would mean for Savic's hostages.

'I don't think we're going to learn anything about this man that will let us slip beneath his skin,' Price said. 'I have my two best shots lined up on him. He must know we have him in our crosshairs, but the man is standing there at the far end of the caravan showing himself almost as if he's taunting us. His shotgun is aimed and ready for action. My betting is he knows we won't risk taking a shot, because even a direct hit between the eyes could cause a reflex twitch that pulls on his own trigger.'

'But then he must also realise he can't wait us out,' Bliss said. 'Not forever.'

'Right now he's still weighing up his options. My guess is before long he will call, at which point we will know his next move.'

Warburton agreed. 'It is his next logical option. He will have demands. In order to make them, he must contact us.'

All Bliss could do was wonder how it had come to this. Strategising any investigation was a difficult task, but eventually he and his team were always able to formulate a plan. That was the point at which Bliss began to feel in control of the situation. The difference this time was that no sooner had they reached a decision and set things in motion, than their killer acted and cut dead the team's activities, forcing them to re-evaluate and react. At no stage over the past three days had Bliss felt on top of this operation, which left a bad taste in his mouth and a sense of dread he was unable to shake.

51

If the armed police officers were any good at all, then by now they had a bead on him and were ready to squeeze on their triggers with every intention of ending his life. Paul knew this to be the case, and accepted it as part of the overall challenge he faced. He also believed they would not take the decision to fire on him unless they became convinced he was about to harm one or both of their colleagues. That fact alone had bought him this much time, and they were in no hurry to force his hand.

It made perfect sense. If they were as good as he suspected, he would be dead before the sound of breaking glass or the shot itself became audible. If they were as good as he suspected, his brain would immediately cease to be able to control both the thought synapses and muscle contractions required to fire his sawn-off Browning. Yet if they really were as good as he suspected, they would also be acutely aware that the reflexive action of his death might accidentally result in a fatal pull on one or both triggers.

So they would not take the shot. Not yet.

Paul took a breath. He felt surprisingly calm. The situation was his to manage. The two detectives continued to kneel on the rough, threadbare carpet in the centre of the caravan. He met the man's gaze and acknowledged him with a flick of the hand.

'You,' he said. 'You call your boss now.' He waggled the mobile and said, 'What number?'

The man licked his lips. 'Speed-dial one,' he replied.

Paul nodded. He pressed the combination of buttons and then held the phone to the man's ear. 'Good. You make sure it is your boss, then I speak.'

Moments later, the policeman's eyes flickered instinctively. Then he said, 'Boss. It's me. Bishop. Don't ask any questions. He wants to talk to you.'

Paul twitched the shotgun, just to remind the detective of its presence and of who had sole control over life and death inside the caravan. He took a deep breath before speaking into Bishop's phone.

'Listen only. I want a four-seat vehicle, with a driver. He must pull up directly outside my door. He will then get out and open the two nearside doors, after which he will climb back in behind the wheel. The man I have here will then come out and get in beside the driver, and close the door once he is inside. I will then come out with the woman, and both of us will slide into the back. At all times I will have my finger on the trigger with pressure already applied. If I see anybody else within fifty feet of us, I will fire. If anybody tries to jump me, I will fire. And if anyone shoots me, I am certain I will still pull my trigger. Nobody is to follow us when we leave. If they do, I will fire. When I have reached my destination, I will allow all three police officers to remain alive and well. This is my promise to you, in exchange for doing exactly as I say. I think by now you know I am a man of my word.'

52

'Okay, I hear you,' Bliss said as calmly as he was able to given the circumstances. 'But you listen to me now, before we go any further, our hostage negotiator wants to...' He stopped speaking because he realised Savic had ended the call.

'He really is a man of his word,' Warburton said beside him, having heard the conversation on the phone's speaker. 'He told you to listen only, and he meant it. He had no intention of listening to anything you said in response.'

'Bastard!' Bliss cursed beneath his breath, not wanting the Serbian to hear his spiralling outrage from inside the caravan.

'Take it easy, Jimmy. I know how you feel, but losing your rag will solve nothing.'

Bliss nodded. He glanced at Price. 'I suggest you redeploy some of your people, Eric. Have them take up positions ready for if or when we stick one of our vehicles outside that door.'

'Are we going to allow that to happen?' Price asked. 'I mean, right here and now we have the best setup we are ever likely to have in terms of taking this man down. We have a clear shot and a green light. If you let him go mobile, we lose it all.'

'We may have no choice,' Warburton answered, stepping in as

negotiator. 'We can delay only so long. He knows we have vehicles here. He's not asked for anything that requires time or external authority to summon up. It's something we are able to deliver. And I mean soon. Within minutes.'

'And if we don't?'

'Then my bet is he'll threaten to shoot one of his hostages.'

53

Paul continued to feel unruffled, but he also recognised that he was about to enter the most fraught period of the entire stand-off. He had made his demands. The police would either comply or they would not. If they did, then at some point during the transition he risked becoming exposed to something more than a bullet. Perhaps an officer secreted behind the vehicle, whose task it was to shift the aim of his weapon. Maybe even somebody hidden in the rear compartment. But he was prepared for all eventualities should they attempt to foil his escape.

He had already decided to keep the woman secure if they ended up going mobile, using the male detective as the first offering of his resolve. If they did not deliver the vehicle and driver, he would threaten to shoot the man. A threat came with one opportunity to comply. Which, in being true to himself, was all he ever gave. He saw no reason to change his methods now.

After five minutes of inactivity and silence he hit redial on Bishop's phone. The call was answered immediately. The voice this time was a woman's.

'Pavle,' she said. 'My name is Diane. I'm going to be negotiating with you from now on. Before we go any further, how are my two officers doing?'

'I do not see my transport,' he said, no inflection in his own voice. A complete lack of emotion was always the hardest thing for them to hear.

'It's being made ready. My two officers. How are they both, Pavle?'

'Ready? One driver gets inside, starts it up, and pulls it around to my door. That's ready.'

'We're having it refuelled. We don't want you to run out of petrol and get angry with our colleagues.'

Paul considered the response. Was it a lie? He did not enjoy being lied to. He rarely gave a second chance when that happened. Was it already time to make his threat? He ran through the various permutations, deciding he had nothing to lose by doing so. 'If you are stalling, let me tell you I have my shotgun pointed at your man's face. This Bishop is your friend, no? I think this is true. So hear me now, I will kill him if you do not comply with my demands.'

'Hey, now there's no need for that, Pavle. There is no question of us not complying. We're siphoning fuel from one vehicle to the other, giving you a full tank. That's all. What could we possibly gain from such a short delay?'

Killing the call, Paul allowed the phone to fall from his grasp, where it bounced once on the carpeted surface and then lay still on the floor. The words spoken by the woman outside sounded composed, her explanation perfectly reasonable.

Too composed.

Too reasonable.

The use of his name showed a certain respect. Perhaps a little too much. Paul did not know what they had to gain by the delay, only that he was being delayed. This was unacceptable to him. It meant they had no intention of complying with his wishes.

He swore and stamped down on the phone. Once. Twice. A third time, much harder, using the full force of his boot heel to crush the glass screen to dust. Infuriated, a low growl emerged from the back of his throat. He saw the two detectives staring up at him with horrified expressions on their faces. Paul grinned crookedly, stamping his foot down one last time.

Whether it was that final fierce and sudden action, a shift in the air caused by the movement, or the vibration rattling through the caravan's steel floor beneath the thin layer of carpet, nobody would ever know. But something about Paul's demolition of the phone caught the attention of the reptile nestling close by underneath the TV stand.

That final brutal stamp had likely caused the snake to fear it was under attack, and the brown, diamond-backed adder did precisely what its instincts told it to do.

The adder coiled and reared and cracked the air as it struck. It bit down hard into the thing that had triggered its distress, and venom flowed into its victim's bloodstream.

Paul cried out in both alarm and pain as the creature's fangs sank deep into his calf muscle, the startled reaction causing him to pull back on the shotgun's trigger.

As the creature recoiled and retreated back to relative safety, the sound of the gunshot inside the mobile home was deafening.

54

Bliss was the first to respond, the first to reach the caravan. He was vaguely aware of the bellowed warnings for him to keep clear as he ran, that he could still be in danger if the shooter had one cartridge left unexpended or had already reached for another weapon.

But Bliss ignored them all.

The shotgun's explosive retort had been swiftly followed by two further shots from clearly different weapons. In pulling the first trigger, the assassin had surely signalled his own death. If not... Bliss did not even want to think about what might be waiting for him on the other side of the caravan door. But as the commotion around him coalesced into a series of animated blurred figures and faces, he drove his feet hard up three steps and wrenched open the door anyway.

The pink mist was thick and cloying.

Bishop lay on his back, blood and viscera spattered all over his face and chest. Too much blood and horrific gore for the victim to have survived. Bliss entered the area and knelt by his friend's side, reaching beneath the slumped form and pulling the man close to his chest.

'Bish!' he cried. 'Bish! Speak to me, Bish.'

It was too late. He knew Bishop had to be gone.

Frantically his eyes scoured his friend's body for the gaping wounds he knew must be there. He needed to locate and compress them, stop precious lifeblood from pumping out onto the caravan floor. Only he could not find them. Broad spatters and trails and smudges of blood. But no open wounds, sucking or otherwise. Bliss saw hard nuggets of what looked like bone, as well as strands of softer, pulpy tissue smeared all over Bishop's face, yet there was no obvious sign of the wounds that had created them.

And then he saw tears forming in his colleague's eyes. They welled and began to slide across the top of his cheek and run down the side of his head towards his ears. Bliss watched in confusion as the trails worked their way through the blood spatters. Bishop's shoulders lurched and his chest rose and fell as he emitted a deep, animal-like howl.

'Boss!' a voice called out from behind him.

'Get help!' Bliss snapped without looking back over his shoulder.

'Boss!' More strident this time.

Bliss swivelled his head. Hunt stood there, looking down at...

Turning the other way to follow Hunt's gaze, Bliss was astonished to discover a child sprawled out on the floor. It made no sense whatsoever, yet the figure was so tiny it could only be a child. But as he blinked, he saw that this child was dressed in the same clothes Mia Short had been wearing earlier in the day. Even as his eyes began to take in the familiar diminutive form, and the dense spillage of blood became more apparent the higher up the body his gaze climbed, Bliss's only thought was to wonder at who this child with the missing face could possibly be.

55

Darkness had become a frequent and unwelcome visitor in Bliss's life. Whenever either personal or professional tragedy staked a claim on his emotions, he felt the chill of its touch and the full weight of its import pushing down on him. Mia Short had been both a colleague and friend and her loss injected a pain into Bliss's heart so piercing he wondered if it would ever dissipate.

This time the black veil of grief settled over him as he sat alone in his office. Several hours had slipped by since the events at the quarry. Having scrubbed himself clean of blood and bone matter and changed into a fresh set of clothes, Bliss volunteered to deliver the tragic news to Short's husband. It was one of the toughest things he had ever done, but he believed he owed it to Mia. Later, having left a family liaison officer with the sobbing man and his two distraught children, he drove himself back to HQ.

For much of this time, Bliss felt as if life was taking place inside a bubble, where sounds were indistinct, vision never sufficiently sharp to be accurate. At any moment when a thousand thoughts and more assaulted his senses, Bliss focussed on only one: the absence of Mia Short.

Pain was not a strong enough word to describe how he felt.

Sorrow was familiar to him. He had previously lost family and friends, as well as his wife in the most horrific of circumstances. But the utter misery brought about by this death had left him reeling and barely in touch with the world around him. He met nobody's gaze when coming back to his office, said nothing at all to those he encountered. If they spoke to him he was unaware of it. Bliss closed the door behind him and slumped down into his chair behind the desk, as hollowed out as he had ever felt.

When a gentle knock came at his door a few moments later, he told whoever stood outside to go away, the instruction barked and unrepentant.

But the handle moved, the door swung inwards and instead of obeying his order, Detective Superintendent Fletcher entered the office. She sealed them inside and turned to face him. 'We've told Waring and Thaw about the outcome at the quarry and they can't wait to dish the dirt on each other,' she said.

Her manner was businesslike. Bliss understood his boss was attempting to lead him back to the path of work as a way of luring him out of his self-imposed darkness. It was a tactic he himself had employed in the past.

'I'm not surprised,' he managed to say. 'Do they understand what they've done?'

'I think they do. Especially Sergeant Waring. He took it badly, I have to admit.'

'Good. I hope it haunts him for the rest of his miserable life.'

'On that we can agree, Jimmy. From what we're hearing it looks very much as if it was Thaw who schemed his way into both circles, and at some point Waring spotted an opportunity he could not resist. As it turns out, both were perfectly happy to see the end of Baker, and just as eager for others to have done their dirty work for them.'

'I bet they were. For one of them it meant climbing higher up the social scale in Baker's absence, while the other boosted his own reputation and income from Thaw's increased business. And all while intimidating those involved in the actual murder.'

Superintendent Fletcher nodded. 'Which was one of the reasons why those thirteen suspects were not hunted down before now. Both Thaw and Waring had them all in their pockets for as long as none of them broke ranks to confess.'

'I'm guessing the situation changed,' Bliss said. *And sounding the death knell for Mia in the process.*

'It looks that way. It was Waring who wormed his way beneath Thaw's skin. He sensed one or two of the suspects were faltering, and it occurred to him that if they did a deal then the whole house of cards would come tumbling down around his ears. He said he'd been wary of it all along, and had always planned on taking action against everybody involved if he felt threatened.'

'Don't tell me. Let me guess. Waring didn't have the means to hire a contract killer, and saw Thaw as the answer in respect of finance and, of course, their previous alliance. Our *colleague* simply decided it was too risky *not* to do something about the thirteen. Both in terms of the chance they might talk, but I suspect also because they might come looking for a payday through blackmail at some future point.'

Fletcher sighed. 'It's a terrible thing, ambition. Mix it with greed and it can become a highly volatile brew. Of course, you have to be that way inclined to begin with. Waring was not lured unwillingly onto the rocks. He sought them out and eventually foundered on them.'

'Leaving behind a trail of misery and dead bodies in his wake.'

Bliss did not think only of Mia at this point, nor even the other officers or Kelly Gibson. His thoughts extended also to those local members of the Sutton End community who had been driven virtually psychotic by Charles Baker and his lust for power and money. So far into the darkness they became consumed by their own bloodlust.

'How did they ever hope to get away with it?' Bliss muttered.

'What made them believe they could possibly regulate such a large number of people?'

'I'm not sure they did. Both of them admitted that the whole thing spiralled out of their control. They expected to stir up emotion and hatred, and a reaction from two or three people, especially from the Roma camp because of the rape victim. Neither of them were aware of how many people became involved in the murder until after Baker was dead.'

'And by then it was too late. No un-ringing that bell, right?'

'Exactly. It became unwieldy not by design, but by chance. They did too good a job of stirring up hatred towards Charles Baker.'

Bliss nodded. Took a breath. A number of actions unravelled after being set in motion. Neither Waring nor Thaw had predicted the escalation, yet their collusion ultimately led to the death of Mia Short. Nothing they said or did now could ever compensate for that.

As for the assassin, Bliss would gladly have put the rifle bullets through the man's head himself. If anything, the killer's own death was over too quickly and painlessly for Bliss's liking. But at least he was gone and would never have his day in court.

Fletcher pulled a folded sheet of paper from her jacket pocket and handed it over. 'I think this explains how Waring saw this working out,' she said. 'It was found on our killer.'

Bliss pulled back the folds and read what was written in black ink on the page. He peered back up at his boss. 'A copy of our assassin's hit list.'

'You see who the last name is on there?'

He read it fully this time then folded it up and passed it back to Fletcher. 'So Thaw was meant to be the final victim. Waring wanted him silenced as well. He needed the man's money, but that was as deep as their partnership ran as far as he was concerned.'

'I can't say I'm surprised. What's one more death among so many? Especially when it not only slams the door on the matter, but effectively seals it.'

'Not quite,' Bliss argued. 'Savic was used to silence everyone else involved, but who was going to silence Savic?'

Fletcher squinted at him. 'I hadn't considered that. I expect Waring had it in mind to tie off that loose end himself.'

Bliss nodded. It seemed likely. 'Did they find the snake?' he asked. Bishop had managed to tell them everything he could remember, including how the adder had struck at Pavle Savic.

'Eventually. Evidently it was a right bugger for the RSPCA to corner.'

'I guess there's some justice in his own pet contributing to his eventual downfall.'

Fletcher agreed. 'But none at all that it should also cause the loss of one of our own,' she said.

'I think it's time I spoke with my team,' Bliss said after a moment of silence passed between the two.

'They're all out there waiting for you. They understand the process, Jimmy. Before you can speak to them about what happened, you have to first come to terms with it fully yourself.'

'And how about you, ma'am?' he asked. 'How are you dealing with it?'

'In truth, I'm riding a professional wave that I hope is taking me back towards sanity without my completely screwing up. I dare say that at some point soon the date I have with a bottle of red wine will cause my emotions to overflow.'

Fletcher paused for a moment, a wistful expression appearing on her face as she continued. 'You and I are not entirely dissimilar when it comes to processing such things, Jimmy. There are differences, of course. Me, I immediately switch into superintendent mode, do what needs to be done, and then later allow myself to wallow. You need time before you can press that professional button. But in the end, we both manage to go on as well as find a way to mourn. It's all we can do, otherwise it destroys us.'

Bliss cast his eyes downward. 'This is going to be the hardest thing I've ever had to do as a team leader. Many years ago, long before your time here, ma'am, I had to speak to my squad following the suicide of one of our own. Penny Chandler and I worked closely with him, and he killed himself after I discovered he was both on the take and a murderer. That was tough, because despite everything he did, he was a much-loved character around the station. I considered him a great friend. But now, with Mia... my mind is a black hole. There's so much to say, but I'm at a loss as to how to go about it.'

'Speak from the heart,' Fletcher advised him. 'Everyone will respect you for it, no matter what words spill out. But first of all, you need to throw off those shackles, Jimmy. I spoke with DS Chandler and DCI Warburton before heading into your office. They told me how you feel about the way events unfolded. So I'm telling you now, before you ask your team to move on, you need to be in a place where you can do the same. Starting by accepting this was not your fault.'

Despite Fletcher's soothing voice and heartfelt assertion, Bliss felt unspoken criticism of him seeping out of the ventilation ducts. Its essence tainted the discoloured walls and fabrics with crimson darkness, imbuing the air with blood and tissue particulates, their toxic vapours swarming around him like a cloud of angry insects waiting to infect him with their poison.

'Inspector,' the superintendent said, nudging him back into the moment. 'Do you accept what I have said? That you did nothing wrong.'

Bliss licked his lips. Tapped his left index finger against his temple. 'In here,' he said. He then tapped the same finger against his heart. 'But not in here.' His hand slipped lower, and he spread it across the slight bulge of his stomach. 'Or in here.'

'Which is perfectly natural. And I know you understand why that is the case, Jimmy. Your gut instinct insists you could have done something different, perhaps even something more. Anything, in fact, that would not have led to Mia's death. Your heart aches for the loss we and Mia's family have suffered, and that ache feels like a harsh rebuke. But inside your head, where reality and logic take over from emotion, you recognise the truth. That's a good thing. A healthy thing.'

'It doesn't feel that way right now, ma'am.'

'Because it's all still too raw. But your team is also in pain and it needs its leader. One final thing you need to be aware of before you go out there to speak with them. DCI Edwards took control of the situation earlier when you rushed out of here to drive over to the quarry. She assumed gold command. There may be a price to pay for that.'

Bliss frowned and shook his head. 'If so, it'd be grossly unfair, ma'am. You say I'm not to blame, but if that's true then the boss was even less so.'

'This is the police, Jimmy. Someone always has to be accountable. Now, come on, I'll walk with you.'

When they entered the major crimes area, the place was teeming with people but the conversation was subdued. Silence gradually washed over the room as everybody became aware of their presence.

'I loved Mia Short,' was how Bliss began addressing his colleagues. 'And that's the simple truth of the matter. I loved her in the same way I love all of you who work by my side and never take a backward step. It's the kind of bond so few people understand, and fewer still get to enjoy. When someone touches your life in such a way, you never forget them. Mia may have been snatched from this world, but she will never be gone from either our hearts or minds.

'Moreover, I respected Mia so much. The colleague she was, the friend, the DI she was destined to be. Fact is, I think if she had ambitions to rise even higher in the ranks, Mia was the type of character to achieve just about anything she put her mind to. We knew her as hard-working, fiercely loyal, and those who let themselves be swayed by her stature soon learned the error of their ways.'

337

This prompted a ripple of gentle laughter. A shared memory of the firecracker Mia Short could be when riled.

Bliss glanced around at his team. He reflected on those words and how he had only come to realise the truth of them as he delivered his speech. Sadness threatened to overwhelm him once more, prompting him to speak. To say anything, hear anything back, rather than allow the utter grief he felt to completely engulf him.

'I do feel guilty. I sent Mia and Bish out there. It should have been me, but it wasn't. Things were more than a little hectic and perhaps I didn't pay enough attention to the possibilities. To the threat we now know existed. But I'll overcome that feeling of guilt. Because eventually I will accept the reality of what happened.

'That a series of criminal and ugly events spurred by pure greed led Mia and Olly Bishop into harm's way at the hands of a contract killer and ex-mercenary from Serbia, who held a firearm on them in the midst of a dangerous and escalating situation. I guess we will never know if Savic would have pulled the trigger had he not been bitten by his own pet. But we do know the surprise at being bitten jarred the man's aim as well as cause him to fire. We could be sitting here just as easily mourning the loss of Olly Bishop, and we must all wish him well while he recovers in hospital from shock.

'Today, though, we rightly mourn Mia. Counselling sessions will be offered to all of you, and I urge you to take advantage of them. If that sounds odd coming from me, well it sounds just as odd *to* me. But trust me when I say you need to talk about this with somebody. I understand that many of you will not want to take this home with you, and I can empathise. So don't. Speak to the counsellor and find your own way back. Take as much time as it needs. None of us will ever forget Mia Short, and nor should we. But I believe we honour her memory best by carrying on doing the job she loved and died for.'

Bliss stood back and lowered his head. Silence followed. Then, after a moment, a slow applause broke out. Within seconds everybody joined in, and when Bliss looked up he saw colleagues weeping and hugging and sharing emotions they so desperately needed to express.

DC Ansari raised her Peterborough United mug and called out, 'Three cheers for Mia Short.'

The entire room erupted into cheers for their late colleague, and the mood changed from one of immense sorrow to an overwhelming sense of great resolve. Chandler made her way over through the throng to hug Bliss.

'Are we okay, Pen?' he asked as they both pulled away. 'After what happened earlier?'

She peered deep inside him. 'Of course. Always. And, if it means anything to you, you were right to hold me back at the quarry. I would have been a liability, someone else you needed to think about when you already had Bish and… and Mia.'

'Just as long as we're still talking.'

This raised a faltering smile together with a fresh glut of tears squeezed from her reddened eyes. 'You and I are fine, Jimmy. Better than fine. We're good.'

When Chandler turned away to speak to Gratton, she was swiftly replaced at his side first by Ansari and then, to his complete shock, DCI Edwards.

'You did well,' she whispered in his ear. 'Mia would be so proud of you.'

Bliss nodded. 'Cheers, boss. I hope none of this comes back to bite you. We've not always seen eye to eye, but you shouldn't have to take a hit for this.'

'I'm not sure if I agree with you,' Edwards said. Her eyes were dull and as flat as her tone. She appeared to still be in a state of shock. 'Our colleague and friend is dead. I can't wash my hands of her death.'

'If they ask me, I'll be in your corner. I won't let it go without a fight.'

She raised a weak smile. 'You know what, Jimmy. Despite everything that has gone on between us, I wouldn't put it past you to defend me.'

Fletcher bided her time as Bliss shook hands with other colleagues, eventually slipping alongside him. Smiling, she hooked an arm through his and said, 'Nail the men responsible for what happened last night. Justice is pedestrian, so it will take time, but as soon as they are convicted, you will be able to look back on these past few days in a completely different light.'

Bliss blew out a long sigh. 'I do hope so, boss. I still find it hard to believe this was put together by those two arseholes. I thought they were holding back on us, but I didn't have either of them down as the linchpin on this.'

'That's probably because neither of them were on their own. You and I both know this did not go the way of many of our operations. It was fast, it was furious, and it left little option but to react to ever-changing circumstances. The thing to keep in mind is that you did precisely that. The one thing nobody will say about you when you hang up your spurs, Jimmy, is that you lacked determination. You have it to the point of bloody-mindedness, and you can take credit for working this out and for identifying the location of our killer.'

'Yeah. Which leads me back to the quarry, which in turn steers me all the way around to Mia again. I wish I'd never figured the bloody thing out.'

Fletcher shook her head. 'You don't mean that. Not really. Large parts of all this will simply vanish from your conscious thoughts. But, you should always remember Mia, no matter how much it hurts to do so. Soon, those awful images that you carry with you right now will fade, and what you will see then is the Mia you knew and loved in life. The happy, smiling face of a team member and friend. I guarantee you it will happen one day without you even being aware of it.'

Bliss shrugged. 'I'm not so sure about that, ma'am,' he said.

'I know you tend to carry your scars internally, Jimmy. That your heart bleeds for those you have lost reveals itself in your character every single day. But in time, the guilt will diminish, those haunting memories along with them, and you will once again be reunited with the true version of our absent friend.'

'That's a pretty big guarantee,' Bliss said, turning to face his boss.

'It is. And the reason I feel able to give it is because your therapist will not be the one who will deliver it to you. She will not be the one who will rid you of your current shackles and set you free. Neither will it be your friends, colleagues, family or bosses.'

'Then who will?'

Fletcher gently squeezed his arm. 'Why, you of course. That same integrity of character now holding you in its grip is the same one that will eventually release you. It has always come from within you, Jimmy. I thought by now you had realised that.'

56

Bliss did not mind the wait. Not when he had such an extraordinary view to gaze out upon. Standing at the Turquoise Coast vista point where he and Chandler now over-looked the bay from which the region took its name, they were close enough to the cliffs at which the Düden Waterfalls spill out into the Mediterranean Sea to feel its spray refresh their exposed flesh.

Bliss turned his face to the sun and breathed in fresh clean air, a cooling breeze ruffling his close-cropped hair. The blazing hot summer had bleached its colour from silver to white, and it did not appear to be in a hurry to change back again now that autumn was in full swing.

Five days earlier, the bureaucratically impaired conglomerate of British and Turkish agencies and offices who jointly worked towards reuniting Chandler with her estranged daughter, finally came through. The British side had been aligned and keen for a couple of weeks, but received pushback from the Turkish National Security Service. Pressure was applied, however, and the MI6 agent resident in the British Embassy in Ankara had intervened with both the NSS and police in Antalya to pave the way for a direct approach to Mehmet Uzun.

It was their acquaintance, Munday, from MI5 who called Chandler personally to report the seismic shift. 'Apparently, your ex was rather aggressive in his opposition to the very notion of you being in contact with his daughter.'

'I can't say I'm surprised to hear that,' was her flat response.

'The local police officers initially used his volatile outbursts as an excuse to back off. However, our SIS man in Turkey explained to Mehmet that paving the way towards a meeting might be the lesser of two evils – the other one being charged with abduction and the possibility of a trial being held in the UK where the abduction first occurred. He did not relent without a fight, but relent he did.'

'Thank you for all your efforts.'

'You're very welcome. Please do me one favour, though.'

'Anything.'

'Tell Bliss to leave me alone. We're done now.'

Chandler came from a sizeable family, but had never considered anyone other than Bliss to accompany her on her journey into a country that existed on the cusp of eastern and western philosophies and convictions. Their visas were rushed through without delay, and they had flown into Turkey the previous evening from Birmingham. Hannah was being driven alone to the appointed location by a senior member of the local police service; an arrangement agreed between parties acting on behalf of both Mehmet and Chandler.

While Bliss took in the stunning view and basked in the warmth of the late-September sunshine, Chandler paced back and forth. Anxious tiny steps, moving her in a subconscious regular pattern that traced a small triangle shape on the ancient paving slabs. There was one way into the vista point and one way out again, onto the main thoroughfare that ran into the heart of Antalya city centre. As she shuffled back and forth, Chandler's eyes never once left the entrance to the slip road.

'What if she's changed her mind?' Chandler said absently, snaring Bliss's attention.

'She won't have.'

'But what if she has?'

Bliss turned away from the ocean and stepped towards his friend. He put his hands on her shoulders. 'Then it will be a case of last-minute nerves, that's all. She'll overcome them, Pen.'

'We can't know that, Jimmy. Not for sure. My daughter came to this country believing I was dead. Why should she care now?'

'Because now she knows you're alive, and there's no doubt in my mind that she is every bit as anxious to see you as you are her. It's human nature. You're her mother. For the past seventeen years you have been a vague memory and a sense of loss to her. She won't pass up on this. Believe me.'

Chandler stood still for a moment. Sighed, hands resting lightly on her hips. 'How come you're Mr Positive all of a sudden? Usually you're the Eeyore of our group.'

'Because I've never been so certain of anything in my life as I am about this.' Bliss stared deep into his friend's gleaming eyes. 'You never gave up on her once in all these years, Pen. Don't do so now.'

'Don't call me Pen.'

'I wouldn't have to if you stopped being such a soppy tart.'

Chandler nodded. She peered up into his face. 'I see you,' she told him.

'What d'you mean you see me?'

'I see the real you. Beneath the bravado I see the pain etched into your flesh.'

'I'm fine.'

'No, Jimmy. You're not fine at all. And I know you don't need me to remind you for the hundredth time that what happened to Mia was not your fault, but I'll do so all the same. Nobody could have foreseen it ending up that way. And if you want to blame yourself for having suggested she act up as DI, then you'd be wrong. Mia would have put herself in the exact same position had she still been a DS. Had she been a bloody DC, for that matter.'

Bliss shook his head. 'You've got it all wrong. I'm not blaming myself, Pen. Not anymore. I understand why you might think that. I do. But I'm past feeling sorry for myself. I know it wasn't my fault. One of the three people to blame is now dead, and the others will wish they were. If I'm feeling a little melancholic, then maybe that's acceptable given the circumstances. I may have changed the way I regard things, but it doesn't make me immune to sadness.

'I miss Mia so much. I can't bear the thought that I will never see her come through the major crimes doors again, her blonde hair flapping around her head, those black leather outfits, the pen-tapping. She was the original "Cuffs and Baton Barbie" and every time I close my eyes I still see her that way. I'm not depressed or climbing the walls, Pen. I'm just sad. So very, very sad.'

Chandler reached up to squeeze his hand. 'I know. I am, too.'

They both heard the approaching engine at the same time. Bliss turned his head. A white Ford Tourneo Connect was coming in off the slip road entrance. Its boxy shape made it look like a cross between an SUV and a van with windows, but all Bliss could focus on was the blue livery and the word 'POLIS' running across the sloping bonnet.

Bliss could feel Chandler's body quaking, and he leaned in to whisper in her ear, 'It's okay, Pen. You've got this. All you have to do is be yourself. You do that and she won't fail to fall in love with you.'

She flicked him a sidelong glance. He read the gratitude in it and he nodded and let go of her hand. Somehow managing not to rush headlong in her excitement, Chandler made her way across the paving slabs to the roadside kerb. Seconds later, the vehicle pulled over and came to a halt directly in front of her. The driver, a uniformed police officer, exited and walked swiftly around to the kerb.

'Miss Chandler?' he said uncertainly. A middle-aged man, dressed all in blue and sporting a beret, he eyed her with no small measure of trepidation. Bliss noticed the officer's gaze slip his way momentarily, assessing any potential threat.

'That's me,' she replied. From her bag she took out her passport, opening it to reveal her photograph and details.

The Turkish cop examined it for what seemed an age, before finally nodding and stepping to one side. 'The agreement is for me to remain for precisely one hour,' he said in halting English. 'Then I have to return Miss Uzun to her home.'

'I understand.'

The officer reached out a hand and pulled the rear door open. Moments later, a tall and lithe young woman wearing a long-sleeved dark blue dress which flowed out and down to ankle-length, stepped out of the vehicle. No hijab covered her hair, which was long and silky and dark brown. Her eyes were dark, wide, and set deep.

A breath caught in Bliss's throat – Chandler's daughter was stunningly beautiful. For a moment there was only silence as the two women stared at each other. Then Hannah nodded once at Chandler, and her mouth formed a heartfelt smile revealing perfect white teeth.

'Hello, mother,' she said softly.

'Hello, Anna,' Chandler replied. 'I'm so very pleased to meet you again.'

Bliss turned away, back to the ocean, his eyes misted with more than the spray coming off the waterfalls still tumbling into the deep blue waters below.

AUTHOR'S NOTE

Sutton End does not exist – so far as I am aware – in Lincolnshire. I invented the town because of the things I write about its inhabitants, and I was concerned about all manner of libel issues arising if I had used a real town as the location in this specific instance.

The Baker's Dozen case is, however, based on real life events which took place in a little rural town in the USA. I have used 'artistic' licence to expand upon the theme, but certainly a similar event appears to have rocked small town America in the past.

At the end of *The Reach of Shadows* I was determined to give Bliss and his team a more straightforward case afterwards, one that kept them on their toes and never let up, blazing across their lives like a comet. That *The Death of Justice* brought both tragedy and then happiness for some was, perhaps, an unequal balance, and I don't expect to escape from my readers on some of what took place and the choices I made. Please know they were made for the right reasons.

ACKNOWLEDGEMENT

I have a few of these to get out there this time, and as usual I'm really happy to. I'll begin by thanking Diane Warburton for paying (to charity) for the opportunity to appear in this book as a character. Diane chose to be on the side of good rather than evil, and to my surprise she not only ended up being a DCI but also spending a huge amount of time on the page. Diane, I hope you like what I did with you. I'll also take the opportunity at this juncture to thank my two main beta readers, Dorothy Laney (my aunt) and Livia Sbarbaro (my friend).

Specific technical gratitude is extended this time to both David Drayton and Holly Gibbs at the John Lucas Funeral Directors in Peterborough's Dogsthorpe area, who were extremely helpful with my questions about the embalming process. Any mistakes or omissions are my own, not theirs, as they were both thorough and professional at all times.

To my Facebook ARC group I once again thank you all for your enthusiasm and support for my work and for keeping my spirits up when they are low.

To my lovely wife for keeping my feet on the floor by using her entire repertoire of witty and abusive put-downs. To my daughter for doing the same thing, but in a much more terrifying and heart-felt way.

Finally, to my readers whoever you may be or wherever you hang your hat. Without you I'm just the bloke who disappears for hours at a time into his office and taps away at the keyboard for no apparent reason. You all make sense of my life right now, and I am so grateful to each and every one of you. Although I will work on other projects, Bliss will be back – book #6 has already been started. I don't intend giving him up without a fight.

Thank you – Tony.

Printed in Great Britain
by Amazon